Reaping the Whirlwind

Praise for *Reaping the Whirlwind*

"Mystery buffs will find a full plate in this book: love affairs, intrigue, murder, and intellectual controversy—all portrayed against an accurate geographical backdrop with historical personages mingling with fictional characters. The result is that this book is an enjoyable means of learning about one of the world's great trials, and it sounds a warning of the dangerous consequences of scientific theory being accepted as proven fact."

—**Richard M. Cornelius, Ph.D.,** Bryan College Emeritus Professor of English and Scopes Trial specialist, Dayton, Tennessee

"Tightly written and fascinating."

—**T. Suzanne Eller,** author of *Blood of the Fathers*

"Rosey's style reminds me of Jan Karon's *Mitford Series*."

—**Norman Rohrer,** founder of The Christian Writer's Guild

"In *Reaping the Whirlwind,* Dow has taken what might have been dry, historical facts and woven them into a tale of intrigue and obsession. Under her capable pen, gray areas become clearly defined, while dark, consistent lines become blurred and change shape as the wind blows. The characters, while obviously living in another day and time, are pleasant to observe; suspects abound, keeping readers guessing. An excellent and surprising first!"

—**Patti J. Nunn,** *Charlotte Austin Review*

"If you love colorful historical characters and a good mystery, you will love this intriguing and intellectually stimulating work."

—**Diana Kirk,** best-selling author of *Songs of Isis*

"An interesting, sensitive, page-turning look into that time in history."

—Linda Hall, author of *Katheryn's Secret*

"Entertaining, educational, thought-provoking."

—Dan Reynolds, Creationism Connection

A TRENT TYSON HISTORICAL MYSTERY

REAPING the WHIRLWIND

ROSEY DOW

NEW YORK

LONDON • NASHVILLE • MELBOURNE • VANCOUVER

Reaping the Whirlwind

A Trent Tyson Historical Mystery

Published in New York, New York, by Morgan James Publishing. Morgan James is a trademark of Morgan James, LLC. www.MorganJamesPublishing.com

Proudly distributed by Ingram Publisher Services.

ISBN 9781636980522 paperback
ISBN 9781636980539 ebook
Library of Congress Control Number: 2022945297

Cover Design by:
Rachel Lopez
www.r2cdesign.com

Interior Design by:
Christopher Kirk
www.GFSstudio.com

To my mother, whose unfailing belief in my writing spurred me on when I wondered if my dreams would ever come true.

Acknowledgments

To Ken Ham of Answers in Genesis, who mentioned the Scopes Trial during a seminar and sparked the idea for this story.

To Dr. Richard Cornelius, who welcomed me into his treasure trove of artifacts and carefully preserved newspaper clippings, who answered all my questions and read this lengthy manuscript. Without you, the historical quality of this work would have been impossible.

And thank you to Morgan James Publishing who agreed to give *Reaping the Whirlwind* a breath of fresh air with a re-release and for their support in helping me share the story for more readers to enjoy.

Author's Note

The 1925 case of *Tennessee vs. John Thomas Scopes* has often been called "The Trial of the Century." Hundreds of publications, including a Pulitzer Prize historical study, have dealt with the trial. In the creative arts, the trial has also been the theme of many songs, plays, poems, a novel, and now this historical mystery. The following issues of the trial have influenced millions of Americans, especially in the realm of education: academic freedom, governmental authority vs. individual rights, separation of church and state, creation vs. evolution, the role of the media, and interrelationships of educators, students, tax-paying parents, and school boards.

Since the Scopes Evolution Trial had many bizarre elements, the reader is advised that the trial is an outstanding example of truth being stranger than fiction. I have been painstaking in my research and meticulous in my attempts at historical accuracy. The reader is assured, therefore, that trial references which might strike the reader as figments of the author's imagination can generally be accepted as historical facts with a couple of exceptions:

Walter F. Thomison, Dayton's doctor at that time, had a clinic near the corner of Market and Main. Because of a doctor's intimate involvement in the fiction part of this story, the author chose to use a fictional character, Dr. Adam St. Clair, instead. Dayton's constable at that time was replaced by Deputy Sheriff Trent Tyson.

Following is a list of people who were actually in Dayton at the time of this record:

William Bailey, owner of Bailey's Hardware

Katherine "Kate" Bailey, William's wife

Clifford Bailey, William's son and friend of John Scopes

Dick Beamish, reporter with *Philadelphia Inquirer*

James Benson, witness

William Jennings Bryan, prosecution counsel

Mary Bryan, Will's wife

William Jennings Bryan Jr., prosecution counsel

John W. Butler, drafter of the Butler Act

Rev. Cartwright, preacher who opened court on Day One

Clarence Darrow, defense counsel

Ruby Darrow, Clarence's wife

Jim "Red" Darwin, owner of Darwin's Mercantile

Maggie Darwin, Red's wife

W.F. Ferguson, Rhea County High School biology teacher

John Godsey, Dayton attorney

Bluch Harris, Sheriff of Rhea County

Paul Henderson, reporter with *St. Louis Post-Dispatch*

Arthur Garfield Hays, defense counsel

Wallace C. Haggard, prosecution counsel

Sue K. Hicks, prosecution counsel

Herbert E. Hicks, prosecution counsel

Jack Hudson, witness

Philip Kinsey, reporter with *Chicago Tribune*

Dudley Field Malone, defense counsel

Benjamin Gordon McKenzie, prosecution counsel

J. Gordon McKenzie, prosecution counsel, Ben's son

Harry Lewis Mencken, reporter with Baltimore's *Evening Sun*

Maynard M. Metcalf, zoologist

George Fort Milton, editor of *Chattanooga News*

W.A. Moffit, pastor of First Baptist Church

Howard Morgan, witness

Luther "Luke" Morgan, banker and Howard's father

John Randolf Neal, defense counsel

Austin Peay, Governor of Tennessee

Bill Perry, reporter with *Nashville Banner*

Charles Francis Potter, Unitarian preacher

George W. Rappleyea, manager of Cumberland Coal and Iron

John Tate Raulston, circuit court judge

Thurlow Reed, barber

Kelso Rice, policeman from Chattanooga

W.F. Roberson, juror

Frank Earl Robinson, owner of Robinson's Drug Store

Clarke Robinson, Earl's wife

Wallace Robinson, Earl's son

F. R. Rogers, citizen of Dayton

Quin Ryan, radio announcer for WGN, Chicago

John Thomas Scopes, defendant

Thomas Scopes, John's father

Harry Shelton, witness

Doris Stevens, Malone's wife

A. Thomas Stewart, District Attorney General

Rev. A.C. Stribbling, pastor of Cumberland Presbyterian Church

Walter White, superintendent of Rhea County schools

Virgil Wilkey, barber

Alvin York, WWI hero

All others are completely fictitious and have no resemblance to any person living or dead. Courtroom dialogue is based solely on the court record.

-ROSEY DOW

Prologue

I like to think of myself as a gardener. A gardener loves flowers.

If he must root out a misshapen plant or snip off a dead head, that doesn't mean he loves his beautiful blossoms less. It means he's a tidy gardener.

He's doing the landscape a favor. No one can blame him.

Chapter One

Dr. Adam St. Clair moved his queen across the chessboard and said, "Check."

Hunched over the small table, Deputy Sheriff Trent Tyson twisted his wedding band and studied the position of his king.

"C'mon, Doc," he complained. "We've only been at it for twenty minutes. Did you have to go for the jugular already?"

St. Clair chuckled. A heavy chin anchored his face to a wide body that had softened during middle age and sagged after that. "You can always forfeit."

"Not on your life! Just sit quiet a minute while I think." Tyson stroked his heavy black mustache and didn't speak again for three minutes.

It was a rainy Monday evening in the spring of '25. The men sat in a room full of lace and fragile fixtures—a spinster's parlor.

Usually, the men played chess at Tyson's house, but today St. Clair's office hours had run late, and he'd asked Tyson to come to the house he shared with his sister, Sadie, instead.

The phone jangled.

Dr. St. Clair grimaced. "I hope that's someone for Sadie. Today I had to talk Essie Caldwell out of an appendectomy. I put twenty stitches in a kid's split head and treated a burned face besides my regular appointments. I'm beat."

"Man is born to trouble as the sparks fly upward."

St. Clair let out an irritated grunt.

"Sorry, Doc. I know you don't believe that rot. Neither do I. Don't know why I brought it up."

"What I need is a two-week fishing trip."

On the third ring, the doctor let out a frustrated sigh and slowly stood. The phone sat on a table three steps away. He picked up the base and pulled the cup receiver to his ear. "Dr. St. Clair." He listened a moment and turned to Tyson. "It's for you."

Tyson lurched to his feet. The edge of his cuff hit a shepherdess figurine, and it toppled onto the chessboard. He grabbed for it and missed. The board landed on the floor, and chess pieces scattered across the tile like an avalanche.

Thoroughly disgusted with himself, he picked up the phone's base and spoke into the mouthpiece. "Tyson here."

"Mr. Tyson, this is Nessa McGinty," a soprano voice said. "Mama told me you were there. I'm sorry to bother you."

His grip on the receiver tightened. "Is Lori okay?"

"Your daughter's fine. I'm in south Dayton. I can't get Mrs. Ida Johnson to answer her door. I'm afraid something may be wrong."

"Give me the address." He pulled a notebook from his shirt pocket and jotted it down. "I'll be there in five minutes. Wait for me on the porch." He let the cup drop into the cradle and spoke to the doctor, who was on his knees retrieving his chessmen. "Ida Johnson won't answer her door. Do you want to come with me?"

Gripping the edge of the table for support, St. Clair heaved himself to his feet. "I'd better come, yes. Miz Ida's had a bad heart for years."

Tyson reached into the front pocket of his jeans for his keys.

St. Clair said, "We'd better take both vehicles in case I have to stay late." He strode to a side door. "I'll fetch my bag from the office, and we'll be off."

Tyson finished replacing the chess pieces as Sadie stepped into the front room. A tiny woman with the bearing of a general, she had been her brother's right hand for forty years. She was also the local midwife, with training as a druggist. St. Clair left most female complaints to her capable hands.

She held a thick volume, one finger marking a page.

"Good evening, Miss Sadie," Tyson said, giving her his rakish smile. "Studying for your doctor's degree?"

"You should do some reading yourself, Mr. Tyson," Sadie said, smile wrinkles appearing around her eyes. She always talked to Tyson as though she were a school teacher advising a naughty boy.

"It would expand your mind."

Tyson chuckled. "My head's already big enough."

The doctor reappeared and Sadie looked at his black case. "What's happened, Adam?"

"We've got to check on Miz Ida," he told her, locking the door. "Nessa just called to say she won't answer her door." He fetched Tyson's trench coat and fedora from the closet.

"Should I come along?" Sadie asked.

"Maybe you should. Miz Ida likes you better than me."

Each man hustled through the dark and drizzle toward his own Model T, with Sadie trailing her brother. Dr. St. Clair's vehicle was practically new with an automatic starter. It burst into a pleasing chug-chug at the touch of a knob.

Tyson's eight-year-old Lizzy always balked and squawked when it rained. On a night like this, she could have made a preacher cuss, and Trent Tyson was no preacher.

He opened the right-hand door—the only front door that worked—and reached across the passenger seat to set the spark and throttle levers. While Tyson pulled the choke wire with his left hand and worked the crank with his right, Dr. St. Clair left his flivver idling with Sadie inside. He hunched his neck down into his turned-up collar and joined the deputy.

"Miz Ida's an elderly widow," the doctor said, standing near Lizzy's fender. "For the past twenty years, she's had a heart condition that gives us a scare every few months. She has Nessa McGinty come in once a day to cook and wash up. As far as I know, Miz Ida hasn't been outside her house in ten years."

St. Clair shoved his hands into deep coat pockets. "Lately she's been restless and depressed. I'm afraid she may have hurt herself or had a heart episode." Tiny droplets made a pattern on his derby.

Finally, Lizzy roared to life and settled into her normal pop-rattle-bang with the motions to match. Tyson scuttled through the door to reset the spark and throttle. St. Clair hurried to his vehicle and turned on the lights.

Tyson waited for him to back out the drive, then pulled Lizzy away from the curb behind the doctor's smart flivver. Before they'd reached the turn, he'd soaked his handkerchief and sleeve trying to keep the mist off the inside and the rain off the outside of his windshield so he could see.

The two automobiles moved a block west on Main Street. Just after the Hicks Brothers Law Office, they swung left onto Market Street, the central thoroughfare crossing Dayton from north to south. A few minutes later, Lizzy's headlamps shone on slim Nessa McGinty huddled under the wide porch roof out of the rain. She wore a knitted cloche hat and a thin black coat. Her face looked chalky in the glaring light.

Ida Johnson's house was the old frame type with a wrap-around porch and peeling white paint. Shrubs hugged the front steps, and a hundred-year-old oak spread its branches across the yard. A street lamp shone through the tree to make weird swaying shadows on the house and lawn. The front steps to the porch had a loose gate that screeched back and forth in the whipping wind.

Both automobiles stopped on the street. Tyson angled his car toward the porch so the headlamps could light their way. Leaving Lizzy chugging, the trio walked in together.

"Do you know how we can get inside?" Tyson asked Nessa when they reached the shelter of the porch roof. "Does she have a key hidden somewhere?"

"The only key is inside the house," she said, her eyes glistening in the harsh light.

Tyson tried the door. It was solid. The only way to get in would be to splinter the door jamb. He moved down the porch, trying windows.

"That's Miss Ida's window," Nessa called. "I tapped on it, but she didn't answer."

Tyson continued around the front and latched the banging gate. When he turned the far corner, a gust drenched him. Light glowed around the edges of a drawn curtain, but he couldn't see anything inside. He banged on the sash and shouted loud and long.

No answer. He hustled back to the others.

"You may be able to get in by the inside cellar stairs," Nessa suggested. "They enter into the kitchen. The door's kept locked, but the latch is old and rusty."

Without bothering to answer, he quickstepped off the porch and hurried around the house. The cellar had a ground-level entrance covered by double doors.

Blackness rose around him like murky water as he eased into the opening. Mold and dust and furnace smoke made the air smell thick. He struck a match and held it high. The heat touched his fingers. He blew at the flame and dropped it in one jerky motion.

A scuffling noise behind him made his skin crawl.

The match had allowed him a glimpse of a set of rough stairs across the room. Moving blindly, he barked his shin, found the railing, and climbed the steps. At the top, he shoved a shoulder against the paneled door. It screeched and gave way.

He felt a switch beside the door and flooded the kitchen with light. A brass key hung on a hook beside the back door. He grabbed it and reached for the latch.

The doctor was first through the door. Calling Miss Ida's name, he hurried toward the front of the house. Nessa and Sadie followed him with Tyson on their heels.

Tyson glanced around. How did the old lady stand it? Less than a minute, and he already craved fresh air.

A frail body lay over a writing table by the window. Half a second behind the doctor, Nessa ran toward the old woman's limp body calling "Miss Ida!" then drew back, horrified. She let out a shrill gasp and both hands flew up to cover her cheeks.

Miss Ida lay with her arms at odd angles as though she'd been boxing with someone. A web of dried foam covered blue lips that drew back against her teeth in a ghastly smile.

Sadie turned Nessa around and urged her toward the door. "Let's wait in the kitchen, dear. The doctor will look at her and tell us what happened." She took the girl's hands. "You need a cup of hot, strong tea. Your fingers are like ice." They left the room, the murmur of Sadie's words slowly fading.

St. Clair straightened and shook his head.

"How long's she been gone, Doc?"

"I'd say two hours. Not more than three."

"Any guess about what killed her?"

"Look at her blue lips. I'd say it was her heart." He glanced at Tyson. "I'll call the undertaker." He picked up the phone standing on the writing table.

Tyson shed his hat and coat and hung them from the back of a chair. His keen eyes started cataloging the room before St. Clair finished putting through the call.

Tyson hated loose ends. They ranked right up there with liars and loudmouthed women. At times like this, a skeptic inside his head woke up and whispered a series of *what-ifs* in his ear. He had to fit all the pieces into the puzzle or the skeptic wouldn't go back to sleep. And Tyson wouldn't sleep himself.

That pesky skeptic had banished him to Dayton six weeks ago because of a bootlegging case he couldn't turn loose of.

He knelt to look under the sofa and let out a soundless chuckle. Here he was digging again. He hadn't learned his lesson.

Nothing hid under Miss Ida's sofa or the chairs. Not even dust.

The outer perimeter of the sitting room had nothing to offer Tyson's probing eyes except bare tabletops and crocheted antimacassars.

St. Clair hung up the phone and turned away to pick up his bag.

Tyson moved to the writing table for a closer look at the dead woman. A moment later, he strode to the kitchen. Nessa sat at the table with Sadie and another woman whose matronly build and lined face showed that she'd lived half a century.

"Do you know Essie Caldwell, deputy?" Sadie introduced them. "She lives next door."

"I'm Ida's closest friend," Essie said, looking distressed. She had a shrill, warbling voice and small, darting eyes.

Tyson acknowledged her presence with a curt nod and turned to Nessa. "Can you get me a damp piece of cotton wool? And a small glass bottle with a cork?"

Holding a steaming cup of tea in both hands, Nessa looked at him as if he'd lost his senses. He repeated his request.

Sadie said, "She's upset, Deputy. And no wonder. I'll get it for you."

She reached into a cabinet and found a flat liniment bottle, clean and clear.

St. Clair strode in. "Ketcher's on his way, Tyson. There's nothing more for me to do here." He stood beside Sadie and looked at Tyson. "Would you mind waiting for him? I need to make some notes in my office records about what happened tonight."

"Sure thing, Doc," Tyson said.

Essie turned in her chair to watch the doctor leave.

Sadie followed St. Clair to the door. "Oh, tell your mother I'll be over to see her tomorrow, Nessa."

"Of course, Miss Sadie." She sent Sadie a weak smile and a limp-handed wave goodbye.

"Would you turn off my flivver, Doc?" Tyson asked. "She's still running."

"Will do." Dr. St. Clair stepped into the night.

"When the undertaker leaves," Tyson told the young woman, "I'll drive you home."

She nodded and sipped tea.

Essie sniffed into a handkerchief. "Poor Ida. I can't believe she's really gone."

Returning to the living room, Tyson swabbed Miss Ida's lips until the last traces of foam disappeared. Forcing the soggy cotton wad into the bottle's narrow neck, he tried to cork it but the cork slipped and fell to the floor. He bent to retrieve it and stopped.

Beside the dead woman's shoe lay a china tea cup in four pieces.

He finished corking the bottle and set it on the table. On hands and knees, he gathered up the china fragments and wrapped them in his handkerchief. He shoved both bottle and handkerchief into his overcoat pocket where it hung over the chair.

A moment later, Nessa watched him walk into the kitchen. Her cheeks had more color, but her eyes had lost their usual sparkle. She'd taken off her hat and her dark braid glinted red in the light.

"I'm sorry to bother you with questions now," he told her, "but it's part of police routine in a case like this."

"What happened to her?" she asked, looking directly at him.

"Doc said it was her heart." Tyson pulled out a chair and sat across from her.

He reached for his notebook and asked, "Does Miss Ida have any relatives that need to be notified?"

"She has a daughter in Chattanooga. Miss Ida and Bella never got along."

"Bella ran off and got married against her mother's wishes," Essie chimed in. "Ida never got over it."

"Do you know where to reach Bella?"

"Miss Ida has a letter box on her writing table," Nessa told him.

"Bella's address is sure to be in it. Her name's Smith, Bella Smith."

"Who had a key to the house?"

Nessa turned to look at the hook beside the door. "That's the only key there is."

"She have a fat bank account? How could she afford a maid?"

Nessa shrugged and touched her full mouth. "I don't know. We never talked about money."

"She had some investments," Essie said, "from her husband's retirement or something."

"He work in Dayton?"

The neighbor woman answered again. "Cumberland Coal. He was a manager for thirty years. Right steady James was, according to Ida. He was real careful with his money."

She would have gone on, but Tyson cut her off. "How long have you worked here, Nessa?"

"Five years, but I don't consider this a job. Miss Ida was more like family to me. She was a lonely old soul that no one cared about." Tears filled her eyes. She blinked and looked away.

"I cared about her," Essie said touching Nessa's hand. "I used to come over for tea three or four times a week. Sometimes we cut out quilt blocks, and sometimes we just talked."

She rambled on, "We both have rheumatism. But Ida didn't have my pleurisy or fainting spells. Lumbago's what gave her the most trouble, if you ask me."

He made a note. "If that's the only key, what if Miss Ida was sick and couldn't get to the door?"

Nessa said, "She'd take the key to her room. I'd tap on the window, and she'd hand it to me." Her blue eyes moved to Tyson. "You have to understand. She was old and . . . a little odd. She even kept her doors locked against Elmer ever since he accidentally killed her rose bush with too much fertilizer."

"Elmer?" he interrupted, jotting something down.

Essie answered. "Elmer Buntley. He lives in a shack behind the post office. He does gardening in summer and odd jobs in winter for a dozen people. You must have seen him around. He wears a brown leather cap with flaps over the ears, and a green plaid coat."

"Elmer never came into the house, then?"

Nessa studied the table, her lips pulled in.

Tyson waited.

"I felt sorry for him," the girl said. "If Miss Ida was taking a nap, I'd sometimes let Elmer in for a hot cup of coffee. I didn't have the heart to see him working in the cold and damp without giving him something."

"Did Elmer come inside today?"

She nodded. "He cut some spearmint for us."

"And you made tea with it."

"Yes, I had a cup and left the rest for Miss Ida. Today was Miss Ida's first cup of spearmint this year. She was enjoying it when I left her."

Essie nodded. "She loved fresh spearmint."

Tyson's eye caught a bit of green on the counter. "Is that some of it?"

Nessa stood and peered at it. "That's not spearmint. I don't know what it is. It wasn't here when I left at four-thirty."

Tyson joined her for a better look. Five four-inch sprigs lay in a matted lump beside a china cup on the counter. "Do you know where there's an envelope?"

"In the desk. I'll get it." A minute later, she handed him one.

Tyson scooped the plant inside and folded it closed. "It's probably not important," he said, "but it won't hurt to save it just in case." He returned to the table, and Nessa sank into her seat.

She rubbed her eyes with the heels of her hands.

"How did Miss Ida feel today? Was she depressed? Anxious?"

"She hasn't been steady on her feet since last winter," Nessa told Tyson. "She managed to get around the house, but she couldn't stand up to cook or anything. Today, she was a little cranky, but that's nothing new."

"You left when?"

"I came at three to make Miss Ida a soft-boiled egg and a piece of toast like I always do. I washed up and left at four-thirty."

"Why did you come back?"

"I forgot my purse." She glanced around the tidy kitchen. "There it is beside the bread box."

A loud knock shook the door. Tyson let in the undertaker and his son. They looked as tall and wide and flat as a rugged barn door. The younger man carried a collapsing stretcher and a white sheet.

They laid Miss Ida out, wrapped her up, and had her in their horse-drawn hearse in minutes.

Tyson had shrugged into his coat, ready to leave, when a lacy paper on the writing table caught his eye. Looking closer, he saw that Miss Ida's head had been lying on an unfinished letter dated that day:

Dear Alice,

I can't wait to see you when you come in June. I've been saving something special.

He folded the page and stuck it into his shirt pocket. Near the lamp was the wooden letter box Nessa had mentioned. Lifting the hinged lid, he looked through the stack of mail inside and chose an envelope to take along.

"Who's Alice?" he asked, wedging a chair against the cellar door.

Smelling of liniment, Essie stood near him. "Alice is Ida's favorite niece, in Chicago."

He turned out the lights and locked the door. Essie trudged across the yard to her house, a two-story building with yellow light streaming from an upstairs window facing the driveway.

Nessa walked with Tyson to the car, her arms tight against her middle in the damp chill. He opened the passenger door, set the spark and throttle, and reached for the crank. Nessa climbed inside as he stepped to the front of the car.

You're way off the beam this time. He scolded the skeptic and gave the handle a twirl. The old lady was locked in with the only key hanging inside the house. And suicide is out.

Besides, only an inhuman fiend would knock off a harmless old lady. In Chicago or New York, he'd consider it. But in Dayton?

The skeptic wasn't buying it. Two or three pieces still didn't fit.

CHAPTER Two

Leaving Front Street, Tyson turned north on Market. He strained forward through the open window to wipe the windshield, and a gust sent his hat flying into the back seat. Rain doused him, and cold water trickled down his collar.

He clenched his teeth and smacked the steering wheel. "Someday I'm going to get a set of windshield wipers and an automatic starter." He'd been making himself the same promise for five years.

Nessa looked over at him and raised her voice above Lizzy's racket. "Sounds to me like you should get a new car."

He grinned. "Lizzy's part of the family. I couldn't bear to part with the old girl." He glanced at Nessa. "I don't see you around the house much. You have a regular job?"

"I clean for the St. Clair's, the Robinson's, and a few others." She snugged her hat down in the back. It covered her forehead down to the top of her pert nose. "I wanted to go to college, but when Dad died we couldn't afford it. His pension barely covers the mortgage. I have to help Mama make ends meet."

"Too bad you can't get more boarders. The house is big enough."

"Dayton's not exactly a booming town," she called back. "There used to be lots of people and all kinds of attractions, but when the mine started wearing out, Dayton did too. There's talk the mine's going to shut down. If it does, I don't know what we'll do."

He wiped the windshield yet another time as they puttered past Darwin's General Mercantile and Bailey's Hardware. The store windows reflected Lizzy's lights and matched the black glare of wet pavement.

"What do you know about Bella Smith?"

"I've only met her a couple of times. She smokes long cigarettes, wears flimsy clothes, and smears on the face paint. Her daughter's a flapper, too. They come to see Miss Ida once or twice a year. Bella ran off with some city fellow twenty years ago. Miss Ida hasn't had much to do with her since then. Even when Bella's marriage broke up, she didn't come back."

"When's the last time Bella came to Dayton?"

"The last I saw her was at the state fair almost a year ago."

He refastened the top button of his overcoat. "You can't blame her. After living in Chattanooga, Dayton takes some getting used to."

"You should make some friends." Nessa glanced at him. "You've been here six weeks, and you still haven't come to church to meet anyone."

Tyson grimaced. "Dr. St. Clair and I play chess every Monday. I enjoy talking to him. He has some fascinating ideas."

Her voice became sarcastic. "I know—Darwinism and all that."

"You ever read Darwin's book?"

"Sure. I dated a college guy a while back, and he lent it to me."

"What did you think?"

"I ditched him. I'm not interested in any evolutionist." As an afterthought, she added, "It was no great loss. The poor guy had two strikes against him. He had a mustache."

Tyson twitched the bristles above his upper lip. Nessa McGinty looked like an innocent kid, but she sure knew how to take the wind out of a guy's sails. They drove the rest of the way in silence.

McGinty's Boardinghouse stood on the southwest corner of Fourth Avenue and Market, a sprawling clapboard structure with a wide front porch holding three rocking chairs. The landlady had half a dozen rooms for rent on the second floor. Tyson rented a two-room suite at the front.

The temperature had fallen ten degrees by the time Lizzy pulled into the driveway. With a quick goodbye, Nessa hopped out and headed for the back door and the family apartment. Wet, weary and disgruntled, Tyson bedded down the Model T and headed for the front door—the boarder's entrance.

A wide, dimly lit hall cut the house in half, with a staircase facing the door along its right wall. He hung his coat in the front closet and dropped his fedora on the shelf. He turned on a lamp on the hall table and drew an envelope from his shirt pocket.

Jiggling the phone cradle, he said, "Mabel?" and waited. A moment later he went on, "See if you can find a number for Bella Smith in Chattanooga, will you? Call me back when you get her."

He leaned against green-striped wallpaper, mulling over the events of the evening. What was it that bothered him about the old woman's death? He couldn't put a name to it.

The phone rang and he grabbed it.

"Here's your party, Deputy," a thin voice said.

"Thanks, Mabel." A click. "Mrs. Smith?"

"Yes?" She sounded as though she was chewing gum.

He gave her the news quickly and succinctly without voicing his suspicions.

"I'll be up tomorrow or the next day," she murmured. "I've got a job. I'll have to get off."

"Let me know when, and I'll open the house for you." He gave her the office number and broke the connection, relieved that she'd taken his call so calmly. Hysterical females made him nervous.

He turned out the light and took the stairs three at a time. It was close to ten, and he was beat.

His tiny sitting room was dark, lit only by the dim glow of a night light in the bedroom. He headed toward the light and leaned over the trundle bed beside his own.

Lori, the darling of his heart, lay with her fluffy curls across the pillow, her face so like Carrie's that he felt a stab in his middle. One pudgy hand lay beside her cheek, the other one—the shriveled, disfigured one—lay on the quilt. He lifted the cover and eased both her arms under it.

Five years ago, his wife had died in a hail of bullets on a street corner in Chattanooga, a casualty in a gang war she knew nothing about. Trent was left with an eight-week-old baby to care for. Six months later an orthopedic specialist told him Lori had a birth defect. Her left arm would never grow.

The little girl stirred and squinted up at him. "Hi, Daddy," she mumbled. "You came home."

"Yes, Chicky." He kissed her forehead. "Go to sleep."

She wrinkled her nose. "You smell good."

He smiled softly and touched her cheek. Her eyes drifted closed.

Tyson slipped off his shoes and emptied his pockets. Loose change and keys he placed on the dresser. Pulling a sheet of white paper from a drawer, he wrapped the items from Miss Ida's house, tied the bundle with string, and, holding it close to the faint light, addressed it to an old friend: Charlie Greene, Pathologist, Chattanooga Police Force.

He undressed in the darkness and slid under heavy blankets.

He had never dreamed he'd end up in a place like Dayton, alone, with a child to raise. Closing his eyes, he let his mind wander.

Trent Tyson had seen a lot of life since he enlisted in the army on his eighteenth birthday. Seven years later he landed in France to fight a war he had no interest in. When he got home he met Carrie, enrolled in the police academy, and got married all within one year.

Fifteen months later, Carrie was gone. He had a baby to raise, and a future to face when he'd rather crawl into the casket beside his wife.

Blotting out his pain, he focused on his career. He studied homicide investigation under a battle-scarred, street-smart warrior. The lieutenant's raw wisdom and keen insight reminded Tyson of his own father, a retired police officer who'd walked a beat for thirty years.

Before long, Tyson was a precinct detective with his sights on joining a homicide division. Another year or two on the Chattanooga force and he would have made it.

Six months ago, he and his partner received a big case assignment. After four months of late-night stakeouts, dangerous shadowing jobs, and hours of sifting through a haystack of facts to find a needle of evidence, they had a bootlegging boss dead to rights.

They celebrated with a steak lunch and then delivered the goods in a fifty-page report. The next day the police chief killed the case.

The crook happened to be an old crony of his.

When Tyson got the word he didn't speak for two hours. That night he stared at his bedroom ceiling until dawn then got up to pace. At eight o'clock he phoned the mayor and blew the whistle.

What had he gotten for his noble gesture? A few days later he stood in the police station clenching a yellow termination slip.

He stared at his wooden cubbyhole as though it had betrayed him, his cheek muscles working in and out, then he shoved the paper into his pocket without bothering to fold it. His years on the detective squad played out behind his eyes like a silent movie. He was twenty-nine years old, keen in mind and body, with success brushing his grasping fingertips.

His ambitions had just vaporized.

Without saying a word, Tyson shouldered past his partner and stormed outside. Bitter cold sucked the air from his lungs. He tucked his head down as though ready to charge and pulled in a ragged breath. If not for Prohibition he would have gotten stewed. He was tempted to do it anyway.

Instead, he fired up the Model T and drove aimlessly around Chattanooga until time to pick up Lori from the sitter's house. A week later he took a train north and stopped in every town along the route, looking for a job. If he had to be a custodian at the jailhouse, he'd take it. A little girl depended on him. In Dayton, Sheriff Bluch Harris's aging deputy wanted to retire, so Tyson got his job on the spot.

Tyson had knocked on fifty doors in Dayton trying to find someone who would board them and watch five-year-old Lori while he was out. Finally, he found McGinty's place. Heddie liked Lori from their first meeting. Too bad she disliked Lori's daddy.

He rolled over to his side on the creaky bed and pulled the quilt around his ears. His thoughts returned to Ida Johnson's sitting room, and he began to snore.

"Wake up, Daddy! It's morning." Lori bounced on his chest, her face glowing. She giggled when he squinted at her, then she buried her face in his neck.

"Morning, Chicky." He patted her back and gave her a squeeze.

She sat up and announced, "Heddie's making pancakes."

"In that case, let's get downstairs before Micky eats them all."

He flung back the covers. She slid down to her trundle bed, still bouncing while he struggled with her buttons, and slipped a yellow dress over her head.

"Go down to the dining room. I'll dress and be there in five minutes."

She watched him with big eyes. "No, you won't, Daddy. You have to shave."

He rubbed his bristly chin. "Oh, yeah. Make that fifteen minutes."

She trotted away, her empty sleeve swaying, and banged out the door. She was finishing her pancake when Tyson reached the dining room. A pink ribbon tied back her dark hair, the work of Nessa or Heddie. Lori thrived here.

She sat in a chair on a thick catalog next to Micky, Heddie's fifteen-year-old son, a stout, likable lad. Micky didn't look up. A six-inch stack of hot cakes had his full attention.

Heddie McGinty arrived with a steaming platter of pancakes when Tyson took his seat. Middle age hadn't affected her much. She had the barest of smile wrinkles and glossy black hair, wavy and thick, pulled up into a French twist. She'd lived in America for forty years but still carried a touch of an Irish brogue.

Wearing a corduroy jumper, her braid lying forward over her shoulder, Nessa came into the room with her tiny mother, carrying a brown bottle and a small spoon—Lori's tonic, Dr. St. Clair's special blend. Nessa McGinty had an internal energy that put springs in her shoes.

Tyson took a second look at the girl's bright eyes. She showed no lingering effects of last night's shock. Suddenly aware that he was staring, he dug into his pancakes.

"Here, Lori. Open wide," Nessa said to the little girl. When the brown liquid disappeared, she kissed the top of the child's head and took a seat beside her. "Miss Sadie said she'll try to visit you tomorrow," she told Heddie, eyebrows raised. "I thought you two quarreled last week."

"Just a little misunderstanding, me love. I called her last night and apologized." She looked meaningfully at Tyson, her chin up. "A person should never be too good to admit he's wrong."

Tyson picked up his coffee cup, fighting irritation. That crack was directed at their last discussion. Opinionated Heddie had started in on the labor union crisis during supper. By eight o'clock Tyson had had enough and tried to ease out gracefully. Finally, he retreated to his room in self-defense.

Heddie adored Lori. That was enough to keep him here. Lately, he had to remind himself of that whenever Heddie started one of her tirades.

He turned to Nessa for a quick change of subject. "If you think of anything more about Mrs. Johnson, please let me know."

"Wasn't that a pity?" Heddie asked. "Poor Ida had such a lonely life." She lifted the bacon platter and left the room.

Nessa smiled, crinkling the corners of her blue eyes. "Please don't take Mama too seriously. She's got a kind heart."

Tyson stifled a wry comment.

"I like Heddie," Lori piped up. "She's taking me to Robinson's yard this afternoon. They have a tire swing and monkey bars."

Tyson reached for the pancakes. For all her faults and outdated opinions, Mrs. McGinty could cook like an angel.

He was finishing his fourth serving when someone knocked on the door.

Micky lurched from his chair to answer it.

"Hi!" a husky voice cried.

Wearing a red coat and matching babushka, Anna Joy Mullins stepped into view. Her wide mouth stretched into a loose-lipped grin; her almond eyes narrowed to slits. She lived next door with her widowed mother.

"Come in, Anna Joy," Nessa called, smiling. "Would you like a pancake?"

"Mama made me scrambled eggs this morning," she proudly replied, beaming.

"I'll be there in a jiff," Micky said. He gulped half a glass of milk and dropped his napkin on the table.

Anna Joy walked to school with Micky. She did household errands for an elderly lady who lived next to the school and returned with Micky on his lunch hour. She could have walked the two blocks alone, but her mother worried that her mentally-challenged daughter would try to cross a street without looking first.

Micky grabbed his book bag and coat and dashed out, Anna Joy trotting behind him.

Nessa's mother finally sat down to her own breakfast.

A light double knock brought Nessa to her feet. "That's the mailman. I'll get it, Mama." She returned with a narrow brown envelope and handed it to Heddie. "It's the pension check."

"Thank the good Lord," Heddie said, tearing it open. "Cumberland Coal is so unreliable. They were late last month and the mortgage is due . . ." Her face blanched. She stared at the check. "They've cut it in half!" She gulped and fanned herself with the slip of paper. "Nessa, Nessa what are we going to do?"

Her daughter grabbed the check. "How can they do this to us?"

Trent sipped coffee. He wasn't sure they remembered he was there. Maybe they didn't want him to know their private affairs.

Nessa slumped against the back of her chair, staring at nothing. In a moment, she glanced at Tyson. "Three years ago, a support piling slipped and hit Dad in the head. He died instantly. His company gave us a full pension for him, just as though he'd worked thirty years and retired. It wasn't as much as we were used to getting, but we've managed to scrape by. Now, this."

A hopeless expression flickered across her face. An instant later, her chin came up, and she looked at Tyson. "How can two women earn eight hundred dollars? If the mortgage were paid off, we'd have plenty to live on."

Lori slid out of her seat. "I'm going up for my picture book."

"Come and give me a kiss, Chicky," Tyson said. "I've got to go to work." She hugged his neck, planted a wet smacker on his cheek, and skipped out.

Turning to the ladies, he said, "I'll think about your problem today. Maybe I can come up with a good idea. We'll talk about it tonight, all right?"

"Oh!" Nessa cried. "I've got to run across to Bailey's!" She darted into the hall and opened the closet. "Bye, Mama. Bye . . . Trent." The door banged after her.

A second later, Tyson looked out the window to see her flying form pause on the sidewalk then run across to Bailey's Boardinghouse on the opposite corner.

Tyson swallowed the last of his coffee and strolled outside to crank Lizzy. She turned over on the second swing. One morning out of fifty she surprised him.

How could two women earn such a sum? Tyson made a hundred a month, good wages for a man. A woman couldn't earn half that much, especially as unskilled as Nessa and Heddie were. He held the question at arm's length and looked at it from different angles.

It was a puzzler.

The day was bright and cool with the fresh smell that follows rain. Trees in the courthouse yard showed the first signs of misty green.

Tyson stayed on Market Street until he reached the south side of town. Leaving Lizzy idling by the curb, he strode into the tiny post office, laid a quarter and his package on the counter, and swapped howdys with the lady clerk.

On his way out he almost tripped over the town vagrant, a scrawny man wearing a hat covered with stars and stripes—a relic from a long-forgotten Fourth of July parade. Dirt filled every crack and pit on the man's face and hands, and his scraggly beard lay matted to a chicken-like neck. He gripped a broom.

"Watch out, Sammy," Tyson said. "I almost clipped you."

"Howdy, Deputy." His voice sounded like a branch scraping a window pane. "See what I got me here?" He held open his tattered coat to show a kitten peeking from its inner pocket. The creature looked as unkempt as its owner. "I found her in a ditch this morning. Crying as though her little heart would break." His breath was eighty-proof.

"That's nice, Sammy." Tyson tried to think up a line to free himself. Sammy would keep talking forever if a person let him.

Sammy's ladder was a few rungs short, but—aside from his potent breath—he was harmless.

"I'm on my way to work," Deputy Tyson told him with just the right amount of impatience in his voice. "See you later." Tyson adjusted his hat and left the steps. Where did Sammy get the hooch?

It was an old question that no one would answer.

Whistling, the deputy returned to Lizzy, still doing her pop-rattle-bang dance.

"Hey, mister!" a boy called. "Got a nickel?"

Tyson slowed up when he saw a cluster of boys hustling his way.

The oldest youngster stood a fraction under five feet, with a shock of unruly hair that was a mixture of blond and red, mostly red. He wore a filthy overcoat that hung to his knees. His shrewd green eyes sized up Dayton's new deputy.

Tyson had often seen the gang hanging around town when they should be in school. Sons of miners and their families lived in shotgun houses on the wrong side of the tracks. This was the first time they'd asked Tyson for money.

"Good morning, gentlemen." Tyson paused six feet from his vehicle, his manner pleasant and relaxed. "Do you mind my asking what you need a nickel for?"

"The bakery sells day-old rolls for a penny," the spokesman said. He tugged at his coat front but kept his eyes steadily on the deputy.

"As it happens, I'm on my way past there." Tyson stepped toward Lizzy. "Care for a ride over?"

A ripple of pleasure swept the group. Deputy Tyson pulled open the door and slid behind the wheel. The boys piled in, five in the back seat and their spokesman in front.

"Why aren't you fellows in school?" Tyson asked casually as they turned north.

"We don't have proper clothes," he replied in a matter-of-fact tone. "Mr. Rappelyea cut back Pa's check again. Pa says we'll have to leave the valley if things don't pick up soon."

An urchin in the back seat added, "My dad says the mine's going bunked. We's a-going to West Virginny this summer."

The car lurched to a halt in front of Peal's Bakery, and Tyson dug into his pants pocket for a quarter. He flipped it to the biggest boy.

"Here. Get yourselves something hot to drink, too."

A dozen eyes widened.

"Thanks, Deputy," said the boy. He clutched the coin and pulled at the door handle. The next moment he turned to glare over the seat at his comrades.

On cue, a whisper of "Thank you's" wafted toward Tyson. The boys tumbled out to the sidewalk.

"Hey, wait a minute," Tyson called after the door slammed.

They gathered around the window.

"You fellows like to play baseball?"

The big boy shrugged. "We don't have no ball or bat."

"I've got both. How about a game Saturday afternoon at three… in the high school field?"

"Swell!" he said.

"Round up some more fellows. I'll see you then."

He pulled away from the curb, and the boys went into an excited huddle. Tyson grinned. Things were looking up.

CHAPTER Three

Near the corner of Main and Market, Tyson stopped in front of Robinson's Drug Store beside the three-story Aqua Hotel. Again, he left Lizzy running. The old girl was so hard to crank, he hated to turn her off.

Narrow and deep, the drug store had glass counters down both sides. Along the walls stood glass-fronted cabinets stocked with Robinson's wares. Several round tables filled the center section next to a fully-equipped soda fountain. A wide sign—F.E. Robinson Co., The Rexall Store—hung on the back wall.

In an ad campaign several years before, Earl Robinson had called himself "The Hustling Druggist," a name that stuck. Robinson had been hustling all his life. Scarcely out of school, he had used the daily train to provide Daytonians with laundry service, fresh flowers, newspapers, and any special-order item no one else could locate. With his profits, he bought into a drug store, then went to pharmacy school to make the most of his investment.

The store smelled of coffee with a vague antiseptic aftertaste. Two men relaxed at a table, their faces half hidden by newspapers.

One of them glanced up, twitched his mustache, and muttered, "Morning, Deputy." The other simply caught Tyson's eye and nodded.

Giving a general hello, Tyson picked up a *Chattanooga Times* from the array of newspapers stacked beside the register.

"Howdy, Deputy," Robinson said. The druggist stood two inches shorter than

Tyson. His easy grin made his chipmunk cheeks puff up. "What can I get you, Deputy? Coffee?" he asked, wiping his hands on the white apron covering his pudgy middle.

"Just a paper this morning, thanks." Tyson plunked a nickel onto the counter. "Say, you need any help in the store, Doc?" Folks had started calling him Doc after he got his pharmacist's degree.

Robinson shook his head. "I just hired me a fellow from the high school."

Tyson sketched a two-finger salute and turned back toward the door. "My flivver's running. I'll see you later."

"Have a good day!" the druggist called. A bell pinged when he opened the cash drawer.

Shoving through the door, Tyson came face to face with a lean fellow wearing round spectacles. Pulling up short, he said, "Good morning, Coach! How's life?"

John Scopes gulped. His cheeks were red spots, his words came in gasps. "I'm late. I'm down to five cigarettes . . . so I ran down to get a pack before school. The grocery didn't have my brand . . . I should have been at school ten minutes ago."

"I'll drive you over."

Scopes's pale eyes lit up. He looked more like a high school student than a teacher. "Thanks!" He dashed inside. The shy teacher boarded with the Bailey family on the opposite corner from McGinty's Boardinghouse.

Scopes's mild manners could be misleading. Last fall when a bully challenged him, Scopes did a fast-ball windup and hurled an eraser at the troublemaker's head. A direct hit. After that, no one dared defy the new teacher again.

Scopes dived into the car and slammed the door. Tyson set the throttle, and they shot ahead with a whoosh and bang.

"You're giving final exams now, aren't you?" Tyson asked.

"They'll start Monday. I'm due to give a physics review in . . ." he pulled out his pocket watch, "half an hour. Mr. Ferguson is sick so I have to give the biology review, too.

"It's tough having to review for a class you didn't teach," Scopes complained. "Mr. Ferguson left me his notes. I'll have to do the best I can, I guess. Biology isn't my field, but with Ferguson sick someone has to do the review. I guess I'm the goat."

The moment Lizzy paused before the school, Scopes scooted out of the car. With a quick wave and "Thanks!" he sprinted across the expanse of lawn toward a side entrance.

Tyson turned around and set a course for the sheriff's office behind the courthouse. This was day number thirty-two as Harris's deputy.

On day one, Harris had pointed to the front desk. "That one's yours, Tyson. You mind the door and the phone. I hope you know how to keep yourself occupied. The most we ever get around here is a traffic ticket or a vagrant."

He chuckled deep in his chest. "*A* vagrant. Sammy Buntley. He's our guest ever' month or so. He stays drunk most of the time, but I can't figure out where he's gettin' the stuff. He doesn't have the brains to run a still."

He paced to a second desk about ten feet behind Tyson's and off to the left. "Dayton's been dry since nineteen-aught-three. Prohibition don't mean a thing to us. We're used to it." He picked up a folded copy of the *Chattanooga News-Free Press*, dropped his bulk into a squeaky metal chair, and flipped open the paper.

Tyson had dropped his hat on a wall peg and looked around. Besides the desks, the office consisted of a single filing cabinet, a closet, and a trash can. A thick door with a small barred window divided the right wall in half: the Rhea County Jail.

For thirty-one days he'd twiddled his thumbs in the office or strolled Dayton's streets looking for someone to shoot the breeze with and kill some time.

Turning onto Third Avenue, Tyson thought of Miss Ida's passing. Maybe today would be different.

He eased Lizzy into a parking space beside the office entrance. A wide brick building with a single door and three windows in front, the sheriff's office had a four-car parking lot across the face of the building and a hitching rail along its side. A motorcycle with a rusty back fender leaned across one parking space.

Tyson slid across the seat and slammed the door behind him.

As usual, his boss had arrived first.

Sheriff Bluch Harris looked like a bulldog wearing a suit and tie. He sat propped at his desk drinking coffee and reading the *Chattanooga Times*—the same paper Tyson carried under his arm.

"Morning, Sheriff. If I'd known you were buying a *Times*, I would have picked up a different paper." He poured himself a cup of coffee from Harris's thermos. It smelled strong, the way he liked it.

The big man grunted and turned a page. "You should-a saved your nickel. This is nothing but a propaganda page. There's another article in here about the Butler Act."

Sheriff Harris scanned the news sheet before him. "It says here, 'Their pot shot at science will prove a boomerang.'"

Tyson set his coffee cup on the front desk. "Pot shot at science?"

"Yeah. The editor claims that outlawing evolution in the classroom keeps children from having a proper scientific education."

Disgusted, the sheriff threw the paper to his desk. "He ought to be run out of town on a rail."

Tyson didn't comment. The topic was too hot to touch. A month ago, Tennessee's legislature had approved Butler's bill outlawing evolution in Tennessee school rooms. The aftershock still rocked the nation. Six states had already introduced anti-evolution bills, but only two had adopted them—and even those dealt only with minor points. Tennessee was the first to make a felony of teaching evolution, including a mandatory fine.

Tempers ignited whenever the subject came up. Tyson had quickly learned to keep his opinions to himself.

Moving slow eyes to his deputy, Bluch eased back in his seat and clasped both hands behind his head, elbows out. "I heard you had some excitement last night."

"Dr. St. Clair and I found Miss Ida Johnson dead in her house. The doc said she had a bad heart."

Watching Tyson, Harris digested the information. "You got another idea?"

Tyson turned his chair to face Harris and sank into the seat.

The sheriff leaned forward, meaty hands folded around his coffee mug. "Let's hear what's on your mind."

"Miss Ida had a shell-shocked look on her face, Sheriff. It didn't seem natural to me. And white foam had dried on her lips. I swabbed her mouth and sent the cotton to Chattanooga to be tested."

Harris's dark eyebrows drew up. "You think she was poisoned?"

Tyson sipped coffee and set the cup down. He told Harris about the locked house and the unfinished letter.

Harris nodded. "Nobody would want to hurt Miz Ida. When I was a kid she used to give me cookies for raking her leaves." He leaned back, grabbed his paper, and shook it out.

Tyson reached for his own copy and opened to the editorial page. At ten minutes to nine, the phone rang. He swiped up the cup receiver. "Sheriff's office."

A shrill voice whined into his ear. "This is Bella Smith. I'll be coming up tomorrow around three."

"I'll meet you at the house," Tyson said.

She rang off and Tyson swiveled toward Harris who was still deep in his paper. "I believe I'll go back to the Johnson house and look around some more. Want to come along?"

Harris turned a page. "You've still got some doubts, don't you?" He shrugged. "Go ahead. I'll mind the store."

Tyson stepped outside. A warm breeze chased brilliant sunbeams across hedges and fields. He folded back Lizzy's canvas roof and snapped it down. A dozen buzzing honeybees hovered over the pink azalea bush next to the hitching rail.

When the engine roared to life, he hopped across to the driver's side of the car, flipped his fedora to the seat beside him, and took off. Five minutes later, Lizzy's tires crunched against the gravel in Miss Ida's driveway. Tyson grabbed his hat and pulled it down tight.

This time he entered the porch by the front steps where the gate had banged last night. Bending slightly forward, hands shading his eyes on the glass, he peered through the window on the front door. Through a crack between curtain panels, he could see a parlor furnished with a camel-backed sofa under a dust sheet and tasseled lampshades. Cluttered tables filled the corners. A thick coating of dust told him no one had used the room in years.

He sauntered around to the kitchen door and turned the key in the lock. Inside, the cellar door hung on weary hinges, its broken lock a sad reminder of the night before.

The dim, musty interior gave him an eerie feeling. The sitting room's heavy chairs seemed like hairy trolls crouched in the shadows, waiting to spring. A floorboard creaked under his foot, and the back of his neck tingled. Something felt wrong here. Something intangible yet very real.

He tried the door on the west wall and found a bedroom, a long, narrow affair with a popcorn quilt on the single bed and an antique chest of drawers beside the window. The room was barely wide enough to fit a ladder-back chair and night table beside the bed.

Pulling out his notebook, Tyson listed everything. A pincushion, brush, and mirror lay on top of the chest of drawers. Beside them, a manila prescription packet had "heart medicine" scrawled on it. A magnifying glass rested on a black Bible with yellowed pages.

He checked through the drawers: clothing and some letters tied with blue ribbon, the newest one dated twenty years ago. He looked under the bed and in the night table.

The grandfather clock in the dining room struck eleven as he started on the kitchen. Fifteen minutes later he tucked his notebook away and stepped into the sunshine.

"Hello!" a warbling voice called from across the drive. "Yoohoo!"

Essie Caldwell ran heavily across the adjoining yard. The wind tugged at the skirt of her house dress.

"I was afraid I'd miss you," she gasped, out of breath. "I've got to . . . catch my breath. Asthma, you know." She dabbed a handkerchief at her face. "Are you looking into Miss Ida's . . . umm… passing?"

"Ma'am, Miss Ida had a bad heart for years."

She waved him off. "I know that, Deputy. But if you're satisfied she died of heart trouble, why are you looking over her house?"

She had him there. He drew in a breath and tried to think up a pat answer that would put her questions to rest.

"No, don't say anything. I know police work is confidential and all that." She leaned a little closer and whispered, "I thought you ought to know that Miss Ida's daughter, Bella, came to see her the night before she died."

The woman looked directly into Trent's eyes, her expression conveying volumes as she raised her eyebrows and lowered her chin. "Bella stands to inherit, you know."

"Did you actually see Bella, Mrs. Caldwell?"

"She came in a motorcar. The noise woke me up around midnight. I saw her get out of the car and go into the house. My bedroom window faces the driveway and there was a moon that night."

He pulled out his notebook. "Would you spell your name and give me your full address?"

He wrote down her statement and continued to his car. When Bella arrived tomorrow she'd have to face some questions. He hoped she knew the right answers.

Restless and irritable, Tyson paced around the office until noon then walked south to Robinson's for an ice-cream-sundae lunch. Charlie Greene wouldn't have the lab results on Miss Ida for at least two or three days. Tyson wished scientific wheels turned a little faster.

Shoving the matter aside, he thought about his landlady's dilemma and stopped at a few stores to ask if they needed a clerk. No one did.

At half past four Lizzy's war dance faded away, and she settled into her parking space at home. Tyson pulled up her roof in case of rain and headed inside the house. As always, he walked through the door with two things on his mind: Lori and supper. He tossed his hat into the closet and remembered he'd left his trench coat in the car. He shrugged. He'd get it in the morning.

"Hi, Daddy!" Lori called from the parlor. She and Nessa sat on the sofa with a wooden jigsaw puzzle of a barnyard before them on a table.

"Hi yourself, Chicky." Tyson planted a kiss on top of her head.

"Hello, Nessa. I've been thinking about your problem." He sat beside his daughter.

Nessa fit a cow's head to its body and asked, "Did you come up with anything?"

"Sorry. I asked Darwin, Robinson, and Bailey if they needed any help in their stores."

She laughed deep in her throat. "So, did I. The answers were all the same." Sobering, she said, "I found Micky a couple of lawn-cutting jobs. Besides that, there are always strawberries to pick.

Mama, Micky and I can work sunup to sundown. We'll make a penny a quart."

Tyson pulled out his notebook. "At that rate, each of you will have to pick two thousand quarts every day for two weeks. And no time off for Sunday."

"Every penny does help. Micky will get a quarter for each lawn. That's fifty cents a week for the summer . . . six dollars?"

Lori held up a puzzle piece shaped like a star. "Look, Daddy. Put this one in."

"Let's see." Tyson smiled down at her. "The barn needs a door, don't you think?"

She nodded and picked up another piece.

"I knocked on a few doors and applied for more cleaning jobs," Nessa went on. "I've got three spring-cleaning assignments—a dollar a day. Mrs. Bailey will take at least three days to do her house. Every year she scrubs the ceiling in her attic and takes a needle to clean out the nail holes." She grinned.

Tyson's stomach gave a groan. "What's for supper? I'm starved."

"Chicken and dumplings."

"Too bad your mother can't bottle her cooking. She'd make a fortune."

Nessa sat up straight, her almond eyes wide. "That's it! That's the answer."

"What?"

Lori looked from Nessa to Trent. She hopped up. "I'm going to see if supper's ready," she said and darted out.

"A lunch room," Nessa said, cheeks turning pink. "We could start a lunch room. We're only a block or two from town. Everyone knows how good Mama's cooking is. At church suppers, her food's always the first to go."

"Where would you have it?" Tyson had his doubts about the practicality of the plan.

"Right here." She scooted out the door calling, "Mama, listen to this!" leaving a stunned young man in her wake.

Tyson shook his head. That girl had more energy than a pack of huskies at feeding time.

At dinner, Nessa and her mother argued the lunchroom idea up and down. Tyson kept out of it. Lori watched the women like a spectator at a tennis match. Finally, Nessa won out.

Tyson grinned behind his glass of tea. Maybe Heddie had a weak spot after all.

Heddie said she had several tables around the house that she could bring downstairs. They'd take the long dining room table to the kitchen and replace it with several smaller ones.

"I've got some red gingham curtains packed away in the attic," she added, warming to the idea. "I can rework them into tablecloths, and I'll wash up my good china."

"Oh, Micky," Nessa said, "I almost forgot. You're cutting grass for the Riesbeck and Harris families this summer. You'll start as soon as the grass gets a little taller."

He stared at her. "I wanted to play baseball this summer. The fellows have picked out teams already."

"You'll have time to play," she told him. "Baseball doesn't take every minute of every day, does it?"

"Speaking of baseball," Tyson broke in, "I'm organizing a little sandlot ball on Saturday at three. I could use a hand. How about it, Micky?"

"Sure, Mr. Tyson." The boy's expression lightened.

"If everything goes right, I want to put together a team from those ragged kids on the street. To give them something to do, you know."

"That's a marvelous idea." Nessa looked at Tyson, wonder in her expression.

He told them about a team he'd organized for street urchins: the Chattanooga Sluggers. "I don't want to mess up your summer plans, Micky, but if you'd like to help me get the boys in shape, I'd appreciate it."

Micky grew thoughtful.

"Think it over and let me know."

"Yes, sir." Micky dug into a fat dumpling.

The phone rang. Nessa threw down her napkin and hurried across the hall.

"Who could that be?" Heddie wondered. "And at supper time, too."

Two minutes later, Nessa rushed into the room, her eyes glowing.

"That was Ben McKenzie, Miss Ida's lawyer. He said he'll be reading Miss Ida's will after the funeral, and I should be present."

"You?" Heddie's eyebrows reached for her hairline.

"Know what this means, Mama?" Nessa wrapped long arms around her mother. "Miss Ida must have left me some money. They wouldn't want me there otherwise, would they?"

CHAPTER
Four

"I didn't know Miss Ida had a nest egg," Heddie said when Nessa turned her loose. "I wonder how much it is."

Tyson touched his napkin to his lips. Who else stood to inherit from Miss Ida?

Nessa dropped into her seat at the table and picked up her napkin. "Miss Ida told me she had something salted away to pay her property taxes and other things. I'd no idea she'd leave *me* anything." She tucked a loose strand of hair behind her ear. "Even five dollars looks big as a house to me now. Why, when school's out Micky will have to..."

"Speaking of school." Heddie interrupted Nessa and pinned Micky under a dark stare. "I hear that new teacher, that Mr. Scopes, is leading the young boys down a merry path."

Tyson glanced at Micky, sitting across from his mother with his head ducked down. The boy's lips formed a pucker.

"Scopes seems harmless enough, Heddie," Tyson said, reaching for a bowl of creamed corn.

"He's skipping awards assemblies with some of the students. They're smoking and telling dirty stories in the school basement."

Her eyes skewered Tyson as if she blamed him, not Professor Scopes, for the problem. The evening train shrieked into town, drowning out Heddie's next sentence.

Tyson slowly spooned a portion of corn onto his plate. Why had he opened his mouth?

Lori held her plate out. "More corn," she said, watching the spoon in Tyson's hand. He gave her some and set the bowl back.

"You got a bum steer, Ma. We weren't telling dirty stories," Micky muttered. "We was telling jokes and laughing."

"Were you smoking?"

"No, ma'am." The red around Micky's ears called his answer into question.

"Why'd you cut class?" Nessa asked.

"Aw, it was one of them boring assemblies they have every month. Some old coot will talk about a do-gooder and give them a plaque or something. It's enough to make a fellow's skin crawl."

"Son, you may be fifteen years old, but you will still show respect in my house." Heddie's back stiffened. "'Old coot is not acceptable while you're under this roof, you understand?"

"Yes, ma'am." He could barely be heard.

"Now, Mama," Nessa said from the other end of the table, "summer vacation starts in four weeks. There won't be any more assemblies this year. Let's not argue about it now." She lifted a cloth-lined basket toward Tyson. "Would you like some more bread?"

Nessa's mother would not be put off. "We'll talk it over later, Micky, me boy." Her eyes filled with tears. "Oh, what would your poor father say about these goings on?"

Nessa turned the conversation toward menu ideas for the lunch room, and the rest of the meal passed uneventfully. Tyson watched the girl from his side vision. She handled her mother like a pro. There was more to Nessa McGinty than a few freckles and flashing eyes.

At a quarter to seven Tyson carried Lori upstairs on his shoulder to get her ready for bed. Nessa followed them for the child's nightly bath routine.

"Do I have to wash my hair tonight?" Lori lisped when her daddy set her down.

"No, honey." Nessa smiled and stroked gleaming curls. "Let's have a bubble bath tonight."

"Goody! Goody!" She bounced into the bathroom with Nessa close behind her.

Tyson left them and started tidying his sitting room—a sparse but comfortable room the size of the parlor. No need to get the ladies of the house to watch Lori again tonight. He'd phoned the doctor this afternoon and asked him to come here. Twenty minutes later, a knock on the front door brought Tyson downstairs. He pulled open the door and saw St. Clair standing there with Sadie.

"Good evening, Mr. Tyson," she said, showing the hint of a twinkle. "I came to visit with Heddie while you and Adam play your game."

"She has to get in her daily dose of gossip," her brother said, smiling broadly. He had a thick book in his hand and seemed in hearty good spirits. He followed Tyson up the stairs to the tune of shrill, little-girl giggles from the regions above.

Tyson's nose told him Heddie had just taken a cake from the oven. He'd have to come down later and check it out. The men took their places on the short sofa. Tyson had set up the chess board on a table before them. Elbows on knees, leaning forward, Tyson moved a knight. "I hope we don't have another evening like the last one," he said.

"Miss Ida had a long life." The doctor used his favorite philosophical tone. "We shouldn't mourn her. When people get so old they can't function anymore, it's time to let the younger generation take over."

"I doubt her daughter would agree with you," Tyson said, dryly.

Dr. St. Clair made his move and leaned back, hands clasped across his belly. As always, he wore a white shirt and black bow tie. "Bella never cared about her mother while Miss Ida was living. Why should she care now?"

"Doc, are you sure it was Miss Ida's heart that killed her?"

St. Clair drew in a breath. "There's no certain way to know, Tyson, besides an autopsy." His voice lowered and he leaned forward. "I shouldn't tell you this, but now that she's gone, I reckon it won't matter." He paused, lips pursed. "Last week I had to tell her she probably had cancer. She may have decided to end her life quickly instead of dying by inches."

His words intensified. "And what if she did? Why dig up that dirt for every gossip in town to hash over? It's best to let the poor woman rest in peace."

Tyson picked up his bishop and set it down. Tilting his head, he looked at his opponent. "You've got some funny ideas, Doc."

Dr. St. Clair replied absently, his mind on the game. "You should read more, Tyson. I brought you a book that will open your eyes to a whole new way of thinking." He set a pawn two paces forward and handed the volume to Tyson. "It's *The New Decalogue of Science* by A.E. Wiggam. You'll find it spellbinding. Keep it as long as you like."

Tyson looked at the book as though it were a box of black widows. "I'm not much of a reader. Not for heavy stuff like that."

"You should exert yourself," St. Clair said. "America's going back into slavery. This time those Bible thumpers are the masters and the rest of us are wearing shackles. First, Prohibition and now the Butler Act."

St. Clair captured Tyson's queen. "Checkmate." His laugh held a gentle note of triumph.

Lori bounded into the room, warm and pink with her hair damp around the edges. An instant later she landed in her daddy's lap. He caught a whiff of Octagon soap.

Tyson lifted her as he stood. "Set up another round, Doc. The night's young."

"I want a piggyback ride!" Lori cried.

"Okay, Chicky." He set her on the couch and knelt down. In a train conductor's drawn-out call he said, "All aboard! Last train for Lilly White's party!"

Lori shrieked with laughter when he bent over double and gave her a bouncing ride into the bedroom. "More, Daddy, more!"

He lay her on the trundle bed and pulled back the turned-down quilt. "Not tonight. Dr. St. Clair is waiting for me." He picked up her rag doll—a motley homemade creation with one eye—and tucked both dolly and girl under the cover. "Night, night."

"Can I go to Robinson's tomorrow, Daddy? I want to play on the swing."

"We'll ask Heddie in the morning." He kissed her forehead and she snuggled down.

The hall clock struck ten before Tyson declared himself the winner of the second game. He tried to give the science book back to the doctor, but St. Clair insisted he keep it. Tyson didn't want to offend him by adamantly refusing.

When the doctor and his sister left, Tyson dropped the volume on the table beside the chess board and immediately forgot it. He checked on Lori, then hustled down to the kitchen to see if he could snag a piece of warm cake. Lucky for him, Heddie was in a good mood that night.

The next afternoon at five minutes to three, Tyson set out for Front Street. Driving through Dayton from one end to the other took about three minutes. He had plenty of time to reach the Johnson house for his meeting with Bella Smith.

Near the Richland Creek Bridge, he rounded a slight curve and stepped on the brake. A bus and a Buick had stopped on the road ahead. To the left of the vehicles, a group of men in hard hats gathered around something near the road.

Seeing them made Tyson remember that a work crew was scheduled to blast out a boulder on the edge of the road. An order had come through to widen a narrow spot.

A mail truck trundled along in front of Lizzy. His prospective baseball team hunkered down in a grassy field off to his left. They seemed to be playing marbles or something on the ground. One of the boys was doing cartwheels around them.

He caught sight of Deputy Tyson's Model T and stayed on his feet long enough to wave.

Tyson sent him a salute in return. A honeybee paused to buzz around the deputy's head and bump the windshield. A second later it found the open window and disappeared.

Sammy stood fifty yards from the roadworks site, facing traffic.

The old-timer looked like a clown figure, wearing his moldy overcoat with that Uncle Sam hat cocked on his head. Shoulders back, chin high, he snapped his arms up and down with precision, directing the vehicles. For once, he didn't look soused.

The bus and the Buick moved ahead.

Somebody from the crew shouted, and Sammy flung his hand up. The mail truck groaned to a halt. Ahead, the blasting crew ran for cover behind an old shed. The boys joined them.

Sammy arched his head forward and squinted at the mail truck. Suddenly, he saluted and waved the truck through. He held a palm out to stop Tyson.

Tyson was tapping his thumb on the steering wheel and thinking about laying on his horn. He was late. Why had Sammy let the mail truck through and not him?

The truck lurched ahead, gathering speed. An ear-pounding boom shook the earth. Rocks and dirt flew high. The mail truck skidded, brakes screeching, and almost overturned when one wheel veered into a shallow ditch. A hailstorm of debris bounced off its roof with flat-sounding smacks.

An instant later, the burly driver jumped from the truck and lit out like his pants were on fire. He grabbed Sammy by the lapels and lifted him six inches from the ground, shaking him until his hat bounced off. He shouted, "Why'd you wave me on?" His nose came within an inch of the old man's pitted beak. "You could have killed me!"

Sammy's face blanched. His mouth opened and shut several times. Finally, he gasped, "The mail must go through."

Tyson hopped out of his flivver and hustled toward the men. "Take her easy, mister," Tyson said. "Sammy didn't mean any harm."

Trembling, the driver turned Sammy loose.

The boys sprinted to the scene. The smallest one ran as fast as he could crying, "Wait! Wait!" but still fell behind the rest. The gang of boys gathered around the adults, their eyes darting from face to face.

The driver staggered back to his truck and sat on the running board, mopping his face with a red bandanna. Sammy stood beside the road, his eyes glazed.

Within fifteen minutes, Tyson had backed Lizzy up to the truck and dragged it out of the ditch. The old girl didn't look like much, and she had a fussy disposition, but she sure could pull.

The crew foreman gave Sammy two bits and sent him on his way. Then he offered Sam Bob O'Toole the old-timer's job. A burst of hall-oo-ahs went up from the gang.

When Tyson finally arrived at the Johnson house on Front Street, a middle-aged woman and a teenage girl leaned against a gleaming Pierce Arrow in Miss Ida's driveway. Both women had the face and hair of a china doll. The girl wore a black coat, unbuttoned to show an icy green sheath that stopped above her bare knees. The woman carried a coat over her arm. Her low-waisted satin dress bulged in the middle. She looked like something from a carnival sideshow.

Tyson parked Lizzy and approached them. He lifted his hat and said, "I'm Trent Tyson. How do you do?"

The woman smiled and held out her hand. "I'm Bella Smith. This is my daughter, Dotty."

The girl stared at him without changing her expression.

Tyson pulled out the house key and handed it to Bella. "Would you mind if I ask you a few questions before I go?"

An undefined gleam crossed her face then vanished. "Sure, Deputy. Is it about Mother?"

"Yes."

"Let's go in and sit down. No sense getting Old Essie the Peeper in a flap. She's got her nose to the window right now."

Tyson glanced at Mrs. Caldwell's house next door.

"Upstairs, second from the right," Bella said, leading the way to the kitchen door. "She's been doing it for years."

The interior felt colder than the outdoors. Bella flipped on a light. "Excuse me a moment, will you?" she asked, dropping her purse on the kitchen counter. "I've got to call the post office and have Mamie get a message to Elmer. He's going to have to relight the furnace." She slipped into her coat on her way to the sitting room.

Dotty perched on a chair at the table. She looked like a fledgling bird that hadn't grown its proper feathers yet.

Tyson palmed his notebook, flipped a couple of pages, and pulled out his pencil stub. "How long since you last saw your grandmother, Miss Smith? Did you visit her often?"

"Last summer Mama and I came up for two weeks." Her eyes had a sunken, hollow look and she didn't seem to focus on anything.

Bella came trotting back and took a seat. "Mamie said Elmer's working right across the street from her office today. He should be here soon." She glanced at Tyson. "What do you want to ask me?"

Tyson rubbed his thumb along the notebook's edge. "The morning after your mother's death, I sent some items to Chattanooga to be analyzed. Until the tests come back, I'll have to ask you to hold off funeral arrangements."

Her eyebrows drew together, her shoulders leveled off. "Say, what is this?"

"Just a precaution. It's nothing to worry yourself about." He shifted in his chair and asked, "Do you have any relatives in Dayton?"

The woman touched the stiff curl on her cheek and pursed her lips. "I'm an only child," she said. "Mother's last relative died ten years ago."

"What about friends?"

"I don't know much about her friends. We didn't get on too well the past twenty years." She paused, watching him. "She never forgave me for marrying Bert." She drummed the table with glossy red nails. Nicotine stains disfigured the first two fingers.

"Your husband is living?"

"Bert ran off with some floozy shortly after Dotty was born. I haven't heard from him since. I divorced the creep five years ago."

"It must have been hard putting food on the table, a woman alone with a small child."

"I've got a good job. A friend in my apartment house kept Dotty for me until she was old enough to go to school." She met Tyson's gaze. "We made out."

"Where do you work?"

Her chin came up. "Win Ho Laundry and Alterations on McCallie Avenue in Chattanooga."

That simple statement explained more to Tyson than she knew.

He made a note and put away the pad.

"When the test results come in, I'm sure you'll be able to go ahead with the funeral."

"How long will it be?"

"Soon. But if I don't hear from them by tomorrow, you'll have to send your mother to the morgue in Chattanooga. Ketcher doesn't have the equipment to keep her here longer. He'll make the arrangements."

"While I foot the bill, right?"

He let the question hang. "Thank you for talking to me." He stood and put on his hat. "I'll call as soon as I hear from Chattanooga."

Watching him with hungry eyes, Bella stayed in her chair while he let himself out.

Tyson paused on the porch steps to take a long breath. The skeptic tugged on his earlobe and whispered, "She's lying."

After a tussle with Lizzy, Tyson crossed the work zone on his way home. Sam Bob handled his new job like a veteran. Sammy had disappeared.

At supper that night, the McGinty family held their sides and howled with laughter when Trent told what Sammy had done. If they knew what lay in store for the old man they wouldn't have been laughing.

CHAPTER Five

When Tyson parked Lizzy across the street from Robinson's Drug Store the next morning, he met Sammy on the sidewalk.

"How's it going, Sammy?" Tyson asked.

"Fine, Deputy," the old man said, grinning. His bare gums glimmered. "Tanks for helpin' me yestiday."

"That's what I'm here for." Tyson watched a shiny Pierce Arrow skim past, and swung his leg out into the street. Just at that moment, a black Studebaker turned onto Main Street, so Tyson jerked back. Sammy didn't see the roadster and kept going.

"Sammy! Look out!" Tyson grabbed for his coat tail and missed.

The vagrant turned around to run back, but the car grazed his side and knocked him down.

Immediately, Luke Morgan, a local banker, jammed on the brakes and rushed to the fallen man. "Are you okay, Sammy?" he asked, kneeling beside him. Morgan looked up at the Deputy. "I didn't see him until too late."

Sammy tried to sit up but moaned and quickly lay back. "My leg! It hurts bad."

Tyson rushed to the injured man. "I'll take him to Dr. St. Clair," he told Morgan. "I saw the whole thing. You aren't responsible. It was an accident."

Sammy groaned and clung to Tyson's shoulder, his left foot poised in mid-air. "I can't walk on it," he said. His face turned pale green; his foul breath came in quick, shallow gasps.

"Can you give me a hand getting him into my car?" Tyson asked the banker. Two cars were lined up behind the Studebaker and a small crowd had gathered on the sidewalk.

Morgan lifted the injured man's hat out of the gutter and came to Sammy's other side. The men hustled him into Lizzy. Repeating his apology and making promises about taking care of the bill, Morgan laid the hat on Sammy's lap and went about his business.

Cranking Lizzy took longer than the block-and-a-half ride to St. Clair's office. Once there, getting Sammy inside was another matter. The leg had swollen until his trouser cuff made a dent around his ankle.

Tyson ran into the office, and in less than a minute he and Dr. St. Clair hurried back with a stretcher. When they stepped into the doctor's inner sanctum the walls and ceiling seemed to exude a strong carbolic smell. Everything gleamed white: the examining table, the instrument tray, the cabinets, the painted walls. On an enamel counter stood a row of glass jars with stainless steel lids. They held cotton balls, swabs, tongue depressors, and metal tools that looked like instruments of torture—and probably were.

Sammy begged the doctor not to cut his new pants. New to him, that is. The jeans were faded and patched and mended.

Like all men of his profession, Dr. St. Clair paid him no mind. He gave the old boy a whiff of ether and ordered Tyson out of the room.

The waiting room had chairs lining its four walls. Two small tables held newspapers and back issues of *Harper's Bazaar*. Potted plants covered two window sills.

Essie Caldwell stood up when he appeared. "Was that Sammy Buntley?" she asked anxiously. "What happened to him?"

"He had a run-in with an automobile. Hurt his leg."

"How terrible! I hope he's all right." She sat down, her brow puckered with concern.

Tyson looked around the room and saw his neighbor, Belinda Riesbeck, and her pixie-faced little girl, Jody. He hadn't noticed them before.

He pulled off his hat. "Hello, Mrs. Riesbeck. Jody, how are you?"

The child gave him an impish grin. "I'm coming to your house after lunch today," she told him. "Lori and me is gonna play paper dolls."

"That's wonderful. Lori will be delighted." He pulled a slightly flattened box from his pocket. "Care for some licorice gum?"

Over the child's head, Belinda smiled a thank-you at Tyson, and he told her about Sammy's accident.

Two more mothers arrived, each with a small boy in tow. Tyson smiled and nodded a greeting, vainly trying to remember their names, then he strolled outside to put up the top on old Lizzy. During the ride home, Sammy would need to stay warm.

Belinda picked up their conversation when Tyson returned to his seat. "Sammy lives with the Baptist parson. His brother, Elmer, threw him out last month." She grimaced. "Not that Elmer Buntley has much of a place to offer him."

"Elmer Buntley is Sammy's brother?" Tyson asked, his thumb toying with his wedding band. Dayton's interwoven family ties still had him baffled.

"Elmer is Sammy's only relative." She leaned forward to fetch Jody a magazine. "Until a month ago, they lived together in a little shack behind the post office. Elmer's always fussing about something. He does our yard work."

On the other side of the room, Essie nudged into the conversation. "Elmer's a busybody, Deputy. He's always trying to tell me how to manage my yard—I've been gardening for forty years."

"I think he's nice," Jody piped up.

Belinda beamed at her daughter. "He's taken a shine to Jody," she told Tyson. "Every Friday he brings her a little present—a flower or a pretty rock or something he's whittled.

"Last month, Sammy made Elmer mad, so he threw Sammy out to freeze in the cold. According to Elmer, Sammy was stealing money from him, but I doubt it. Pastor Moffit felt sorry for Sammy and put a cot in his back pantry for the poor man."

"I guess I'll have to take him to the parson's place then," Tyson said, thinking aloud.

"I'll bring him some soup," Essie promised, delighted with herself for thinking of it.

Dr. St. Clair leaned head and shoulders through the doorway. "He's ready, Tyson. The leg was broken. I had to cast it." He pulled the door wider. "Come on in."

Sammy lay on the table with his eyes closed. White plaster covered his left leg from knee to toe. He groaned and tried to open his eyes.

"Sammy, Deputy Tyson's going to take you home now," Dr. St. Clair said, speaking softly yet clearly. "Can you sit up?" He handed Tyson a manila pill packet. "Here's some pain medicine for him. I wrote the directions on the envelope." He reached for the stretcher propped nearby. "I think we'd best give him a lift to the car, don't you?"

Sammy moaned again when they shifted him from the stretcher to the car's seat. His casted leg got tangled with the good one, and the men took several minutes getting him situated.

Tyson whizzed west to Cedar then north one block and pulled into Pastor Moffit's driveway. The parsonage was only five years old, a small, sturdy place with a wide porch and neat yard.

When the tall, lean preacher opened the door, an orange kitten darted out. A two-year-old tyke scooted past her daddy's leg and nabbed the fugitive. It was the same kitten that had peeked out of Sammy's coat pocket when Tyson met him at the post office.

Pulling off his fedora, Tyson quickly told Pastor Moffit about the accident.

When he finished, the preacher shook his head. "I'm mighty sorry." His voice sounded deep and mellow. "My wife is due to have a baby any day now. She has five kiddos to chase already. I can't burden her with a sick man, too."

Tyson glanced at Lizzy where Sammy slouched across the back seat. "Isn't there any place else Sammy can go?"

"Deputy, before we took Sammy in, I called every home in my parish. No one would take him. He's too dirty, too uncouth, and too unreliable. I couldn't stand to see him sleeping outdoors, so I set up a cot in our sunroom."

Tyson sucked in a long breath. "I guess there's no choice but to carry him back to his brother's place. I'll talk turkey to Elmer and make him let Sammy stay."

"I'll get you his things." Moffit disappeared for thirty seconds.

He reappeared holding a cracked satchel and brown paper sack. "We got him some clothes from the missionary closet." He shook his head, sadly. "Sammy has the idea that you keep on one set of clothes until they wear slam out. I tried to make him take a bath when he first came, but he threatened to sleep outdoors first, so I gave it up." He handed the satchel and bag to Tyson, then paused, watching the deputy. "We'd like to see you in church sometime, Mr. Tyson."

"Yeah. Sometime. Maybe." Tyson said, embarrassed. He didn't like being embarrassed. "Sammy's in pain. I've got to get him settled. Thanks, Pastor." Slipping his hat on, Tyson jogged to the driveway, threw Sammy's things into the back seat, and climbed in the driver's window. He backed Lizzy into the street, away from Moffit's kind, knowing eyes. Trent Tyson was never comfortable around a preacher, but Moffit made him edgier than most.

Sammy sat up straighter when Elmer Buntley's shack came into view. It was a square structure with a tin roof and one window. Mismatched boards made up the walls and the crooked door. Along the front of the house, three rose bushes sprouted tiny leaves.

When Lizzy stopped close to the house, Tyson saw a rusty padlock gripping a hasp next to the doorknob. Frustration tightened his jaw. What should he do now?

Beside him, Sammy sat up and stared. “Elmer works for Kilpatrick on Friday mornings,” he said, carefully forming the words. “Across from the post office.”

Mumbling something about coming back, Tyson set out toward Church Street. Fifty feet to his right lay the railroad tracks.

Sam Bob and his pals were pitching cinders against the depot’s red siding. Those kids were like a bad penny.

Elmer was raking twigs and limp leaves in a yard the size of a postage stamp. He scowled when he caught sight of Tyson. In spite of milder weather, the gardener still wore his coat and a fur-lined cap with the ear flaps down. The coat had once been dark green. Now it was mostly black. Clenching the rake handle, his filthy hands looked callused and chapped.

“Your brother had an accident,” Tyson told him briskly. “He’s got a broken leg.”

“What’s-at got to do with me?” The old man fixed watery blue eyes on Tyson.

“You’ve got to let him stay with you,” Tyson said mildly, returning stare for glare. “There’s no place else for Sammy to go.”

Elmer let his eyes move away from the officer’s. He rubbed his nose with a brown forefinger. “I’ll unlock the door,” he said shortly. He dropped the rake on top of the pile of debris before him. “I’d best not have no trouble out of him. I’ve had all I’m gonna take.”

Ignoring his remark, Tyson headed back to Sammy. He heard Elmer’s shambling work shoes on the pavement behind him.

Sammy and his brother were of the same short, slight build, but years of hard work had put iron into Elmer’s muscles. He strongarmed Sammy inside the shack and laid him on a ratty sofa.

A filthy, tattered curtain stifled the feeble light coming through the only window. The sofa and a wooden chair stood against one wall, near a table holding a single-eyed hot plate and a dish of moldy cheese. On the other side of the room, a double bed and dresser looked like auction rejects of twenty years before.

“Here’s a blanket for ya,” Elmer ground out, throwing a stained bit of wool at Sammy. “I’ll be back when I’m finished at Kilpatrick’s.”

He banged out the door without a second glance.

“He got rid of my bed when he kicked me out,” Sammy told Tyson. “He said he didn’t want me askin’ to come back, so he broke up my bed and burned it.” His hands were trembling. “My leg’s hurtin’ something fierce.”

Tyson handed Sammy a pill and poured a glass of water from a greasy pitcher on the table. He dropped the medicine packet on a small stand beside the couch and quickly excused himself.

Relieved to have gotten away so easily, Tyson drove home. It was nearly noon. Close enough for a lunch break.

Ten minutes later, he regretted the move. When he opened the front door, someone shouted, "Whoa!"

Tyson peeked through the six-inch opening. He saw the back of Micky's woolly head and his brown flannel shirt.

"We're moving a table, Mr. Tyson," the teenager said. "Hold on a minute." He leaned into his load and moved away. Tyson stepped inside. The house reeked of ammonia and Bon Ami cleanser.

Nessa appeared in the hall wearing a damp canvas apron. "Hello, Trent. You're home early." Dust smudged her nose and one cheek. "I'm afraid you'll have to eat in the kitchen."

Beyond Nessa, the dining room looked like a tornado zone. The windows stood bare, and the beadboard walls glistened wet. A bucket of dirty water sat on the floor.

Nessa followed him into the kitchen. "Here's your sandwich." She pulled a cloth-covered plate from the ice box and gave it to him along with a bottle of milk. "Mama went into town with Lori. She'll be back soon. I've got to be over at Robinson's in half an hour." She darted down the hall.

Tyson pulled a chair away from the long table and laid down his cheese sandwich to pour a glass of milk. He should have gone to the soda fountain for a root beer float.

"Hi, Daddy!" Lori called. She skipped through the back door with her hand in Heddie's. "Robinson's pig had babies. Wanna come with me to see them? When Jody comes, we're going to walk over and look at them."

Heddie left Lori on her father's lap and went to check out the dining room.

Tyson swallowed milk. "I met Jody at Dr. St. Clair's office today. She told me she's coming to play paper dolls with you."

Lori nodded, making her curls bounce. Her eyes were sweet pools of light. "But first we'll go see the pigs."

He popped the last bit of bread and cheese into his mouth and downed the rest of the milk. "I have to get back to work." He bent to kiss the top of her head.

She smiled into his eyes. He said goodbye with a pat on her cheek and whistled his way out to the car. Just being around Lori always lifted his spirits. She had the dearest angel face on God's earth.

God's earth? Where had that thought come from? Tyson figured God was a figment of someone's active imagination. If God actually did exist, how could anyone know that for sure?

He reached through the car window for Lizzy's crank. Maybe he would read the book St. Clair gave him. What could it hurt?

The sun felt warm on his back as he bent over Lizzy's front end and worked the crankshaft. He stopped long enough to pull off his light jacket and throw it on the seat. In spite of the beautiful weather, Lizzy chose today to show her worst side. She brought out the worst in Tyson, too. Finally, he gave up and walked to the office. It was just over the next block, why work up a sweat on a day like this?

Maybe Charlie Greene would call this afternoon. With the mail what it was, Charlie would have received the package by Wednesday or Thursday. Today was Friday.

Tyson and Greene went back to their academy days. Greene was a chemist who had become tied up in a murder case. By the time the police arrested the killer, Charlie had developed an appetite for criminal pathology.

Strolling past the brick courthouse, Tyson reached the sheriff's office at two minutes past one.

"Where've you been?" Harris asked from his desk. He had a black book in his hands. "You have an accident or something?"

Tyson dropped his hat on the front desk. "Not me. Sammy." He told the sheriff what happened. "Elmer wasn't happy about keeping him," Tyson said, "but he had to do it."

"If he had refused, we'd have to send Sammy to a public nursing home in Chattanooga. That would have been a shame." The sheriff lay the book on the table and picked up a pencil.

Tyson leafed through his notebook, trying to put the skeptic back to sleep.

An hour later, Jonas Ketcher phoned to say he'd put Miss Ida's body on the afternoon train to Chattanooga. Tyson hung up the receiver and poured himself a cup of coffee. Waiting was harder on him than having a tooth drawn. Finally, five o'clock rolled around and he called it a day.

Lori greeted him at the front door. "We saw the piggies, Daddy."

She had a sober look that made Tyson kneel to her level. "Did you have fun?"

She shook her head, her eyes big. "The mother pig ate one of her babies."

"While you were there?" He drew her into his arms.

She nodded. "Why did she do that, Daddy?"

"She's just a pig, Chicky. Pigs don't know better."

"I don't like pigs."

"Hey, how about a walk to the river? We can skip rocks."

"Now?"

"Right now. Let's go." He paused at the dining room to tell Nessa and her mother he was taking Lori with him. Tyson held the little girl's hand until she grew tired, then he put her on his shoulders.

He told her funny stories, gave her bouncy rides, anything to take her mind off the unpleasant afternoon. She seemed okay but stayed close to him until bedtime. He read to her from a storybook until she fell asleep, her hand on his arm.

Though the plant may be sound, if it will not bear fruit it is good for nothing but to be cut off at the roots. Why keep it around?

Saturday morning Tyson was up early and hard at work before breakfast, moving and rearranging furniture. He and Micky carried several heavy pieces to the attic. Lori hopped from chair to chair, stood where people wanted to walk, and made herself a lovable nuisance.

After all their labor, Heddie fed them bread and jam for breakfast the second day in a row and soup for lunch. Tyson's stomach didn't take it kindly. At twenty past two, the phone jangled. Nessa nabbed the receiver, listened, and handed it to Tyson.

"It's Dr. St. Clair. For you."

The hair on Tyson's neck got a prickly sensation. He took the phone from Nessa's hands and held the cup to his ear. "Tyson here."

St. Clair's voice had an edge. "Can you meet me at Buntley's shack on Church Street, Tyson? I just got a call from Elmer." He paused. "Sammy's dead."

CHAPTER Six

"Sammy probably had a heart attack or a stroke," St. Clair continued, "but in such a case, I'd like someone else along."

"Sure, Doc. I'll meet you there." Tyson clicked the metal cradle several times. "Mabel, get me Sheriff Harris's house, will you?" He turned to look at Nessa, who watched him with an anxious expression. Before he could tell her anything, Harris came on the line. Tyson spoke into the receiver. "Dr. St. Clair just phoned me. Elmer Buntley found Sammy dead a few minutes ago."

"People don't die of a broken leg," the sheriff muttered heavily.

"You want to come along?"

"I'll be there before you will." Harris broke the connection.

Tyson told Nessa what had happened and asked her to keep an eye on Lori. He snatched his hat and coat from the closet and called to Micky, who was coming down the stairs. "I'll be back in time for the game."

When Tyson arrived at Buntley's shack, Harris stood near the door, his motorcycle nearby. Elmer slouched beside the sheriff, his eyes wide and scared. Without his cap, Elmer's head looked like a brown egg with a few wispy hairs on top.

"I thought he was sleepin'," Elmer's reedy voice quavered when Tyson reached them with his trench coat over his arm. "I shook him, and he was stiff." Elmer's Adam's apple bobbed under its thick layer of stubble.

Elmer stepped aside to let them in. He sank into a wooden chair as though his legs had given out, and dropped his face into trembling hands. The table held an untouched lunch of greasy soup and hard bread.

Harris centered in on the old man, his tone even and soothing. "Adam St. Clair will be here any minute, Elmer. Would you like a glass of water or something?"

While the sheriff casually switched from reassuring phrases to questions, Tyson moved around, notebook in hand. Sammy lay with his head resting on the left arm of the couch, his feet propped on the right one. The cast gleamed white in the dimly lit room.

One look at his face and Tyson's pulse sped up by half. That surprised, pained look he'd seen on Miss Ida lay mirrored on Sammy's bearded maw. A web-like patch of foam had dried over tense, drawn-back lips.

After Miss Ida's passing, Tyson had put some containers into his coat pockets. This time he'd arrived at the scene prepared. He slipped a small corked bottle and an envelope from his pocket.

Pulling a bit of cotton from the envelope, he dampened it with water from the pitcher on the table and swabbed the man's mouth until all traces of foam had disappeared. Forcing the cotton ball into the bottle, he corked it and returned it to his pocket.

A nasty blanket covered Sammy from his matted beard downward. Even his hands were out of sight. Tyson pulled the blanket back. Clenched into rock-hard knots, his fists lay on his stomach. Yesterday's dirt was still intact. Tyson couldn't check the palms. Those tight fingers might have been made of marble.

The dead man's pockets held an odd assortment of junk. Making a small pile on the table, Tyson listed every item: a broken pocket knife, seventy-three cents, a small lump of bruised weeds, three pebbles, and ten feet of string.

Dr. St. Clair arrived just then, so Tyson moved to the other side of the table and placed everything from Sammy's pockets into a side pouch of the dead man's cracked satchel. Even with his clothes sack, the possessions of Sammy Buntley wouldn't fill a single dresser drawer.

"Morning, gentlemen," Dr. St. Clair said, moving into the room. He spoke a few words to Elmer, then moved to the body. The doctor felt the lifeless neck. Bluch and Elmer fell silent, observing the doctor's practiced movements.

Tyson continued his survey. Inches from Sammy's head lay the cluttered table where Tyson had set Sammy's medicine envelope the day before. Tyson soft-footed around St. Clair for a closer look. The manila packet was still there propped against a smudged glass, though moved a little from its original position. Tyson placed it in the satchel. The glass contained an inch of clear liquid. Probably water.

Tyson pulled out a second bottle and—carefully gripping the glass as close to its rim as possible—poured the liquid into the bottle and corked it. The glass he wrapped in a scrap of newspaper from the table and placed it into the satchel. He recorded in his notebook that he'd touched the glass near the rim.

St. Clair covered the body and straightened. "My guess is that he's had a heart attack," he announced. "He'd look more peaceful if he'd had a stroke."

"He had dried foam on his mouth, Doc," Tyson said. "That mean anything?"

"Maybe." The good doctor shrugged. "Would you like me to test it for you? I have a little lab behind my office, you know." He reached for the derby hat he'd laid on the table.

"Don't worry yourself, Doc. I'll take care of it."

Sheriff Harris spoke. "You finished, Tyson? I need to find a phone and call Ketcher. Hang around 'til he comes, will you?"

St. Clair picked up his bag and followed his boyhood friend, Harris, from the room.

For the first time, Tyson took a good look at Elmer who sat staring at the mound on the couch. His chin and jowls shook.

Pulling up the only other chair, Tyson sank to the seat. Was that genuine grief on the old man's face?

"What time did you find him, Mr. Buntley?"

The gardener darted a guilty look Tyson's way. "Two-fifteen, like I told Bluch." He pulled a wadded handkerchief from his back pocket and pressed it against his eyes.

"Did he act sick this morning?"

"No, sir, Deputy. I fried us some eggs for supper. He ate all I gave him. An hour later he took his pain pill and went to sleep. He was still sleepin' when I left for work this morning. That's all I know." He rubbed a forefinger along the side of his nose. "I went out at daylight to finish Kilpatrick's yard before noon.

"Today's my afternoon to work at Riesbeck's," he complained. "I'm late already."

So much for overwhelming grief.

"As soon as Ketcher comes, you can be on your way." Tyson changed tactics. "How long did you work for Miss Ida?"

Elmer's bony head jerked up. "Twenty-five years." His eyes bored into Tyson. "She was a shrew, that one. Never a good word for anyone. Always harping on something." His eyes strayed back to the couch.

"Her daughter's already moved in," Tyson commented, hoping to draw him out.

"Yesterday." Buntley nodded, brightening a little. "She's a right smart one, Bella is. And much better to be around than her mother, I can tell you."

He glanced at the deputy. "She's keepin' me on. Said I know more about the yard than anyone else, and I may as well stay." His rough fingers pulled a watch from his shirt pocket. Its crystal had a crack at two o'clock.

The clop-clop of horses' hooves announced Ketcher's arrival. Father and son did their work in short order.

"I'd like to take Sammy's satchel and clothes with me," Tyson told Elmer as they left the shack. A flick of his hand showed Buntley didn't think Sammy's things were worth mentioning.

Tyson continued, "I'll drive you across town if you like. Riesbeck's live on my block."

"I know where they live," he answered crossly, then went on in the same tone, "I'd be grateful."

Lizzy's pop-rattle-bang provided their only conversation on the drive north. Elmer hunkered close to the door, staring morosely at the passing storefronts, his lipless mouth pressed into a tight line. Tyson didn't feel like talking either.

The moment Lizzy's wheels stopped turning, the old timer lit out across the street. He stopped long enough to pick a stray daffodil bobbing beside the sidewalk.

When Tyson reached the second floor of his house, Nessa and her mother were coming down the attic stairs with their arms full of red gingham. "You're back," Nessa said, smiling. "Lori's on your sofa drawing in her notepad."

"What about poor Sammy?" Heddie asked.

"Doc said it may be a heart attack. Elmer seems pretty broken up—in his own way."

"That tough old cob?" Heddie's eyebrows came up. "If he has a heart, it's a piece of flint. Never has a kind word, he hasn't."

"Now, Mama," Nessa said. "You know he loves children."

"I know nothing of the kind." She headed for the stairs. Her black brogans clumped on every step.

"Roast beef and baked potatoes for supper," Nessa said, smiling, and followed her mother.

When Tyson stepped inside the open door of his sitting room Lori looked up from her work. He leaned over for a hug.

"Is it time for baseball yet, Daddy?"

Tyson glanced at his watch. "Three and half hours to wait. Think you can make it?" He touched her cheek.

"Micky said he'll let me mark the score on the chalkboard."

"You don't say." He lifted the satchel from the table.

"What's that, Daddy?"

"Something I found. I want to see what's inside."

Her eyes widened. "Me, too."

"You can look but don't touch, okay?"

She nodded then reached out a finger. Tyson pretended to bite it. She giggled.

He undid the clasp and turned the satchel over, shaking gently.

Sitting beside his daughter on the sofa, he opened a new page in his notebook and pulled out his pencil. He listed:

- a dog-eared Bible
- a prescription packet, six pills left
- a folded, faded tintype of a couple in wedding clothes
- two stale biscuits
- a rusty locket with no picture inside

On the bottom, he found a black glass bottle. Pulling out the cork, he sniffed. Moonshine. Grimacing, Tyson re-corked the bottle.

In the clothes bag, he found some hole-infested socks and undershirts, two faded flannel shirts, and a pair of jeans. Tyson looked over the pathetic pile before him and wished he'd

been kinder to Sammy while he'd had the chance.

Digging into his coat pocket, he pulled out both specimen bottles and the clump of weeds. He wrapped them in newspaper with the drinking glass and the moonshine bottle, then he packed them in a small carton he found in the bottom of his closet.

He made a list of instructions and tied the parcel with string. Charlie Greene's work address was soon scrawled on the outside. If Tyson hurried, he could reach the post office before it closed at noon.

"Be back in two shakes, Chicky." He kissed her crown and dashed down the stairs. Lizzy made a flying trip in twenty minutes.

Afterward, he stowed the satchel and sack in the back of his closet, planning to take them to the office on Monday.

Promptly at three, Tyson and Micky arrived at the ball field, arms loaded with equipment and Lori in tow. Fifteen boys stood under the trees at the back of the lot.

"Howdy, fellows!" Tyson called. "Micky, here, is my assistant. He'll divide you into teams, and we'll play ball."

The boys, ranging in age from eight to eighteen, crowded around loose-limbed Micky who called most of them by name. Sam Bob O'Toole stood at dead center, his buddies close to him.

While they got organized, Tyson set a piece of coal-blackened board against a tree. He drew a chalk line down the middle, wrote Red and Blue on top, and handed Lori the chalk. "Here, Chicky. When Micky tells you, put a line on the board, okay?"

Her curls bounced. She gripped the chalk as though her life depended on it.

When Micky had the boys ready, Tyson said, "Red Team's up to bat. Let's play ball!"

To say the boys needed practice was like saying the Grand Canyon needed a little fill dirt. But they swung and they ran and they slid until everyone was dusty and sweaty and feeling great. When they changed sides, Tyson noticed Nessa sitting in the grass next to Lori. The young woman watched every move of the players and shouted advice twice a minute.

She waved at him and called, "Great game, Coach."

An hour later, he shouted. "Time to break it up. It's a draw—two to two. Next week we'll practice swinging and pitching."

Nessa stood and brushed off her khaki skirt. Picking up the scoreboard she fell into step with Tyson and his daughter. They walked home with Micky half a block ahead of them.

"It's nice of you to spend time with the boys," Nessa said.

"I enjoy it. Once they get the hang of the game, we'll have a grand time."

"You think I could play?"

"You?"

"Sure, I always play with Micky and his friends. I'm a first-class shortstop."

"If you really want to," Tyson agreed. "You can be on Micky's Blue team. They could use some help."

"I hope supper's almost ready," Tyson went on when they reached the corner of Market and Fourth. "I could eat a whole cow."

The smell of well-done beef greeted them at the front door. Nessa hurried down the hall toward the family apartment and Tyson headed straight for the stairs. He had to get Lori washed up and changed for supper then change himself.

Suddenly, Lori jerked his hand toward the parlor. "Grandpa!"

Tyson spun around.

Vic Tyson's white beard made him look like Robert E. Lee, only Vic was taller and slimmer than that other southern gentleman.

"Lori, honey!" Vic Tyson scooped up his granddaughter and squeezed her until she squealed.

Trent watched them with mixed emotions. What was his father doing in Dayton?

"Hi, Dad," he said, finally. "When did you get in?"

"Half an hour ago, Trent. Your lovely landlady fed me tea and cake and let me wait in here."

Trent held out his hand to shake. "It's good to see you. How've you been?"

"Just dandy, my boy. I thought I'd take a little train ride and check up on my sweetheart." He kissed Lori's cheek.

"That's great, Dad. Umm, if you'll excuse us a few minutes, we have to get cleaned up for supper."

Vic set Lori down. "Mrs. McGinty rented me a room. We'll have plenty of time to catch up."

"Hurry, Daddy." Lori darted down the hall. "I want to get back to Grandpa fast."

Tyson took two steps at a time toward his daughter who was already at the top of the stairs. Every six months or so, Vic appeared at Tyson's door and two things happened: he interfered in Tyson's affairs, and he overstayed his welcome.

With her squirming and chattering, changing Lori was no small matter, but somehow they made it down to supper on time.

Vic was standing in the wide door to the dining room talking to Nessa when they reached the stairs. His hearty southern drawl drifted upward. "When I retired five years ago, I decided to see some of the world. I've been to New York, Miami, Los Angeles. . ."

He caught sight of Tyson and Lori. "Trent, my boy. I was just telling this lovely young lady how I retired from the Nashville Police Force. Come give me some sugar, Lori honey." A loud smack followed.

Vic lifted the little girl. "You're cute as a June bug on a Saturday night."

The good china was set out and crimson tulips filled vases on two tables. Red gingham softened the window's corners. The dining room now held five tables ranging in size from two seats to six.

Tyson sat at a four-seater next to a larger table where Micky read a wrinkled comic book about Deadeye Dick. Watching his father, Tyson pursed his lips. Why hadn't he inherited some of his dad's finesse with the ladies? Nessa was staring at the older man, enjoying his story. Her pleased fascination irritated Tyson.

"Mrs. McGinty! Let me help you with that." Vic took two platters from Heddie's hands and placed one on each table.

"Please call me Heddie," the landlady said, smiling up at him. "Everyone does." She had tortoiseshell combs in her hair.

"And you all must call me Vic." His look included Micky and Nessa. After he pulled out chairs for the ladies, he settled into a seat beside his son.

"I hear you've had some trouble lately, son." Vic helped himself to beef, served Lori a small piece, and handed the platter to Tyson.

"I've sent some things to the lab. We won't know for sure if there's foul play until the results come back."

"If you need my help, just say the word. I may have been a beat cop instead of a high-class detective like you, but I can still sniff around."

"Thanks, Pa." He dug into his mashed potatoes.

The newcomer entertained everyone with stories of his police days, and when the meal was finished he helped clear the table.

Tyson took a reluctant Lori up to bed while Vic dried plates for Heddie. Tonight marked the first time Tyson had heard Nessa's mother laugh.

On Sunday, Vic escorted the McGinty family to church. They insisted on taking Lori, so Tyson had an enjoyably quiet morning.

At noon, Heddie invited Vic to sit at her table. While Lori napped, Vic talked the ladies and Tyson into playing Mah-Jongg. He was at his charming best and kept everyone laughing. At least, Tyson smiled a few times.

By the end of the game, Tyson noticed a change in Nessa. Her face had a watchful expression, and she smiled only slightly at Vic's jokes. She lingered behind the older folks to help Tyson put away the game.

"What's the matter?" Tyson asked, stacking tiles into the long box. "You don't look happy."

"Is your father always so charming?"

"Ever since I can remember. While my mother was living, it wasn't so pronounced, but since she died ten years ago he seems to get more expansive every year." He chuckled dryly. "He's not a bad sort. He's a gentleman to the core."

He ran tense fingers through the froth of curls tight against his skull and again wished he'd inherited some of his father's ways. He glanced at the freckles on Nessa's nose. Lately, he was wishing it more and more.

Nessa changed the subject and hurried away the moment the last tile landed in the box.

Sammy's shell-shocked face still haunted Tyson on Monday morning. Bluch Harris hadn't arrived when Tyson reached the office, so he settled down to read the morning news. He'd reached the classifieds when the phone jingled.

"Sheriff's office, Tyson speaking."

"Hey, Tyson! How's you-all a-doing?" The timbre of Charlie Greene's voice put squeaky chalk to shame.

"Charlie!" Tyson's pulse rate picked up. "How are Renee and all the little Greenes?"

"Great, Tyson. I've got some results for ya." Papers rustled. "Ida Johnson may have died from poison."

Tyson's throat tightened down.

"You still there, Tyson?"

"Sure, Charlie." He picked up the phone base and leaned back in his seat. "What kind of poison?"

"A weed. It grows all over. *Tanacetum vulgare.* Commonly called tansy. The same plant you sent to be analyzed."

"I know what it is," Tyson said. "We were in the same class, remember?"

Greene coughed. "She may have taken it accidentally. Some folks drink tansy tea to kill intestinal worms. If they get too much, the tansy kills more than the pests. It may also be used to induce abortion."

"No chance of that," Tyson commented dryly. "She was seventy-two."

Charlie chuckled. "The cotton swab you sent was soaked with it, but the broken cup was clean. Nothing but spearmint tea and sugar on it.

"How poisonous is tansy, Charlie? How much does it take to kill a person?"

"It's pretty potent stuff. Two or three cups of tea may be enough. There's also oil of tansy, which is much more concentrated. A quarter teaspoon of that would do the trick." The pathologist went on, "The coroner will want to check out the body and have an inquest. When can you get her down here?"

"She's already in Chattanooga. We shipped her to the morgue a few days ago. Dayton doesn't have a cooler."

"The medical examiner has a couple-a cases ahead of you, Tyson. It'll take two or three days."

"Did you get my second package? I mailed it Friday."

"The mail arrives in an hour. I'll see if it's there."

"I have a nasty suspicion you'll find the same thing."

Charlie's voice tightened. "You got something cookin' up there, Tyson?"

"We've had two deaths this week and neither party was ill."

"What makes you think they're connected?"

"They had the same pose, the same grimace, the same foam on their mouths, everything."

"I'll try to shove your stuff to the top of the list," Charlie promised. "Talk at you later." A click cut the connection.

Tyson let out a slow breath and dropped the receiver to its hook. He was still staring at the wood grain on his desk when the sheriff came in fifteen minutes later.

CHAPTER Seven

"You don't say," Sheriff Harris muttered when Tyson told him the news. Harris flipped his gray trilby to a peg by the door and lumbered toward Tyson with his neck stretched forward, frowning. "Any chance she could have taken it accidentally?"

"One in ten million. As bitter as the plant is, she couldn't have swallowed more than a mouthful without knowing it."

"Yeah, that's right. Ma used to have to whip us to get us to take it when we was kids." He paused by the front desk and Tyson smelled Brilliantine hair tonic.

"What if she wanted to drink it?" Harris went on. "She was lonely and sick. She may have gotten tired of living."

His deputy considered it. "Maybe. Dr. St. Clair said he'd just told Miss Ida that she may have cancer."

The sheriff sank to his desk and picked up a sheaf of papers. "There you have it. I'm sure that's the answer."

"We'll have the medical examiner's report in a few days."

"Fine." He shuffled pages. "I've got to get this budget report to the commissioner's office by morning."

Tyson spent the next half hour sharpening pencils with his pocket knife and laying them end to end on his desk. He cleaned his nails and rearranged his top desk drawer. He wanted to stroll down Market and shoot the breeze with some of the fellows, but the possibility of a call from Charlie kept him tied to the phone.

Disgruntled, he went to lunch half an hour late. A beefy aroma met him at the boardinghouse door, and his irate stomach began to grumble. He hung his hat over the newel post and stepped into the dining room to find everyone dipping deep into their soup bowls.

"Daddy, Daddy," Lori chanted. She waved her spoon and grinned up at him.

Tyson touched her face. "Hey, Chicky. Did you think I wasn't coming?" He took a seat next to her, the last empty chair at the family table.

Vic handed him a plate of rolls. "We were beginning to wonder what happened to you, boy."

"I was waiting for a phone call that never came." He smeared butter on a spongy roll and bit away half of it.

Nessa said, "We're opening for business on May fifth. I'm copying the menus, and Micky's painting a sign for out front."

"The trouble is," Heddie went on, "we won't open soon enough to make this month's mortgage payment."

Vic looked concerned. "Why don't you visit the banker and tell him what you're doing? He'll probably give you some extra time."

"That's a grand idea. I'll go first thing in the morning." Heddie smiled at him. "It's nice to have a man around who knows about these things."

Nessa looked at Tyson. "Dad always handled the finances."

Heddie stood and said with her gentle trill, "I'll fetch the dessert."

"Dessert?" Eyebrows raised, Tyson looked at Nessa.

"Strawberry shortcake." She smiled, anticipating his reaction. "The first for this year."

His eyes widened. "I'm glad I didn't wait on that call longer than I did."

When Heddie returned, Vic got to his feet to help her with the serving dish and coffee pot. Her dimples showed when she thanked him.

Tyson took a second look at Nessa's mother. He glanced at Nessa who stared back at him with a bland expression pasted on her face.

Micky had his dessert finished in less than two minutes. He dashed out, racing the bell that signaled the end of lunch hour.

Trying to scoop up a fat strawberry, Lori tipped her plate into her lap. "My strawberry!" Her face puckered.

"I'll get a towel." Nessa sped toward the kitchen, her braid swinging behind her.

"Don't worry, Chicky," Tyson told his teary-eyed daughter. He lifted the plate and scooped shortcake and whipped cream off her skirt. "Nessa will have you fixed up in no time."

"Here's a new plate, love," Heddie said, serving a new portion. "You can change your dress before our walk."

"To the school playground and maybe to the river." Vic smiled at his granddaughter.

Tyson helped Nessa repair the damages. A few minutes later, Lori went upstairs with her daddy for a new jumper. Vic and Heddie were waiting at the bottom when they returned.

"Let's go, Lori honey," Vic said, taking the child's hand. "We must get to those swings before school lets out."

Tyson returned to his seat at the empty table and picked up his fork.

Nessa arrived a minute later. Sliding into her chair, she said, "I've got dish detail today."

He grinned. "You don't seem anxious to get started."

She cut herself another piece of shortcake. "This is my only weekday afternoon off. I intend to enjoy it." Her expression darkened. "Not that I can enjoy much these days . . . with the mortgage due in three more weeks." She took a small bite and chewed. "Do you think the court will probate Miss Ida's will soon?"

"Not likely." Tyson told her about the lab findings. "There will have to be an investigation, I'm afraid."

"That could take months!" She lay down her fork.

"I hate to say this, but it could take longer than that."

"Who would have hurt Miss Ida?"

"You can answer that better than me." He popped a last bit of red-laced cream into his mouth.

Nessa leaned back, gazing into the middle distance. "I can't think of a single likely person."

"What about Elmer Buntley?"

Eyebrows pulled down, she turned toward him. "Elmer's grumpy, but he's not vicious enough to kill someone."

"You ever hear of Lizzy Borden?"

She shook her head. A dark strand of hair clung to her cheek. She scooped it back.

"Lizzy Borden was a Sunday school teacher in a Massachusetts village. One morning both her parents were found axed to death. No one was around but Lizzy."

He leaned forward. "Don't you see? No one is above suspicion. A murderer looks just like anyone else."

She shivered. "I know everybody in town, Trent. They're nice folks. Church-going people, most of them."

"Well, there is a chance she committed suicide. . ." He paused, thinking. "Or is there? I forgot about the letter."

"Letter?"

"The unfinished letter on Miss Ida's writing table. She was writing to someone named Alice."

"Her niece."

"Miss Ida was looking forward to a visit from Alice." He thumped a fist to the table. "That cuts it. Suicide is out."

He gazed out the window at a Model T skimming by, then looked back. "Say, I've got an idea."

Nessa watched him, waiting.

"How would you like to be my eyes and ears around Dayton?" he asked. "You go in and out of people's homes every day."

"You mean I'm invisible?"

He chuckled, watching her full red lips curve upward. "I wouldn't say that, exactly."

She traced the rim of her coffee cup. "What would I do?"

"Give me all the latest gossip. Tell me what makes this town tick."

She grinned. "You mean things like Essie Caldwell has a rabid crush on Dr. St. Clair?"

"You're joking."

"Why do you think she's always at his office? She's a bit of a hypochondriac, but not that bad."

Tyson chuckled. "At her age?"

She looked at him archly. "Just because a person gets old doesn't mean they get cold." She pursed her lips. "Let's see… what else? John Scopes is interested in a girl from Morgan Springs. He goes to the hotel there every Saturday night to dance with her. And then there's…"

Tired of her games, he broke in. "Are you still working at the Johnson house?"

"Sure. Bella asked me to stay on."

"Great. Find out if Bella came to Dayton the night before her mother died."

Nessa's smile faded. "You can't be serious."

"I have a witness to it."

She crossed her arms tightly to her waist. "This is scary."

"Why do you say that?" He grinned. "All we have to do is find an invisible man who walks through locked doors to bump off little old ladies."

She smiled wryly. "Piece of cake, right?"

He took a swallow of coffee. Nessa began stacking plates in front of her on the table.

"Not to change the subject," Tyson said, "but what's going on between my dad and your mother?"

Her hands paused. "You noticed, huh?"

"It wasn't my imagination?"

She shook her head and reached for a dessert plate. "Mama's gone on him, I'm afraid."

"Oh, no." Under his breath, he added, "Not again."

She clinked the plate onto the stack and looked intently at him. "You mean he's a wolf?"

"Not exactly a wolf. No." He hesitated, choosing his words. "Pa is honest as the day. It's just that he charms the ladies everywhere he goes. Last time he came to visit me, he courted Lori's babysitter until I wanted to belt him."

A scheming gleam came into her eyes. "We've got to do something."

"Do something? What?"

"Stop them." She leaned toward him. "Do you want a stepmother?"

He thought about Heddie and her meddling ways. "Absolutely not."

"Well, I don't want a stepfather either. We've got to do something."

"I don't think there's anything to worry about, Nessa. Pa hasn't married yet, and Mom's been gone for ten years."

"But what if he decides Mama is the one? Mama's more than willing. My daddy was a mine foreman. He never held out her chair or used flowery words. Vic's a white-haired Rudolph Valentino. I wouldn't be surprised if he started kissing hands soon." She squinted at the white tablecloth. "We've got to break them up."

He grinned at her intensity. "You talked me into it. I'll talk to Pa and you can deal with Heddie." He held out his hand. "Want to shake on it, partner?"

She grasped his hand and squeezed. "Partners. In crime and romance. Or should I say un-romance?" She chuckled.

Tyson laughed deep in his chest. "You are one of a kind, Nessa McGinty," he said. He meant it, too.

Suddenly he remembered Charlie Greene's call. He scraped back his chair and sprang up, glancing at this watch. "I've got to get back to the office. I'm expecting a call from the lab in Chattanooga." He rushed into the hall and picked up his fedora. "See you later."

Not stopping to crank Lizzy, he hustled across back lots on a diagonal to the office.

The parking lot was empty when he arrived. He heard the phone when he fit the key into the office lock. Flinging back the door, he lunged for the receiver.

"Hey, Tyson!" Charlie's cheerful voice squeaked into his ear. "I've got something interesting here."

Tyson perched on the edge of his desk. "C'mon Charlie, give."

"You were right. The second case was tansy poisoning."

"What about the liquid?"

"Pure water. I'm sending the glass to the fingerprint lab. You may have to wait a while for those results." He cleared his throat. "Just for curiosity's sake, Tyson, what've you got over there?"

"I don't know, Charlie. I haven't got that far yet. I'll send Sammy's body to you in the morning."

"Fine. If I can do anything else, just give a holler." He rang off.

Settling into his chair, Tyson reached into his pocket for a piece of Black Jack chewing gum.

Five minutes later Bluch Harris stepped through the door. He glanced at Tyson and chuckled. "You look like a cow on the cud."

"Chew on this for a while," Tyson said. He relayed Charlie's findings.

Harris headed for his desk, making Tyson shift his chair to keep him in sight. The sheriff lowered his bulk into the seat and said, "Tansy's common around here. This time of year, people are all the time gathering poke salad or some kind of herbs. Maybe some accidentally got mixed in with their pickings. Or, maybe both of them took poison on purpose. Suicide. We talked about that before." He fumbled around on his desk and picked up a toothpick.

"Two suicides in one week?" Tyson lifted his chin. "No way, Sheriff. Too much of a coincidence."

"Yeah, I guess you're right." He blew out a bushel of air. "I can't imagine something like this happening in my town." With a scowl, Harris looked even more like a bulldog. "I'd have a talk with Adam St. Clair if I was you. He knew both Sammy and Miss Ida for years."

"I'm playing chess with him tonight." Tyson got out of his chair to open the closet door. Reaching deep inside, he found Sammy's old satchel where he'd stashed it earlier. He dumped its contents on his desk.

Did a vital clue hide in this pile of junk? Had Sammy pulled up some tansy somewhere along the road? Even if he had, the little sap that would have stayed on his hands wouldn't have harmed him.

"Sheriff," he glanced at his boss, "we'll need to send Sammy's body to Chattanooga."

Scanning a sheet of paper before him, Harris nodded absently. "Make the arrangements."

After three minutes on the phone with Ketcher, Tyson looked around for his hat. Finally, he realized it was still on his head.

"Be back in a while," he told Harris and left the office. He spent a few minutes walking home and cranking Lizzy. Finally, she coughed to life.

Whizzing through the commercial center on Market Street, he kept moving south. Did some link connect Miss Ida and Sammy? Did they know one another? Unlikely. Miss Ida kept to herself.

Did they have the same friends? What friends? Miss Ida hadn't been in society for years. Everyone in town knew Sammy, but a close friend? From what Pastor Moffit had said, there were none. Sammy's own brother hadn't wanted him.

The afternoon train rumbled into town as he crossed the Richland Creek Bridge and turned right into Front Street. He wanted to have another chat with Bella.

She came to the door on the second knock and looked surprised to see him. Or was it another emotion?

"Good morning, Deputy," she said, smoothing down her cotton gown and forcing a smile. She had dark circles under her eyes.

"The lab called this morning," Tyson told her. "I thought you'd like to know the results."

"Of course." She pulled the door wider. "Come in."

Dirty dishes lay in the sink. Through the dining room door, Tyson saw a table piled high with clothes and other personal items.

"Don't mind the mess," Bella said. "I'm sorting through Mother's things." She gestured toward the kitchen table. "Won't you sit down?"

"No, thank you. I'll only be a minute." He tried to soften his tone. "I'm afraid there will have to be an autopsy."

Her face blanched under the pancake makeup. "Why?"

"Your mother had traces of tansy on her mouth." He watched her reaction. "Do you know what tansy is?"

She backed up to a chair and sat. "It's a poisonous plant with yellow flowers. It grows all over the back lot." She stared at Tyson. "Are you saying my mother was poisoned?"

"The autopsy will tell more."

"You people never give a straight answer. Why else would they do an autopsy?" She looked down at her clenched hands.

Tyson waited a moment then asked, "Why did you lie about the last time you saw her? A witness saw you come here the night before she died."

Stark fear creased Bella's face. Her breast rose as though she was fighting for breath.

"Please be honest with me," Tyson said. "You'll only put yourself in jeopardy."

"I . . . I came to borrow money. My rent was overdue. That's all it was, Deputy. Honest."

He moved to the door. "The autopsy report won't be ready for a few days. I'll get back to you when I know more."

She nodded but didn't look up.

Tyson let himself out and paused on the porch. He had an idea Bella was still lying.

Looking at his watch, he saw it was too late to catch Ben McKenzie at his office. That visit would have to wait.

When he reached home Tyson glanced into the neighbor's yard and saw Elmer Buntley bending over one of Jenny Mullins's rose bushes. Mrs. Mullins's rare yellow roses owed their fame to Buntley's loving care. Tyson crossed the grass for a friendly chat with the gardener.

"Good afternoon, Elmer. I'd like to talk to you."

Buntley sent up a suspicious look before he straightened, brushing off his earth-covered hands. "What about?" he snapped.

"It's about Miss Ida. How did you get on with her?"

Elmer's mouth had an impatient twist. "I told you she wasn't easy to work for."

"Did you actually quarrel?"

His eyes narrowed and he worked his rubbery lips in and out half a dozen times. Finally, he muttered, "We didn't have no words, if that's what you mean. Mostly she griped and I listened."

He rubbed his nose, adding another layer of grime. "She got mad at Nessa for giving me coffee and cookies. Locked the door on me, she did. The old bat only paid me two bits a day to stoke her furnace and carry out the ashes. It didn't hurt her none to give me a hot cup now and then."

"Where were you the night she died?"

Those watery eyes darted about like a rat looking for a hole. "Where I always am. At home. Alone." His voice rose to a whine. "Look, Deputy, why the third degree? I ain't done nothing wrong."

"Elmer, do you know what tansy is?"

He shrugged. "Sure. It's a weed some folks take for worms. My mama gave it to us when we was kids, me and Sammy."

"Why'd you throw Sammy out?"

"Say, what is this?"

"Just answer the question, Elmer. I'm trying to put some facts together. You happen to be the only one who knows the answers."

The old man stared at the ground. "Sammy kept getting into my money jar. No matter where I hid it, he always found it. Whilst I was out workin', he'd blow my wages on liquor. I finally had enough and I threw him out." His rounded shoulders sagged even more. "Drink's what killed him," he continued. "It finally affected his heart."

"Sammy's heart was good as yours," Tyson said.

Elmer's head came up. "Dr. St. Clair said he had a heart attack."

"Dr. St. Clair was making an educated guess. He was mistaken."

Tyson hesitated, wondering how much to tell. Drawing in a full breath, he plunged ahead. "I have reason to believe Sammy may have been poisoned."

The old man's eyes widened. His mouth fell open. In a moment, he blurted out, "Poisoned! How?"

"That's what I'm trying to find out." The sun went behind a cloud, and a chilly wind whipped past. "We've ordered a full autopsy, Elmer. Sammy's body leaves for Chattanooga in the morning."

The gardener's rheumy eyes showed he had trouble absorbing the news.

"If you think of anything that may help, let me know, will you?"

Elmer nodded.

Tyson left him staring at the rose bush as though it had suddenly spoken aloud.

CHAPTER Eight

That evening a table lamp cast a soft glow over the second-floor front sitting room of McGinty's Boardinghouse. Rain played a gentle tune on the window glass. Tyson relaxed on his short sofa beside Dr. St. Clair. A chess board lay before them.

St. Clair had begun the game with the Ruy Lopez opening: king's pawn forward two.

Tyson studied for five minutes before he reached for his own king's pawn. He set the piece down and leaned back. "I got a call from Chattanooga today," he said. "Sammy died of tansy poisoning, too."

"Poison?" St. Clair's brow creased. He looked up from the board.

"How can that be?"

Tyson scraped a thumb across the seven o'clock stubble on his chin. "I wish I knew, Doc."

"Surely it was accidental. Elmer's got a surly disposition, but he wouldn't hurt a fly."

"What makes you think Elmer did it, Doc?"

"Who else had opportunity?"

"This afternoon Elmer seemed truly shocked when I told him about the lab report." Tyson brushed gentle fingers through his curly top. Was the gardener a psychopath? Did he have a split personality? There had been reports of such cases in the papers lately.

Dr. St. Clair moved a knight. "Didn't Elmer Buntley work for Miss Ida?"

"He works for half the people in Dayton," Tyson said abruptly. The whole business irked him. He had a hard time keeping his mind on the game.

The first match ended in short order. Grinning over his victory, St. Clair set up a second one while his playing partner padded to the bedroom to check on Lori. In the evening Tyson liked to shed his shoes and soft foot around in his socks.

"You can't forget suicide," St. Clair said while he waited for Tyson to open the second game. "Neither Ida nor Sammy had much to live for."

"I don't buy it, Doc. It's too much of a coincidence that they'd both choose the same method right down to the same poison. Besides that, Miss Ida wrote a letter to her niece saying she couldn't wait to see the girl. Ida Johnson didn't kill herself."

"Have you got any other leads?"

"As far as Miss Ida goes, I've got some people with opportunity but no motive strong enough for murder." He reached for a pawn. "I'll have to keep sniffing around." He grinned suddenly. "That's the fun part of this job, isn't it?"

St. Clair grunted. "I don't know as I'd call that fun. Now, stitching up a mangled hand and seeing it work again. That's a different story." He looked up. "Did you read any of Wiggam's book yet?"

"Uhm . . . I've been real busy, Doc."

"Start on chapter three if the beginning discourages you. You'll find it fascinating."

"Speaking of fascinating, I hear you have a lady friend."

St. Clair stared at him like he wondered if Tyson had lost his mind. "Where'd you get a fool idea like that?"

"Local gossip."

He turned his attention to the board. "That's all it is. Hen talk." He reached for a pawn. "Who are they hooking me up with this time?"

"Essie Caldwell."

He nodded reluctantly. "Now, I can see how some people would get the wrong idea about her. She's in my office twice a week certain she's on the brink of death. Yesterday, she was having chest pains."

"Sounds serious."

"Right. Two hours before, she'd stuffed herself with cooked cabbage. So, I prescribed an antacid, and she left thinking I'm Pasteur."

His expression softened. "I'm being too hard on her, I guess. She twitters like a canary, but Essie does have a mind under all that hairdo. She does odd jobs for me in my lab on Thursdays. We've had some good discussions."

"The same as you and I?"

"I hate to deflate your ego, Tyson, but you aren't the only one I talk to." The doctor made his move. "Check."

An hour later Tyson cornered the opposing king. Shortly afterward St. Clair said good night.

With his collar unbuttoned, his suit coat over his arm, Vic paused in his son's open doorway while Tyson put away the chess game. "How's the case coming, Trent?" he asked, stepping inside.

"It isn't."

Vic took a seat on a straight chair nearby and listened while Tyson related his talks with Bella and Elmer.

"I believe Elmer," the younger man concluded, "but I know Bella must be lying. I can feel it. The trouble is, I don't know which part of her story is false."

"What about her job in Chattanooga? She's come to live in her mother's house, hasn't she? Did she quit or what?"

Tyson reached into his shirt pocket for his notebook and flipped it open. "She worked at Win Ho Laundry." He tapped a finger on the page. "I'll call Jim Crabill, my old partner, and ask him about it. He'll talk to me." Tyson smirked. "He's about the only one left who will."

"You got a bad deal in Chattanooga, son. I'm glad to see you're doing so well in Dayton."

Tyson sent a startled look toward his father. *Who said he was doing well?*

Vic continued, "You're sitting pretty here. Wonderful people to watch Lori, nice house and all."

Tyson tucked the wooden box of chessmen on a shelf under an end table and leaned back on the sofa. "Say, Pa . . ."

"Yes?" Vic stroked his bearded cheek.

"Do you like Heddie?"

"Like her?" His eyebrows lifted a fraction. "She's a fine woman—honest, hard-working, dedicated."

"She's also a shrew when she's crossed."

Vic fastened dark eyes on Tyson. "Have you been annoying the poor woman? After she's been so good to you?"

"Dad," he said, irritated, "she thinks William Jennings Bryan walks on water. And she'll argue 'til she's blue if a fellow doesn't agree with her."

"Will she now?" Vic grinned, delighted. "You and I have never talked about it much, Trent, but I have to tell you I agree with her. It's wonderful the way Bryan has taken up the banner against evolution. He speaks in universities all over the nation."

"Come again?" Tyson stared at his father. Was this the same man he knew so well?

"I've been meaning to tell you . . . I gave my life to God three months ago in a Billy Sunday campaign." He touched his chin, his expression sad. "Your mother was a godly woman. I never did right by her."

Vic stared at the faded roses on the carpet until Trent felt edgy and cleared his throat. "Sorry to cut you off, Pa, but it's getting late. I've got to get up for work in the morning."

Instantly Vic's expression cleared. He stood and smiled. "Don't you wish you were footloose like me? No more razor-nicked cheeks and gobbled breakfasts for this man." He picked up his coat. "Tomorrow I'm making a kite for Lori. We're going to the ball field to fly it."

Tyson followed him to the door. "It's good of you to spend so much time with her."

"I wouldn't miss a minute of it." He said good night and went out.

The moment the door closed, Tyson's expression darkened. His father's announcement had cut him deep. For twenty-two years he and his dad had been allies against a Bible-quoting woman who loved them with all her heart. She'd preached and pleaded, prayed and scolded to no avail.

Trent Tyson had always been proud to classify himself as a free thinker. Now his father had defected to the enemy camp. Tyson rubbed his face with both hands. The world had suddenly gone out of kilter.

When he looked up, he saw *The New Decalogue of Science* on the end table beneath the lamp. Moving slowly, he picked it up, stretched out on the sofa, and opened to chapter three.

"Wake up, Daddy! It's morning!" Lori tugged at his shirt.

"What?" He blinked at her. He lay on the sofa with a book on his chest.

"Why didn't you go to bed, Daddy? You're still wearing your clothes."

He reached out to kiss her cheek. "I was reading, and I fell asleep."

"I didn't know you read books." She tried to pick up the heavy volume, but it slid out of her hand. "Does it have pictures?"

"Nope. I wish it did." Yawning, he sat up and peered at his watch. "Let's get you dressed. I'm going to be late for work."

She followed him into the bedroom. "Grandpa's going to make me a kite."

"So he told me. Hold still a minute so I can get your buttons."

After wolfing down two eggs and a biscuit, Tyson reached the courthouse at ten minutes past nine and parked Lizzy in front of the office. He opened the front door and popped his head inside to say two sentences to the sheriff.

Seconds later, he strode south toward Second Avenue. Ben McKenzie had his office facing the south side of the courthouse square. Last year, the lawyer returned to private practice after nine years as a District Attorney General of Tennessee. Tyson had met McKenzie a few times. This was his first visit to his office.

A sign on the brick building said, "McKenzie and McKenzie, Attorneys at Law. Established 1888." It had an arrow pointing upward.

Buttoning his suit coat, Tyson stepped through the heavy door, climbed twenty steps, and entered an airless waiting room. A stout, dimpled woman sat behind a desk.

"May I help you?" she asked, her eyes pausing on his badge.

"I'd like to see McKenzie."

She laid down her pen. "Would that be Ben McKenzie or his son, Gordon?"

"Mr. Ben McKenzie. It's a police matter."

She got out of her chair and, shoes clumping on the oak floor, stepped to a thick door directly behind her. She tapped twice and stepped partly through.

Turning to Tyson, she said, "You may go in."

He strolled past her into a room lined with weighty books, dense furniture, and not a speck of nonsense.

Behind his desk, McKenzie's bony cheeks were red-veined and mottled, his nose long and sharp. He looked far older than his fifty-nine years. When the attorney stood to shake hands, a humorous gleam in his eye chased away Tyson's gloomy first impression.

"Good morning, Deputy. Tyson, isn't it?" He pointed to a chair. "Have a seat. What can I help you with today?"

Tyson told him about the lab report on Miss Ida. "I need to know what's in her will, Mr. McKenzie. Was there enough at stake to provide a motive for murder?"

McKenzie's lipless mouth drew into a pucker. He studied the man before him. "Have you received a report from the coroner?"

"They're doing a complete autopsy now. We haven't got the official report yet."

McKenzie hesitated. "I'd rather wait until the coroner's report, officer. If there was indeed foul play, then, by all means, I'll let you see the will. Until then, the will remains privileged communication between Mrs. Johnson and her attorney." A smile softened his refusal. "Forty years ago, Miss Ida entrusted me with her affairs. I know some other fellows would pull out the will without a fuss, but now that she's gone I'd rather be a little too strict than too lax."

"Wouldn't she want her murderer caught?"

"If the coroner confirms that she was murdered, you'll have the will and welcome."

Tyson tapped his fingertips against the hat brim on his lap. "I see."

He stood. "I'm sure Chattanooga will be acting on this soon. I'll check back with you then."

"Let me know if they schedule a hearing. I'd like to attend."

"I'll be sure to do that." Tyson shook hands with the lawyer and let himself out.

He glanced at the clock over the outer door as he passed beneath it. Ten o'clock. Time enough to get a haircut before lunch.

On the landing, he tightened down his fedora against a strong breeze. Disappointing that McKenzie wasn't more cooperative. Understandable though.

Tyson paused on the sidewalk, thought about cranking Lizzy, but turned east instead. Main Street was only two blocks from here. He may as well walk.

An hour later he stepped out of Wilkey's Barber Shop and crossed the street to Robinson's. He had a white arc around his ears and smelled of hair tonic.

"Oh, Mr. Tyson!" A shrill voice behind him made him turn.

He waited while Essie Caldwell shuffled toward him. Her spring coat flapped open to show a narrow skirt that slowed her progress.

When she was within ten feet of him, she wheezed, "Mr. Tyson, I remembered something else you may like to know."

He looked at her with what he hoped was polite interest. "Yes, ma'am?"

"It's something Miss Ida said the last time I saw her. We were sitting in her kitchen drinking catnip tea for our rheumatism." The lady's hat glinted from hundreds of ebony sequins. "I don't know if it's important or not."

Moving automatically, he pulled out his notebook and flipped to a page marked "Ida Johnson."

The woman spoke as though reciting from memory. "Ida said, 'Essie, lock your doors at night. There's shady goings-on in Dayton.'"

"Do you know what she was referring to?"

Her head bobbed. "I hear cars coming and going at all hours of the night."

"Did they stop at Miss Ida's house?"

"Well . . . sometimes. Sometimes just on the street, going past."

Scrawling a few words on the paper to satisfy her, he smiled.

"Thank you, Mrs. Caldwell. You've been very helpful." He tugged the brim of his cap, and she trotted away, her coattail flapping in a strong breeze.

Tall, rawboned, and sour-looking, William Bailey trudged past her, facing away. He bent over and picked something off the ground, looked at it, and dropped it into his pocket. The owner of Bailey's Hardware repeated the procedure several times until he disappeared around the corner toward his store. Tyson gazed after him, wondering what a prosperous man like Bailey could find so interesting on Dayton's sidewalks.

The Hustling Druggist was hustling when Tyson pushed into the store. Five people waited in the soda fountain line with six more at the tables, an overflow crowd in the small shop. Two young men darted around filling orders for ice cream, drinks, and hot dogs. Doc Robinson scrambled back and forth between the fountain and the cash register, filling orders and helping a chubby recruit learn the ropes. Today the shop had a sweet smell, a blend of soda pop and chocolate syrup.

Standing at the back of the ordering line, Tyson nodded to Gordon McKenzie at a tiny round table with George Rappelyea, manager of Cumberland Coal. Ben McKenzie's oldest son leaned back in the chair, listening to Rappelyea and fiddling with the straw in his empty soda glass. Gordon had a round face with a matching belly.

Rappelyea bent toward him, talking fast, his hair standing up like black wool with fine white streaks in it.

McKenzie saw Tyson. He lifted his fingers without moving his fleshy hand from the table and nodded a greeting.

"Can I help you, Deputy?" a gangly soda jerk asked.

Tyson stepped forward. "I'll have a double strawberry sundae with vanilla ice cream and walnuts, please."

He carried his gleaming dish and a glass of root beer to a table.

Rappelyea stood as Tyson passed. The short man grabbed his straw skimmer and reached inside the crown for a slip of paper. He bounced with nervous energy, his New York accent thick. "Here's an invitation to a party my wife's giving on Saturday night, Deputy." His thick glasses reflected light. "Good day." The little man dashed out the door.

"Mind if I join you?" Tyson asked McKenzie.

"Help yourself."

He sat down and reached for his spoon.

McKenzie crumpled another of Rappelyea's invitations and dropped it into his empty soda glass. "How's life treating you, Deputy?"

"Fair to middlin'." Tyson savored the cold ice cream. "What's your opinion of the Butler Act, Mr. McKenzie?" Tyson ventured cautiously.

"I'm for it."

Tyson glanced at him. Gordon was a few years shy of thirty and had already served as a Rhea County judge. "What do you think of the bill itself? Will it hold water?"

The lawyer straightened and rested an arm on the table. "The bill was poorly worded. It allows some legal loopholes that should have been closed up. I wish the legislature had taken time to revise it before they voted.

"Governor Peay claims the law will never come to court. If it does, I pity the man who has to put teeth to it." He stood and dropped a two-cent tip to the table. "I've got an appointment in twenty minutes. Nice talking to you, Deputy." He put on his hat and strolled out.

Tyson drew the spoon across his ice cream, taking his time over the rich strawberry sauce, Robinson's secret recipe. He read the invitation to Rappelyea's party. The New Yorker had married a lively Southern girl six years his junior. Still in her early twenties, she frequently held parties for the young people.

Tyson scraped the bottom of the dish, sucked the glass of root beer dry, and left the drug store. Lizzy cranked on the second swing.

When he reached home for his lunch hour, Nessa met him near the stairs, a plate of cookies in her hands.

"Mama packed Vic and Lori a picnic lunch," she told him on their way toward the dining room. "I'm afraid we're only having egg salad sandwiches today."

He chuckled. "You couldn't have timed it better. I just ate a sundae." Taking a seat next to Micky, Tyson picked up a sandwich.

Nessa set down the plate and took a chair across from Tyson. "We'd best enjoy our dining room while we can," she said. "In a few days, we'll have to eat lunch in the kitchen."

Her brother added, "The last coat of varnish is drying on the sign. I'll put her up tomorrow." Micky glanced at Tyson. "I've decided to help you train your baseball team, Mr. Tyson. The fellows at school have too many players as it is. I may as well give my time to the ones who need it."

"First rate, Micky. We'll talk over some strategy when we get a chance."

The boy picked up three sugar cookies and scrambled to his feet. "I've got to run." The door thumped after he dashed out.

Tyson looked at Nessa. "I've got a few questions for you. About Miss Ida."

"Have you learned anything new?"

"Charlie Greene says Sammy had tansy poisoning, too."

Her lips parted. "What a horrible coincidence!"

"I'm not so sure it was a coincidence."

"Why not?"

"Think about it. Two deaths from the same substance in less than a week's time? How many people have died of tansy poisoning before this?"

She paused. "I've never heard of one."

He lifted a cookie. "What time did you serve Miss Ida's supper the night she died?"

"It was about four o'clock as usual."

"And what time did she have tea?"

Nessa wet her lips. "I'd say about four-thirty. I washed the dishes and laid out things for breakfast. Then I took in her cup."

"Did you cut the spearmint yourself? You said it was fresh."

"Ye-es." She turned to stare out a narrow window beside the table. Tyson waited. Sometimes silence drew out more information than a barrage of questions.

She sent him a worried look. "You know, now that I think about it, Elmer brought me the spearmint. He'd been digging in the backyard and came across a new clump, just sprouted, so he cut a handful and brought it in."

"Was that near the house?"

"There's some along the fence row close to the drainage ditch on the back lot."

Tyson sipped iced tea. "Do you have time this afternoon to show me exactly where it grows?"

"I'm helping Clarke Robinson until four. After that, I could go with you."

He helped her clear the table, and they stepped outside together. From the front walk, Tyson saw Elmer Buntley working in Jenny Mullins's yard.

"I'd like to talk to Elmer before I go to the office," he told Nessa. "See you at four."

The girl hurried away with one hand holding down her hat and the other hand on her whipping skirt. It was a great day for kites. He couldn't wait to hear Lori tell about her day with Grandpa.

Watching Anna Joy help Elmer mulch around the flowers lining the walk, Tyson stepped across the grass.

"Hi, Mr. Tyson," the Mullins girl called. Her smile stretched from ear to ear, her almond eyes squinted closed.

"Hello, Anna Joy." Tyson grinned at her, then turned to Elmer.

"I have a few more questions to ask you, Mr. Buntley. Could you spare me a few minutes?"

The gardener straightened up and stared at him. "What is it now?"

Anna Joy trudged to the wheelbarrow at the corner of the house to get another bucket of wood chips.

Tyson said to Elmer, "Did Sammy like tea made from herbs?"

Disgust creased his grizzled face. "Sammy didn't want nothing but moonshine. Otherwise, he drank water and complained the whole time."

"Elmer, do you know where he got the stuff?"

The gardener's eyes shifted away. He twitched his shoulders. "Every few days he used to disappear in the middle of the night. When he came back he'd have a couple-a bottles with him. I don't know where he went or who he saw."

The gardener brushed wood chips from his filthy coat. "I tried not to know, Deputy. I didn't want to get mixed up in no bootlegging outfit. Those folks'll kill . . ." He looked startled. His watery eyes moved to Tyson. "Is that what happened? Did they poison him?"

"I've sent the bottle to the lab. We'll know in a few days." Tyson jotted something in his notebook. "When was the last time Sammy went out at night?"

"I wouldn't know. He lived with the parson for six weeks."

Tyson tucked the notebook away. "Thanks, Mr. Buntley. I won't hold you up any longer." He waved to Anna Joy. "Bye, now."

She set down her bucket so she could put all her energy into a smile. "Bye, Mr. Tyson."

As Lizzy puttered toward the Baptist parsonage on Cedar Street, Deputy Tyson considered Elmer's statement. The bootlegging angle might be the answer. He'd phone Chattanooga PD later and talk to his old partner.

Parking Lizzy, Tyson noticed that the grass around Pastor Moffit's house needed clipping. Amazing how much it grew in a few days. Tyson paced up the fieldstone walk and knocked firmly.

When the door opened, the preacher's weary face relaxed into a smile. "Good morning, Deputy. Care for some lunch? We're just sitting up to the table. I have to warn you, though—my cooking's not made for company." His smile widened. "We have a new baby boy."

"Congratulations. As for lunch, no thanks. I've just eaten."

Tyson reached for his notebook. "I'll only take a minute of your time. I need to ask you a couple of questions."

"Daddy," a small voice called from inside. "Can you cut my meat for me?"

The preacher turned and said, "Get Joey to help you, Suzy." He looked at Tyson. "I need to get back to the children."

"I'll keep it short. When Sammy Buntley was staying with you, did you notice if he left the house in the middle of the night?"

His wide brow tensed. "He slept in the sunroom, Deputy. All he had to do was slip outside. We'd never know it."

"You never heard a closing door or his footsteps?"

The preacher grinned. "Not me. I sleep the sleep of the dead. But my wife may have."

"I don't want to trouble her."

"No problem, Deputy. She's changing the baby. I'll ask her." He left the door open and hurried away.

As soon as he disappeared, a towheaded six-year-old boy skittered into the enclosed porch. He stopped halfway across the room, his brown eyes round.

"Howdy, partner," Tyson called softly, squatting to the child's level. "What's your name?"

"Bobby."

"I hear you have a new brother."

The child nodded. "He's all red. And he cries loud."

Moffit returned, and Tyson stood.

"Go finish your lunch, Bobby." To Tyson, he said, "One morning about a week before Sammy left us, Molly noticed mud on the porch floor that hadn't been there the evening before. She didn't hear him go out, so we've no idea about the time."

"Thanks, Pastor." Tyson turned to leave.

"Mr. Tyson." Genuine concern shone through Moffit's eyes. "God is real. And he loves you."

Tyson cleared his throat. Every time he came near this man, he got a mini-sermon and ended up feeling like a heel. "Uh, thanks, Pastor Moffit. Good day."

As Tyson cranked Lizzy, the preacher's words pulsed through his mind with every swing of the handle. *God is real. God is real.*

He felt more relieved than usual when the old girl finally kicked in.

Shortly before two o'clock Deputy Tyson reached his empty office and picked up the phone. Minutes later he had Jim Crabill on the line.

Chapter Nine

"Hey, Tyson!" Jim boomed. "How's life in the big city?"

"Great, Crabill. Just great." Tyson pushed aside the irritation he always felt at Crabill's constant ribbing. "I need a favor."

A low chuckle. "Shoot."

"I need you to check out a Chinese laundry on McCallie Avenue. Win Ho Laundry and Alterations."

"I know the place. What's the problem?"

"I have an idea it's the source of some white lightening that's coming into Dayton."

"You don't say. We're heading that way this afternoon. I'll case the joint for you." Crabill paused. "Maybe we'll raid the place… just for fun."

Tyson grinned. Crabill hadn't changed on that score. "Thanks. Call me if you get something."

The deputy clicked the metal armature twice then said, "Get me Chattanooga 556, will you, Mabel?" He popped a piece of licorice gum into his mouth.

In a moment the receiver squawked.

"Morning, Charlie. Did you get my box?"

Greene's shrill laugh answered him. "You sure are a busy fellow, Tyson. I thought they'd put you to roost up there in strawberry land." Static blurred his next words.

"What's that?"

"I said, I stayed late to finish your work last night."

"Next time I come to town, I'll buy you lunch."

"I was hoping you'd say that." He cackled again. "Your liquor bottle was clean. Nothing but hooch inside and the victim's prints outside." He paused. "Your water glass had two sets of prints on it, one set came from the dead man. I'll send the final results to you with this report."

"Thanks, Charlie. I'll talk to you later." As Tyson set down the phone, the sheriff came in, a newspaper in his hands.

Tyson told him the latest from Chattanooga. "Ben McKenzie won't produce Miss Ida's will until after the coroner's report."

Harris nodded. "He's a stickler, old Ben is. A good lawyer, though. He and I grew up together." The sheriff leaned back in his chair with both hands on his head, elbows out. "Ben McKenzie, Adam St. Clair, and I used to go skinny dipping in The Blue Hole up in the pocket."

Tyson chuckled. "Must have been a lark."

"Kids today don't know what fun is." He unfolded his *Chattanooga Times*.

At four o'clock Tyson stepped outside and looked down Third Avenue, the street running along the north side of the courthouse, to see if Nessa was waiting for him. She stood in front of Robinson's sprawling brick house. On the northeast corner of Third and Market, the unusual structure consisted of two wings at right angles with a circular porch filling the corner between the wings and a turret-like room over the porch roof to form an apex.

Nessa waved and started toward him while he cranked his darling Lizzy. The car chitty-chugged to life as she reached him.

"We can't stay too long," she said when they were inside the vehicle. "I've got to help Mama with supper."

"It should only take about fifteen minutes."

"Bella went back to Chattanooga to close up her apartment," the girl said. "She'll be back in a day or two."

Tyson parked on the street. Elbow to elbow, he and Nessa strolled toward a two-acre stretch of green behind the Johnson house.

Nessa peered at the ground as they moved. The grass had grown into a thick carpet with several taller stalks jutting high above their fellows.

"That's the spot," she said a moment later. Jagged-edged spearmint mingled with weeds and grass beside a rusty barbed-wire fence at the back of the property. "Last year, I used to come out and cut it on summer afternoons. Spearmint is always refreshing at the end of a hot day."

Tyson scouted around for signs of the poisonous plant.

"There's the tansy, if that's what you're looking for," she told him. "Over by that fence post."

Tyson plucked a few spiky blades and sniffed them. They smelled bitter. He dropped the leaves into an envelope and placed them in his pocket.

Nessa drew in a deep breath, her eyes on the mountains to the west. "I always love this place. It's so peaceful out here."

Tyson's eyes drifted over her face. "I like it more all the time, myself."

She darted a glance at him, flushed, and turned quickly away.

"Let's get you home," he said, as if it were his own idea.

On the ride north, he told her about his conversation with Crabill that afternoon. "If Sammy had something to do with bootleggers, that could be a clue."

"Sammy Buntley?" Nessa didn't buy it. "He couldn't do much more than sweep or carry out trash. How could he be involved with a bootlegging outfit?"

"It's the only thread I can come up with."

"I think you'd better keep looking."

At home, they found Anna Joy Mullins stacking blocks with Lori on the parlor floor. Both girls wore ponytails and dark jumpers. Anna Joy's had navy plaid fabric. Lori's was a solid brown to match her hair.

The moment Tyson's daughter saw him she hopped up and came for a hug. She quickly pulled away and ran back to her friend. "Me and Anna Joy are making a big castle." She held her arm straight out to show how big.

"Hello, Anna Joy," Nessa said, walking closer. "What a great job. You've been working hard."

The two-inch blocks lay neatly arranged in a rectangular shape with taller columns at each corner.

Anna Joy grinned and rubbed her pudgy hands together. "Lori put the top ones on," she said, proudly.

Nessa knelt on the carpet. "How about a wall around it to keep bad guys out."

Lori plopped down near Nessa. "Will you help us?"

Tyson sat in a chair nearby. "I'll help you, girls. Nessa has to cook supper."

"I forgot!" Nessa jumped to her feet. "Mama's going to be frantic if the meal's late." She scurried out.

Tyson slid out of his chair and stacked blocks for nearly an hour until the phone rang. He got up to answer it.

"Hello." A woman's mellow voice spoke. "Would you tell Anna Joy it's time for her supper?"

"Certainly, Mrs. Mullins." He put the receiver down. "That was your mother, Anna Joy. Time for supper."

The almond-eyed girl nodded vigorously and leaned toward Lori. "Let's put the blocks in the box."

When she left, Lori snuggled into her daddy's lap. "I like Anna Joy."

"It's good you have a friend." He stroked her curls.

"She never teases me about my arm like those other kids did in the nursery school."

An old ache on the upper left of Tyson's chest started throbbing again. He lifted Lori's chin so he could look into her eyes. "I love you just the way you are. You know that, Chicky."

She flung her arm around his neck. "I love you, too, Daddy. You're my best-est friend. Even best-er than Anna Joy."

Pressing his eyes shut, he squeezed her and set her down. "Time to get washed up for supper."

The next morning two autopsy reports arrived by special delivery on the early train. Tyson tore into the envelopes and scanned their contents.

At the time of her death Ida Johnson had tansy residue in her stomach but no plant particles. She had eaten within the last four hours: beef and potatoes, corn and limas. Her heart was diseased but not fatally so. She had a tiny malignant tumor in her right breast. No traces of tansy appeared on her hands.

Sammy Buntley's report was almost identical to Miss Ida's except he had eaten vegetable soup and bread. He had a moderate level of laudanum in his blood, the painkiller Dr. St. Clair had prescribed. His liver was in the beginning stages of cirrhosis. No traces of tansy on his hands, but residue in his stomach, in his mouth, and on his lips. No plant particles there either.

Cause of death in both cases: poisoning.

Tyson dropped the papers on Harris's desk. The sheriff picked them up. "Well, what do you know," he said after a moment.

"Where do we go from here, Sheriff?"

Harris dropped the papers and studied his deputy, standing beside him. "You want to give it a go?"

"Absolutely." He told the story of Carrie's death. "If there's a bootlegging outfit involved, I'll nail 'em so tight, they'll have to turn in a written request to breathe."

"Sic 'em." The sheriff handed the autopsy report back to Tyson. "Just let me know how things are shaping up."

Tyson pulled out his notebook and drew a clean sheet of paper from his desk. He spent the rest of the morning organizing his data and studying it. If Bella and Sammy were involved with bootleggers how did Miss Ida fit in? Surely, the old woman hadn't any connection to a gang. The idea was laughable.

He left his car in the parking lot and walked home for lunch. The air felt light and warm with a mild breeze that made him want to tie a hammock to a tree where no one could find him.

Lori and Heddie met him at the corner of Third and Market. They'd just left Robinson's backyard playground.

"Daddy!"

He bent to pick her up. "We timed that right, didn't we, Chicky?"

A commotion ahead caught Tyson's attention. A block and a half north, some teenage boys sauntered toward them. One of them chanted something. Chasing him, Anna Joy shrieked and waved a green cola bottle over her head.

Tyson set Lori down. "Heddie, take her into the house, will you? I may be late for lunch." He let his long legs eat up distance until he came within reach of the sobbing girl. "What's going on here?"

The culprit stiffened and turned pale. He was a full head shorter than any of the others. "Nothing, Deputy."

A red-haired kid said, "Just a little fun, that's all."

Tyson stared him down. "It doesn't look like Anna Joy's having fun."

She sniffled. "He said my shoes were clodhoppers." She wiped tears with one hand while the other hand aimed the bottle at her tormentor's head.

Tyson caught it from her with a quick swipe. "Let's get you home, Anna Joy. Your mother will be worried." He turned a hard look toward the boy who started the problem. "If I hear of you teasing her again, I'll put you on work detail for a month, cleaning the street. You got that?"

"Yes, sir." The bully kept his head down.

Tyson took Anna Joy's arm and led her home. Jenny Mullins came to the door as soon as they reached the porch. She had a square face with puffy cheeks and a salt-and-pepper bun. The moment she saw Anna Joy's tear-smudged face, her expression grew concerned.

She reached for the girl. "Are you hurt, deary?" She pulled her daughter into a featherbed hug. Anna Joy sobbed against her shoulder.

Mrs. Mullins looked over her head. "What happened, Mr. Tyson?"

"Some boys were teasing her. I gave them a stern warning. If they bother her again, let me know and I'll take care of them."

"She has a bad temper," the mother told Tyson. "I worry about her sometimes." She spoke into the girl's ear. "Come inside, child. I'll get you some tea and cookies."

Tyson took that as dismissal and cut across the grass to his own front porch. He came into the dining room in time to hear Vic's "Amen" after the blessing. He paused at the door, shocked. It was the first time he'd ever known his father to pray.

When he took his seat Heddie passed him a bowl of pinto beans. "What happened with that poor child?" she asked.

"Anna Joy wasn't hurt," he filled his plate and set the bowl back, "but I've never seen her so mad."

Micky said, "She was still mopping the kitchen when I stopped for her. Mrs. Abbot said she'd ask somebody else to walk Anna Joy home. She must have picked the wrong ones." He lifted his glass.

"Next time I'll wait, even if I'm late."

"Can I go and see her this afternoon, Daddy?" Lori asked. "I'll take her my picture book. She likes it."

He touched her curls. "That's nice of you, Chicky." He looked at Nessa. "Will you have time to call Mrs. Mullins and ask if Anna Joy's up to a visit?"

"Sure." She smiled at Lori. "When I'm done at the St. Clair's house this afternoon, I'll take you over myself."

Tyson looked down at his daughter. "As long as Anna Joy's okay. As upset as she was, she may be too tired today."

Lori nodded. She crumbled cornbread into her bowl of beans, leaving a wide patch of crumbs on the tablecloth around it.

Half an hour later Tyson gave his daughter a peck on the cheek and headed back to the office. The sheriff met him at the door.

"Chattanooga called," Harris said. "The coroner released his report this afternoon. It'll go in the mail tomorrow." He reached for the doorknob. "I'm going over to Wilkey's. Be back in a couple of hours."

Tyson picked up the phone. "Mabel, get me Ben McKenzie's office, will you please?"

Twenty minutes later he sat back, satisfied. In a few days, he'd get his hands on that will.

Monday turned out to be rainy and miserable. Shortly after noon, Tyson got a call from McKenzie.

"Good afternoon, Deputy. I just got the paperwork from Chattanooga. If you're free, you can come over at three this afternoon to see the will."

"I'll be there," Tyson said, "and thanks for the call."

McKenzie chuckled. "I may be hardnosed, but I'm not unreasonable."

They said goodbye, and Tyson glanced at his watch. He paced from the door of the jail to the filing cabinet and back again. If both old people had been murdered, were their deaths connected?

He sat down and stared out the front window. He had to come up with some physical evidence or he was going nowhere. Tyson paced the office, scanned his notes, chewed his thumbnail, and deliberated. If a bootlegging operation was the key to Miss Ida's and Sammy's deaths, how could someone poison them?

A jangle broke into his thoughts. He scooped up the receiver.

"Sheriff's office, Tyson speaking."

"This is Sam Smith at the *Chattanooga Times.* We hear you have a couple of unsolved murders up there."

Tyson stiffened. "Pull in your neck, Smith. We don't have anything to report yet."

"OK if I check back with you in a couple-a days?"

"Suit yourself." He hung up without saying goodbye. Just what he needed, a bunch of newshounds yapping at his heels. It would be a cold day in Tahiti before Trent Tyson gave them anything.

At three sharp, McKenzie's secretary told Tyson he may enter the inner office. At his desk, McKenzie looked up from reading a long paper.

"Here it is, Deputy. I was just refreshing my memory." He handed the page to Tyson. "Miss Ida wasn't a wealthy woman, but she did have a few pennies squirreled away."

Sinking into a chair, Tyson skimmed the close-set type, then went back and read it slowly.

Nessa would receive a thousand dollars. Miss Ida's niece, Alice Benton, got two thousand. Bella got the house and all remaining assets. That was it.

Tyson rubbed his thumb over his lower lip. "It's not much."

"Not enough to kill for." The lawyer cocked his head, thinking.

"Of course, if Bella were in desperate straits . . ."

"It's something to consider." The deputy pulled out his notebook and jotted down a few things. "Thank you, Mr. McKenzie."

He handed the will across the desk.

"Find out who did it, and we'll probate this document."

"I'll do my best." Tyson stood. "I just hope the guilty party gets nervous enough to make a mistake. I'm short on concrete evidence at this point."

"You calling in Chattanooga PD?"

"Not yet. The sheriff and I are going to nose around first."

Tyson strolled out of the office and descended the steps. Preoccupied, he crossed the block toward the sheriff's office. Call in the Chattanooga force? Not by a long shot. What if the murderer happened to be an old pal of some big whosis?

He shook his head to clear his brain and reached through Lizzy's open window for the crank, suddenly hankering for an ice cream soda. It was late enough to stop in at Robinson's for a few minutes then call it a day.

The drug store felt cool after the warmth of the street. Though not up to scorching summer temperatures, the weather had risen to just above the comfort zone. Tyson let the jingling door close behind him and edged between several occupied tables on his way to the counter.

At a table on the left, the Hicks brothers, Herb and Sue, had their heads together, deep in conversation. Well-known local attorneys, the men looked alike—dark-haired and slight—but Sue wore glasses. His mother had died during his birth, so a grieving father had given the boy his mother's name.

"I'll take a double strawberry soda and a glass of water," Tyson told the young soda jerk.

Carrying his drinks, Tyson found a seat in the corner. A few minutes later Belinda Riesbeck arrived with Jody. Wearing a white sailor suit with a red tie, the little girl clutched a hand-carved train engine.

While her mother ordered, the child sidled up to Tyson, eyeing his ice cream. "My mother's getting me a sundae."

"That's great, Jody. What flavor?"

"Vanilla with strawberries on top."

"That's my favorite, too. Say, that's a nice engine you've got there."

She proudly held it out for him to see. "Mr. Buntley made it for me! He says he'll make some cars to go with it, too."

Her attention drifted to Tyson's silver badge. "Did you catch any bad guys today?"

He grinned. "Not today. Maybe tomorrow."

"Jody," her mother called. She sent a polite smile to Tyson. "I'm sorry if she's bothering you."

"No bother. Jody's my little friend." He looked into the child's deep blue eyes. "You must come over to play with Lori soon."

"Can I, Mama?"

Belinda smiled. "Sure, baby. Now come and eat your ice cream before it melts."

Jody perched on the dainty chair and dipped a long-handled spoon into her dish. She chattered happily, her eyes in constant motion.

Ten minutes later Jody gave Tyson a parting wave as she and her mother left the store. They paused at the door to let George Rappelyea come in.

Rappelyea carried a folded copy of the *Chattanooga Times*. More agitated than usual, he marched to the cash register and thrust the paper at Robinson.

"You and John Godsey are always looking for something that will get Dayton a little publicity. I wonder if you've seen the morning paper?"

Tyson glanced their way. What was Rappelyea up to now?

"Sure, I've seen the paper," Doc said. "Why?"

"Did you see this?" Rappelyea pointed to a spot on the creased page and waited while Doc read it.

The pharmacist did, aloud. "We are looking for a Tennessee teacher who is willing to accept our services in testing the Butler Act in the courts. Our lawyers think a friendly test case can be arranged without costing the teacher his or her job. Distinguished counsel have volunteered their services. All we need now is a willing client. The ACLU."

Robinson's head tilted slightly to one side, his eyes narrowed. "What do you have in mind, George?"

"Why don't we take them up on it? Get Ferguson or someone else to stand trial? It would be the show of the century."

"I'm listening," Robinson said, watching the small man before him.

"The ACLU promises to cover any fine, so we can't lose. Look, Doc, I've got connections with the ACLU. I'm from New Yawk, remember." His voice intensified. "What a boon for Dayton!"

"We'll have to talk to Walt about it," the druggist said, referring to Walter White, the county school superintendent. "I'll phone him this afternoon."

Rappelyea retrieved his newspaper and stuck it under his arm. "Let's meet here tomorrow and talk it out."

"Sure, George. Around three."

The mining manager stiff-legged out the door.

Tyson slowly stirred bits of fresh strawberry in the bottom of his soda glass. If a trial of that size came to Dayton the crowds would be unbelievable. Harris would have to call in some more boys to help out. Dropping a few pennies to the table, Tyson left the store.

That evening over the chess board Tyson discussed Rappelyea's scheme with Dr. St. Clair.

The doctor sat straight, his eyes alive. "What a chance to do the country a service," he said. "If the Butler Act is overturned in Tennessee, those Bible thumpers may lose ground in other states as well." He gently tapped his fingers on the table, considering the news while Tyson studied his move.

In a moment he went on, "I hope it's a healthy week for Dayton. This is one trial I want to see."

The next morning Tyson greeted Sheriff Harris with a detailed account of Rappleyea's brain wave.

"You've got to be jokin' me, Tyson," Bluch said, heavily. His face suddenly brightened. "Think of all the booze hounds we'll catch… and the fines we'll collect. We may be able to get some new filing cabinets and a typewriter."

Tyson buried his face in the *St. Louis Dispatch*. If a trial that size came to Dayton, crowd control and traffic would be a nightmare. He was against it. But then, what did he know? He was only a deputy.

Harris drifted out. The phone rang and Tyson grabbed it, clamping his jaw and hoping it was another reporter calling.

CHAPTER
Ten

"Hey, Tyson! This is Crabill."

Holding the receiver to his ear, the deputy grinned. "What'ya got, Jim?"

"You were right on the money with that laundry place. It's a front for a booze and gambling joint in the basement. We want to bust the place, but I thought I'd call you first and see what you've got cooking."

"I'm wondering if they're supplying Dayton. Bella Smith, the daughter of a local woman, has been doing secretive runs up here in the middle of the night. Her mother and a local drunk were murdered. I'm wondering if somebody bumped them off for knowing too much."

"In that case, we'd better hold up. Can you get a handle on it from that end?"

"I need someone to do surveillance on Bella Smith. She's moved to Dayton but still makes runs to Chattanooga." He gave a description of Bella's Pierce Arrow as well as her address. "Can you take care of that for me?"

"Will do. You won't be seeing our man, but we'll put a tail on her." The line went dead.

Since the weather was sunny, Tyson decided to walk home for lunch. Today was the grand opening of McGinty's Lunch Room. There may not be a parking spot left for Lizzy.

Micky's sandwich sign stood near the street corner. Chest-high, it shouted in green and gold: "McGinty's Lunch Room. Open 11–2."

Below in smaller letters: "Closed Sunday." Tyson had helped the boy carry it out that morning.

Last weekend the family—boarders included—had manicured the yard and scrubbed the house's white siding. Heddie's azaleas had held onto their scorching pink blooms a few extra days in honor of the occasion.

Nailed to a wooden post beside the front steps, a chalkboard listed today's specialties. To make it, Lori had spent an hour rubbing soft coal over a piece of board. Afterward, Nessa scrubbed Lori for an hour.

Three men sat in the dining room when Tyson stepped into the hall. A white ruffled apron around her slim middle, Nessa met him with a tray of water glasses in her hands. She'd wound her hair into a knot and tied it with a pink ribbon.

"How's it going?" Tyson whispered.

"Our first customers are looking at menus this minute." She pulled in her lower lip then let it out and tried to smile. "I'm so nervous, I can't think straight."

He grinned down at her. "Relax. You've known these folks all your life, remember?"

"I'm not worried about them. It's the mortgage that's bothering me. What if this doesn't work?"

He didn't answer. His mind was occupied with the scent of dusky perfume. Charming.

She focused on his eyes. "What's wrong? Is my nose smudged?"

She looked so rattled that Tyson chuckled. "You're the one with all the faith. Why don't you start using it?"

"Touché." She drew in a breath, pulled up a wide smile, and aimed for the dining room like a gladiator facing a lion.

Tyson followed her.

"Ready to order?" she asked sweetly, setting the tray on the round table where the men waited, grinning at her.

Tyson sat at a small table in the corner. When Nessa had gathered up the menus he raised a finger to catch her attention. She tucked a fat notepad into her apron pocket and hurried toward him, a question on her face.

"Hand me a menu. I'm a paying customer today."

Smiling softly, she handed him a piece of thick paper covered with careful script. Tyson took the page and stared at it as she hustled toward the kitchen. He didn't see the Soup of the Day or the Sandwich List. What he saw was the light in a young woman's eyes.

Two elderly couples appeared in the doorway, a group of local businessmen close behind them. The grand opening was off to a smashing start.

Tyson finished his potato soup in short order, paid his tab, and left. Red Darwin and Luther Morgan needed his table.

A few minutes before three, Tyson eased into the drug store. Maybe he was nosy, but he wanted to see what George Rappelyea was up to. Moments later, Tyson settled into a chair near the front windows with a tall root beer float in front of him.

Bubbling with enthusiasm, Rappelyea arrived first. As usual, his suit looked as though he'd slept in it for the past two nights. His hair resembled a thorny bush. The mining boss got a cream soda and sat at a table close to the cash register. He and Tyson were the only customers in the store. Robinson remained behind the soda fountain while a clerk filled gooey containers with ice cream toppings.

Wearing a linen suit, Walter White arrived next, a solid man in build and in character. Behind White, the small-framed Hicks brothers walked with Wallace Haggard, a muscular young giant who looked more like a football player than an attorney.

Throwing down his towel, Robinson set four colas on a tray and brought them over.

While Doc handed out drinks, Rappelyea took the lead. He placed the ACLU ad on the table. "We're meeting today to tawk about setting up a test case on the Butler Act," the mining engineer said in his broad New York accent. "If we can find a teacher who's willing to stand trial, Dayton will get nationwide publicity and maybe draw in new commerce. "I called the ACLU yesterday," he went on. "They'll provide number-one lawyers and guarantee to pay the teacher's fine. We only provide someone to sit in the defendant's chair."

"Who would we use?" Sue Hicks asked. "Ferguson is a family man with children."

Rappelyea shook his head. "I tawked to him last night. You can count him out. He's too scared his reputation will be ruined."

"I don't blame him," Sue said. "A family man has to think about those things." He reached up to adjust his round spectacles.

Superintendent White spoke up. "How about John Scopes? He doesn't teach biology, but he's a science teacher."

"Is he still around?" Haggard drawled. "The term ended four days ago. I thought he'd be home in Kentucky by now."

Robinson said, "He's still here. He came into the store yesterday. He said he met a blonde, and he's waiting around to have a date with her."

Their laughter filled the store.

"Sounds like John," Rappelyea said. He flipped a straw skimmer back and forth between his hands. "Let's get him here and ask him."

White rubbed his heavy jaw. "I saw him playing tennis at the school an hour ago. He may still be there."

Rappelyea darted to the door and thrust his head outside. "Hey, Jimmy!"

A medium-sized boy came near. He wore a plaid, golf-style hat and suspenders. "Yes, sir?"

"Would you go over to the school and ask Mr. Scopes to come here? I'll give you two bits if you bring him back."

The child took off at a run.

Fifteen minutes later Scopes burst through the door, huffing. His cheeks glowed and glistened. He paused to wipe his face with a wrinkled handkerchief. His shirt had wide sweat stains under the arms and down the chest.

Rappelyea stepped outside to pay his messenger, then returned, smiling widely. "Good afternoon, John," Rappelyea said, rising.

"I'm sorry about my appearance," the young teacher panted. "I was playing tennis."

"That's quite all right," Robinson told him. He lifted a chair from another table and set it down for Scopes. He turned to the fellow at the fountain. "Bring another soda, Bobby."

George Rappelyea opened the game. "John, we've been arguing, and I said that nobody could teach biology without teaching evolution."

"That's right," Scopes said. His puzzled expression showed he wondered where this was leading. A chain smoker, he reached into his pocket for a cigarette. Haggard lit it for him.

"The biology book we use at RCHS teaches evolution," Scopes said, puffing smoke as he spoke. He laid his cigarette in a black ashtray and crossed the room to the shelf of textbooks on the back wall. He returned holding *Civic Biology* by G.W. Hunter. The young teacher scanned the table of contents, then opened the book and lay it on the table. The page described man's development from lesser animals, complete with drawings.

"You've been teaching this book?" Rappelyea asked. "Sure. I got this text from the storeroom when I subbed for Mr. Ferguson during exams." Dragging deeply on his cigarette, Scopes let the smoke gently billow out as he scanned the circle of intent faces before him. "What's this all about?"

"You've been violating the law," Robinson said. "Here, read this." He handed over the *Times*. All eyes watched the young man's face as he read it.

Scopes placed the newspaper on the table. "I still don't get it."

"Would you be willing to stand for a test case? Would you be willing to let your name be used?"

"You don't have to do it, John," Sue said. "If you have any qualms whatsoever, say so now." He and Scopes were good friends.

"I never taught evolution," Scope protested mildly. "All I did was review for the exam."

Sue said, "That's not the point here. The question is: are you willing?"

"I don't know. I don't like the idea of having a police record."

Rappelyea said, "But it won't be the same as a criminal offense. The fine is one hundred to five hundred dollars, and the ACLU has promised to pay it. They'll provide you the best lawyers free of charge. You'll help the country get rid of a bad law."

The discussion lasted several minutes. Scopes removed his glasses to rub his eyes. His face pensive, he listened to the arguments.

"Will you let your name be used?" Robinson finally repeated.

Abruptly, the young teacher nodded. "I agree that it's a bad law. I don't care. Go ahead."

Glancing at his watch, Rappelyea said, "I've just got time to run over to the justice of the peace and swear out a warrant." He looked at Tyson. "Come along, Deputy, will you? You can serve him."

At Tyson's nod, the mining engineer stood and lifted his skimmer off the table. "We'll get a bunch of scientists and preachers down here. H.G. Wells and a lot of the big boys." He bounded outside.

Tyson finished his soda and strolled outside. He crossed the street and walked a block to the office of the justice of the peace in time to meet Rappelyea coming out.

"It's ready," the small man announced, as though it were a personal achievement. "The bond is a thousand dollars."

Without a word, Tyson received the document from the bald, spectacled official and dropped it into his inner coat pocket. Scopes accepted the warrant, glanced at it, and ground his cigarette into a glass ashtray. "If that's all, I guess I'll get back to my game." More handshaking followed, and John left with Sue Hicks.

Robinson walked to the wall phone behind the counter. Giving a number, he waited. "*Chattanooga Times*? This is F.E. Robinson of Dayton. We've just arrested a man for teaching evolution." Pause.

"John Scopes of Rhea County High School."

A few minutes later he clicked the armature to break the connection, then called the *Nashville Banner*.

"I'll wire the ACLU," Rappelyea said. He dashed through the door and down the street. Running his thumb across his wedding band, Tyson gazed through the window until the mining engineer disappeared around the corner onto Market.

The group dispersed. Tyson sauntered out with the last of them. Heading for home, he followed Walter White a short distance down Market Street.

Outside of Darwin's store, White met Bob Gentry, stringer of the *Chattanooga News*. The school superintendent said, "Something has begun that's going to put Dayton on the map."

The date was May 5, 1925.

When Tyson reached home Nessa met him at the front door, her face shining. "We made twenty dollars today, Trent. Mama ran out of soup and she had to send Micky to the grocery for more bread."

"I helped wash dishes," Lori piped, tugging Tyson's pants leg. "I rinsed."

He stooped to pick her up. "Sounds like your faith's working after all," he told Nessa, grinning.

Vic appeared in the parlor door. "Heddie's cooking is the ticket. As long as she can keep dishing it out, they'll keep coming."

A chuckle came from the kitchen. Heddie called, "It's flattering you are, Vic Tyson."

The old man rubbed his beard to hide a smile. "I'd best watch what I say. She's got good ears."

"Where were you during lunch?" Tyson asked his father.

"Filling plates in the kitchen. Lori was my first mate."

The little girl's ponytail flipped around when she nodded. "I put pickles and lettuce beside the sandwiches."

Tyson gave her a squeeze. "I feel like a shirker. Maybe I should mop the floor or something."

"Paying customers don't have to work," Nessa told him, smiling into his eyes. She leaned toward Lori and touched her back. "Do you want to play outside with Anna Joy this afternoon? I'll fill the wash tub and you can go swimming."

"Goody-goody!" Squirming to get down, she grabbed Nessa's hand and pulled her toward the kitchen. Laughing, the young woman trotted after her. A moment later, the back door banged.

An ironic twist on his lips, Tyson stared at his father's calm face. "Since when are you interested in kitchen work?

"The ladies needed help." Were his cheeks pink? Hard to tell through the beard.

Tyson's eyebrow twitched. "You're heading for a fall, Pa. I wish you could see it."

With his son close behind him, Vic turned back into the parlor. "Whether falling is good or bad depends on where you land."

He chuckled. "If I were tumbling into a banana cream pie, I wouldn't mind much, would you?"

"Heddie's no fluffy dessert. I wish you could see that."

"Simmer down, boy. I'm afraid we'll just have to disagree on that point. You're the one wearing blinders, not me."

Tyson sat on the sofa and pulled at the knot in his tie. "You'll never guess what happened at Robinson's Drug Store this afternoon."

Vic took a seat, and Tyson filled him in.

Halfway through the story, Heddie came in with two glasses of lemonade. When she heard the topic of conversation, she stayed to listen.

"God be praised!" she exclaimed when Tyson finished. "Think of the boarders we'll have, the lunchers." She clasped her hands. "This is the answer to our prayers."

"Looks like an answer to an evolutionist's prayer to me," Tyson remarked dryly. "If there is such a thing."

Vic said, "I wish Bryan would come. He's got those atheists pegged but good. He'd nail 'em to the wall."

"Glory be! I forgot my potatoes." Heddie rushed out.

Tyson stood. "Guess I'll wash up for supper." His coat hooked by a finger and hanging over his shoulder, he took his time climbing the stairs. Who would have thought McGinty's Boardinghouse would turn into a den of Holy Rollers? And his father right in the middle of them.

The next morning, the *Nashville Banner* put Scopes's arrest on the front page. Always on the ball, Robinson had ordered extra copies of both the *Times* and the *Banner*. Tyson bought the last newspaper in the store.

He waited until he got to his desk to read it. Harris was in the office ahead of him, an open copy of the *Times* in his hands. He didn't look up when Tyson came in.

The *Banner's* front-page article said, "J.T. Scopes, head of the science department of the Rhea County High School was charged with violating the recently enacted law prohibiting the teaching of evolution in the public schools of Tennessee." It went on to say that this was a test case under the auspices of the ACLU.

Tyson grunted. "At least they got most of it right."

"Wait until the Associated Press get hold of this," Harris muttered. "Hard telling what they'll say next."

When Tyson arrived home at four-thirty that afternoon, the parlor was humming like a hive of bees. He opened the door and looked inside.

Heddie and Nessa sat on the sofa with Belinda Riesbeck. Jenny and Anna Joy Mullins sat across from them in soft chairs. Between them, a pile of cloth and cotton lay on the coffee table. All had brown felt in their hands—some were cutting, some hand stitching, some stuffing cotton into floppy forms. Lori and Jody had wooden blocks spread out on the carpet in a system of roads.

Lori was first to notice Tyson. "Daddy!" She ran to him for her hello hug.

Embarrassed to have interrupted a hen fest, Trent backed into the hall and knelt to talk to his little girl.

"Daddy, Heddie said there's gonna be a big hoopla here." Her hand patted his cheek. "Will there be cotton candy and clowns like we saw in Chattanooga that time?"

"It'll be a circus all right, Chickabiddy, but not the kind you're thinking of."

Nessa lay her workmanship on the coffee table and followed them into the hallway. She wore a navy jumper over a pale yellow blouse.

Tyson stood and whispered to Nessa. "What're you working on? A church bazaar?" Lori skipped back into the parlor, leaving the door ajar.

"We're making stuffed monkeys to sell as souvenirs during the trial. They'll be collector's items." She leaned closer. "Is John Scopes in jail?"

"Of course not. The worst he can get is a fine. And he won't even have to pay that."

Tyson's eye caught a movement. He watched Anna Joy lean toward Lori and hand her two clear blue marbles. Lori laughed, delighted, and gave one marble to Jody. The girls began rolling them through their roads.

Heddie bit off a piece of thread and said, "Darwin got his ideas from the devil himself. I'm glad there's a law to keep his teaching out of our schools."

Tyson stepped into the doorway and spoke without thinking. "Now, Heddie, I wouldn't go that far," he said. "What's wrong with kids learning science? There's no sense keeping young people in the dark ages because of some head-in-the-sand religionists."

"So, believing that God made the world is sticking your head in the sand?" Heddie demanded, piercing him with her intense stare. She twirled a length of thread off a wooden spool. "Can you look at pretty Nessa and see a monkey in her family tree?"

Tyson clamped his lips to hold back a loud laugh. With Heddie in that tree, monkeys didn't seem so bad. He swallowed a grin, but Nessa caught the mirth in his eyes.

"Trent," she said, "this is more serious than you realize. If God didn't make the world, what purpose do our lives have? Why are we here?" She pointed to his badge. "Why do we have laws? What keeps us from acting like animals and killing each other without remorse?"

Tyson sobered, observing her intent expression. She was incredibly lovely.

What's more, he didn't have an answer for her.

He shrugged. "I don't know, Nessa. I'm not a scholar, never claimed to be one." He turned away. "I'll be in my room until supper's ready."

At that moment Lori made a retching sound. Her face turned red. She retched again.

In a flash, Trent picked her up and turned her over his arm with her head far down.

"Bring it up, Lori! Bring it up!" he kept saying, as though his words would clear her throat. A muffled gurgle was the only answer.

The child's face darkened to purple. Nessa flew to him. She pressed the child's back with both hands. The marble popped out on the floor.

Gasping, Lori wailed. She reached for her daddy's neck and clung to it as though it were a life preserver. Clutching her, Trent sank into an armchair. He felt light-headed. His legs had turned to jelly. He put his face next to Lori's. "Are you okay now, Chicky?"

Lori nodded, still crying. She snuggled her head close to Trent's neck and lay quiet.

"I's sorry," Anna Joy said, her almond eyes glistening with tears. She knelt in front of Lori, her chubby hand on the child's arm. "I's sorry, Lori."

Lori reached out to hug her friend, then returned to the safety of her daddy's arms.

Nessa gave Anna Joy a hug. "Don't worry, Anna Joy. She's okay now."

Fifteen minutes later, when his knees would support him up the stairs, Tyson carried Lori to their rooms to clean up for supper.

The choking episode brought back in full force the tumult of emotions he'd felt after Carrie's death. The fear, the rage, the unspeakable dread.

Changing his daughter and brushing her curly mop of hair helped him regain some equilibrium, though his insides still felt shaky.

After supper, he tucked Lori into her trundle bed and sang her to sleep. Then he picked up Wiggam's book.

Looking fresh as a newly picked peach, Nessa stopped Tyson on his way out the door the next morning. "Would you drive by Dr. St. Clair's office and pick up some tonic for Lori? I've got about two doses left."

"Sure." He pulled on his hat. "I'll get it on the way home."

No news came from Chattanooga PD that day and no blazing inspiration hit Tyson's brain. He killed time listening to Harris's speculations about the upcoming trial and keeping his own opinions to himself.

Finally, he headed home early and called, "Lori?" when he stepped through the door.

"In the kitchen, Daddy," her shrill voice answered.

Belinda and Jody sat at the table with Nessa and Lori. Lori and Jody were pulling green stems off strawberries and dropping them into a wide basin. Both girls had rosy, fruit-dotted chins.

"Trent! You're home early." Nessa sliced berries into a third basin.

"Not much going on at the office," Tyson said, "so I thought I'd head home."

"Did you get Lori's tonic?"

He snapped his fingers. "I forgot it." Heading back toward the door, he said, "I'll get it now. Be back in twenty minutes."

St. Clair's waiting room stood empty when he arrived. The door through the dividing partition was locked and so was the inner sanctum. Tyson stepped outside onto the porch and knocked on the outer door of St. Clair's living quarters.

Sadie parted the curtains on the door and looked out, then opened the door. She wore a spotless white apron over her brown calico dress. She smiled when she saw the deputy. "Good afternoon, Mr. Tyson. Are you looking for Adam?"

He slipped off his hat. "Is he around? I've come to fetch some tonic for Lori."

"Just a moment. I'll get him." She disappeared through a doorway off the living room.

Wearing an open-necked shirt, Dr. St. Clair stepped into view. He had a heavy gray book open in his hands.

"Howdy, Trent. What can I do for you?"

"I've come to fetch some tonic for Lori."

"Come along to the office. I'll get it for you." He checked the page number and lay the book on a nearby table. Keys jangled as he found the right one and unlocked both doors.

Leaving the examining room door ajar behind him, he reached for a tall brown jug and a small, flat bottle of the same dark glass.

"I hear there's going to be a trial here soon," the doctor said, glancing back at Tyson.

"Yeah." The deputy stood near the white counter and bent the brim of his fedora between his fingers. He didn't like the antiseptic smell in there.

"It'll be history in the making," St. Clair went on. "A giant step forward for science—if we win." He dug around in a drawer and pulled out a funnel. "I wonder who they're going to have representing the different sides."

"The Hicks brothers and Haggard are in on it, but I'm not sure if they're defending or prosecuting."

"I wish they'd bring Clarence Darrow down here. He's the man to take on those dim-witted fundamentalists. Without notes, he spoke for two days in the Loeb-Leopold case and kept those college boys from hanging. That was after they'd confessed to killing their thirteen-year-old cousin with a hammer just to see if they could get away with it." The doctor nodded approvingly. "The man's a genius."

Tyson said, "I was on the Chattanooga Force at the time. The trial was a popular topic at headquarters. You wouldn't have agreed with their viewpoint."

"Darrow's the man for our time," St. Clair insisted. "I'd love to see him in action."

Tyson's expression sharpened as a thought came to him. "Doc, I've got a couple of questions for you."

The doctor chuckled softly. "Legal or medical?"

"Scientific." Tyson reached into his shirt pocket for a piece of Black Jack. "How is it that men have laws to control their actions when animals don't? If we came from the same ancestors, I mean."

Watching thick dark liquid ooze slowly into the funnel, St. Clair said, "We've reached a higher plane. Man is evolution's crowning achievement. And he keeps getting better." He set down the jug and pushed a wide cork into its opening. "Think of people all over the world. You can see how some people are more developed than others."

"How so?"

"Well, some live in huts and wear loincloths. Others drive Cadillacs."

"But they all have the same kind of arms and legs. They all walk upright and have some type of government." Watching St. Clair's face, Tyson took the tonic bottle from his hand.

"Have you read any of Wiggam's book yet?" St. Clair asked, moving to the sink to wash out the funnel.

Tyson put on his hat, preparing to leave. "I got through the third chapter last night."

"He makes some fascinating points around chapter five. Keep reading. When you're through, we'll talk more in-depth."

Tyson said goodbye and strolled back to his car. He was disappointed that St. Clair hadn't given him any satisfying answers.

Chugging north on Market, he decided to dig out some answers himself. Maybe he ought to start with Darwin's book instead of Wiggam's. The next chance he got, he'd ask the doctor if he could borrow it. Meanwhile, on to chapter five.

CHAPTER Eleven

By the next week, Harris had taken to prowling around Dayton, listening to the latest gossip and sizing up the town's attitude.

In some quarters controversy ran high enough to erupt in a fight. The sheriff wanted to be nearby if that happened, and quash the trouble before it got out of hand.

That left Tyson in the office minding the phone, with little to occupy his time. He started carrying Wiggam's book to work.

"Tyson?" Harris barked into the phone the next afternoon.

"Here, Sheriff."

"Come on over to the courthouse. Some men are in the courtroom discussing Chattanooga's bid to have the trial there instead of Dayton. They're getting rowdy. I could use some help."

Tyson stood and reached for his hat. "Be there in two minutes."

Cutting across the lawn, Tyson stretched his legs toward the back door of the courthouse. He reached it in twenty-five paces and hustled inside. Jogging up wide steps, he met Harris at the double doors on the second floor.

Wearing black garters over his white shirt sleeves, barber Virgil Wilkey stood in front of the open doorway, legs wide, hands behind his back, blocking the officers' way.

Behind him, George Rappelyea's voice echoed in the near-empty room. "We ought to boycott Chattanooga for sticking its nose into Dayton's business!" he said, standing in front of the judge's bench and shaking his fist. Two camera flashes exploded, making the little man blink.

Several called out, "Hear, hear!"

Tyson rocked back on his heels, lips pursed, watching. Harris let his meaty jaw sink to his chest, his eyes on the short mining engineer.

Face flushed, Rappelyea shouted, "The state has no business in the schoolroom ordering teachers to keep scientific facts from children. Lots of people of Dayton agree. There are as many evolutionists in Dayton as there are monkeys in Chattanooga!"

Slim Thurlow Reed pushed his way to the front and shouted, "You can't call my family monkeys!" He lunged at Rappelyea and bit him on the shoulder.

Letting out a startled, angry cry, Rappelyea cuffed the man on the ear. They set to, fists raised.

"Break it up!" Harris pushed Wilkey aside and lunged between the red-faced, huffing men. He put his hands on both chests, separating them. "That's all, folks! Let's call it a day."

Tyson shouldered his way to the center of the crowd amid cries of "Nail him, Thurlow!" "Run him out of town!" and "Give him one for Scopes!" Because Rappelyea had signed the warrant, many Daytonians thought the mining engineer had betrayed his friend.

"Go on about your business!" Bluch Harris called, skimming a fierce eye across the crowd.

Slowly, the men filtered out of the room and down the stairs. When the last fellow ambled out, Harris mopped his big face with a red bandanna handkerchief. "That was a close one. George had best pull his horns in or he'll get himself into real trouble."

"That man seems to look for trouble," Tyson remarked as he and Harris returned to the office. When they reached the parking lot, Tyson stared at the sheriff's motorcycle. A small wooden sign hung from its back: "Monkeyville Police." Was anyone immune to local hysteria?

The sheriff threw a wide leg over the motorcycle seat and hit the starter. Over the roar of the engine, he shouted, "I'm heading into town for a few minutes. I'll see you later." With a little gunning of the engine, he rolled away, his sign rattling against the rusty back fender.

Tyson slowly stepped inside the office. Five minutes later, feet propped on his desk, he was deep into Wiggam's last chapter when the phone jangled. It was Crabill.

"Hey, Tyson. We've got some news for you."

"Spill it, Crabill."

"You were right on the money about the laundry. It's part of a larger operation coming from outside the city. We know where the still is, but we don't know who's heading up the outfit."

"You may as well go ahead and bust the laundry, Jim. Finding the boss may not be good for your health." Tyson's tone showed his deep bitterness.

"I know what you mean."

"You get anything on Bella Smith?"

"Yeah. She's picking up the stuff at two a.m., then driving to Dayton. She leaves the trunk of her car unlocked. An hour later, somebody comes and lifts the goods for her."

"You get an ID on him?"

"His name's Zach O'Toole. He's a coal miner that lives on the wrong side of the tracks."

"Is he in the clink?"

"Not yet. We're holding off for a while, trying to sniff out some bigger game." He paused. "That help you any?"

Tyson grunted. "Not much. If the murders *were* booze-related, I can't figure out how the victims could have gotten the poison."

"Did someone slip them a doctored chocolate bar or something?"

"Lab reports show their stomachs contained only what they ate for dinner. Neither cook had a decent motive."

Sheriff Harris came through the door and hung his trilby on a peg. He carried a small paper sack. Glancing at Tyson, he headed for his desk.

"It's your baby, Tyson," Crabill continued. "I'll give you a call if we find anything else." The line went dead.

Tyson replaced the cup receiver.

"Bad news?" Harris asked, shifting in his chair for a comfortable position.

"Bella's laundry job is a front for trafficking moonshine. She hauls the stuff to Dayton in the wee hours and unloads it near her mother's house. Zach O'Toole makes the pickup."

"Look, Tyson," the sheriff said, opening his thermos, "maybe Bella knocked off her mother for being too nosy about her comings and goings."

"Bella was there too early. Miss Ida didn't die until the next night. And how does Sammy fit in? He wouldn't have blown the whistle on her. He'd cut off his own supply if he did."

"How about Elmer? He had a grudge against both parties."

"Bad enough to knock them off? He had a fight with Miss Ida last year. Why didn't he do it back then?"

Harris considered a moment. "Maybe the two cases aren't related."

"No way, Sheriff. The same kind of poison only four days apart? That can't be a coincidence." Tyson stood up and started pacing. His shoes thumped on the wooden floor. "If we haul Bella in for questioning now, we'll blow the big sting operation Crabill's setting up in Chattanooga."

"I guess we'd best sit tight then." Harris reached into the sack for a cookie.

Tyson pulled out his notebook and studied the pages he'd practically memorized. Fifteen minutes later he tucked the tablet into his pocket and stared through the window at the back of the courthouse, where a work crew was building a tall scaffold. Dayton had already started dressing up for its big date.

After lunch, curiosity drew Tyson to Robinson's Rexall. The drug store was the news center of town these days. Conversation focused on the upcoming trial no matter when a fellow came around.

A delivery van passed Lizzy. Tyson turned to stare and almost caused an accident. On its side, someone had painted a chimp and "Monkeyville Express." Further down the street, a billboard showed a monkey drinking soda, another had a picture of a long-tailed primate holding a bottle of patent medicine.

Even the home of the hustling druggist had changed since Tyson's last visit. A wide sign above the fountain advertised, "Simian sodas, 5 cents."

Doc Robinson leaned across the counter, confiding to Tyson a fact that the whole town knew by now: "William Jennings Bryan is coming as a special prosecutor. He announced it this morning on the radio."

Tyson picked up his ice cream sundae—butterscotch today. "You don't say. My landlady will be delighted. He's one of her favorite speakers. Almost better than Billy Sunday."

Robinson said, "According to Bryan, the World's Christian Fundamentals Association invited him in, and the Hicks boys seconded the motion."

"Doc, this is turning into a first-class brawl."

The druggist chuckled. "You've got that right. I only hope a few thousand folks will want to see the punches firsthand."

Tyson found a chair near the front door. Sipping sodas, Sue Hicks and a shaggy-haired, unshaven man in a wrinkled suit sat at the next table. Tyson nodded at them as he dropped his hat on the table and sat down.

He was halfway through his sundae when the bell on the door jingled and John Scopes walked in.

Sue stood. "Dr. Neal, that's John Scopes now."

Scopes walked to the table and shook hands with the men.

"Boy, I'm interested in your case and, whether you want me or not, I'm going to be here. I'll be available twenty-four hours a day."

"Thank you, sir," Scopes said, excitement in his voice.

When they were seated, Sue explained that John Neal was a constitutional expert, the head of a private law school in Knoxville. What he didn't say was that two years before, John Neal had lost a position at the University of Tennessee's school of law for choosing a textbook with radical views.

The next year he opened his own law school and then ran for governor of Tennessee. He lost to Austin Peay who had just signed the Butler Act into law.

Neal was a man with a mission.

The two lawyers put their heads together with Scopes over the small round table and talked in excited, low tones.

Tyson finished his ice cream and walked down Market Street toward Lizzy. *The New Decalogue of Science* hadn't given him much insight into Dr. St. Clair's philosophies. Wiggam wrote in flowery, scientific terms about improving the human race by an evolutionary system called *eugenics*. From what he could understand, eugenics meant teaching people to choose marriage partners who were healthy and smart. It also meant sterilizing the handicapped, the insane, the hardened criminal, and those with epilepsy.

Something about the whole issue rankled in Tyson's mind. He thought of his dear little Lori. Would she be sterilized if eugenics became popular?

He planned to leave the book at St. Clair's place this afternoon and borrow another one. Maybe Darwin made more sense.

The next ten days brought a series of frustrating events. Crabill continued to block Tyson from questioning Bella Smith. The town council had a royal battle over where to hold the trial. Until they reached an agreement, the sheriff's office couldn't make plans for crowd control and traffic patterns.

A premature United Press article announced that the trial would be held in a ballpark seating ten thousand, with short sessions to keep tourists in town as long as possible. Pure speculation, news reports became wilder as time went on.

Gossip lines vibrated and swelled with rumor and conjecture. John Scopes received a telegram from Clarence Darrow and his partner, Dudley Field Malone, offering their services free of charge. Darrow's reputation held so much controversy that even the ACLU defenders couldn't agree on whether to call the Chicago lawyer in.

Daytonians argued his good and bad points from morning to night. "Darrow volunteered because Bryan threw his hat in the ring," Heddie declared when the lunch rush died down on Saturday. Tyson and Micky sat in the kitchen finishing their meal while Nessa wiped down tables, and Vic and Heddie washed the dishes.

The widow told Vic, "Bryan hits at Darrow in his column every chance he gets. Darrow writes letters to the editor about Bryan. They want to fight it out man to man."

"What's so bad about Darrow?" Nessa asked, stepping into the room with a tray of dishes in her hands.

Tyson said, "He's a radical criminal lawyer who defends hopeless cases." He looked at Heddie. "Darrow's dynamite in the courtroom."

"He's an infidel," Heddie declared. She dried her hands and poured leftover soup into a large bowl.

Tyson swallowed a sharp answer. "Everybody's entitled to his opinion, Heddie," he said and scraped back his chair. "How about a round of Mah-Jongg, Micky? Are you through working?"

"Swell." The boy popped a last bite of strawberry pie into his mouth.

"Count me in," Nessa said. "I'll be finished in fifteen minutes." She sat down and lifted her spoon.

"Me too!" Lori chimed.

"How about a walk with me and Heddie, honey?" Vic asked while he stacked saucers in the drainer. "We can go to the schoolyard and play on the swings."

"Yeah!" She slapped the table until the silver rattled.

Tyson lifted her hand and kissed it. "I think we get the point, Chicky."

She leaned her head on his shoulder and giggled.

Half an hour later the trio met in the parlor, Tyson and Nessa on the sofa, with Micky in a chair across from them.

Between turns, Nessa said, "You look worried, Trent."

He leaned back and let out a wide breath. His hand pushed at the hair above his brow. "It's Miss Ida and Sammy." He told her about Crabill's call. "Until Chattanooga PD finishes their investigation, I can't say anything to Bella or O'Toole."

"I haven't seen anything suspicious," she said.

"Hey, what is this?" Micky said, looking at Nessa. "You going undercover or something?"

Nessa waved him off. "No, silly. Nothing that exciting." She elbowed Tyson. "It's your turn already."

An hour later, Tyson was ready to place his final tile when a blood-chilling scream sounded outside. A second scream sent the three players running out the front door and around to the back of the house.

In Mullins's yard, Elmer Buntley had Anna Joy in a half nelson.

Raising a hoe, the girl hacked at a rose bush. A second bush stood bent and bare.

"Stop it!" Buntley yelled, trying to pull her back. "Are you crazy?"

Shrieking hysterically, Anna Joy broke from his grasp and turned on him, the hoe raised high overhead. Mrs. Mullins burst out of the house like an avenging angel, with Essie Caldwell trotting behind her.

Tyson raced toward the dueling pair. Elmer reached up, finally made contact with the hoe handle, and wrenched it from the girl's hands.

Anna Joy pummeled him with her fists.

Mrs. Mullins and Tyson reached them at the same moment. Both grabbed the crying girl and dragged her away from the gardener.

Shoulders squared, Essie stepped in front of Elmer, blocking him from following.

"He called me a retard!" the girl screamed, kicking and struggling to get away.

Clamping down on her daughter's arms, Mrs. Mullins turned on Elmer. "How dare you!" she shouted above her daughter's sobs.

Anna Joy stopped struggling to watch the argument. Her chest heaved and tears coursed down her red face.

"You're finished here," Jenny Mullins said between clenched teeth. "Gather up your tools and get out!" She looked as though she wanted to pick up the hoe and have a go at him herself.

Essie said, "You heard her, Elmer." She took a step forward, hands on hips and fire in her eye.

Elmer slunk away. Jenny made cooing noises at her daughter. "Let's go inside, honey. We'll get you in a nice hot tub, and you'll feel better." She glanced at Tyson. "Thank you, Mr. Tyson. We'll be fine now."

Essie followed them into the house.

Tyson walked over to join Nessa and Micky. They stood in a huddle, looking at the slashed rose bushes.

"Elmer had no right to call her names," Nessa blurted out. "He was cruel. There's no excuse for that."

They strolled back inside to their game and Tyson won the day.

But he didn't feel like celebrating.

At a quarter to three, Tyson and Micky headed toward the baseball field with Nessa. Vic and Heddie were already there with Lori.

This time the little girl got to put six marks on the board. The Blues won four to two. Nessa had made two of the winning four runs. Tyson allowed himself a secret grin as they gathered up the gear. She was quite a gal.

When they reached home at five-thirty, Dr. St. Clair's car sat in Jenny Mullins's driveway.

"I wonder what's happened," Heddie said, a worried look on her face. "Nessa, take the stew off the stove while I go to Jenny, will you, love?"

She was back in time to set two gingham tables in the dining room. "Anna Joy couldn't get over her tantrum, so Jenny called the doctor. He and Sadie came to give her a sleeping draught. The poor child will be right as rain in the morning."

Nessa carried a large tureen of mulligatawny stew into the room and everyone forgot about their neighbors' problems.

A stunted plant may produce a dazzling flower, full of light and beauty. But don't be fooled; if left to reproduce, it can spoil the whole garden in one generation.

Shortly after dawn, hoarse cries brought Tyson to his feet before he'd fully opened his eyes. He felt for his pants on the back of a chair and peered out the window. The noise seemed to be coming from Mullins's again. He slipped his bare feet into shoes, nabbed a shirt, and jogged down the stairs.

The house next door was dark except for a single light on the second floor. Tyson reached Jenny's back porch door and turned the doorknob. Locked.

He pounded on thick oak. "Mrs. Mullins! It's Deputy Tyson. Mrs. Mullins!"

The screams quieted by half. Tyson traced the woman's movements by the racket she made. It seemed an eternity before she unbolted the door.

"What's happened?" he asked.

Her eyes had a wide, glazed look. Her mouth hung open, and her breath came in great gasps. A moan rumbled deep in her throat.

Tyson gripped her shoulders. "What is it?"

"Anna Joy . . . Anna Joy . . ." She reeled. Tyson caught the stout woman when her eyes turned up and her knees gave way. Grasping her limp body under her arms, he pulled her into the living room and laid her on the sofa.

Wearing robes, Nessa and Heddie appeared in the kitchen door. Heddie had her hair in pin curls with a silk scarf tied over it. She looked like a skinned chicken.

Fear all over her face, Nessa said, "What is it, Trent?"

"Stay with Jenny. Something's wrong with Anna Joy." He raced up the stairs three at a time.

To the right of the stairs, a yellow glow directed him to the girl's room, a frilly affair with pink wallpaper and ruffled curtains.

Anna Joy was lying on the single bed, covers askew; her face was twisted, the lips drawn back against her teeth. Her eyes stared at the wall.

Tyson felt her neck but he knew the answer before he touched her cold flesh. She'd been dead for more than two hours.

Tears rushed to his eyes. He dashed them away. This was no time to let emotion cloud his judgment. He must think. He rubbed his bristly jaw with a trembling hand.

Deep breaths, Tyson. *You've got a job to do*. Swallowing hard, he closed his eyes and opened them again.

On a small desk by the window seat lay a stack of note paper and a pencil. He picked up a page and began listing everything he saw.

"Trent?" Nessa called from below. Heddie's Irish brogue came softly from the living room, murmuring Jenny's name.

Tyson walked to the head of the stairs. "Stay where you are, Nessa."

Terror and dread reached her voice. "What is it?"

"She's gone. Call Dr. St. Clair, will you? If Jenny wakes up, don't let her come up here."

Tears dripped from Nessa's cheeks onto her quilted robe. Biting her lips, she turned away.

Tyson shut the door to the girl's room. The place must stay sealed until he finished.

First, he checked for bruises and defense wounds. She had bruises on her upper arms, probably from last night's struggle. He looked closely at her face. Horrified, he looked again.

Damp white foam covered her lips.

He returned to the top of the stairs. "Nessa?"

Loud sniffs came from below. "Yes?"

"Fetch me a clean bottle and some cotton." He moved down the stairs.

He heard rustling in the kitchen. In a moment, Nessa came toward him carrying what he asked for.

Twenty minutes later he heard a car's engine and glanced out the window. Dr. St. Clair had arrived. Tyson stayed at the job.

The very normality of the room made it all the more frightening. He cataloged items that nearly every girl's room contained:

picture books and stuffed dolls, glass figurines, clothes, and shoes.

Sliding his notes into his shirt pocket, he picked up the specimen bottle and went out. He removed the key from the inside lock, secured the door behind him, and slipped the key into his pocket. No one would touch the body besides Jonas Ketcher. Then Anna Joy would go to Chattanooga for the ME's autopsy.

St. Clair was kneeling beside the grieving mother when Tyson arrived downstairs. Still on the sofa, she threw her head from side to side, crying and moaning. Nessa stood nearby, her freckles lost in the red sheen on her cheeks, her hand pressed over her nose and mouth.

Heddie bent over next to Dr. St. Clair. The doctor had a hypodermic in his hand.

"Hold her arm, Mrs. McGinty," he said. "This will help calm her down."

A moment later, he stood and noticed Tyson. "What's happened?"

"Anna Joy shows the same signs that Sammy and Miss Ida did."

Astonishment blanked out the doctor's expression.

"I've sealed the room," Tyson told him. "I'll make arrangements to have her transported to Chattanooga for a complete autopsy."

His angry eyes bored into Dr. St. Clair's. "I don't know what's going on in this town, but I'm gonna find out if it's the last thing I do." He turned toward the door. "I'm going home to make some calls."

CHAPTER Twelve

"I'll come along," Nessa said, following Tyson into the kitchen. "Mama can stay here while I get dressed and make breakfast."

They walked outdoors. Morning light made the world feel bright and clean. Nessa stared at the two mangled rose bushes and shuddered.

"When you're through with official business, you ought to call Jenny's married daughter in Nashville," she said when they reached their own door. "I got her number from the ledger beside Jenny's phone." She handed him a slip of paper.

They walked to the front porch of the boardinghouse. It seemed natural for Nessa to stay with him. In the hall, Tyson reached for the phone, and Nessa shuffled toward the back of the house. Now that the excitement was past, Tyson felt as though he'd already worked a full day. He checked his watch. Seven a.m.

By noon Tyson had almost finished his inspection of the Mullins house. Anna Joy's body was on its way to Chattanooga in the back of a hired truck. Heddie sat with sleeping Jenny while four ladies—Mrs. Kate Bailey, Mrs. Clarke Robinson, Mrs. Maggie Darwin, and Essie Caldwell—stood on the back porch waiting for Tyson to let them in, an unusual way for these church-goers to spend a Sunday morning. Jenny's married daughter, Sandra Dennis, had yet to arrive.

After taking time to fetch a few envelopes and paper bags from his room, Tyson had combed Jenny's house looking for clues. He dumped out trash cans and sifted their contents. If Anna Joy had swallowed tansy, how did she get it?

Standing at the gauze-curtained kitchen window, he stared blindly, his brain reviewing the house and its contents. Brushing his mustache with his index finger, his eye drifted to the window sill, where a green glass vase held a fist full of wilting weeds. Suddenly he came out of his brown study and realized what he was looking at.

He pounced on it. Dumping the water in the sink, he spread the clump out on the table to examine the spiky leaves. *Eureka.* He pulled a paper bag from his pocket and carefully slid the limp stems inside.

Minutes later he opened the door to tell the women outside, "You may come in now. Heddie is with Mrs. Mullins. The doctor had to give her a hypo to calm her down. He said she'll sleep all day."

Clarke Robinson, the wife of the hustling druggist, was a slim, immaculate woman with intelligent eyes and a brunette pompadour hairstyle. She stepped toward the deputy and asked, "Has Sandra Dennis been notified?"

"Yes, ma'am. I phoned her early this morning. She should be arriving soon."

Mrs. Robinson looked at the others. "If Jenny's sleeping, there's no need for all of us to stay."

"I need to get lunch for my men." The speaker was a small, gray woman with an anxious mouth. "John and Clifford went to church with Mr. Bailey this morning. If I'm not home when they get back, they'll be prowling around my kitchen like two hungry bears."

John Scopes boarded at Bailey's white clapboard house on the northeast corner of Fourth Avenue and Market. He and Bailey's red-haired son, Clifford, were fast friends.

The lady wore a faded house dress, black stockings, and thick black shoes. "I'll bring a hot meal over later."

"Thank you, Miz Bailey," Mrs. Robinson said.

The little woman stepped off the porch and headed for home. She lived within sight of McGinty's property.

"I'll stay." Maggie Darwin stood tall and matronly, with a gray bun high on her crown. She hefted a satchel. "I brought my painting things along in case I had to wait." Maggie's hand-painted china had occupied the front window of Darwin's General Mercantile for twenty-five years.

"I'll stay, too," Mrs. Caldwell chirped. "Jenny and I are close friends. I'd like to stay with her."

"As you wish," Mrs. Robinson said. "My family will be needing their lunch, too. I've got a thousand things to do this afternoon. The Lady's Aid is planning several fund-raisers for the trial. I'm trying to get some ideas together for our meeting tomorrow."

Mrs. Darwin set her satchel on the kitchen table. Mrs. Caldwell hurried toward the stairs.

Before Tyson headed home he took a walk along the back border of Jenny Mullins's yard. The center lay trimmed and neat under Elmer Buntley's care, but the adjoining field grew almost a foot high. Kicking through the tall grass, he found what he was looking for. A patch of tansy near the southwest corner. Unfortunately, it looked as though it hadn't been touched this spring.

Frustrated, Tyson crossed the yard and entered his home. The place was quiet. Everyone had gone to church. Or had they? The smell of frying chicken drew him to the kitchen. He hadn't eaten breakfast.

Nessa stood at the stove, a giant white apron covering her navy dress. She turned toward the door when he stepped through. She held a fork in one hand and scissors tongs in the other.

"Can a fellow still get some breakfast?" he asked.

"How about a couple of hot drumsticks with some macaroni and cheese?"

"Dish her up. I'm game." He slid into a chair at the end of the table.

"I was too upset to go with the family this morning," she told him, "so I stayed behind to cook." She slid a heaping plate in front of him and poured a glass of iced tea. Moving quickly, she lay the last of the frying chicken onto a wide pan and slid it into the oven.

She sat across from Tyson and looked him straight in the eye. "What happened to Anna Joy, Trent? I want to know."

He finished chewing and sipped tea. "It's tansy poisoning again. I'm ninety-nine percent sure of it."

Her face paled. She drew in a quivering breath. "What is happening in this town?"

"I found a vase full of tansy in the kitchen. Maybe Anna Joy pulled the plants and chewed on some of them." He shrugged. "I'm grabbing at straws, I guess. Who would chew on something that bitter?"

"We've got to find out who's doing this." She pulled her elbows tight and shivered. "Anna Joy was a gentle, sweet soul. I don't know how Jenny is going to get on without her. That child was all she had." Her eyes swam with tears.

Tyson had an urge to pull her into a hug, to comfort her. Instead, he leaned forward, looking into her eyes. "If it's humanly possible, I'm going to find the answer, Nessa."

"Tell me what to do and I'll help. Anything."

Tyson's next sentence died in his brain. His eyes stayed on hers for a long, taut moment.

Suddenly, she darted from her chair to pull plates from the cabinet and set the table.

Tyson slowly picked up a piece of chicken. What was wrong with him? There was a lunatic on the loose, and he was acting like a lightning-struck calf.

With Lori on his shoulders, Micky came through the front door. "Hey, Nessa, is lunch ready?" he called. "I'm starving!"

Tyson lurched out of his chair to take his daughter in his arms and carry her into the parlor for a serious chat. Sitting on the sofa, he held her close. She picked at his shirt buttons while he spoke.

"So you see, Chicky," he ended, "Anna Joy had to go away. She won't be able to play with you anymore."

Lori's innocent eyes looked up at him. "Will I get to see her when I die?"

He folded his arms about her. "One day we'll all be together again. You and me and Mommy . . . and Anna Joy." How he wished he could believe that.

Lori touched his cheek. "Don't be sad, Daddy. It'll be okay."

Tyson squeezed her to him and closed his eyes tight. He wished he could believe that, too.

Finally, he turned her loose and she skipped to the kitchen to talk things over with her Grandpa while Tyson called the sheriff. He should be home from church by now. The phone rang twice before Harris picked it up. "Tyson here. Could you meet me at the office?"

"Now? I just got home."

"Sorry, Sheriff. It's an emergency."

"Give me half an hour. The wife's putting a roast on the table."

Moving in slow motion, Tyson reached for his fedora on the closet shelf and set out walking. The hazy sky hung over the town like a warm, damp dishcloth, with not a single breeze for relief.

Tyson sat on a bench in the shade of a willow oak on the courthouse lawn until Harris's motorcycle puttered up.

"What's happened?" Harris asked when Tyson met him inside the office. The sheriff leaned against Tyson's desk. He had on a black suit and a string tie.

"It's Anna Joy Mullins, the daughter of the family next door to me," Tyson said.

"What'd she do?"

"She's dead."

Harris's face sagged. He reached around the desk to grab Tyson's chair and drop his bulk into it. Chin against his chest, eyeing his deputy, he muttered, "Give it to me one piece at a time. Nice and slow."

Ten minutes later, Tyson said, "There's no way Anna Joy could be tied up with Sammy or Miss Ida. And Elmer didn't see the girl after the fight. Her mother was with her constantly."

"Looks like I was right after all," Harris drawled, relaxing. "It's spring, and folks are digging in the ground. What we're seeing is a series of accidents. I'm telling you, boy, tansy grows all over around here."

"Then we need to get out posters and warn folks about it."

Harris grabbed the phone. "I'll call the *Times* and have them print us up some flyers with pictures of the plant in bloom. We can have them by day after tomorrow."

While Harris was on the phone Tyson shook the damp clump of tansy out of the envelope and spread it across a south-facing window sill to dry. When he finished, he went directly to the lavatory and carefully washed his hands.

The sheriff stood to take off his coat. He hung it behind his own desk chair and sat.

At the front desk, Tyson drew a wad of scrawled notes from his pocket and carefully copied them into his notebook, filling the last page. He slipped a rubber band around the covers and dropped the notebook into his bottom desk drawer. Then he reached into the top drawer to pull out a fresh tablet. He dated it and slipped it into his shirt pocket.

Half an hour later he finished writing his report and dropped it on the sheriff's desk. "I'll see you in the morning."

The sheriff merely nodded, picked up the report, and started plowing through Tyson's square handwriting.

Tyson walked home, hands deep in his pockets, taking his time. Maybe Anna Joy's death was unrelated to the other two. Maybe it was a freak accident. She loved to dig around in the soil and pull up things. Maybe she had gotten hold of the wrong weed this time.

He drew in a deep breath and hoped the medical examiner would shed some light on a very dark subject.

He reached his corner at the same time as Mr. Bailey and watched the big man bend over to retrieve something from the sidewalk.

Tyson's eyes narrowed when he realized it was a worthless pencil stub, too small to be of any use. What was Bailey doing collecting those? Shrugging, Tyson turned west at the corner.

Dr. St. Clair's Model T stood in Jenny's driveway. Instead of entering the boardinghouse, Tyson headed over to have a talk with him.

He met the doctor coming out the back door. "How's Mrs. Mullins, Doc?"

"Awake but still overcome."

"Can I talk to her?"

"I gave her a mild sedative that should calm her without putting her to sleep. If you don't upset her, you may ask her five or ten simple questions. I doubt her nerves can stand more." He started to go, then turned back.

"Are we still on for chess tomorrow night?"

"Sure, Doc. I need to rest my mind for a couple of hours. This business has me tied in knots."

St. Clair's lips formed his usual gentle smile. "I feel that way myself. I'll see you at half past seven, then."

Tyson rapped on the Mullins' door. A minute later a short, mousy-haired woman arrived.

She opened the door wide and stood on the threshold. "Yes?"

"Mrs. Dennis?"

At the lady's nod, he said, "I'm Deputy Trent Tyson. I phoned you earlier. The doctor told me I could ask Mrs. Mullins a few questions."

"Come in. I just took Mother some tea. Excuse me a moment, please." She hurried toward the stairs. A few seconds passed and she reappeared, "Come up please, Mr. Tyson."

Wearing a flannel bed jacket, Jenny Mullins lay propped in her wide four poster, sipping broth, when Tyson stepped in. Her puffy cheeks sagged. The cup trembled in her hands. A square tray lay beside a hurricane lamp on the bedside stand.

"Should I leave you alone?" Sandra asked.

"If you don't mind," Tyson said. "This shouldn't take five minutes."

Nodding, she went out.

He sank into the cane-bottomed rocking chair beside the bed and kept his voice low. "I need to ask you some questions, Mrs. Mullins, about what happened."

Jenny held her wavering cup out to him. He took it and placed it on the tray. She glanced at him, her eyes swollen and red, then stared at the nine-patch quilt, waiting. Her breath came in shallow, silent gasps.

"What did you eat for dinner last night? Can you remember?"

She tried to speak, cleared her throat, and tried again. "It was creamed chicken over toast with succotash, Anna Joy's… favorite. Strawberry pie for dessert."

His pencil flew over the notebook. "Describe to me what happened when you brought your daughter inside after her argument with Elmer Buntley."

Jenny's pale hands plucked at the cover. She stared at the footboard.

"Essie and I got her upstairs to her room. I told her to undress while I went to the kitchen to fetch hot water from the stove reservoir. She took a hot soak in the tub for half an hour."

The woman swallowed hard. "I thought she'd calmed down, but when I got her into bed, she started up again. She was crying and throwing things. When she broke her favorite figurine, I thought I'd better call the doctor. Whenever she gets like that he has to come and give her something to calm her down. Last night was one of her worst spells."

"She went to sleep after the doctor left?"

"Yes, about twenty minutes later. When she dozed off, Essie went home, and I went to bed. I got up around midnight and heard her crying. She said her stomach hurt. I gave her some more sedative and a cup of hot tea. A few minutes later she went back to sleep."

"What kind of tea?"

"Chamomile. It grows in our backyard." She turned tortured eyes on Tyson. "What was it, Mr. Tyson? What happened to my baby?"

Tyson hesitated. "I sent her for an autopsy. I asked them to rush it, but we'll have to wait until at least tomorrow for the results."

He tucked the notebook into his pocket. "I'll let you know as soon as I get any news."

She nodded. Two fat tears trickled down her wrinkled cheeks. "She was all I had left."

Tyson swallowed to loosen his tight throat. He stood. "Try to rest. I'll hold off any more questions until you feel better."

He found her daughter in the kitchen, washing out a small pan. "You may want to go to her, Mrs. Dennis."

With quick, practiced movements, she set the pan in the drainer and dried her hands. She hurried past Tyson without a word.

By the time Tyson reached home, Heddie had supper on the table: creamed chipped beef over toast and green beans boiled with bacon.

Conversation came slow and heavy. Nessa touched her napkin to her eyes instead of her mouth.

Lori said, "Is Anna Joy in heaven with Mommy?"

"Yes, Chicky," Trent said, fighting his own weakness.

"Good." She nodded, satisfied. "Mommy will take care of her."

To Lori, Mommy was an angel who lived in the sky and had all sorts of wonderful talents. The child couldn't remember Carrie at all, a fact that tormented Trent like no other.

Everyone felt relieved to be away from the table. Nessa was leading Lori upstairs for her bath when Micky said, "Uh, Mr. Tyson, could I talk to you a minute?"

"Sure, Micky. Let's go into the parlor."

Tyson relaxed on the camel-backed sofa. What kind of problem could Micky have that needed his help? Tyson didn't feel like hearing anyone else's woes at the moment.

The boy settled into a chair, his hands rubbing the navy broadcloth covering his knees. "Mr. Scopes asked me to testify against him before the grand jury."

CHAPTER Thirteen

Tyson leaned forward, sure his ears had deceived him. "Mr. Scopes asked you to testify *against* him?"

The boy nodded. "He said he needs some of his students to testify that he really did teach evolution."

"Did he teach it?"

"Well . . . no."

"Do you want to do it, Micky?"

"I'd like to help Mr. Scopes." He cleared his throat. "I thought you may be able to steer me right, you being a policeman and all. Don't people go to the slammer for lying on the stand?"

Tyson studied the boy's eager face. "If Mr. Scopes truly wants you to testify against him, no one will press charges for perjury."

"There are seven of us fellows," Micky went on. "We're supposed to meet Mr. Scopes tomorrow evening, so he can give us the scoop."

Tyson's lips twisted together. The more he heard about the trial, the less he liked it. Sure, the Butler Act was bad, but this type of staging went against his justice-oriented grain.

The Grand Jury was scheduled to meet at ten o'clock Tuesday morning. Since Chattanooga's attempt to drag the evolution trial into its own courts, Judge Raulston had put a rush on the indictment. The grand jury wasn't scheduled to meet until

August, but Dayton didn't want anyone stealing its thunder.

Monday evening after supper, Micky went to Bailey's house for a coaching session with Scopes. Heddie's lips tightened when he left, but for once she kept her thoughts to herself.

Lori sat quietly in her chair until Tyson stood up. Then she asked, "Will you read to me after supper, Daddy?" Her wide blue eyes gave a better argument than fifteen minutes of pleading.

"Sure, Chicky." He lifted her into his arms. "Dr. St. Clair is coming to play chess tonight, so we'll have to do it right away."

"I want to hear about Puss 'n Boots."

He carried her upstairs to their sitting room and selected a book from the stack on a side table. Tyson felt her soft curls against his chin, and his heart squeezed until he felt physical pain. He wanted to pray for God to protect this precious life from harm.

But he couldn't.

How can a person pray to an idea, a myth, a phantom? He shook off the impression and opened the storybook.

Dr. St. Clair's knock interrupted Tyson's last two lines at the end of the story. Nessa answered the door.

"Good evening, Lori," the doctor said, beaming at his little patient a few minutes later. "How are you this fine evening?"

Lori watched him, a knowing expression on her cherub face. "I'm cheering up Daddy," she told him.

Tyson gave her a hug and lifted her as he stood. "You've done a fine job of it, Chicky. I feel much better." He smiled over her head at the doctor. "Lori's going to bed now."

"Good night, Dr. St. Clair," she called over her daddy's shoulder.

He settled her into the trundle bed and kissed her cheek.

When he arrived back in his sitting room, Dr. St. Clair was setting up his side of the chess board. "I feel like a winner tonight, Tyson," he said. "You'd best look out for yourself."

Tyson ran stiff fingers through his curly top. He felt like a loser.

The men played in tense silence. St. Clair was engrossed in the game, but Tyson couldn't get his mind off Anna Joy Mullins. He kept seeing her laughing face while she played with Lori.

"I'll check on Mrs. Mullins before I go home," St. Clair commented in the middle of the game.

"She was able to answer a few questions this afternoon, but I didn't press her. She couldn't concentrate very well." Tyson shook his head sadly. "My heart goes out to the poor woman."

The doctor nodded. "Mine, too. I wish there were some pill or injection I could give her to take away that kind of pain." He moved his bishop.

While Tyson studied his next move, Dr. St. Clair rested his chin on his hand and seemed to look deep within himself. He said, "I wish it were possible to discover which unborn babies would turn out like Anna Joy, so we could eliminate them before their parents became attached to them. It would save so much heartache."

Shocked, Tyson suddenly forgot the game. "It would also deny them much joy. Anna Joy was a sweet, happy child. Most of the time she had the disposition of an angel."

"Didn't you read Wiggam's theory on eugenics?"

"I read it from cover to cover. But something about it doesn't seem right to me, Doc. I don't want my child choosing her mate because he's healthy and smart. I want her to pick someone with good character qualities like honesty, loyalty, and kindness."

He leaned a little forward. "And I don't want someone rejecting her because she's handicapped." His blood pressure rose just thinking of it.

"What about the insane?" the doctor insisted. "Do you believe they should propagate more people like themselves?" A scornful expression flitted across his face and disappeared. "If we want our society to improve, we must decrease the number of unproductive people. Think of where we could go with one hundred percent of the population contributing to the general good."

He leaned forward, eyes burning. "We could stamp out diseases like epilepsy and diabetes in one generation." He chuckled and his mild manner reappeared. "Arguing will get us nowhere, Tyson. How far have you gotten in *The Descent of Man*?"

"I'm just getting started." Tyson moved a pawn.

St. Clair smiled. "When you finish it, we must set aside a Monday evening for a good talk." He looked over the board before him and moved his queen. "Check."

Tyson drove Micky to the brick courthouse at nine o'clock the next morning. The grand jury didn't convene until ten, but Micky needed moral support, so he came along when the deputy had to report to work. Wearing his black Sunday suit and tie, his woolly hair brushed straight back, Micky looked as though he were the chief mourner at a funeral. His nervous frown added to the impression.

Several motorcars were parked on Market Street, and a huddle of men waited on the lawn. Some had press cards tucked into the ribbons on their straw skimmers. Four held bulky cameras.

John Scopes and Dr. Neal stood a few steps apart from the rest. Neal looked as though he had crawled out of bed and come to the courthouse without consulting a mirror. His hair needed cutting and brushing. His clothes had deep-set wrinkles that hadn't gotten there overnight.

Scopes glanced at his pocket watch as Tyson and Micky reached him.

"Good morning, gentlemen," Tyson said, shaking hands with the teacher and his lawyer.

John Scopes had a stiff set to his shoulders. "Howdy, Deputy."

He looked toward the boy. "Micky? Are you ready?"

The young man cleared his throat. "Yes, sir. I remember what you told me."

Looking pinched by ties and stiff collars, a group of teenage boys soon gathered around. Tyson scanned the group and recognized a couple of Micky's friends, Howard Morgan and Harry Shelton. Morgan was a timid freshman. Shelton was a senior with a sullen attitude.

John grinned at his recruits. "I appreciate your help, boys. You're doing a service to your country."

Neal stepped closer to Tyson. "Superintendent White is acting as plaintiff instead of George Rappelyea," he told the deputy. "White's association with the county schools gives him more influence."

Tyson asked, "John, is it true you're taking Clarence Darrow into the case?"

"I'd be an imbecile not to," Scopes declared. "He's the best defense lawyer in the country. I've always admired him. He'll give those religious fanatics a run for their money."

"Careful, boy," Neal said, "the question is not whether evolution is true or untrue. It's freedom of education that we're fighting for. That's what this case is really about."

Vic arrived at the same time as a carload of starched lawyers and, at fifteen minutes to ten, the men—not a single woman present—moved toward the front doors of the courthouse. They marched up the outside steps, across the porch and foyer, and straight up the wide stairs to the second-floor courtroom.

Prosecuting attorneys led the way. First in line, tall, lean Tom Stewart, the district's hard-nosed attorney general, held a briefcase. After him marched Sue and Herb Hicks, Wallace Haggard, and stout Gordon McKenzie.

Tyson recognized Walter White nearby. The school superintendent wore a gray pinstripe suit that fit closely across his broad shoulders.

A wiry man with a round paunch and a projecting lower lip, Judge Raulston paced beside Tyson and his father. A lay preacher for the Methodist Episcopal church, the judge had a firm reputation as a conservative Christian.

Thirteen jurymen filed into the front row of theater seats. Nine of them wore bib overalls. Tall double windows appeared at close intervals along three walls of the square room, letting in light but little air. Reporters scattered throughout the room. Tight springs squeaked when they pushed their seats down.

Cameras flashed. Last-minute questions came rapid fire from reporters to the prosecutors and the judge. Judge Raulston smiled and struck a pose—Bible to left breast—for a camera shot. He wore a business suit instead of a black robe. This was the biggest case Raulston had ever tried, a boon for a country judge born in the Tennessee mountain town of Gizzards Cove.

Tyson, acting as bailiff today, called the session to order. Sheriff Harris stood by the door, looking somber and watching the crowd. Vic sat on the end of the third row, near the door. He may have to leave early. Heddie would need his help in the kitchen come eleven o'clock.

Seated with his fellow witnesses in the second row, Micky McGinty swallowed hard and gripped the arms of his chair. Beside him, Howard Morgan's eyes were wide as dinner plates.

After the jury was sworn, Judge Raulston read the Butler Act and Genesis Chapter One. District Attorney Stewart stood and made a brief opening statement about the law being violated. He called Walter White to the stand. Through White's testimony, the offending textbook, *Civic Biology*, was entered into evidence. Stewart read portions of the text, then called Howard Morgan.

"Did Mr. Scopes, use this textbook in your classroom?" Stewart began, his voice mild, unthreatening.

"Yes, sir." The boy kept his eyes on the floor.

"Did Mr. Scopes talk about man coming from apes?"

"He talked about Tarzan of the apes."

Stewart smiled. Faint chuckles rose from the audience.

Three more questions and Howard stepped down. The others testified in the same brief manner.

Tyson noted that despite Scopes's frantic coaching, the boys knew little about evolution. The prosecution didn't seem to notice their weak testimonies.

Stewart closed his argument in short order. He simply stated that a law had been broken, and the case should be brought to open court.

Judge Raulston turned to the jury. "If you find that the statute has been thus violated you should indict the guilty party promptly. You will bear in mind that in this investigation you are not interested to inquire into the policy or wisdom of this legislation."

Giving his son a slight nod, Vic slipped out when the jury left to consider. Minutes later, the jurors returned with a decision to indict Scopes.

Judge Raulston set the trial date for July 10, said, "Court is adjourned," and rapped the gavel.

Immediately reporters moved in. The judge's chest swelled when he said, "It has always been one of the great passions of my life to ascertain truth in all matters, especially relative to God, but I am not so much worried over the question as to whence man cometh as I am to whither he goes."

Tyson didn't care for Raulston's pious attitude. If Scopes had a biased judge, would he get a fair trial?

Micky moved into a huddle with his classmates, their faces alight with excitement. The boys hustled down the wide stairs to the first floor and outside.

Tyson followed the last stragglers from the courtroom and closed the swinging double doors behind him. When he reached the yard, he saw Scopes and Neal waiting under a spreading tree with the Hicks brothers. Scopes leaned his back against the bark, one knee up, a cigarette in his mouth. He threw the cigarette away when he saw Stewart heading toward them. The district attorney handed Neal a paper, spoke to him briefly, and strode toward his shiny Model T parked in front of the sheriff's office.

"Mr. Scopes." An eager young man with a *Chattanooga Times* badge on his jacket pushed toward John. "What do you think about the court's finding?"

"I'm ready to go through with it."

The reporter pressed closer, his short pencil racing across a steno pad. "What's your position on the Butler Act?"

Scopes cleared his throat. "I believe the Butler Act is unnecessary because evolution doesn't necessarily rule out the existence of God."

Neal interrupted. "That will be all." He put his hand on Scopes's elbow and hurried him away. His next words drifted faintly back. "Keep your opinions to yourself, boy. We're not here to argue evolution, just test the law."

The disgruntled reporter regarded the backs of the defendant and his lawyer and said, "This was the crime established in the jury room."

The crowd slowly dispersed, and Tyson ambled to the office.

Sheriff Harris entered behind him and dropped a long envelope onto Tyson's desk. "Here are the flyers about tansy that I ordered. See they're distributed, will you?"

Tyson tore off the manila covering. Across the top of slim white paper, bold black letters shouted, "Danger in your Back Yard!" followed by a statement about tansy and the three deaths that had resulted from it. A picture of the plant in bloom made a border on the left side.

Dayton being the expansive metropolis that it was, Tyson finished circulating the flyers around noon. When he arrived home for lunch, Heddie was standing at the stove, ladling up a steamy white soup. Vic piled sliced turkey onto thin brown bread while Lori placed pickles beside finished sandwiches.

"Hi, folks!" Tyson said. "How's business?"

"Marvelous," Vic said without looking up. "Want some turkey on rye?"

"Sure." He nabbed a plate and gave Lori a peck on the cheek as he passed her. "No hug today, Chicky. Not with that messy hand."

She lifted her briny paw toward his face. He jerked back. Little girl laughter filled the kitchen. She said, "Grandpa's going to take me to the state fair, Daddy."

"That's right." Her grandpa nodded, smiling down at her.

Tyson glanced around. "Where's our star witness?"

"Micky?" Vic asked. "He changed his clothes and trotted off to the Blue Hole for a swim with some of the guys. They're feeling rather smug at the moment, from what I gather."

"They did quite well," Tyson said, "for as little coaching as they had."

"Coaching!" Heddie muttered. "My Micky'll not be testifying in the real trial. He's had his fun. Let someone else do the dirty work."

She carried a tray of china bowls to the table, set it down, and wiped her hands on her terry cloth apron. "Had a meeting with Mr. Harris at the bank this morning, I did," she told Tyson, her features grim. "We have to pay one month's payment by Friday or he'll foreclose. The bank's in trouble, he says."

"Sorry to hear that." Tyson sat down and dipped into potato soup, thick and buttery. "Mind if I ask how much the payment is?"

She hesitated, her pride still intact. "Sixty-five dollars," she said finally.

"I'll pay my board a month ahead," he offered. "That'll give you twenty."

Vic nodded. "I'll do the same."

The woman looked from father to son. "It's generous of you, but I hate to take your money."

Vic gave her a gentle smile. "This isn't charity, Heddie. We owe you that money."

"Not yet you don't, Vic Tyson."

Nessa rushed in. "I need four more specials and a roast beef on sourdough." She grabbed the water pitcher. "The district attorney is here with both McKenzies. Old Ben is keeping them laughing."

"Smile pretty for 'em," Tyson teased.

She scrunched her face at him and hurried away, heels clicking on the linoleum.

"Perhaps you'll be able to make the payment with your lunch room earnings by then," Tyson said to Heddie's back as she ladled more soup.

She shook her head. "You should see my grocery bill. We're making only ten percent profit from all this work. And I had to buy a bigger soup pot on Monday." She made a clicking sound with her tongue. "Five dollars, it was."

"I'll cash a check this afternoon," Tyson said, rising. "I'd best get back to the office before Harris comes looking for me."

"Him?" Heddie said, eyebrows high. "He's eating a second helping of potato soup this very moment."

"Is that so?" He sat. "Well, give me a second bowl, too. I can't let him get ahead of me, can I?"

Lori giggled. "Daddy, nobody can do that. You run faster than anyone!"

A little after ten the next morning, Charlie Greene called the office. "That you, Tyson? I just got an autopsy report on a girl from Dayton, one Anna Joy Mullins."

The deputy picked up his pencil, his heart quickstepping. "Go ahead, Charlie. I'm listening."

CHAPTER Fourteen

"No need for me to read it all out," Charlie Greene's shrill voice went on. "It's almost the same as the last two you sent down here. The victim died of tansy poisoning, no plant particles, no residue on the hands."

Tyson drew in a slow breath, the cup receiver pressed tightly to his ear. "You're not surprising me. I've been expecting it." He rubbed his jaw. "That doesn't make it any easier to hear, though." He dropped the pencil to the desk. "Thanks, Charlie. Whenever I get down that way, we'll get together for Mah-Jongg or something." He hung up, pulled out his notebook, and leaned back in his chair.

Were the three deaths connected? It seemed impossible. Sammy and Miss Ida had Bella as a common factor. Anna Joy was a child in a sheltered environment. What could be the connection there?

He thought of Elmer Buntley and his struggle with the girl. But then, Buntley didn't have opportunity between the time of the fight and Anna Joy's death. Tyson decided to pay the old-timer another visit anyway.

He tapped a thumbnail against his scrawled notes. What kind of crazed monster would murder a harmless child?

He massaged his face with both hands. The air was hot and humid, but Tyson felt chilled to the bone.

After work that afternoon he found Nessa sitting on the front porch in a squeaky rocking chair.

"Hello, Trent," she said as he started up the four wide steps in front of her. "You look like you swallowed a green lemon."

He grunted. "You're not far wrong."

"Want to talk about it?"

"Where's Lori?"

"She went on a walk with Mama and Vic. They'll be back in half an hour."

He relaxed in the rocking chair beside her, their arms almost touching. "I got a call from Chattanooga. Anna Joy's autopsy report."

She waited, watching his face while he told her the findings. "There's a maniac loose, Nessa. I can feel him."

She tightened up and rubbed her upper arms. "The invisible man."

"Somehow we've got to smoke him out."

"How?"

"A killer has to have two things: motive and opportunity. I've been beating my brains out trying to find a motive. I've come up with a couple of possibilities for Miss Ida and Sammy, but Anna Joy? Who would want to kill her? It doesn't make sense."

"She and Elmer had that fight."

"But afterward, her mother came along and took her in the house." He looked at her. "After Anna Joy went to sleep Jenny went to bed."

"Could someone have come into the house during the night? What about her window?"

"It was open. I checked it that morning." He scraped his thumb across his lips. What about Jenny herself? Was she tired of caring for a handicapped child? Tyson shoved the thought away. It was too horrible to even consider.

Nessa glanced toward the house next door. "Jenny's going to sell her house and move to Nashville with her married daughter."

"I think I'll go over there after supper tonight." He felt in his pocket for his notebook. "It's funny how Elmer Buntley's name keeps coming up. With Miss Ida, Sammy, and now Anna Joy."

"He works for half the people in Dayton."

"Yeah, for Bella Smith, too. How are things going over there?"

"They're a sloppy bunch," she said, wryly. "The kitchen's a mess every time I go in. And the rest of the place isn't much better."

"Are you cleaning the whole house for them?"

"Bella's paying me twice what Miss Ida did, so I guess by rights I ought to do twice the work." She glanced at him. "Dotty's been real depressed lately."

"Any idea why?"

"She won't talk about it. I get the feeling it's something that happened before they came here." She smoothed down her daisy-covered skirt. "One funny thing, Elmer has taken a shine to Dotty.

He's at the door most every day asking for her. One day I came to work and he was standing at her bedroom window where it opens onto the porch. Dotty has Miss Ida's old room, you know.

"Some mornings, Dotty goes out to help Elmer or Essie Caldwell with their gardening. She seems to brighten up a little when she does that."

"Think Elmer's invisible enough to be a suspect?" he asked.

Nessa grinned. "He doesn't smell invisible."

Placing his elbow on the rocker's armrest, he leaned toward her, a tender look on his face. "Neither do you." He gazed into her eyes, so blue and alive. "Sometimes I wish…"

"Trent, don't." She cut him off, her expression sad and a little desperate.

"Don't what?"

Her face flamed scarlet. "Don't . . . anything."

Still close to her, he murmured, "There's been some kind of electricity between us ever since I drove you home that night in the rain. You can't deny it."

"I'm a Christian, Trent. I can't date an . . ."

"An infidel like me." The corners of his lips drew down and in.

He waited for the anger that always blossomed inside him when someone referred to his spiritual condition. Strangely, this time he only felt empty. He took a few slow, deep breaths and drew back a little, still watching her.

Nessa twisted her hands and chewed her lips. Her voice was shaky. "I didn't mean to offend you. Please don't think I feel I'm better than you. I don't. But my faith is important to me. More important than anything."

"Does that mean we can't be friends?"

"No! Of course not." The words gushed forth. "I still want to help you with your investigation." She pointed toward the sidewalk. "There's the folks."

Vic and Heddie turned into their driveway, past the sandwich sign announcing open-faced roast beef with gravy for Saturday's special.

Lori let go of Vic's hand and bounded toward her daddy. "We watched the fish down at the dock!" She landed in his lap with a thud.

Tyson stifled a grunt and clasped her to him. "Maybe we can go fishing tomorrow, Chicky. Would you like that?"

Vic looked at the sky. "I wouldn't count on it, son. Looks like rain's brewing east of here. We may be getting some liquid sunshine tomorrow."

Nessa shaded her eyes and looked up. "I hope it doesn't stop our baseball game."

Sinking into the third rocker, Heddie touched a handkerchief to her forehead. "Maybe rain will cool things off a mite."

Booming thunder shook the house. The wind whipped Lori's hair into her eyes.

"Let's get inside," Vic said, reaching for the front door. "We're in for it now."

They hustled into the hallway. Simmering chicken made Tyson's stomach groan. Lunch's turkey sandwich was long gone. Since the dining room was set up for the next day's business, the group moved toward the kitchen.

"We'll have to make the parlor into a dining room," Heddie said, reaching for the flour bin. "People are turning away because they can't find a seat. Jenny's loaning me four tables."

"You planning on doing that tomorrow, Heddie?" Vic asked.

She set a mixing bowl on the table and filled it with brown flour. "If it rains, there won't be much else to do. We'll have an off day in the Lunch Room for sure."

After a second plate of chicken and dumplings, Tyson stepped into the hall. He reached into the closet for his hat, his umbrella and a flashlight then strode to the parlor door. "Nessa, I'm going over to talk to Jenny."

The girl sat next to Lori on the sofa, a puzzle spread out before them. Nessa nodded. "Don't hurry. I'll look after Lori."

The child pushed a wooden piece into place. "Come back and read to me when you get done, Daddy."

"I'll do that." He ducked outside and had his pant legs soaked the minute he stepped off the porch. Lights from the Mullins's house showed him the way. Tonight, he followed the lane down to the sidewalk and back up Jenny's drive. The grass was too flooded to walk through.

Jenny drew up short when she saw him at the door. "What is it, Deputy? Something about my daughter?" She pulled the door wider and stepped back. "Come in out of the rain."

"I need to ask you a few more questions." He folded the umbrella and propped it against the door frame where it immediately began forming a puddle. "I'd also like to take another look at her room."

Jenny's gripped hands folded across her fluffy middle. "Sandra left this morning. I'm glad you came." She led the way to the stairs. "I've cleaned the room, so I don't know what you'll find."

"I want to look outside. Is there any way someone could have climbed into her window that night? Has anyone ever done it before?"

Her brows drew together. "Never. That window is twenty feet from the ground." She opened the bedroom door and flicked on the light.

Tyson pushed aside pink chintz curtains and peered through the glass. Why had he chosen a night like this to check out a hunch?

Water ran down twelve mullioned panes on the double-hung window. The lock was still undone. Gripping the sash, he shoved it up and stuck his head outside. Chilly rain cascaded over his hair and dripped off his ears.

The flashlight beam touched the grass and slithered up the siding.

A drain spout climbed the wall three feet to the right of the window. To the left, two thick branches brushed the house, causing a screeching, swishing sound similar to the *yeowing* of a cat.

"Here's a towel, Mr. Tyson," Jenny said, handing him a wad of fleecy blue when he'd had enough of wind and rain. "Did you see anything?"

"There are a couple of possibilities if the fellow were small and wiry." He took off his hat to wipe his face and hair. He rubbed his felt fedora, leaving bits of blue lint across the brim.

He handed the towel back to her. She took it away and returned while he made a few notes.

"Think back to the last few days before the accident, Mrs. Mullins. Did you have any visitors? Did anything unusual happen to Anna Joy?"

"Nothing except that fight with Elmer."

"Were there many episodes like that?"

"Last week was the second time. About a year ago, she stamped through a plot of irises when Elmer wouldn't let her help him weed the flower garden. He said that she was pulling out the good plants, and he made her quit."

"Why did she help Elmer? Wasn't he paid to do the yard?"

"She wanted to." Her eyes glistened. "She loved to dig in the dirt, plant seeds, and see life come out of the ground. It made her feel like she had done something important." She swallowed hard and dabbed at her eyes.

"Were there any tantrums when you and she were alone?"

She looked up, fire in her eyes. "Never. We never quarreled. Anna Joy was the sweetest child..." her face contorted, "...to walk God's earth."

He waited a moment for her to regain composure. "Think carefully, Mrs. Mullins. Have you ever seen Elmer climb a tree?"

"He's older than I am, Deputy." Doubt registered in her eyes, followed by an inspiration. "You know, I do believe last summer he climbed our water oak to trim some branches that had overgrown the house. I was afraid they'd fall and put a hole in my roof."

Tyson scratched out a note. "How long have you known Elmer?"

"More than fifty years. We went to the same school. He quit about the time I was in second grade."

"Has he always been so grouchy?"

"He always had a bad attitude. But he really turned sour after his mother died. He and Sammy lived with her right until the end. They were both in their forties." She raised expressive brows. "It didn't seem natural to me."

"What happened to her house?"

"The state sold it for back taxes. It's the Caldwell place, next door to Miss Ida. Essie's husband did a sight of work on it the two years before he passed on. You'd not know it was the same property."

Tyson leaned against the window sill, considering. "So, Elmer and Sammy had to fend for themselves. One of them a drunk and the other one uneducated."

She nodded. "That's right. Elmer has been gardening for people since he was a boy, but a body can't live decent on a few cents a day."

He rubbed his jaw. "Did Anna Joy have any life insurance?"

A spasm creased her face. "Why do you ask that?"

"It's part of the routine," he said, mildly. "Please, don't upset yourself by reading things into my questions."

She twisted her apron between pale hands. "Yes, she did. When she was born, my husband said we ought to take out a policy on her." Her lips quivered. "He thought we ought to have enough to cover burial costs in case she…"

"I understand. That was wise of him." He hesitated. "I got the autopsy report today."

Jenny sank into the rocking chair beside the bed, white to the lips.

"Anna Joy died of tansy poisoning. Do you know what that is?"

She nodded but didn't speak.

"She had no plant residue on her hands or in her stomach. That means she probably didn't get it accidentally."

Jenny's jaw went slack, her eyes widened in horror. "What are you saying? Someone poisoned my baby?" Her breath came in ragged sobs. "Who would do such a horrible thing? My Anna Joy?" Stiff fingers covered her open mouth then lowered to tear at the buttons on her dress. Her head leaned back and a deep, guttural moan came out.

Tyson rushed to her and helped her onto the bed. He leaned over her and spoke directly into her face. She was gasping like a tired runner. "I'm going out to use the phone, Mrs. Mullins. I'll be right back." He bounded out the bedroom door and down the stairs.

Sucking in a deep breath, he tried to still his shaking hands. Seeing the woman in such a state brought back the memory of his own raw anguish when he lost Carrie.

"Mabel? Get me Dr. St. Clair, on the double."

The doctor arrived in less than ten minutes. He gave Jenny an injection and she sank into a stupor. Every dozen breaths, a groan shook her body.

Outside in the hall, Tyson told St. Clair, "I had to tell her that someone poisoned Anna Joy." He shook his head, his face full of pain.

"It had to be done," St. Clair told him.

"That doesn't make it any easier."

"Sadie will stay with her tonight," he said. "Would you mind fetching my sister? You can use my car." He pulled a ring of keys from his pocket and held them toward Tyson.

"Sure, Doc."

Driving through the rain in the sleek Model T, Tyson tried to get a grip on his emotions. He was a law officer. A case shouldn't get to him like this.

Sadie seemed worried when she answered his knock. Tyson stepped inside out of the rain and pulled off his hat.

"Adam called," she said. "I keep a suitcase ready for emergencies." She pulled a raincoat from the rack. Tyson took it from her and held it open for her to slip into it. "I hope Jenny's okay," she said, pinning on her taffeta hat. "I hate to see her go through such a hard time."

"A death is never easy, and losing a child is especially hard." He picked up her case as Sadie flipped open her umbrella.

Ten minutes later, he parked the doctor's flivver in Jenny's driveway and walked with his sister to the door. Closing her inside, he hustled toward his back door.

Heddie and Vic sat at the kitchen table close together, looking at a Sears catalog.

The sight of the old couple so cozy with one another set Tyson's teeth on edge. He'd done his best to dissuade dear old dad, but Vic wouldn't listen. He'd have to take his medicine.

Tyson hung his coat and hat over the back of a chair to drip dry, muttered a noncommittal greeting and goodbye in one breath, and paced toward the stairs. In his sitting room, Nessa sat with Lori on the sofa, her head cuddled against Nessa's shoulder, a book in the child's lap.

"Hi, Daddy!" She wore a pink robe with white flannel peeking from underneath. Her cheeks looked as rosy as the cotton fabric about her.

He looked at his child's contented face and fear clawed his vitals. What helpless innocent would be next?

CHAPTER Fifteen

After a dream-filled night, Tyson woke to the sound of thunder and pouring rain. He looked down to see Lori snuggled against his side, sound asleep. He couldn't remember her coming in with him.

She must have kicked off her own covers and came to share his. Closing his eyes, he savored the warmth and softness of a stormy morning. The horrors of last night seemed far away.

An hour later he opened his eyes at the insistence of a hungry five-year-old as the clock in the next room struck eight. A boom like a drum roll made Lori dive to his chest and hide her face.

"There's nothing to be afraid of, Chicky. We're safe inside." He rubbed her back. "I smell sausage."

"Heddie's making pancakes this morning. Nessa told me last night."

He threw back the covers. A drafty chill made him want to retreat under the down-filled quilt. There'd be no baseball today. Maybe he'd pay a call to Elmer Buntley's shack instead. The old man would surely be at home in weather like this.

Just after ten o'clock he held an umbrella aloft and stepped into the weather. He ran to Lizzy and ducked inside. What on earth had possessed him to come out? He pulled his hat tighter and waited for a break in the rain.

Fifteen minutes later he puttered south on glistening Market Street. Plate glass windows showed well-lit but empty shops on both sides. The sidewalks were bare.

Twin streams ran down each edge of the street. Tyson dabbed at the windshield with his handkerchief, then gave it up and slowed to a crawl.

As he'd figured, Buntley was at home. The gardener let Tyson stand under his umbrella in the downpour while he decided whether to let the deputy inside.

"I need to ask you a few things about Mrs. Mullins and her daughter." Tyson hunched tighter into his collar. A gust blew water down his neck. He hardly noticed. How could he get more wet than he already was?

"What d'ya want to know?"

Tyson pushed his face toward Buntley. "May I come in?"

Watery blue eyes stared into his. Finally, the old man edged away and let the door swing in the wind. In one motion, Tyson closed the umbrella and sprang inside. Hinges shrieked when he shut out the rain.

"Did you ever see Jenny Mullins arguing with Anna Joy?" he asked.

The gardener's voice had a creaky quality that made the hair on Tyson's neck stand up. "Just after school was out I came on them scuffling in the kitchen. That wildcat girl was throwing a fit because she wanted to pick strawberries, and Jenny had to finish canning what she'd already picked." He rubbed his nose with his long finger. "She weren't no angel that girl. No matter how folks like to paint her up."

He sent the deputy a sly glance. "Jenny took the strap to her, she did. She was a-crying harder than Anna Joy and a-saying, 'Why did God punish me like this?' over and over. I felt sorry for the poor soul."

Tyson didn't have to wonder which poor soul he referred to. Buntley's sympathies certainly weren't with the girl.

"How long's it been since you climbed a tree, Mr. Buntley? You look pretty wiry for a fellow your age."

"You've got to be joshing, Deputy. I'll be sixty-two my next birthday."

"Mrs. Mullins said you trimmed her water oak last spring."

His Adam's apple bobbed. "Come to think of it, I did. I forgot about that time." He stretched his turkey neck closer toward Tyson, his eyes hard and mean. "You know, I'm getting a mite tired of you nosing around here, asking me questions like I'm some kind of criminal. I don't like folks pushing me."

Tyson met his stare. "Mr. Buntley, I could take you to jail as a material witness. Would that make you feel any more kindly toward my questions?"

The muscles in the old man's grizzly jaws worked in and out. "I reckon it wouldn't."

"Then don't push your luck." He reached for the greasy doorknob behind him. "I'll talk with you more later." He ducked into the rain and splashed out to Lizzy, still idling in the puddle-filled rut that Elmer called a driveway.

Cold and miserable, he backed into the street. Which of them was lying?

The Lunch Room stood empty when he returned. In the kitchen, Heddie stirred a giant pot of chili simmering on the stove. A pan of cornbread sat in the center of the table.

Tyson eyed the food. Just the ticket for a cold, damp deputy sheriff.

Nessa kneaded bread at the counter. Flour covered her lower arms and apron front. She smiled when Tyson came in. "You look like you need a cup of hot coffee."

"You're a mind reader." He hung his dripping coat from the back of his chair and set his fedora on the end of the table.

Heddie said, "I just came from sitting with Jenny."

"How is she?"

"She won't speak to anyone. She only stares at the wall."

He sat. "Do either of you know how Jenny and Anna Joy got along?"

Nessa watched him, hands hovering over the bread dough.

Heddie said, "They got along the same as any mother and daughter."

"Did Jenny seem burdened about having Anna Joy around?"

Nessa turned toward him, dread in her eyes. "What are you getting at?"

He told them what Buntley had said.

"It's a dirty lie," Heddie said, eyes flashing. "Jenny never did such a thing."

"Now, Mama. I saw Anna Joy get a whipping once. And Jenny cried then, too." Nessa bore down on Tyson. "But that doesn't prove anything. Jenny did not hurt her own child."

He nodded. "You're right. It doesn't prove anything. It does leave a question, though. Jenny claims she never fought with Anna Joy."

"Every mother gets tired." Heddie declared. "She may even say things she doesn't mean. But that doesn't prove that she'd commit murder."

He held up both hands in surrender. "You've made your point."

Nessa picked up the dough and squeezed off a glob.

Heddie pointed her stirring spoon at Trent. "This afternoon you and Micky can turn the parlor into a second dining room."

"Does that mean we have to carry the sofa to the attic?"

"No, to our apartment." Nessa grinned. "Don't look so relieved. You'd think we're slave masters around here."

"Many a truth is spoken in jest." He held up a hand to block the dishtowel she'd raised. "Didn't you mention coffee?"

Heddie disappeared into the family quarters and closed the door. Nessa dusted off her hands and reached for the coffee pot. "You got me so stirred up about Jenny, I forgot." A moment later, she set a steaming cup in front of him.

"I talked to Elmer again this morning." He picked up a spoon and reached for the sugar bowl. "I feel like a yo-yo, hitting the same targets again and again and getting nowhere."

"Have you ever considered praying about the situation?"

He smirked. "Is this where the sermon starts? If so, I've got some things to do upstairs."

"You're a cynic to the core, aren't you?" She slapped a wad of dough into a small mound and dropped it into a pan.

"I wouldn't say that."

"Prove it." She eyed him archly. "Come with us to church tomorrow."

How she talked him into it he never did figure out. Maybe his emotionally wrought-up state had weakened his resistance.

At ten-thirty the next morning he stood at the bottom of the stairs wearing a silk tie and holding Lori's hand.

"Will you take me to my class?" she asked, looking up from under the brim of a white hat with pink streamers down the back.

"Sorry, Chicky, we're not going to your usual church. First Baptist is having a special speaker today, so we're going over there instead." He eased the stiff collar where it pinched his neck.

Black mesh covering her hat and eyes, Heddie bustled down the hall. Nessa hurried after her mother. She pulled on tan gloves, calling, "Hurry up, Micky! We're going to be late!"

Vic soft-shoed down the stairs. His white hair gleamed beneath a pearl-gray hat with a rolled brim. He wore a double-breasted suit the same color as the hat and had white spats over his shoes.

Tyson glanced at his father and felt like a crow at a peacock convention. He cleared his throat and adjusted his dress fedora, a replica of his usual one, only newer.

Lori skipped over to her grandfather, leaving Tyson to walk with Nessa. Not that Tyson minded.

The storm had blown itself out during the night. Enjoying the breezy, warm morning the group headed east and met the Bailey family at the corner. The hulking, stiff-faced owner of Bailey's hardware walked beside his meek wife, Kate. Red-haired Clifford strolled ahead. His best friend, John Scopes, was still in New York meeting with the ACLU to discuss Clarence Darrow's role in the case.

Heddie called, “Good morning,” to her neighbors. Kate smiled and nodded but didn’t pause to chat.

Tyson and Nessa lagged behind.

“You’re looking smart this morning,” she said, smiling up at him. Her head reached to his cheek.

He grinned. “You don’t look so bad yourself. That bluish-green color suits you.”

She laughed. “It’s called teal.”

Roadsters lined both sides of Cedar Street. Folks in their Sunday best filled the sidewalks leading to the brick church. Set close to the street, the building had a high white belfry above its double doors.

The interior felt dim and cool. Tyson filed into the second row from the back with the rest of the family. Mr. and Mrs. Bailey sat just ahead of them. The church was almost full.

Pastor Moffit spotted them as soon as they sat down. “Nice to have you with us today.” He shook hands down the pew and paused before Tyson. “It’s an honor to have you, Mr. Tyson. I hope you enjoy the service.”

Nodding amiably—he hoped—Tyson worked the brim of his hat between thumb and finger. The pastor moved away to shake a few more hands before hurrying to the platform.

Nessa leaned close to whisper, “There’s Ben McKenzie.” Tyson nodded. The lawyer sat with his wife in the fourth row ahead of them.

The guest speaker—a seminary professor with a bald pate and an extensive vocabulary—expounded on the evils of evolution. Tyson listened carefully. Unfortunately, the man’s education overcame his ability to communicate.

The building grew warm. The sermon grew long. Heads began to nod. Ben McKenzie’s chin sagged against his chest.

A stealthy movement caught Tyson’s eye. He leaned forward a little to see over the pew ahead of him. Bailey had a pencil stub in his hand, his baleful eye on old Ben’s head. In a flash, the hardware-store owner flicked the pencil. McKenzie jerked erect, his wide eyes fastened to the preacher. A moment later, he casually reached up to rub his grizzled head.

Tyson stifled a chuckle.

Nessa elbowed him and sent a warning look. He innocently raised his eyebrows and turned toward the speaker.

At ten past twelve, Moffit reclaimed his podium. “Thank you, Dr. Jasper, for an enlightening message. If there were no Creator, human life would have no purpose, no hope. We would be of all men most miserable." Moffit raised his hands. "Let's stand for a closing hymn."

Strolling home, Tyson told Nessa, "You know, that preacher said more in his closing statement than the professor said in an hour."

"I wish you could accept it, Trent," she said, softly. Her eyes melted into his for a long moment. "I wish it with all my heart."

Tyson remembered her words and her look as he mounted the stairs to his room. He removed his coat and tie, then paused by the dresser. Slowly, deliberately, he pulled off his wedding band and dropped it into a tiny drawer with his handkerchiefs.

On the morning of the state fair, McGinty's Boardinghouse buzzed with excitement, everyone talking at once and making constant reminders. A few minutes past nine they all packed into Lizzy and chugged toward the ball-field-turned-fairgrounds. Vic kept Micky busy providing answers about the town, the locals, and the day's activities.

Lori wore a blue sailor dress and matching hat with long streamers. Tyson picked up his favorite bundle and set her on his shoulder.

"You've got the best seat, Chickabiddy. You can see more than the rest of us."

She squirmed with excitement. "I want to ride a pony!"

"Everyone meet back here at noon," Heddie said. "We'll eat at the car and go to the concert afterward."

Craning his neck looking for friends, Micky hurried toward the center of the activity.

"I'm hankering to sit in the shade with a dish of strawberry ice cream." Vic smiled down at his landlady. "Care to join me?" They strolled away with Heddie's hand on his arm.

Tyson and Nessa stared after them with matching frowns.

"I tried to talk to Mama," Nessa said, flipping her braid off her shoulder, "but she wouldn't listen."

"Same here," Tyson told her, a twist to his lips.

"I want to ride a pony!"

"Why are we wasting time?" Tyson asked Nessa, grinning suddenly.

"Let's go!"

That evening, Lori had milky splotches down the front of her dress. Candy-apple goo smeared her face. Nessa hustled her upstairs for a bath while Heddie saw to supper.

Heddie called the family to the meal as the phone rang. Micky swiped it. "Mr. Tyson, it's for you!"

Tyson spoke three sentences into the mouthpiece and took his chair in time for the blessing.

Dipping beans from the bowl to his plate, Vic said, "We met Herb Hicks at the festival. He just got a telegram from New York. Darrow is taking Scopes's case."

Tyson sat straighter. "Is he now! How did that work out?"

"Scopes insisted. Legally, the boy does have the final word. It is his case, after all."

"Was Darrow at the ACLU meeting?"

"No. But his partner, Dudley Field Malone, was there. Malone did some fancy whispering into Scopes's ear. Hicks said that when Bryan committed himself to the case, that turned the tide. Clarence Darrow wants a grudge match."

Tyson looked at Heddie. "You'll make a pretty penny out of this development, you know. People will pour into Dayton to see those old enemies come to scratch." He lifted a fork full of beans. "I have to admit, I'm looking forward to it myself."

"Bryan's a crafty old warrior," Heddie declared. "How do you think he got to be a politician? He can talk the birds right out of the trees, he can."

Nessa said, "I wonder how long the trial will last. We'd best make up some terrific menus."

An hour later Tyson and his dad enjoyed a few minutes of quiet in the upstairs sitting room. Tyson put his stockinged feet on the coffee table. "So, what do you think of our fair town, Pa?"

"It's a friendly little place." Vic leaned back in a soft chair, his legs straight out before him. "I wouldn't think your office would have much business."

"Generally, we don't."

"I have to admit, I've been hankering to give you a hand on those poison deaths you've been working on." A knowing expression crossed his features. "You've been so interested in talking over your case with a certain young lady that you've forgotten your own father."

Ignoring the remark, Tyson said, "Glad to have you along, Pa. Matter of fact, I just got a call from my old partner in Chattanooga telling me I can interview Bella Smith." He told about the bootlegging investigation Crabill was working on. "How'd you like to visit her with me first thing in the morning?"

Bella's daughter, Dotty, opened the door to Tyson and Vic and stopped chewing gum long enough to stare. She wore a sea green sheath. A double strand of white beads hung to her hips.

Tyson made the first move. "Good morning. Is your mother at home?"

The girl finally remembered her manners. "Yes, sir." She slowly opened the door. "Please, come in."

Tyson looked at the girl's sagging mouth and puffy eyes. Dotty had been crying, and not just an April shower either.

CHAPTER
Sixteen

Dotty glanced at the dishes piled high in the sink. "Don't mind the mess. Nessa will be here later to wash up." She licked her lips. "I'll tell Mama you're here." Beads rattling, she hurried across the smudged linoleum and into the living room.

In a moment Bella appeared and blinked her kohled eyelids. The air about her hung thick with cheap perfume. She plucked at the stiff curl on her cheek. "What can I do for you, gentlemen?"

Tyson said, "I've got a few questions for you, Mrs. Smith." He glanced at Vic. "This is my father, Vic Tyson. He's visiting from Nashville."

Bella smiled at Vic, teeth gleaming. "Nice to meet you, Mr. Tyson." She turned calculating eyes on Tyson. "Won't you sit down?"

They chose seats around a table cluttered with the remains of a toast and coffee breakfast. Tyson pulled out his notebook. "Can you tell me where you were on the night of April 19?"

Her eyes narrowed. "I don't keep a diary, Deputy. That was more than a month ago. I have no idea."

"It was the night before your mother died. Does that bring it to mind?"

She stared at Tyson. Her fingers drifted from the curl to her ruby-coated lips.

"Isn't it true that you brought a trunk load of liquor to Dayton under the excuse of visiting your mother?"

Bella's face flushed. Chin high, she stared at Tyson.

"I've got two witnesses that saw you, Mrs. Smith. For your own good, you'd best come clean."

She seemed to shrink. "I… I came up to see Mother."

"What time was that?"

"I don't know. Late."

"You've got one last chance. I want the truth."

"And go to the slammer? No thank you."

Tyson leaned forward, elbow on the edge of the table. "Look, we want your boss. If you'll give us evidence to nail him, you'll get a lighter sentence. Otherwise, it's five years." He raised his eyebrows. "It's your choice."

Bella's eyes filled with tears, but her voice stayed strong. "I've got a daughter."

"You should have thought of that before."

She sighed heavily and stared at her hands twisted in her lap. "When Bert left me, I was desperate. I had no job, no money. Dotty had just started school. She needed clothes and things." She pulled a wrinkled handkerchief from her pocket and blew her nose.

"Every Saturday night Bert and me, we used to make the rounds of the speakeasies in Chattanooga. A friend of mine from the Win Ho Laundry told me they needed runners. They'd buy me a car and all I had to was drive to Dayton or Morgan Springs late at night, unlock the trunk, and get lost for a while."

She sniffed. "I got a girlfriend in Morgan Springs. I'd pop in on her every couple of weeks."

"Who picked up the liquor?" Tyson prodded.

"I don't know, Deputy. I'd come back after an hour and the booze would be gone."

"Where did you get it?"

"I'd drive to the back door of Win Ho and a big, burly fellow would fill my trunk. His name's Al Hurst."

Tyson licked his pencil tip. "What other names do you know?"

When she finished he had almost a full page, both men and women.

Bella looked at Tyson like a canary watching a hungry cat. "What are you going to do?"

"Have you got twenty dollars?"

She nodded.

"Give it to me, and I'll hold it as bail. I'll write up the papers when I get back to the office."

Bella reached under the table. With her hands out of sight, she fumbled at her skirt and came up with a crisp twenty-dollar bill.

Tyson stood. "I'll be in touch. Meanwhile, don't leave town. If you do, I'll have to sic the big boys on you."

"I'll be here," she said, sullen anger in her voice.

The men crossed the porch and strode to the sidewalk. Vic stood in the shade of a wide maple while Tyson cranked Lizzy. On the opposite side of the street, a lady knelt on an old rug, weeding a plot of orange marigolds.

At the engine's first rumble, Tyson dove through the door to set the spark and throttle. Vic slid in behind him.

When they were on their way, Tyson called over Lizzy's rattling, "What do you think of Bella Smith?"

Vic glanced at his son. "If Mrs. Johnson had gotten wise to Bella, what would the old lady have done?"

Tyson shrugged. "I don't know. I never met her. She lived like a hermit, never even went to church."

"In that case, I don't see her getting involved. She'd probably just shut her eyes to the whole affair."

"That's what I figured, too. Miss Ida willed her house to Bella even though they didn't get along. If she'd do that, I can't see her turning Bella over to the police."

Tyson maneuvered Lizzy into a parking space near the Aqua Hotel. "Let's see what's going on at Robinson's—"

A gunshot cut off his words. It sounded like it came from the barbershop.

Doc Robinson burst out of his store, white apron flapping, and dashed toward the barbershop across the street.

Vic lunged out of the car, Tyson behind him. At Wilkey's door, Tyson collided with a scrawny blond fellow wearing a white cloth around his neck, the left side of his hair trimmed close, the other side shaggy. His eyes wide with fright, the young man stopped to glance both ways then started east as fast as his long legs could take him.

Tyson grabbed him from behind. "Wait a minute!" Tyson said. "What happened?"

Chest heaving, the fellow jerked away. "He tried to shoot me!"

"Who?"

"George Rappelyea." A glimpse of Tyson's badge calmed him by half. He reached for the knot behind his neck. "I was in the barber chair when George came in. We got to talking about the trial and evolution and all. I told George I believed that God made the world in six days." He stopped talking long enough to swallow.

"We started arguing, and George pulled out a gun." A bewildered look spread over his face. "Then he started shootin' wild."

Tyson pulled out his notebook and turned to a blank page. "Would you mind giving me your name?"

"Charles Simmons. I live in Morgan Springs."

Tyson tucked away his pencil. "You can go your way, Mr. Simmons. I believe you're the victim of a practical joke."

Simmons touched his head and said, embarrassed, "I think I'd best go back and finish my haircut."

When they arrived at Wilkey's Barber Shop, a stocky man was grappling with a short fellow in a rumpled suit: Virgil Wilkey and George Rappelyea. Vic was trying to pull Rappelyea off the barber and dodge fists at the same time. Tyson stepped in to help pull them apart, and Vic got a grip on panting, wild-eyed Rappleyea.

Wilkey shook his fist at the mining engineer. "He staged a shooting in my shop!"

"Mr. Rappelyea," Tyson said, reasonably, "this is the second time you've tried to foment a fight. If you can't stay out of trouble, I'm going to run you in."

With his right arm squeezing Rappelyea around the chest, Vic looked like a pro linebacker holding a junior varsity quarterback.

Face red, hair askew, Rappelyea quit struggling and his glare crumpled into a sheepish grin. "You can't blame a fellow for trying, can you?" He shrugged out of Vic's grasp, straightened his coat, and picked up his hat from the floor.

Angry murmurs filled the small room, now packed with men who had heard the shot and come to investigate.

Rappelyea looked around and drawled, "Aw, can't you guys take a joke?"

Vic was in full form. He turned toward the ranks with his hands palm outward. "Okay, break it up. Show's over."

Simmons eased into the right barber chair. "Finish this off for me, will you, Virgil? My wife's waiting at the grocery."

Virgil reached for a comb to restore order to his own ruffled fringe. His wide grin showed in the big mirror covering the back wall.

His fellow barber, Thurlow Reed, sidled close for a whispered conference. The same height as Wilkey, Reed was ten years younger and much slimmer.

Rappelyea strolled outside, Tyson behind him.

Quick-stepping to get in front of the little man, Tyson said, "George, I was serious about no more fighting." He pinned him with a hard look. "I know what you're up to, and I'm asking you to use some common sense. The last thing we need here is a riot or an injury."

"Yes, sir." Avoiding the deputy's eyes, he clamped his straw hat over that mop of hair and strode down the street, a man with places to go.

Tyson went back inside. "I'll give you fellows the same warning I just gave George."

Virgil Wilkey pinched his mouth together in a droll expression. "Have a seat, Deputy, while I fill you in on the facts of life." He picked up his clipper and turned it on.

"I'll stand, thanks," Tyson said.

"That fight at the courthouse was pure Hollywood."

Thurlow Reed nodded. "Rappelyea waltzed in here that morning and asked Virgil to belt him a good one during the speech. He said it would make good publicity for the trial."

Virgil chuckled. "Trouble was, I couldn't do it and keep a straight face, so Thurlow stepped in." He glanced at his friend. "He did a right convincing job. Don't you think so, Mr. Tyson?"

Tyson looked from one to the other, his face serious. "For your sakes, I hope this is the last shenanigan. Next time someone's going to be cooling their heels in the pokey."

Reed grinned. "Like the man said, the show's over." He applied the clippers to Simmons's head.

A small bell tinkled as Tyson pulled the door open. Outside, Vic chuckled. "Your quiet little town ain't so quiet."

"I wish the trial started tomorrow. A full month of this and my nerves will be shot. Look around. The whole face of the town has changed."

Vic gazed at the ape-laden billboards, the banner hanging across Main, and the shops with stuffed chimpanzees in their windows. "I'd say they have monkey fever."

Tyson grunted. "You mean money fever."

They reached Lizzy, and Tyson paused to close the door properly. In his haste, he'd left it ajar.

All the tables in Robinson's were filled. Tyson said hello to Belinda Riesbeck and Jody, Ben and Gordon McKenzie, Clifford Bailey, and Howard Morgan. As he and Vic waited in the line moving toward the counter, Tyson heard the barber shop incident rehashed four different ways.

Usually cool, the shop felt closed and warm today. The mingled aromas of sundae syrups and antiseptic seemed cloying.

"Morning, Deputy," Doc Robinson said when they reached the front. "Good thing you came along when you did."

"Good for who?" Tyson handed over his nickel. "I'll take a paper."

"Here, take two. These are two days old. They just came in on the morning train. One from Washington and one from New York."

Tyson dug out another coin.

"I hope Rappelyea simmers down," the druggist said, moving closer. "There's talk that some folks want to run him out of town. They say he's a traitor for swearing out a warrant on John Scopes."

"Doc, you'd best get John back here before something worse than a little playacting happens. He's the only one who can calm down that kind of gossip."

"I've got his dad's number in Paducah. I'll give him a call and see if John's there yet. He may still be in New York."

Tyson tucked his papers under his arm and left the store with Vic. Fifteen feet down the sidewalk, he threw the newsprint onto Lizzy's back seat and reached for the crank.

"Let's stop by the courthouse," Vic said. "I'd like to see what's going on. They've finished painting the trim outside, even the clocks on the tower. Now they're working on the inside."

Father and son stepped inside the brick building. The odor of fresh paint made Tyson catch his breath. Dipping into cream-colored paint, a dozen men worked in the lobby, the upstairs hall, and the courtroom—some on ladders, some kneeling over baseboards, some with rollers on long handles.

Men wearing gray coveralls positioned new rows of theater seats in front of the current ones, greatly reducing the inner sanctum where the bailiff and the court reporter worked. Along the back wall, a platform hovered eight feet in the air.

Vic nodded toward it. "What's that for?"

"Movie cameras. There will also be a table for three radio microphones. WGN from Chicago has arranged to broadcast the entire trial live to the tune of a thousand dollars a day."

"Looks like I came to town at just the right time," Vic said. "At least I've already got a room. They'll be scarce in a few weeks."

"Some people are planning to move into the mountains and rent out their homes to folks coming in." Tyson shook his head. "I never saw the like."

Dodging traffic, they walked to the next door down the hall.

"This is the press room." Tyson pushed it open. Four long tables had telephones lined up on them like black tuba players in marching formation.

"Let's get out of here," Vic said. "That paint smell is starting to get to me." They ambled down the stairs.

Tyson said, "There will be a public address system reaching the yard and four auditoriums across town. Harris told me they're hoping for twenty thousand people."

Vic rubbed his beard. "For Heddie's sake, I hope he's right. That many people can eat a lot of sandwiches."

Father and son parted ways on the lawn. Vic sauntered north toward home, and Tyson crossed the grass to the sheriff's office. Unlocking the door, he dropped his newspapers onto the desk, flipped on the switch for the noisy fan screwed into a corner of the ceiling, and opened every window in sight. He picked up the phone. Time to report his chat with Bella. Crabill would be interested in her list of gang members.

Five minutes later he finished the conversation with, "I've arrested Bella. She's out on bail."

"I'll put her into the trial rostrum with the rest of the gang,"

Crabill said. "We nailed twenty of 'em before dawn this morning. When I get a trial date, I'll let you know. Just make sure she shows."

"Will do." He cradled the earpiece. If only he'd gotten a warrant to search Bella's Chattanooga apartment before she moved out. Maybe it wasn't too late. He opened a drawer. If he could get the magistrate to sign a search warrant, he'd have a go at Miss Ida's house this afternoon.

The magistrate was a cooperative fellow.

Bella blustered, but she couldn't keep the deputy out.

Gripping a broom in the kitchen, Nessa didn't speak to him when he entered the house. She sent him a look that told him she was sorry to be there working during Bella's humiliation.

For two solid hours, he peered into drawers and make-up cases, into flour bins and jewelry boxes. All he needed was a tiny vial of tansy oil. He sniffed perfume bottles until his head ached.

Nothing.

Bella followed him to the door. The haughty tilt to her chin couldn't hide a spark of fear in her eyes. "You're barking up the wrong tree, Deputy. All I did was drive a car. I never did nothing else illegal."

He left the house with enough frustrated energy to chew the big oak off at the stump. He cranked Lizzy with a vengeance.

Crabill called the next day to tell him Bella's trial date was set for June 9, the following Tuesday. Tyson phoned the lady with the good news.

On June 8, Tyson got home from work to find Vic in the kitchen helping Heddie shell peas. "Howdy, Trent," he said. "What's cooking?"

"Bella has to appear in Chattanooga tomorrow."

Heddie said, "Essie Caldwell is going to look after Dotty while Bella's gone."

Tyson looked at his father, eyebrows raised. "I don't know why you're asking me anything. Just ask the local grapevine."

Vic chuckled. "I always said that women would make the best detectives. They can find out more in two minutes than a trained officer can manage in two weeks."

Heddie dropped six peas into the small bowl on the table between them. "Saw Essie at the market this morning, I did." She sounded defensive. Her cheeks turned pink.

Vic grinned at her. "That's because you're a friendly sort, Heddie. Folks tell you things."

Tyson's lips twitched. He could think of a few things he'd like to tell her himself.

The next morning, he drove Bella to the crowded, noisy courthouse in downtown Chattanooga. Hot bile rose in his throat when he shouldered between the same kind of thug that had snuffed out his innocent Carrie. The dank odor of unwashed bodies made his stomach churn. Easing into a back seat, Tyson endured.

Mercifully, Bella's name came near the top of the roster. Because of her cooperation, she got thirty days. She was lucky.

Unfortunately, she didn't feel lucky. Black tears streaked down her cheeks. She smudged them around with a dingy handkerchief. "Ask Essie Caldwell to look after Dotty for me, will you?" she called to Tyson, as the officer led her away. "Dotty needs help."

Tyson stared after her. Dotty wasn't the only one.

CHAPTER
Seventeen

Two weeks after Bella's conviction, Clarence Darrow made his first visit to Dayton with a crew of reporters. Tyson and his father were sipping cold sodas at Robinson's when the lawyer left the Aqua Hotel to meet with Scopes.

"So that's the great Darrow," Tyson commented dryly, brushing his mustache and eyeing the stoop-shouldered warrior as he passed the drug store's windows. Just shy of six feet tall, the lawyer walked with a stiff-legged gait, his toes kicking high. His craggy brow jutted out over his eyes like a seamed cliff over an ocean cave. A straw hat cocked on his head, his coat unbuttoned, he still managed to look shrewd.

Gordon McKenzie came into the drug store a few minutes later. He ordered a double strawberry sundae and approached Tyson's table. "Mind if I join you?"

"Help yourself," Trent said. "Did you see Darrow?"

"Who hasn't?" Gordon asked. "He's got the whole town shanghaied. The Progressive Club held a banquet for him last night." He dipped a long-handled spoon into the cool confection.

"I heard about it," Tyson said. "I even had free tickets, but I couldn't go. Lori's got a cold, and I didn't want to leave her."

"That Darrow's a slick one," Gordon continued. "He was born and bred in the city but to hear him talk he walked behind a plow with a pacifier still pinned to his shirt." He laughed at his own humor.

Vic twirled the straw in his glass. "I read about his case with those two college kids last year. They should have hung, both of them."

Tyson asked, "Didn't he blame their crime on what they'd learned in school?"

Gordon nodded. "That's right. He said the boys weren't responsible for their actions, that Nietzsche actually was responsible for the crime because of his philosophy books."

"You're over my head, McKenzie."

"Friedrich Nietzsche was a German who believed that a super-race should rule the world. He thought some people were farther up the evolutionary ladder than others. According to him, Jews and blacks were on the bottom rung."

McKenzie sucked his spoon clean. "From a lawyer's viewpoint, it was a masterly stroke. Nietzsche's been dead for twenty-five years. No one can prosecute him anymore."

Tyson checked his watch. "Hey, I've got to go." He stood and picked up his hat. "Are you ready, Pa? I need to see what Harris is up to."

"I believe I'll stay a while," Vic said. He turned toward Gordon. "Are you on the defense or the prosecution team?"

Tyson pushed through the door and paced north on Market. In seconds his hat band felt tight and sticky. He slipped it off and passed a handkerchief over his brow. The moment he replaced the fedora, it felt sticky again.

In the sheriff's office, Tyson found Harris talking on the telephone. "I could use eight," he said, his wide face leaning into the earpiece. He glanced at Tyson and continued, "All right. I guess I'll settle for six. Have them report on the eighth of July to get oriented.... Right." He dropped the receiver into its holder and made a note.

"That was Chattanooga PD," he told Tyson. "I'm borrowing six officers to help us during the trial. It's all they could spare." He jabbed a finger at a town map spread before him on Tyson's desk. "We'll rope off six blocks—Market Street from the courthouse to Main, and one block east and west of Market on Main. No vehicles in the business area, only pedestrians."

"What'll I be doing?" Tyson asked, perching on a corner of the desk.

"You'll take the courtroom patrol with one of the Chattanooga men. One man will be outside on the courthouse lawn, and the rest of us will patrol the town.

They spent the rest of the afternoon discussing traffic and crowd control. The big event was finally in motion. And not only for the sheriff's department. That day, Heddie signed up her first new roomer—Paul Henderson with the *St. Louis Post-Dispatch*.

Tyson greeted him with a handshake before supper. Henderson stood just over six feet tall with dark hair and eyes. He had classic good looks and a sparkling smile but with an immature cast that would make most women describe him as a nice boy. The reporter gave Tyson an open-faced grin.

"You're staying through 'til the trial's over?" Tyson asked.

"That's the plan." Henderson touched his dark bow tie. "I'm here to cover until Darrow leaves tomorrow. I'll stay during the trial preparations and follow on through." He gazed at Tyson. "Care to comment on the case?"

Tyson took a mental step backward. "No thanks. Let's keep things off the record if you don't mind. Living together, it would be best, don't you think?"

The reporter nodded, then smiled broadly at Nessa coming toward them. He turned his nod into a tiny bow. "Good afternoon, Miss McGinty."

Nessa flushed. "Please call me Nessa. Everyone does. Dinner's ready. You may be seated in the dining room. Mother and I will serve the food in a moment."

"Thank you." His eyes followed her progress back to the kitchen.

Tyson's collar suddenly felt warm and tight. "I'll fetch my daughter from the kitchen," he said.

The men parted at the dining room door. Tyson entered the kitchen and found Lori sitting at the table sorting paper doll clothes. Her nose looked red from much blowing, but her eyes were clear and bright.

Nessa was filling a tray with bowls of mashed potatoes and succotash. Baked chicken perfumed the air.

"Why the class act with the new boarder?" he asked.

Heddie answered, "He's not just a boarder, he's a *trial* boarder. Fifteen dollars a week."

"Which means he gets to eat in the Lunch Room free," Nessa added, touching her hair. "And we do his laundry for him."

"Let me carry that for you," Tyson said, stepping forward.

She stared at him. "Why?"

"You can't wear yourself out waiting on the first bird to settle here. There will be more flying in every day." He eased in close to her and lifted the tray. "Open the door, will you? Come along, Lori."

Watching him keenly, Nessa held the door and followed him into the dining room.

Two days later, Heddie stopped Tyson on his way out the door. "Trent, would you mind if your father moved in with you? I know it will be tight, but one of you could sleep on the sofa, couldn't you? I'll only charge for one room." She looked uncomfortable, almost apologetic. "It'll only be until after the trial."

He said, "That's fine, Heddie," when it really wasn't. On the other hand, the lady needed money. What else could he do?

He stepped into the morning sun and adjusted his fedora. Guess who would be sleeping on the sofa. Certainly not Gentleman Vic.

When Tyson returned home that afternoon, Nessa met him on the front porch, a cloth-covered basket on her arm, her freckles dark against pale cheeks. "Trent, something awful has happened."

"What is it?"

"Jody, Belinda Riesbeck's little girl. Dr. St. Clair just diagnosed her with rheumatic fever."

He immediately thought of all the afternoons Jody had played with his Lori.

Nessa went on, "She came down with a high fever and joint pain last night. She was worse this morning and had a rash, so Belinda called the doctor." Her eyes filled with tears. "The poor little tyke."

She blinked hard. "The house is under quarantine. I'm going to leave this basket on the doorstep."

Tyson wished for words to comfort her but came up empty. Was life nothing more than trouble and pain and fear?

For the next two weeks, Dayton residents waited in tense anguish, but no other children contracted the dreaded disease.

Meanwhile, George Rappelyea targeted his energy toward fixing up an abandoned house a mile outside of town. Known commonly as The Mansion, it had been empty for more than ten years, with no plumbing, no electric, and no protection from insects. Its only benefit was eighteen spacious rooms.

Rappelyea recruited several young people to help him sweep and clean, then he brought in Oriental mats and iron cots.

"Don't see why he's taking the defense team out there," Heddie said one afternoon while they were clearing up the Lunch Room. "Only a tramp would feel at home in that mausoleum."

As the trial drew near, Heddie focused more and more on the news. She read the latest papers and listened to the four-foot-tall radio in the family apartment several times a day.

One Saturday afternoon after the family's noon meal, she slapped the *Chattanooga Times* with the back of her hand. "That Unitarian preacher from New York—Charles Francis Potter—says, 'Take ten of the hundred reasons for doubting the Bible's literal truth and drop them from airplanes if necessary on cities of the South.'

"How can he call himself a preacher and say something like that?"

Vic stood and touched her shoulder. "What say we take a walk? Clear the fog from our brains."

"My brain's not foggy," she declared. "I'd like to tell them infidels a thing or two."

"Well, *I'd* like to walk a while and then go to the baseball game. Want to come along?" He smiled down at her.

Her expression softened. "Let me get my hat."

"Me, too!" Lori called, sliding out of her chair.

"Of course, honey," Vic said, kneeling to wipe a smudge from her cheek. "We couldn't go without our little sweetheart."

Micky stood. "I'm going to warm up with the fellows before the game." The clock struck two-thirty as he darted out the door.

Lingering over his peach cobbler, Tyson smiled at Nessa. "How's Jody doing?"

"Some better, thank God."

Tyson touched her hand. "You look tired."

"I'll be glad to get back to normal. The strain is starting to get to me."

He pulled his hand back and frowned. "I'm afraid getting back to normal will be impossible for some of us in this fair town."

"You mean Jenny."

"And Bella. And even Elmer, crusty as he is."

She stood and gathered plates. "I'd best get this cleaned up. The game starts in twenty minutes." She wiped her forehead with the back of her wrist. "I'm not looking forward to playing in this heat. I wish it would rain."

Nessa got her wish on the evening of July 6 when a thunderstorm swept through the valley, pounding roofs and rattling the big boardinghouse. The lights blinked, faltered, and brightened.

Tyson lit a candle in the sitting room when he made up his sofa bed that night. If the night light went out, Lori would wake up frightened of the dark. Funny how she always seemed to know even in a deep sleep.

The next morning dawned sunny and hot as though the storm had never happened. At nine, Tyson headed south to the depot instead of to the office.

Already more than a thousand people milled about the loading platform and under the trees along Railroad Avenue. William Jennings Bryan would arrive in three hours.

By eleven, more than fifteen hundred people had assembled, two hundred of them reporters.

"It must be close on a hundred degrees," Harris remarked to Tyson at twelve-thirty. Sweat made a broad streak down the back of the sheriff's blue shirt. "Wouldn't you know he'd be late."

"I just hope they get here soon. I haven't had lunch."

"Nobody has."

Heddie had closed the Lunch Room today in honor of Dayton's hero. Nessa stood with Micky and Lori in a shrinking block of shade made by the depot cupola.

Tyson strolled toward them.

"Should we wait?" Nessa asked. "It's getting late."

"I'm hungry," Lori said from her perch on Micky's shoulders.

Tyson said, "This is a once-in-a-lifetime happening. You'll miss it if you go now." He dug into his pocket and pulled out a silver dollar. "Here, Micky. Let me hold Lori. You can run to Peale's for some buns and three sodas. He hefted his little daughter. "Where's Vic and Heddie?"

"They wandered off." Nessa shrugged. "We may as well give up, Trent. It's a hopeless cause, keeping them apart."

When Micky returned, Tyson walked back to his post beside the tracks. His hat felt like it held hot coals. He sipped his Coca-Cola and wished away the minutes.

At one-thirty a whistle split the air. Harris hustled down the platform to urge three pressmen to stay back. The Royal Palm limited from Miami screeched, sparks flying, to a halt, a special delivery. Usually, this train barreled through Dayton at full speed.

The "Great Commoner," as the press had christened him, appeared on the rear platform. He wore striped trousers, a dark coat, and the pith helmet that became his trademark during his stay. In his hand was a black Gladstone bag. Doffing the helmet, he uncovered a shiny bald head with a white fringe around his ears. He spoke to the reporters crowding the steps.

"Just say that I am here. I am going right to work, and I'm ready for anything that is to be done."

Cheers and applause wafted toward him. An old crusader, Bryan had traveled up and down the Chautauqua circuit fighting for women's suffrage, income tax, and Prohibition. Secretary of State under Wilson, three times he'd campaigned for the presidency as the Democratic candidate.

Everything about Will Bryan was round: his face, his eyes, his belly. A man near Tyson whispered, "That feller's mouth is so wide he can whisper in his own ear." At sixty-five, Bryan still made an impressive presence, though today he looked drawn with fatigue and heat.

Tyson felt sweat trickle into his collar. Heat and fatigue left no one untouched on a day like this.

A hired companion pushed Mary Bryan's wheelchair to the edge of the steps, where two men helped to lift it down. A lawyer in her own right, Mary Baird was the only female in her class at law school and the only one to pass the bar exam after two years of study. Mary refused to let constant arthritis pain keep her at home.

As soon as two black porters had loaded their luggage, a car sped Bryan and his wife to the home of F.R. Rogers, which Bryan had leased for the duration of the trial.

The Progressive Club scheduled a banquet in Bryan's honor that night. Tyson had two free passes in his pocket. This was one gathering he wouldn't miss.

After work that afternoon he found the older Tyson on his sofa, shirtsleeves rolled up, reading the *Chattanooga News-Free Press*.

"Want to come along to the banquet, Pa?" Tyson asked.

Vic folded the paper and reached for his shirt buttons. "I reckon so. How often does a man get to hear Bryan in person?"

Men in suits and ties filled the banquet hall when Tyson and his father arrived. Two cloth-covered tables laden with china and crystal stretched thirty feet along bare walls. Slim-necked bottles in wicker baskets stood at intervals along the tables. A patriotic bunting draped the speaker's platform at the room's narrow front.

Tyson and Vic found seats on the left, one seat away from John Neal. Dr. St. Clair, looking fine in a black suit and bow tie, sat on the opposite side next to Doc Robinson.

William Jennings Bryan made his entrance at ten 'til six. His trek across the room lasted five minutes because he stopped to shake hands and say a few words to nearly every man there.

With knowing eyes and tight lips, Dr. John Neal observed his opponent's progress.

Bryan grabbed a young waiter's arm as he passed. "Would you ask the kitchen if I could have a dish of radishes with my meal?"

The fellow blushed, nodded, and hurried away.

Bryan finally chose a place across from Neal near the center of the room. When John Scopes stepped up, the Great Commoner sprang to his feet to shake the defendant's hand. "Haven't I met

you somewhere before?" Bryan asked when they took seats across from one another.

It was John's turn to blush. "You spoke at my high school commencement. We had the same alma mater."

"Salem High?"

"I was in the class of 1919."

"Please, refresh my memory about your commencement."

Scopes said miserably, “Four of us broke out laughing during your commencement address.”

“Yes.” The big man leaned back, brow creased, remembering. “I distinctly recall that.” He smiled. “Please tell me. What was so amusing? I’ve wondered about that for six years.”

“The minister who gave the baccalaureate sermon had false teeth. Every time he came to an ‘s’ his teeth would make an odd whistling sound. By the end of the sermon, my friends and I had to pinch ourselves to keep from laughing.”

“Did I make that sound?”

John nodded. “We couldn’t hold back, sir. The whistle hit us so unexpectedly, we just busted out all at once.” He swallowed hard. “I’m sorry it happened.”

Bryan chuckled. “Don’t worry yourself, son. I believe I may have laughed, too.” He took on a concerned, fatherly expression. “Tell me, are you a Christian?”

Chapter Eighteen

Scopes considered the question an instant before saying, "I have deep religious feelings, Mr. Bryan."

"That's not the same, son."

Vic spoke softly but clearly. "Christianity is a deep faith in Jesus Christ as the Son of God."

"Why, thank you, sir," Bryan said, turning his benevolent gaze on Vic. "I couldn't have put it better myself."

Scopes hurried on, "I believe God is love and love is God. I try to live a life of love. Fundamentalists want to force everyone to hold the same prejudices and outdated ideas that they do. They're trying to keep the country in the dark ages."

Bryan leaned forward, speaking gently, "You have no idea what a black and brutal thing this evolution is."

Neal put his hand on John's arm and the young man stopped, a look of uncertainty on his face. "I don't mean to be disrespectful, Mr. Bryan. You asked me what I believed and that's my answer."

"That's good," Bryan answered, smiling. "We shall get along fine. We may be on opposite sides of the issue but there's no reason why we can't remain friends. If you lose the case and have to pay a fine, I'll cover it for you."

A hundred men found their seats, and a team of waiters began serving beef, potatoes, corn, white bread with butter, and yellow pound cake.

Scopes ate little. His potatoes and corn sat untouched.

Bryan asked, "Are you going to eat your side dishes, John?"

"No, Mr. Bryan. I'm stuffed."

"May I have them?"

Tyson held out a bread basket. "Would you like some bread, Mr. Bryan?"

"No, thank you. I'm diabetic. I've given up white bread." He dipped into Scopes's potatoes, smothered with gravy.

From his side vision, Tyson watched the guest of honor, amazed at his appetite.

After the waiters removed plates and cutlery, Bryan stepped to the podium. He spoke and moved with flawless grace. His voice carried easily to those hovering around the back doors.

Ten minutes into the address he touched on the matter at hand. "What is the secret of the world's interest in this little case? It is found in the fact that this trial uncovers an attack upon the Christian religion.

"If evolution wins, Christianity goes. Not suddenly, of course, but gradually, for the two cannot stand together. They are as antagonistic as light and darkness; as antagonistic as good and evil." The room swelled with cheers and applause when he finished.

The night's festivities over, hordes pressed to the platform. Tyson and his father slipped out a side door.

"Bryan made a great speech," Vic said as the Model T chugged toward home.

"You think he was right?"

"Sure. Evolution teaches there's no God. Two opposite viewpoints cannot stand together. It's impossible."

Shifting into low gear to make a turn, Tyson asked, "Would it matter which side came out on top? Would our society change so much?"

The following morning Harris met Tyson at the office door. "The boys from Chattanooga will be here in an hour. This morning I'll give out assignments and show them around. His expression hardened. "We're going to make it tough for anyone to even think about crime. Bootleggers had best head for the hills." He reached past Tyson for the doorknob. "Let's go."

They set out on foot. Townsfolk, reporters, cameramen, and tourists filled the street. Harris rubbed a blue bandanna across the back of his neck. "I wish this heat would break."

Outside the courthouse, a white-haired man had set up a table and piled it with books. He was busy hanging up a banner. All Tyson could read so far on the strip of white cloth was "Hell and . . ."

Tyson asked Harris, "Who's that?"

"Who?" He looked around. "Oh, that's T. T. Martin, head of the Anti-Evolution League. He wrote a little book about evolution in the schools. I guess he figures this is a good place to make some sales."

Two teams of men were hanging banners on the side of the courthouse itself. Dozens of people milled about beneath the shady trees in the yard.

Tyson and Harris strolled down Market Street. They passed Bryan standing on the steps of a grocery store with a group of admirers around him. He wore his pith helmet and carried a palm leaf fan. His gray starched shirt had been cut into a V at the neck. The sleeves had been shortened to elbow length.

Tyson caught a few of Bryan's words, ". . . if defeated, I'll push for a Constitutional Amendment . . ."

Sitting on the back of a low-slung yellow sports car, John Scopes waved to the crowd like the guest of honor in a parade. Beside him, a teenage girl's bobbed hair blew free in the breeze as she smiled widely. Tyson was surprised to see John's arm linked with hers.

A stocky man of medium height sauntered toward Tyson and Harris. His slicked-black hair had a center part. The white straw hat perched on the back of his head held a card in its blue ribbon band: Press.

He handed over two business cards. "H.L. Mencken of the Baltimore *Evening Sun.*" Pencil poised over a stenographer's notebook, he asked, "What preparations have you made to handle the crowds expected in Dayton this week?" He had a throaty voice with a mild lisp on the "sh" sound. His Baltimore accent held a tinge of New York squawk.

Harris's chest expanded with importance. "We've got six policemen coming . . ."

Tyson drifted away. He'd heard of Mencken. Who hadn't? The man lived to shock his readers. Heddie often complained about his irreverent articles.

Darwin's Mercantile had a new sign: DARWIN IS RIGHT—inside.

Hawkers stood behind stands for hot dogs, baked goods, and souvenirs. Nessa and two young ladies held their hand-sewn monkey toys and chanted to each passerby, "Remember Dayton with a monkey. A dollar each." Tyson caught her eye as he passed and got a smile in return.

The Aqua Hotel's garish yellow paint jolted the senses when Tyson rounded the corner of Market onto West Main. Stretched across the street in front of the drug store, a banner announced proudly: Where It All Began.

The store's dim interior felt good after walking in the hot sun. On the left wall of the crowded store, Robinson had put up a bulletin board with notices tacked on it: Darrow arrives at three o'clock tomorrow afternoon. Bryan speaks at First Baptist Church on Sunday morning.

"Beamish specials, 5 cents," had been chalked on the back wall in wide letters.

"What's a Beamish special?" Tyson asked the soda jerk.

"A new formula Richard Beamish brought from Philadelphia."

"Is that the reporter from the *Inquirer*?"

"Right."

"I'll try one." He handed over a nickel and drank it standing up. He had to get back to work.

Robinson shuffled toward him. "When are you blocking off the streets?"

"Late tonight," Tyson told him, setting down his empty glass. He pulled out his watch. "I've got to move."

The sun seemed brighter, the air ten degrees hotter when he returned to the sidewalk.

Just outside the store, a pint-sized reporter stopped a mountain boy wearing overalls. "What do you think about the evolution case?" he asked.

"Case of evolution?" the red-haired fellow drawled. "Land sakes! Who's got it?"

Grinning, Tyson walked on. At this point, he wasn't sure if he favored the Bible thumpers or the liberal press. He ambled back to Market and spotted Harris half a block away.

In mid-stride Harris whirled around to grab a husky reporter by the arm. "That'll be two dollars, sir!"

The newsman gaped. "For what?"

"For swearing on the street. You can pay up now or come to the courthouse."

"Aw," he muttered. "I'll pay." He dug into his pants pocket and came up with two pieces of silver.

Harris carefully buttoned the man's fine into his shirt pocket and elbowed through a crowd gawking at a poster of a chimpanzee holding a coconut.

Harris met Tyson in front of Darwin's store. The sheriff said, "Keep a lid on pranksters. We've had three incidents in the past hour." Stepping into the street, he raised a hand, and a long, open sedan filled with blue-capped men braked beside him.

"Howdy, boys!" Harris called. "Let me in. We'll drive to the office." A burly fellow opened the back door, and the sheriff pushed in, leaving Tyson on the sidewalk.

The day was a series of frustrations: congested traffic, fist fights when local controversy became too personal, and the added effort of keeping his own lip buttoned when the religious element got too pushy.

He had an hour off for supper, then back to work. Tyson's head felt like he'd been plugged with a crowbar. His feet felt like roasted sausages. With street lights to chase away the night, the party ran late.

Tyson fell into bed at midnight and rolled out at six. Even Heddie's hotcakes didn't make him feel better.

At the office by seven, Harris started in without delay. "Can you meet Darrow at the station this afternoon, Tyson?"

The deputy nodded and sank into his desk chair. At a quarter to eight, he set out for Market Street. The carnival spirit of a state fair permeated the town. Toting long rifles, mountaineers gazed about in wonder, pausing to spit tobacco juice in the gutter. Among them stood Alvin York, a hero from the Great War who single-handedly captured over a hundred Germans while behind enemy lines.

"Morning, Deputy," Sam Bob O'Toole called from Darwin's front step later that morning. He and his cronies were hawking tiny American flags and Chinese paper fans spread on a small table. "Want to buy a flag or a fan?" He leaned forward to whisper, "They're three cents. Mr. Baker's giving us a penny for each one we sell."

Tyson grinned and dug into his pocket. "I'll take one of each."

He reached Nessa soon after leaving the boys. "Here." He handed her his purchases. "A present for you."

"Thanks." She tucked the flag into the brim of her blue felt hat and slipped the fan into a pocket. "We've sold five monkeys already."

She pointed down the street. "There's Micky. He's selling cookies and rock candy."

"Deputy! Oh, Deputy!" He turned to see Essie Caldwell hurrying toward him.

She arrived a moment later, puffing. Tyson looked at her, mildly irritated. What useless information did she have for him today?

"I couldn't get Dotty to answer my knock this morning. I tried at seven-thirty and then at eight-thirty just before I came into town."

She peered at him. "I'm worried."

He checked his watch. Eight-forty-five. "I'll call the sheriff's office and see if I can get someone to cover for me." He pushed into Bailey's store to use his phone.

Harris answered on the first ring. When Tyson told him Mrs. Caldwell's problem, he said, "I'll send Kelso Rice down."

Ten minutes later a husky red-haired Irishman marched into view. His nod gave Tyson the go-ahead.

"Do you have a key to the house?" Tyson asked Essie.

"Yes. I was knocking on Dotty's bedroom door this morning."

"Oh. I thought you meant the outside door."

"Deputy, if she was all right she would have at least answered me," Mrs. Caldwell declared, trotting to keep up with his long stride. "Dotty and I are good friends."

"How was she last time you saw her?"

"Awfully depressed. That's what worries me. When she and Bella first came to live in Ida's house, Dotty was like a flower reaching for the sun. She kept telling me how glad she was to get out of the city. But since her mother's…trouble…there's been many a time I've noticed that she'd been crying."

They reached the drive, and Essie led the way to the kitchen door. She sifted through the contents of her purse looking for her key. Tyson keenly remembered his late-night visit here with Dr. St. Clair six weeks ago. The hair on the back of his neck stood up.

Essie threw the door wide and trotted inside. Rounding the corner to the living room, she darted toward Miss Ida's old room and pounded the door, calling, "Dotty! It's me, Mrs. Caldwell. Open up, dear!"

No answer. The silence was deafening.

Tyson's mouth went dry. He stepped forward and turned the knob. It was a heavy latch in a heavy door.

"Step back," he said. Raising his foot, he aimed his heel for the lock assembly in the door jamb. Five hard kicks and it splintered away from the wall.

Essie Caldwell rushed ahead.

Tyson grabbed her arm. "Let me go in first."

Dotty lay under a white sheet, her hair clinging damply to her face, her breathing deep and unnatural. The window was closed, the room stifling.

"Dotty!" Tyson slapped the girl's cheeks.

No response.

Essie clutched her hand. "Dotty! Wake up!"

"I'll call Dr. St. Clair." Tyson hurried to the living room and picked up the phone.

"Put ice on the back of her neck," St. Clair said when Tyson told him what had happened. "I'll be right over."

The ice brought a moan from the girl, but her eyes stayed closed.

Her face looked ghostly.

Tyson left Mrs. Caldwell with her to throw open the window and take a quick look about the room. On the dresser lay a bottle labeled “Sleeping Tablets.” Tyson unscrewed the top. Empty. He looked at the floor. Two tablets had fallen. He’d almost stepped on them. He picked them up and dropped them into his pocket.

The sound of the back door opening drew him toward the kitchen. He met the doctor at the living room door.

“How is she?” St. Clair asked, his face grim. He’d arrived without his hat, unusual for him.

“She moaned a couple times, but she’s still out.” Tyson held out the empty bottle. “I found this on the dresser.”

The doctor reached for the bottle, read the ingredients, and gave it back to Tyson. “Where is she? If she took a handful of those, we don’t have a second to lose.”

Essie looked up from bending over Dotty’s still form. “Thank God you’re here, Doctor.” She stepped back to give him room.

He set his bag on the edge of the bed and used his thumb to lift Dotty’s eyelid. He felt her neck below her ear.

“Find a basin,” he told Mrs. Caldwell. “And bring a pitcher of water, washcloths, and a towel.

The stout lady bolted from the room. He pulled a syringe out of his bag. Selecting a small vial, he filled the hypodermic. “Adrenaline,” he told Tyson.

A moment later, he said, “I’ll have to ask you to hold her head and shoulders up. I’m going to give her a strong emetic. She may have some tablets left in her stomach.”

“How can you get her to drink that if she’s unconscious?”

“I’ll use a rubber syringe with a long spout. Normally, I wouldn’t do this for fear she’d aspirate fluid, but I’ve got to chance it.”

Essie burst through the door with the things St. Clair had requested.

The doctor poured water from the pitcher into a glass on the bedside stand. He stirred in some black powder and drew it into the syringe. Dotty swallowed convulsively until the medication was gone.

“Hold her up now, Tyson.”

Essie rushed to help. Their efforts were soon rewarded with violent retching.

“That’s what I was hoping for,” St. Clair said. “She still had some undissolved pills in her stomach. He let out a slow breath. “There’s a thread of hope. Lay her back now.”

Essie washed the girl’s face and pushed her matted hair away from her neck and cheeks. The woman’s hands trembled as she worked.

The girl’s face contorted. She sobbed softly.

"Dotty!" Essie said, her voice quiet yet urgent. "Wake up, child!"

St. Clair reached for her limp wrist.

"Mama?" she mumbled flopping her head from side to side. "Mama...my baby... my baby." Tears trickled from the corners of her eyes toward her ears. Suddenly, her thin voice rose to a reedy screech. "Oh, God! My baby!"

Chapter Nineteen

Tyson watched Dotty's convulsive sobs with growing horror. She couldn't be more than sixteen. Did she have a baby?

"She needs constant care," St. Clair said. "I can set up a bed at my clinic."

"I'll look after her," Essie said, quickly. "I don't have any responsibilities, living alone like I do." The woman's eyes filled with tears. "Her mother's coming home this afternoon. And to have to face this!"

St. Clair packed his bag.

"What does she mean, 'My baby'?" Tyson asked, pointing the question at no one in particular.

"She may be hallucinating," St. Clair told him. "It happens in some cases like this. When she wakes up she may believe the dream actually happened."

Leaning down and holding the girl closely in her ample arms, Essie made shushing noises. Dotty's cries subsided to deep, low sobs.

St. Clair snapped the bag closed. "I'll check on her this afternoon, Essie. Try to get some fluids into her, some food if she can take it."

Intent on Dotty, Essie nodded without looking up.

The doctor seemed reluctant to leave. His eyes stayed on his patient. He seemed to have forgotten Tyson was in the room. Still watching Dotty, he moved to the door, said, "Call me if you need me," and slowly turned away.

St. Clair let himself out without saying goodbye. Tyson picked up the phone on the writing desk in the living room. His collar felt two sizes too small. Would anyone be in the office to take the call?

On the fifth ring, Harris answered.

"It's Tyson," he said into the cup receiver. "I'm at Miss Ida's house. Dotty, Bella's teenage daughter, took some sleeping pills. Looks to me like attempted suicide."

"You're kidding," Harris's deep voice rumbled. "Why'd she do that?"

"She keeps crying and asking about a baby. We can't make any sense of it." He paused. "Look, Sheriff, can you do without me for a while? I think I ought to hang around here a few hours."

Harris breathed twice. "I'll leave Rice patrolling Market Street and send one of his pals to help him. But, Tyson…"

"Yeah?"

"Be at the train station at three, okay?"

"Sure, Sheriff. I'll be there. It's only a couple of blocks from here."

Dotty slowly ran down like a neglected wind-up toy. She fell into a troubled sleep, mumbling from time to time and moving her hands. Essie stayed near her, fussing about the room, tidying everything in sight. Finally, she sank into the straight chair beside the bed and rested her head in her hands.

"I should get something ready to eat for when she wakes up," she said after a while. She slowly got to her feet.

Tyson followed her to the kitchen. "Why did she do it, Mrs. Caldwell?"

"She's always been a moody child, deputy."

"Do you know why she keeps crying for a baby? Did she have a little brother or sister who died?"

"Dotty's an only child." She set a small pot on the stove and opened the ice box.

"Any idea why Dotty's been depressed lately?"

Essie tucked a loose gray strand behind her ear. "I asked her about it, but she always denied that anything was wrong. A few weeks ago, Bella told me Dotty was mooning over some boyfriend in Chattanooga, a bad sort." She took a quart jar from the ice box and poured some vegetable soup into the pot. "Maybe Dotty was depressed about him."

"I doubt it. You said she was happy when they first came to Dayton. Besides, she'd be more likely to run away with the fellow than try a stunt like this." He stared at the porcelain tabletop. "You don't think she's expecting a child, do you?"

Mrs. Duncan's eyes became dark indignant points. "She's just a child herself."

He glanced at his watch. "I hope Bella gets here soon. She should have been released two hours ago."

At ten o'clock Nessa arrived for her normal day's work. With growing dismay, she listened to Essie's version of the morning. "I'll come back this afternoon if you need me," the girl said. "I don't have any more jobs after the Lunch Room closes."

"You're a dear," Essie said, hugging her. "Later, I'll need to run across to my house and get a few clothes so I can stay the night." She released Nessa and automatically smoothed her hair. "I'd best go in and sit with Dotty in case she wakes up."

Nessa sent Tyson a worried look and quickly stacked dishes from the sink to the counter. She had to be home in less than an hour to serve tables.

Tyson pulled a chair out and sat. "Did Dotty ever mention a boyfriend or a baby?" he asked.

Nessa shrugged and turned on the faucet. "She talked about someone named Ricky in Chattanooga. But she didn't seem to miss him much. She said he was too rough for her liking."

"She keeps crying about a baby."

"I'm afraid I can't help you with that one." Dishes rattled in the frothy sink.

"If she wakes up while you're with her, ask her what she meant, will you?" Tyson asked.

"Of course." She threw him a towel. "I'm in a hurry. Care to dry?"

The Pierce Arrow pulled into the driveway fifteen minutes after Nessa left. Essie bustled through the kitchen to the back door and pulled it open. Tyson stood up from his seat at the table.

Bella had dark circles under sunken eyes. Her hair clung limply to her skull. She paused in the doorway, looking from Essie to the deputy. "What are you doing here? Haven't you done enough?"

Her voice sounded rusty as though she hadn't used it much lately. She smelled stale.

Essie took a step toward her. "Dotty's had an accident."

"What happened?" She dropped her purse to the floor and latched onto Essie's arm. "Is she okay?"

"She's sleeping. I just fed her a few spoonfuls of soup."

Bella trotted toward Dotty's room. Tyson followed her.

She bent over her daughter, calling her name and shaking her. Dotty slept on. Bella dropped into the chair.

"She took a handful of sleeping pills, Mrs. Smith," Tyson said, watching her closely. "Why would she do such a thing?"

Her lips trembled. She looked a hundred years old.

"She keeps asking about a baby," Essie added from the doorway.

Tears slipped from Bella's eyes. She covered her face with her hands and groaned.

Essie handed her a handkerchief.

"She had a boyfriend in Chattanooga," Bella said, finally, her words coming out in harsh gasps. "I knew he was a bad one. She broke off with him when we moved here."

Tyson leaned forward. "Why does she keep asking about a baby? Is she in a family way?"

"No!" Bella's head came up to glare at him. "I know she's not. I know it for a fact."

Tyson checked his watch: two-thirty. "I must go to the station to meet someone, but I'll come back later today. I'd like to ask Dotty two or three questions when she wakes up."

Essie put her arm around Bella's shoulders. "I'll stay with you all day, dear. Don't worry about a thing."

Tyson cranked Lizzy and chugged toward the tiny depot. The railway station was almost deserted when he arrived. Of the half-dozen people milling about the platform, four were reporters. Tyson found a bench in the shade.

A few minutes later, Elmer Buntley eased his lean frame down beside Dayton's only deputy sheriff. Irritated, Tyson tried to ignore the man's stench. He glanced at his watch. The train was due in five minutes.

John Scopes and his girlfriend arrived in the yellow sports car and joined the men on the platform.

Buntley darted a guilty glance at Tyson. "I remembered something I thought you may be interested in."

Tyson gazed at him, waiting.

The gardener hitched up the right strap of his bib overalls. "That afternoon when you brought Sammy to my house, we had a fight. Not a bad one, but…" He broke off and stared at the sleeper cars left on the siding to house a few of Dayton's visitors.

In a moment, he sighed and went on. "I told Sammy he was a vagrant who couldn't hold down a job for love nor money. He shook his finger in my face and said he had a job. He'd been working for six months."

"Who'd he work for?"

"He wouldn't say, Deputy. He said that was his business. Said if I found out, I'd probably spoil things for him."

Tyson reached into his pocket for a piece of Black Jack. "That's an interesting story, Buntley, but it seems like a dead end to me."

"Wait." He gripped the bench with a leathery, dirt-stained paw. "Sammy hinted that he knew some wicked secret about somebody. He said, 'My boss man will pay me pretty to keep my secret, Elmer. Then *you* can come and live with *me*.'"

Tyson pulled out his notebook and scribbled something. "You don't have any idea who it is?"

"My guess is someone north of town." Elmer scratched his white stubble, making his jowls shake. "I saw Sammy heading that way a few mornings last week. I didn't pay it no mind, because he wanders all over looking for handouts."

A shrill whistle cut through their conversation. Tyson stood. Buntley got to his feet too.

"I'll keep it in mind, Elmer. Let me know if you remember anything else."

The old man's faded eyes filled with tears. "Whoever fed Sammy that poisoned weed ought to feel the noose, Deputy. Sammy never hurt nobody." He trudged heavily away.

Tyson looked after him. Why the new story now?

The train screeched to a standstill. Newsmen spread out along the platform, scanning the steps to see which one the famous Darrow would choose to make his appearance. Tyson stepped forward in time to see nine men and one lady descend from the last car. None of them was Clarence Darrow.

But one of them was George Rappelyea, looking like a cat who swallowed a goldfish. He'd taken the morning train to Chattanooga to meet the defense team and ride back with them.

From the hungry look in their eyes and the much-used paper tablets clenched in their sweaty palms, five of the newcomers were reporters. "Is Mr. Darrow on this train?" asked a slim fellow with *Post-Dispatch* on his badge.

"He'll be along later today," Rappelyea replied. By far the smallest man present, he looked unusually fine in a new white coat and black bow tie. He nodded toward a suave man with a perky little lady on his arm. "Meet Darrow's partner. This is Dudley Field Malone and his wife, Doris Stevens."

Malone had a vibrant smile. "Good afternoon, gentlemen." His slicked-back blond hair and receding hairline made him appear bald at first glance, but still, he was a handsome man, an Irish Catholic who specialized in quick French divorces.

He introduced his wife to the reporters, then turned toward a stocky man whose hair, close-cropped around the ears, lay in curly mounds on either side of his center part. "This is Arthur Garfield Hays, attorney for the ACLU."

Hays's only resemblance to Malone was the expensive cut of his striped summer suit. He had a long, heavy jaw and a nose that revealed his Jewish heritage—an association by birth alone. Hays proclaimed himself an agnostic.

Hays nodded at the newsmen but didn't make any comment.

Rappelyea added, "Meet Reverend Charles Francis Potter, pastor of the West Side Unitarian Church in New York. He's going to speak for our side."

"For your side?" a reporter asked. He turned to Potter. "How can a preacher be on the side of evolution?"

Potter's chest swelled. His voice resonant voice boomed, "True Bible scholars see no conflict between evolution and the Bible."

Reporters put pencils to paper as the defense team moved away. Hays's stiff leg caused a pronounced limp. Malone held himself with a formal erectness, but Hays's shoulders sloped into a casual curve.

On the edge of the platform Scopes lifted a suitcase from the stack placed there by a porter.

Dr. Potter called, "Hey, boy, what are you doing with those suitcases?"

Rappelyea touched the preacher's sleeve. "That's all right, Doc. That's only Scopes."

Flushing, the preacher tucked in his chin and followed his party to Rappelyea's waiting roadster.

Rappelyea and his party motored down Greer Street toward Market with Lizzy puttering close behind them. The sky darkened with black rolling clouds. A cooling gust warned of a coming storm.

When they headed north, Tyson turned south and parked in front of the Johnson house once more.

A few fat drops spattered the windshield. Tyson raced the downpour to the porch and won by a hair.

Essie met him at the door. She spoke in a whisper. "You just missed Nessa. Dr. St. Clair and Sadie were here for a while, too." She backed up a step, so he could come inside.

"What did the doctor say?"

"He said she'll probably sleep for twenty-four hours, but then she should be right as rain."

"Where's Bella?"

"Sleeping. She's all in with a bad case of nerves. The doctor gave her a pill and told her to lie down.

"Can I use the phone? I need to check in with the sheriff."

"You know where it is." She picked up a paring knife on the table. "I'm fixing them a good hot supper: boiled ham and potatoes. Bella looks like she's lost twenty pounds."

A clap of thunder shook the house. The wind flapped the curtains.

The wide porch would keep the rain out of the house, so they could leave the windows open, a blessing after the squalid heat of the past few days.

Tyson lifted the phone and spoke a few words to Mabel.

When Harris answered, Tyson said, "I just left the station. Darrow won't be in until the last train." He listened a moment. "I'll be there." With a heavy sigh, he set down the phone and returned to the kitchen.

"Did Dotty say any more while I was gone? Did she give any clue about why she took the pills?"

"Not a thing. I wish I knew what's troubling her."

The small light over the sink flickered.

"Oh, no," she said. "I hope the electric's not going out. I don't know where Bella keeps her candles, and I don't want to wake her."

"They shouldn't be too hard to find." Tyson began opening cabinet drawers. "Here's a bundle." He drew a pack of matches from his pocket and lay them on the counter. "Would you come with me to take a peek at Dotty? If she's awake I want to ask her just one question."

"Surely." Moving quickly, she ran water over her hands and touched them to a snowy dishtowel.

Dotty's face seemed almost translucent against the white pillow, her features slack. At once, Tyson sensed something was wrong.

He touched the girl's face. "Dotty? Can you hear me?" He pressed a forefinger to her neck.

Shocked, he stared at the girl's still form.

"What is it?" Essie asked anxiously.

Tyson looked at her as though she were a mile away. Finally, he found his voice. "She's dead."

CHAPTER
Twenty

"Dead!" Essie stared at him, then at the girl on the bed. Her lips trembled. "The doctor just said she was fine."

"Something must have happened after he left," Tyson said. "Don't touch anything. Phone St. Clair while I take a look around."

Weeping openly, Essie left the room. Tyson closed the door behind her and switched on the lamp. Another violent gust sent gauzy curtains sailing out over the bed, then sucked them out the window.

The night table contained a small tray with a water glass and pitcher on it. Both were half full. He pulled open a small drawer. Inside lay a bottle of sleeping tablets identical to the one he'd found on top of the same table that morning.

Using a piece of note paper from the drawer, he scooped up the small bottle and dropped it into a paper bag from his pocket. As it fell, he heard the faint clinking of pills.

Tyson skirted the bed to reach the window. Anyone could have come onto the porch and ducked inside. They wouldn't have had to take a single step to reach the bed.

He looked at the floor inside and outside the room. No marks.

But with the dry hot spell they'd been having recently, that wasn't surprising. The rain continued full force to erase any tracks in the dust outside.

Suddenly a human shriek rose above the wail of wind and rain.

The bedroom door burst open. Bella charged inside and threw herself at Dotty. "Wake up!" She shook her daughter, screaming, "Wake up! Wake up!"

Puffy-eyed, Essie edged inside the room. She pulled at a knotted handkerchief. "She woke up and wanted to see Dotty. I had to tell her."

Tyson took Bella gently but firmly by the shoulders and led her out to the living room sofa. Essie sat beside her crying into her handkerchief.

With intense relief, Tyson let St. Clair in a few minutes later.

The doctor carried his black bag in one hand, his dripping hat in the other. "What on earth happened?" he demanded.

"It looks like she got more pills," Tyson told him, leading the way to the living room where the mother's hysterical cries continued.

"Calm her down, will you? I'll be in the bedroom."

St. Clair set his bag on a small table beside the sofa and pulled open the spring-loaded top. He pulled out a vial and held it to the light.

In the bedroom, Tyson got on his hands and knees to look under the bed. He pulled out several drawers and lifted the throw rug. Nothing . . . nothing . . . nothing. In her condition, he couldn't imagine that the girl could have poured pills from a bottle and not dropped some.

He took a sample of the water in the glass, then wrapped the glass in paper and slid it into a wide inner pocket of his suit coat.

Sinking to the chair beside the bed, he jotted down Dotty's words and made a few more notes.

Dr. St. Clair came to the door. "I'll check her out and then call Ketcher," he said quietly.

"She's going to Chattanooga," Tyson said. He pulled out his watch. "Tell Ketcher to put her on the evening train."

"You think something's suspicious?"

Tyson grimaced, his eyes on Dotty's face. "I have some doubts. In a suicide case, that's enough."

"This is awful tough on Bella." St. Clair set his bag on the edge of the bed. "First her mother, now this. She doted on the girl, you know."

"How well did you know them, Doc?"

"I delivered Dotty. Bella came home to her mother about the time Dotty was due. That no-account husband of hers couldn't be depended on to help her. He left Bella home alone six nights out of seven to play poker or shoot craps."

"Why would a teenage girl want to kill herself? She had a whole life ahead of her."

"Any number of reasons: depression, loneliness, fear." St. Clair bent over the bed to lift the dead girl's eyelid and feel for a pulse. A formality for the death certificate. "What time did you find her?"

"It was ten past four. She was still warm. I found another bottle of pills in the nightstand. She must have taken more after I left."

"Did she say anything to you, Doc? Did she tell you why she did it?"

"She kept moaning about not knowing something. She didn't say what." He stood up. "With her background, and having made a recent move away from friends and familiar surroundings, she could have been depressed. Adolescents don't think like adults. Small things look huge to them."

He picked up his bag. "I gave Bella a hypo to make her sleep off her hysteria."

Tyson said, "Essie's planning on staying here tonight." He followed St. Clair to the door. "Thanks, Doc. Dayton doesn't know how much they should appreciate you."

The doctor gave him a weary smile. "I don't need a gold watch or a plaque. In my business, there are rewards no one can see."

Ketcher and his death wagon pulled into the driveway for the second time in weeks. Dotty would leave on the same train that brought Darrow.

Tyson drove home and deposited his hat in the closet. Brushing at the dark curls above his forehead, he looked for Nessa. He found her in the dining room, setting up for the next day's business.

"Hi, Trent. We've got a full house tonight. Mama would have set up cots in the hall if we'd had them." She glanced at him and looked back again. "What's wrong?"

"Dottie died this afternoon."

Holding a bundle of spoons against her waist, she gasped.

"Here." He pulled out a chair. "Sit down."

She sat. "But, the doctor said she'd be all right."

"I found another bottle of pills in the drawer beside the bed. I'm afraid she took more of them."

She laid the spoons on the table as though they'd break. Tears welled up. She pulled out her handkerchief. "My nerves are already bad. This is the icing on the cake."

"Did something else happen?"

Looking around, she spotted her purse and picked it up. "It's in here. I found it when I got home." She drew a slip of white paper from an outside pocket and handed it to Tyson.

A black, childish scrawl said, "Danger. Tyson means trouble."

He turned the paper over. "Where did you go today?" He held it toward the light from the window.

"I finished doing floors at Robinson's place, then I went to Bella's. After that, I walked home to serve lunch."

"Through town in the rain?"

She twisted her hands together. "It wasn't coming down too hard just then. A couple of times I had to wait in a shop doorway until it eased off."

"Anyone else waiting there, too?"

"A few people. Some reporters. Elmer was at Bailey's Hardware. He asked about Dotty. After lunch, I walked back to Bella's so Essie could go home to shower and pack a case." She sniffed gently. "What should I do now?"

He let out a long breath. "Be careful. Okay?"

"Trent, I don't even want to go outdoors anymore. I feel so vulnerable."

"Whenever I'm available, you've got an escort. All you have to do is ask." He touched his notebook. "I'm sorry to have to ask you this now, but can you tell me exactly what happened while you were at Bella's house this afternoon? Please try to remember every detail, even if it seems unimportant."

She cleared her throat and swept a dark strand from her cheek. "Essie left around three. A few minutes later, Dr. St. Clair and Sadie

came to check on Dotty. They were in the room for twenty minutes and then they left." She studied him. "That's all that happened while I was there."

"Did you see Dotty?"

"When the doctor left I went to sit with her. She was crying and mumbling. Something about a baby. She said, 'I didn't know,' a few times. I couldn't make any sense of it."

"You're absolutely sure that's all?"

She stared at the red gingham on the table. "Wait. There was one thing. After Sadie and the doctor left, Sadie came back to the kitchen door and knocked. She said she forgot her purse. She ran into the bedroom, stayed about two minutes, and ran back." Her lips twisted into a half smile. "I thought it was funny, her so old and moving so fast." She shrugged. "That's it."

He tucked away his notes and stood. "You're a trooper, Nessa. And I was serious about being your escort. Any time."

She looked up at him and smiled with the corners of her mouth tucked in. "I'll remember that."

He stepped toward the door. "I've got to be at the station when Darrow comes in at six."

The rain slacked off during his drive back to the depot. Less than fifty people waited to greet Clarence Darrow. Two movie crews set up tall tripods at opposite ends of the platform, their cameramen standing ready. John Scopes waited near the tracks with Neal and Rappelyea.

When the train arrived, Darrow was the only passenger to descend. A dark suit hung on his frame like an empty potato sack. He held a small valise. Scopes stepped forward to embrace him, then Darrow answered a few questions for the reporters.

Rappelyea took the case and led the small party to his car. "I've fixed up a place for the team outside of town, and we're having a banquet tonight in your honor."

"That's fine. Fine." Knuckle-and skull, no-holds-barred Darrow had put on a veneer of casual good humor. He stopped to shake hands with a couple of bystanders as he passed through the tiny crowd. Anyone who didn't know better would have thought he was on vacation just stopping by to say howdy to his grandbabies.

Rappelyea caught sight of Tyson as both men reached their cars, parked together in the depot lot. The small man spoke to Neal, then came around to where Tyson cranked Lizzy. "Deputy, the Progressive Club decided to hold a banquet in Darrow's honor tonight." He lowered his voice. "It's a last-minute job. Since they honored Bryan when he came in, they figured they ought to do the same for Darrow." He held out two tickets. "We'd like to have you come. Seven-thirty."

Tyson straightened and accepted the red slips of paper. "Thanks for thinking of me, George. I'll try my best to be there."

"That's all we can ask." Rappelyea hot-footed back to his car, turned the key, and set off.

Tyson worked his arm until Lizzy sputtered to life. Two fat drops hit his sleeve as he hopped inside. He checked his watch: six-twenty. He'd have to head straight home and change if he planned to arrive at the banquet in time to eat.

A surge of rain washed against the windshield. Tyson took the detour around downtown's roped-off area and rattled toward home. No one in his right mind would be on the street tonight. He blessed the rain for keeping the crowds at bay and made a dash for the front porch.

Looking worn, Nessa met him in the hall.

"Hi," he said. "I'll be going out tonight. Can you watch Lori for me?" He hung his damp hat on the closet door knob and followed her into the kitchen.

"Of course." She swiped at her forehead with the back of her wrist. "Lori's never a problem."

In a chair pulled off to one side, Paul Henderson had his face buried in the *Chattanooga Times*. Lori was laying silverware on the table. At the counter, Micky stacked dollar bills, the day's take.

"Darrow came in on the six o'clock train," Tyson said. "The Progressive Club is having a banquet for him." He reached into his pocket and pulled out two tickets. "Anyone want to go with me?"

Henderson folded the newspaper. "I'll go."

Tyson looked toward him, mildly surprised. "Fine, Paul. We'll have to leave in forty-five minutes."

Easygoing as ever, Henderson relaxed on Lizzy's front seat while Tyson fought the elements. The reporter said, "I was supposed to hear Bryan speak at the Morgan Springs Hotel tonight."

"You'd have a hard climb up Walden's Ridge in this weather," Tyson said.

He chuckled. "The boys will try it. Anything for a story."

Considering the short notice, people turned out for the gathering in surprising numbers. In honor of the storm, someone had set up the dining hall for a candlelight dinner, making the affair resemble a wedding reception instead of a town function. Tyson and Henderson found seats near the platform.

Darrow moved around the room, joking, slapping backs, and chatting.

Henderson said, "Look at him. He's courting the townspeople like a dandy sparking a cutie at a box social."

"You know him?" Tyson asked.

"Sure. I've followed his cases for years, sometimes right in the courtroom."

Tyson sipped water. He looked up to see Darrow shake hands with Ben McKenzie, make a comment, and move on.

At precisely seven-thirty, waiters appeared bearing wide trays covered with loaded plates. Except for turkey instead of beef, the menu matched the last banquet right down to the yellow pound cake. They had scarcely finished dessert when Doc Robinson stood, welcomed Clarence Darrow to Dayton, then called him up to speak.

Wearing the same worn suit he arrived in, the man known as the Great Defender stood to one side of the podium, hands thrust deeply into his pockets, chin tucked down like a shy school boy.

He made the expected thank yous, then began his speech. "I was born in a little town like this one. I went to school for a while, and then I quit school and started my education."

Light chuckles rippled across the room.

"I was one of the town loafers and got to like the tinsmith. He was reading law, but he didn't have time to read much because he was so busy working. So, since I was the town loafer, I found time to read law to him while he worked. "I finally read so much law I got to liking it. Then the tinsmith and I went to take our bar examinations. Afterward, we adjourned to a nearby establishment for refreshments. There, the results of our examinations were later announced, and at the bar, at four o'clock in the morning, we passed."

A gust of hearty laughter swept the crowd. Darrow grinned.

"I started practicing law. For a while, I was playing poker on the side and practicing law, and I almost starved. But then I started playing poker and practicing law on the side, and I made enough money to go to Chicago and open an office!"

Paul's face creased into an approving smile. "He's a poker player all right," he whispered to Tyson. "That man's got more degrees than most people ever dream of."

Darrow spoke for several minutes about individual freedoms and the danger of keeping scientific knowledge from children. By the time he stepped down, he'd won the heart of a town primed to hate him.

The crowd milled about and started to disperse. Paul scribbled in his notebook. Finally, he tucked it into his inner coat pocket and stood. "You think Heddie would mind if I use your phone to call St. Louis tonight?" he asked Tyson. "I need to give some of this to my office. I'll cover the bill, of course."

"Certainly." Tyson answered, remembering the benefits of being a "trial boarder." On the way out, Tyson glanced over his shoulder to see Ben McKenzie laughing at a comment of Darrow's and grabbing the defense lawyer's hand for a hearty shake.

When the men arrived, the house was dark. Tyson turned on the hall switch before he climbed the stairs and left Henderson to phone in private.

Pulling at his tie, he stepped into his room and stopped short. On his sitting room sofa in the soft glow of a lamp, Nessa sat reading a book.

CHAPTER Twenty-One

Nessa looked up and smiled gently when he walked in. "I promised Lori I'd stay here 'til you got home. The storm frightened her. Even Vic couldn't calm her down. She wanted her daddy." She lay the book on the table and stood, smoothing her twill skirt.

"How did the dinner go?"

"Darrow's as wily as an old fox. Bryan's got his work cut out for him." He told her some highlights from Darrow's speech.

"The rain's stopped," she said, stepping to the window. "What a relief to have a cool night. Maybe the courtroom won't be too hot tomorrow."

He walked close to her under the pretense of looking out the window over the back of her shoulder.

She murmured, "Something's bothering you. Is it Dotty?"

He spoke softly near her ear. "This morning we got to her in time to save her. Then somehow this afternoon she got more pills."

His voice tightened. "I should have thought to look in that drawer. She may be alive if I had."

She glanced sideways toward him. "If she wanted to die that much, she'd have found a way. You can't blame yourself."

"I sent her body to Chattanooga for an autopsy. In two or three days I should know more."

Her hair brushed his shoulder when she turned toward him. "You've got enough on your mind without this, too."

"I've got to be at the courthouse by seven tomorrow morning."

"I want to come."

"To the trial? Why?"

"Curiosity, I guess. I won't be able to go tomorrow, but maybe Monday. We'll probably never get to hear Bryan in person again."

He grinned down at her. "If you stroll downtown, you'll get to hear him plenty. He's doing so much talking, I wonder if he'll have any voice left to do his prosecuting." He eased his face closer to hers. "I wish you'd take Lori and go away from here for a while."

His eyes drifted over her face.

"You trying to get rid of us?"

"You know better than that. I may look heartless, but I worry over people I care about."

That warning look came over her face.

He backed off. "Good night, Nessa. Thanks for taking care of my little girl."

"You don't have to thank me. She's a joy." Moving slowly, she picked up her book and shuffled out.

Tyson stood unmoving, looking after her until the door gently closed behind her. Staring out the window at the darkness, he reached up to unbutton his shirt.

Before dawn the next morning, Tyson's bare feet hit the floor beside his sofa. Folks were probably already standing in line at the courthouse door to get the choicest seats. He ought to be among the first ones there.

In the kitchen, Nessa's tired face softened into a smile when he strode in. With a fork, she whipped eggs in a bowl and poured the yellow mass into a frying pan. They sizzled and gave off a tempting aroma.

Tyson poured himself a cup of coffee. "The temperature is already seventy-five, and it's only six-thirty. Looks like the storm didn't break the heat wave."

Paul appeared in the doorway wearing a dark suit and carrying his shoes. "Morning, folks. I was afraid I'd wake somebody so I didn't dress my feet."

"Scrambled eggs okay?" Nessa asked him.

"Fine and dandy," he said, sitting beside Tyson and slipping into his wingtips. "You sure have been treating me good." He smiled at Nessa. "I appreciate it."

During the next fifteen minutes, six more men joined them at thé kitchen table. The *Nashville Banner's* Bill Perry sat beside Dick Beamish, propagator of the Beamish special and reporter for the *Philadelphia Inquirer*. An owlish man, Beamish stood under five six and weighed about two hundred pounds. A black ribbon kept his pince-nez in place.

Two telegraph operators and two photographers made up the rest of Heddie's tenant windfall.

The men swallowed eggs and buttered bread. They gulped coffee to brace themselves for a long day. Donning hats and tightening ties, they strolled one block south on Market.

A banner hung over the courthouse entry: "Read your Bible Daily for a Week." On a signpost nearby: "Be a Sweet Angel." A tall fence held the admonition, "Sweethearts, Come to Jesus."

Two dozen backless benches sat under the trees. Water pipes for new outdoor privies crossed the lawn at odd angles. A chimp wearing a vested suit and spats stood on a basket to turn the handle on a tinny-sounding organ. Two women set up tables along the street.

The fellow with the book booth beside the courthouse had already opened for business. His sign read, "T. T. Martin Headquarters, Anti-Evolution League." And below in smaller letters, *The Conflict—Hell & the High Schools,* the title of his book. A dozen folks lingered before a table loaded with Bryan's books as well as his own.

Twenty men already stood before the courthouse double doors, waiting for someone with a key.

"Good morning, Henderson," a fellow reporter called when McGinty's boarders arrived. "The early bird catches it, right?"

Henderson sent him the thumbs-up sign and lounged against the porch railing, elbow-to-back with the man ahead of him.

Two wagons full of mountaineers drew up outside the cordoned-off area at Market and Third. Wearing denim overalls, their whiskered faces sober and gaunt, they plodded to the end of the growing queue.

Movie cameras on tripods stood in strategic positions, ready for the arrival of the star actors in this premier.

The sun moistened faces and dazzled eyes. Tyson felt in his back pocket for his handkerchief. Yes, it was there. He'd be needing it mighty bad today.

Carrying a pot of red geraniums, a grizzled old man stumped to the head of the line. He handed the flowerpot to someone and rattled a ring of keys. Soon fifty men tramped up the wide staircase and through the double doors across the hall at the top.

At front and center of the room, the judge's bench gleamed with a fresh coat of high-gloss varnish. The court's custodian placed the flowers on the front corner of the bench.

Reporters found seats at a press table beside the prosecution's table, on the railing around the sanctum, and in three rows reserved for them behind the jury's front seats.

"Quin Ryan!" Beamish called. He shook hands with a wavy-haired fellow slouched behind a mike labeled "WGN," the massive Chicago radio station. With his round face creased into a wide grin, Beamish said, "Long time no see, but I've been hearing plenty. I catch your program most every day."

Ryan's full mustache spread out when he grinned. "I've been wondering where you get fodder for your column. Now I know."

Beamish chuckled and pretended to shoot him with an index finger.

From a back corner, a cameraman on a ladder called, "He's got you pegged, Beamish!" He swiveled his camera and spoke to his partner below him. "Hey Charlie, there's Mencken!"

Wearing a straw hat and a vaguely cynical expression, the *Baltimore Sun's* star contributor sauntered to the press table and took a chair next to Quin Ryan. Beside Mencken came Philip Kinsey of the *Chicago Tribune*. Darrow's hometown had sent the troops *en masse*.

John W. Butler dropped his heavy frame into a chair at the press table, too. The legislator who drafted the bill on trial today had come to cover the story for a national syndicate. A crowd of pressmen gathered around him, and he gave more comments than he collected.

The windows stood wide open but little air moved inside the room. The thermometer showed above eighty degrees and was still climbing. Tobacco smoke filled the atmosphere and added to the heat.

From his place at the door, Tyson caught a flash of blue serge. He looked around.

"A good morning to you," Kelso Rice said, smiling widely. He stood even with Tyson in height but outweighed him by twenty pounds. His shoulders strained at the uniform.

Tyson smiled. He liked the big Irishman. "Welcome to the circus, Kelso. You're bailiff today, aren't you?" At Rice's nod, Tyson said, "You're welcome to it. I'll hold up the door frame."

Sheriff Harris arrived and glanced into the courtroom. "Judge Raulston don't want anyone smoking in there. Y'all take care of letting the boys know." With that, he disappeared down the stairs.

Rice stepped inside and shouted over the din. "No smokin' when court takes up. Anyone caught smokin' will be fined two dollars."

Amid disgruntled mumbles, cigars and cigarettes slowly found their way into brass spittoons set at intervals across the floor. Kelso took his position to the right of the bench, shoulders back like a soldier on guard duty.

Judge Raulston arrived at eight-thirty with his wife. Behind them, his two daughters carried handfuls of daisies. The judge walked about the room shaking hands and beaming. He wore a new tan suit with a striped tie and carried two thick volumes under his arm: a Bible and a book of statutes.

His four-year-old daughter cuddled in her mother's lap and watched the crowd with her thumb firmly in her mouth.

"Take off your coats, gentlemen," the judge said. He spoke with a slow drawl that made a hearer want to finish his sentences for him. "You don't have to put on city manners here. I'm just a reg'lar mountaineer judge." He held his head high and threw back his shoulders when a photographer held up a camera. The judge's bottom lip stuck far out, making his tight smile look more like a grimace.

A moment later, he said, "There will be no smoking in this courtroom, gentlemen. With the crowded conditions and the heat, I hope you'll understand."

"Maybe the trial won't last long after all," a reporter called.

Raulston chuckled.

Distinguished in an expensive suit, Dudley Field Malone arrived at that moment smoking a cigarette and oozing good humor.

Tyson eyed Malone's double-breasted coat, expecting him to take it off. He didn't.

John Neal trudged in with a half-smoked dead cigar between his teeth. Thick-necked Hays stopped beside the press table to chat with reporters. About the same height as Neal, Hays looked much sturdier despite his bad leg.

John Scopes walked in with his white-haired father, Thomas Scopes, an adamant Socialist. The defendant wore a hand-painted bow tie, no coat, and had his blue shirt sleeves rolled to the elbow.

He looked like a timid teenager. The older Scopes shook hands with his son and found a standing place near Tyson at the door.

Scopes walked straight from the door to the defense table across the room. The defense had its back to the wall.

Darrow was the last of the team to arrive. His coat over his arm, he wore a tan shirt with a white string tie and loud purple suspenders—a style outdated by twenty years. Without his coat to add width to his shoulders, his head seemed unusually large. His twinkling, questioning eyes gave the impression that he found the situation amusing.

A reporter asked Malone, "Are you going to wear suspenders like Darrow?"

Malone laughed. "I refuse to get dressed up for the occasion," he said, tugging his coat sleeves.

Judge Raulston shook hands with the defenders and assigned each of them a title, some earned and some arbitrary.

Farmers and mountaineers continued to pour into the courtroom. When they filled three hundred seats, three hundred more crowded in to sit on window sills and stand two deep along three walls.

A rumbling, expectant hum filled the room. The heat continued to build. So did the odors.

Applause broke out shortly before nine when Will Bryan arrived with his party—tall, spare Tom Stewart, the district attorney general; Ben and Gordon McKenzie; sedate William Jennings Bryan Jr., who practiced federal law in California, and the Hicks brothers.

A male companion pushed Mary Bryan's wheelchair. She and Mrs. Raulston were the only women present.

Already wilted by the heat, Bryan had removed his collar and rolled his sleeves above the elbow. His tiny bow tie hung slightly askew. He carried a Gladstone bag in one hand and a palm leaf fan in the other. The fan did double duty. It created a breeze and chased flies.

Applause swelled when Bryan shook hands with Darrow. The head defender shambled to the prosecutor's table and said to Ben McKenzie, "Well, I see you, too, wear suspenders."

McKenzie grinned. "Yes, Colonel Darrow, we have to keep our pants up down here in Tennessee just like you do up there in Chicago."

Darrow chuckled.

The judge banged the gavel. "The court will come to order," he said. "The Reverend Cartwright will open court with prayer."

Tyson shifted from one foot to the other. He reached for his handkerchief. It was nearly ten o'clock and the process was just getting started. He glanced at Malone, still buttoned into his coat at nearly one hundred degrees, and wondered what the man was made of.

Sheriff Harris arrived just before starting time and stood on the opposite side of the door from Tyson.

District Attorney Tom Stewart stood to his full six-foot-four height. In a deep, solid voice he asked for a new indictment against Scopes because the hastily called grand jury may not have been legal.

Judge Raulston read the first chapter of Genesis and the Butler Act. Three boys—Howard Morgan, James Benson, and Jack Hudson—had been called to appear again, but one was missing.

After some confusion, Howard Morgan said that Jack was hiding in the woods. The Hudson boy liked Mr. Scopes and didn't want to hurt him by testifying against him. Scopes rushed out to find the boy and bring him back.

The audience sweltered.

Half an hour later, Scopes returned with Jack tagging shamefaced along. The boys' testimonies were entered into the record and, despite inconsistencies, the grand jury indicted Scopes.

Discussing the procedure for jury selection, Raulston told Darrow, "I will give you any information I can, Colonel—anything you want to ask me."

Darrow said, "Thank you."

Ben McKenzie called out, "If the court please, about the only thing I know is that Colonel Darrow and I are the only two suspender men in the courtroom."

A few men chuckled.

In a sweaty daze, Tyson dreamed about the cool water flowing past the docks east of town. He jerked to full attention when Gordon McKenzie cried, "Pa!"

Ben McKenzie slumped across the prosecutor's table, overcome by the heat.

Rappelyea and Herb Hicks carried the old campaigner into the hall while Sue ran for water and a towel. Tyson removed the man's tie and fanned him with a handkerchief. A few minutes later, Gordon took his father home.

Back in the courtroom, photographers constantly interrupted the proceedings: turn your head this way, Mr. Darrow; lean forward, Judge. At eleven o'clock Vic slipped out. Time to get to the Lunch Room. During the next thirty minutes, three spectators fainted and had to be carried out.

Shortly before noon, Judge Raulston instructed Sheriff Harris to find one hundred jury candidates for the afternoon session. He banged the gavel and dismissed until one-thirty that afternoon.

More than five hundred men poured down the wide staircase, out the door, and into blazing sunlight. When Tyson reached the yard, vendors and thrill-seekers crowded the entire area. Behind the courthouse, four steers roasted over a massive barbecue pit. Men conducting carnival games vied with hot dogs and souvenir merchants for space along the sidewalks.

In the center of Market Street, a black quartet sang, "The Old Book and the Old Faith." Ten yards away a wild-eyed young man in a threadbare suit stood on a stool and shouted out the evils

of evolution.

Like hundreds of others, Tyson set off in search of drink and food, in that order. Micky had moved the Lunch Room sign closer to the courthouse. A smaller sign near the corner of Fourth Avenue announced: Roast Beef and Mashed Potatoes, fifty cents a plate.

People lined up past Lizzy's parking spot all the way to the sidewalk. Tyson hustled around the side of the house toward the back door. On the wide front porch, he noticed several sawhorses holding doors to make two tables. Planks lay across stacked cement blocks for benches. Micky had been busy that morning.

The kitchen was chaos. Essie Caldwell helped Heddie fill plates while Micky kept dishes washed for reuse. Vic burst through the door for another tray full of dinners. There were no orders today—just hand over four bits, take a plate, and find a seat.

Tyson downed a quart of water and swallowed a roast beef sandwich. He had to get back on the street.

Ten minutes later, Harris met Tyson at the corner of Market and Second. Voice lowered, he leaned toward his deputy, "I just heard a rumor that there's gonna be a moonshine party over at the Morgan Springs dance tomorrow tonight. I'm going to raid it."

"You want me along?" Tyson asked.

"Naw. Rice and the boys will enjoy making the bust. It'll remind them of home." He pulled out a pocket watch. "Darrow's wife is arriving in fifteen minutes. Want to come with me to meet her?"

They arrived at the depot as Ruby Darrow stepped off the train. Auburn-haired and vibrant, Ruby was thirty years younger than her husband. She wore a straight-lined silk dress in a deep terra cotta color with one kick pleat from hem to thigh on the left side.

A hat of the same silk had a turned-back brim that came low over her eyes. A wide feather formed an S from its crown across the brim and onto her shoulder. She carried a silver mesh handbag. The moment her feet touched the earth, she became the talk of Dayton society. She hugged her husband and handed him her tickets.

"Quite the happy couple, aren't they?" Tyson said.

"To look at them," Harris told him, turning away. "I read somewhere that she made a big boo-boo on some of his prize speculations a few years ago, and they've been estranged ever since."

The Darrows linked arms and moved toward Rappelyea's automobile. When the sheriff and deputy arrived at the courthouse, Darrow and his wife were already on the lawn, mingling with the crowd as though this were a family reunion. When Darrow strolled toward the courthouse steps, Ruby walked across the street with Clarke Robinson.

Half an hour later Judge Raulston called the court to order. Bluch Harris reached into a hat holding slips of paper containing the names of the first twenty jury candidates. He pulled one out, glanced at it, and said, "W. F. Roberson, number twelve."

CHAPTER Twenty-Two

For more than two hours, Clarence Darrow and District Attorney Tom Stewart questioned men for the jury. Finally, they agreed on twelve—all white. Nine were farmers, eleven church members. One couldn't read.

Thomas Scopes ran his finger around the inside of his sweaty collar and nudged Tyson. "Say, brother, that's some jury!"

Close to five o'clock, Tyson closed the double doors on the courtroom after the last man strolled out. When he reached home, Nessa and Heddie sat on the front porch snapping string beans. They looked as weary as he felt.

He found a seat at the table across from Nessa's half-filled basin. The painted-door table felt smooth under his hand. An evening breeze carried the sweet scent of honeysuckle.

"Jody had a setback last night," Nessa told him, pushing her hair off her cheek. "Belinda phoned me this morning. She was in tears."

Heddie added, "Her husband is in Nashville on business. It's almost more than the poor girl can stand."

"When will he be back?" Tyson asked.

"Tomorrow, thank the Lord." Nessa poured him a glass of lemonade from a pitcher on the table.

He took a long, cool drink. "M-m-m. Nothing better."

Nessa tilted her head, watching him with a half-smile. "Here's a bit of gossip for you. That Malone lawyer brought a woman with him, and he's staying with her at the Aqua."

He broke off the end of a bean. "That's his wife."

Heddie's eyebrows lifted. "Their last names are different."

He shrugged. "Maybe she likes her maiden name."

Heddie glanced at Nessa. "Who ever heard tell of such a thing!"

Nessa said, "I also heard that Ruby Darrow rented Luke Morgan's house this afternoon. Of Dayton Bank and Trust."

Heddie tsked. "I never could see a fine lady like her living in the Mansion. She took one look at the place and started shaking the bushes for something better."

"Smart lady," Tyson commented, draining his glass.

Heddie said, "Speaking of bankers, we made nearly a hundred dollars today."

Nessa leaned her head back against the siding on the house and closed her eyes. "And to think we'll have to face that crowd again on Monday."

Heddie patted her arm. "Sufficient unto the day…"

Tyson let out a slow breath. "I'm going to hide in the house for half an hour. If Harris wants to shoot me, I'll cock the gun for him."

Nessa pulled out a smile. "I don't blame you one bit."

In the upstairs bathroom, he splashed water on his face and buried his nose in a soft towel. His head buzzed with wherefores and heretofores.

The camel-backed sofa never felt better. He relaxed and closed his eyes.

The next thing he knew, Lori pulled on his arm. "Hi, Daddy! See my flag?" She brushed it against his nose. "Grandpa got it for me. We just got back."

Tyson drew her close to his chest. Her nose glowed red from the sun. She was sweaty and smelled fine.

"That's wonderful, Chicky." He sat up. "I've got to work late tonight, so Nessa will put you to bed."

She plopped down beside him. "I like Nessa. She's my best friend."

"You have several best friends, don't you?"

Wide-eyed she asked, "How many years will the trial last, Daddy?"

He chuckled. "Only ten or so." He kissed her forehead and stood up. "I've got to get a bite to eat and go back to work. Want to see what Heddie has in the kitchen?"

Downtown Dayton stayed quiet for most of Saturday. The defense team took a riverboat ride as guests of the *Chattanooga News*, then gathered at the Mansion to discuss their battle strategy. Many reporters escaped the heat with a jaunt to the mountains.

That afternoon, Tyson arrested a college man for disturbing the peace. Red-faced and shaking his fist toward heaven, he stood at the corner of Market and Main denouncing Christianity. Tyson stepped in when three farmer boys stopped to watch the stranger, a wicked glint in their eyes.

"If you behave yourself and keep quiet, I won't put you in jail," Tyson told the atheist. "That'll be five dollars."

Sputtering, the city fellow paid up and shut up.

A few minutes later Tyson met Harris and Rice in front of the Aqua. He told them of his arrest and handed the fine to the sheriff.

Rowdy teenagers filled the street. They played practical jokes and shouted insults at one another. Around six o'clock most of them crowded into open roadsters and—hooting and laughing—headed for the dance at the Morgan Springs Hotel.

At seven Tyson took a last patrol around the outskirts of town before heading home. He saw a camp meeting in the woods beside the school. The next day he heard that H.L. Mencken had gone to the service and got "converted."

At breakfast Sunday morning, Nessa said, "Would you drive us to church this morning, Trent? William Jennings Bryan is preaching at the South Methodist Church, and we'd like to go."

Tyson sipped coffee. The trial boarders were still in bed. He wished he were, too.

"Please, Daddy?" Lori's bright eyes smiled up at him.

He glanced from one eager face to the other and held up both hands in surrender. "You talked me into it."

Heat shimmered on quiet streets as they drove south to the church. Tyson tugged at his soft collar, wishing for a cool glass of tea and the morning paper in his own sitting room.

Having the whole family in the car made for a tight squeeze. Tyson backed out of his driveway thankful that the church was only eight blocks from home.

As they passed the North Methodist Church Heddie said, "Charles Francis Potter is supposed to speak at our church this morning."

"Who's he?" Vic asked.

Tyson answered before Heddie had a chance. "He's a Unitarian minister from New York. George Rappelyea brought him down to help the defense."

"He thinks the Bible is full of fairy tales," Heddie said, eyes flashing.

"And Pastor Byrd *wants* him to preach?" In the front with Lori and Tyson, Nessa turned to talk to her mother in the back seat.

"The deacons aren't happy," Heddie told her. "I wonder what's going to happen this morning."

"You want me to drop you off here, Heddie," Tyson asked, "so you can witness it firsthand?"

She harrumphed. Swallowing a smile, Tyson drove on.

Half an hour before service time, Lizzy found a parking spot in front of a brick church with two vestibules facing the street. Folks in Sunday best crowded the sidewalk and pushed inside both entries.

Inside, a center aisle stretched to the front between long wooden pews. Muted stained-glass colors contrasted with white plastered walls. A massive oak pulpit stood on the far left of the platform.

Tyson and Nessa found seats halfway back in a crowd of three hundred. Vic and Heddie sat across the aisle with Lori between them. Micky found a place with friends in the back. Tyson caught sight of Judge Raulston's family on the front row.

William Jennings Bryan smiled widely at his audience's cheers and applause. Raising a hand to quiet the crowd, his voice reverberated through the building.

"When the Christians of this nation understand the demoralizing influence of this godless doctrine, they will refuse to allow it to be taught at public expense." He leaned his head back and bellowed, "Christianity is not afraid of truth because truth comes from God."

Tyson forgot the time, the heat, the girl by his side. The man with the message had his full attention.

On the drive home, Nessa and Heddie chatted happily with Vic. Lori cried because she was hot and tired and hungry. Tyson mulled over ideas he'd never considered before.

After dinner, Vic and Tyson sat together in their room, sleepy-eyed with their bellies full of roasted chicken and all the trimmings. Lori snoozed on her trundle bed.

Minus collar, coat, and tie, Tyson lounged in the wing-backed chair. "What did you think of the message, Pa?"

"Will Bryan makes more sense than any preacher I've ever heard."

"That's not a good answer," Tyson retorted, stretching his legs straight out before him. "You haven't heard many preachers."

Vic smiled. "You've got a point there." Leaning back on the sofa, the old man rested black sock-clad feet on the coffee table.

"When you're in that courtroom tomorrow, open your ears. You're letting prejudice muddy your thinking." His eyes drifted shut, stopping the conversation.

Tyson picked up his Sunday copy of the *Chattanooga News.* On the front page, John Scopes was kissing a blonde, his eyes wide in surprise. Tyson chuckled. Somebody had shanghaied young Scopes for a sizzling photograph.

He set down the paper and, on impulse headed downstairs to the phone. "Hello, Doc?" he said a moment later. "Would you bring me Wiggam's book on eugenics when you come tomorrow night? I'd like to take another look at it."

As he replaced the receiver he heard the back door close. He stepped to the kitchen to see who was there. Chicken and sage smells clung to the air.

Belinda Riesbeck stood by the door with a wadded handkerchief across her eyes. Throwing down her towel, Nessa hurried across the room to put her arms around the distraught mother.

Wondering about Jody's condition, Tyson stayed in the doorway to allow himself a quick getaway if Belinda turned on the waterworks in earnest. He pictured Jody at the drug store, scooping ice cream from a dish and angling her wide blue eyes toward everyone around her.

"I had to get away for a few minutes," Belinda said in a moment. Her voice quivered. "I've been in that house for two weeks without so much as a walk out in the yard.

"Elmer Buntley brought her a stuffed monkey this afternoon. She was so taken with it that I knew she wouldn't miss me. And her daddy's there."

"Is she worse?" Nessa asked.

Belinda lowered the handkerchief and blinked hard. Nessa urged her to a chair at the table.

"She seems better," Belinda said. "She wanted her dolly yesterday. And today she ate a good dinner, almost her normal amount."

"What's worrying you then?"

Concentrating on the crumpled cloth in her hands, Belinda drew in a sobbing breath, clawed at her top lip with white lower teeth, then went on in a rush: "The doctor says her heart is permanently damaged. She won't be able to get out of bed. Ever."

Tears spilled down Nessa's cheeks. Belinda squeezed her eyes closed. Her composure gave way, and Nessa knelt beside her to hold her once more.

Tyson eased up the stairs. In a pain-filled daze, he pulled off his shirt, draped it over a chair, and lay on the sofa. His eyes were dry, but his heart cried bitter tears.

A somber mood hung over the house for the rest of the day. That evening Nessa walked to her own church. Vic accompanied Heddie and Lori to the courthouse yard to hear Bryan speak again. The trial borders went along, notepads ready.

Alone and depressed, Tyson stayed on the sofa and pulled out his notebook. After a brief flip through the pages, he put it away and stretched out, his head on the soft armrest, his thoughts wandering.

Back from church, Nessa paused at the stairs to call, "Trent? Are you there?"

Flicking quick fingers through his curly mop, he wished he had thought to put on his shirt before this. He put his head through the open door. "What is it?"

"Pastor Byrd canceled Dr. Potter's engagement this morning because of a big ruckus among the deacons. But that's not all. Pastor Byrd just resigned." She hesitated. "Would you like a sandwich or something?"

He grinned. "Be right down."

Monday morning, the courtroom was as jammed as it had been on Friday, but with a different crowd. Today half the spectators were women, and many of the rest wore suits instead of overalls.

Over the weekend, workmen had installed three fans high above the crowd. The jury and many in the audience held paper fans bearing a toothpaste ad with the slogan "Do your gums bleed?"

Malone again had the distinction of being the only man with a coat on. Using a linen handkerchief with discretion, he looked cool. And drew much attention because of it.

Near the defense table, Ruby Darrow perched in a chair, smiling for cameras and joking with Mencken at the press table nearby. Today she wore jade crepe with a deeply scooped neck and flared three-quarter sleeves. Looking bored, Doris Stevens sat with her.

Mary Bryan's wooden wheelchair stood directly behind her husband. Her gentle face had deep lines, and pain tightened her mouth.

Again, the judge postponed opening court to pose for photographs. As he prepared to go to the bench, Darrow hurried over to him. "Isn't it out of order to have a preacher open court with prayer? Particularly as the case has a religious aspect?"

Judge Raulston stared at the defense attorney. "I've opened my court with prayer since I was first elected." He took his seat and banged the gavel. "Everyone bow for prayer as court opens."

A black-coated minister strode into the sanctum and called on "the creator of the heaven and the earth and the sea and all that is in them." Darrow slouched deeper into his chair. His massive brow made his eyes seem like small, iron points.

Tyson didn't miss a word. Today, the gladiators might draw steel.

At the final "Amen," District Attorney Tom Stewart read the indictment in a full, throaty voice.

Immediately John Neal came to his feet. He made a motion to throw out the indictment. He rambled for half an hour about the Butler Act being unconstitutional since it supported the establishment of religion.

Constitutional argument is dull at its best, but at temperatures nearing a hundred, an open-mouthed, fish-out-of-water expression slowly conquered the crowd as they droned on for more than two hours. Only the attorneys, the judge, and a few die-hard reporters listened closely. Even Scopes seemed asleep.

Beside the door, Tyson shifted on aching feet and moved away from the door molding digging into his spine. Kelso Rice looked at his watch and sent Tyson a how-much-more-can-I-take look. Mercifully, the judge hit the gavel five minutes later.

After lunch and additional legal arguments, Darrow stood, smiling and relaxed. "If the court please—"

Several men edged toward the door. Whispers grew louder until Raulston banged his gavel. "No talking, please, in the courtroom."

Darrow moved to the center of the sanctum, facing the judge. He clenched both fists and shouted, "There is nothing else, Your Honor, that has caused the difference of opinion, of bitterness, of hatred, of war, of cruelty, that religion has caused." A sweeping gesture split his sleeve at his left elbow.

He scanned the silent courtroom, brow lowered, eyes piercing. "The Butler Act makes the Bible the yardstick to measure every man's intellect. Are your mathematics good? Turn to First Elijah 2 for instruction." His oversized head drew down between his shoulders. He shoved fists deep into his pockets.

Working his audience like a blacksmith plying the hammer to a glowing rod, he continued for two hours. Suddenly his head jerked forward, spouting words like bullets. "If today you make it a crime to teach evolution, tomorrow you may ban books and newspapers. After a while, we will be marching backward to the glorious ages of the sixteenth century when bigots burned the men who dared bring any intelligence and enlightenment and culture to the human mind."

Abruptly breaking the spell, Judge Raulston called for adjournment.

Hisses came from the ranks as Darrow found his seat. One voice said, "They ought to put him out!"

H.L. Mencken glared at the crowd and murmured, "Morons!"

Defense attorneys pumped Darrow's hand and congratulated each other on a good day's work.

Ruby came up to inspect the damage to her husband's shirt sleeve. "Clarence," she said, "don't you think you'd better put on another shirt?"

He smiled. "Well, Ruby, don't you think it's too hot today for two shirts?"

After the initial rush to reach Darrow had passed, Ben McKenzie sauntered over to the Great Defender and clasped his hand. "That was the greatest speech I have ever heard on any subject in my life," he said.

"It's mighty kind of you to say that," Darrow said, embracing him.

Tyson stepped outside in time to see a wide streak of lightning slash the sky. A heavenly drum roll followed. Spattering rain made him jog home.

Lori and Nessa met him at the door. "I saw you in the courtroom, Daddy!" Lori said when he scooped her up.

Nessa smiled. "I took her upstairs for a little peek this afternoon." She touched the child's arm, and they shared a slant-eyed grin.

"Are you still playing chess with Dr. St. Clair tonight?" Nessa asked.

Tyson smacked his thigh. "I almost forgot him with so much going on." He let out a loose-lipped gust of air. "Yes, he's coming. I phoned him yesterday." He looked into the dining room and down the hall. "Where's Vic?"

"In your room."

"I'll see if he wants to play Mah-Jongg with the doc and I tonight."

"I'll put on some coffee for you all," she said.

"Put me down, Daddy! I've got to help Nessa."

He set her on her feet and she darted away without a backward glance. Thunder shook the house when Tyson reached his room. Rain pounded the windows. He found Vic stretched out on the bed.

When Tyson suggested Mah-Jongg, his father said, "Sounds like a fine way to spend the evening." He glanced at his watch. "Time for dinner." He reached for his shirt hanging over the bedpost.

"What did you think of Darrow's speech today?" Tyson asked, sinking into a straight chair while Vic buttoned up.

"He's some speaker."

"His argument sounded convincing, but . . ."

Vic reached for a collar. "But you've still got doubts, that it?"

"Much as I hate to admit it, I do. The problem is, I just can't put my finger on the problem." He paused, tapping his hand on the bedside table. "We all believe in personal freedoms, Pa. Everyone should have the right to his own religion."

Vic loosened his belt and tucked in the shirt tail. "Personally, I think the concept of a national school system is the problem. With the mishmash of people in America, how can a single organization teach a set of values that everyone agrees on?"

"You should read *The Descent of Man*," Tyson said. "Darwin is real convincing. I started reading it before the trial started, but lately, I haven't had time to finish it."

Vic picked up his hairbrush and peered into the mirror. "Is that a leather-bound book, green with red print on the cover?"

"Yeah."

"It's right over there. Micky's been coming in here to read it."

He touched the brush to his beard.

"I hear Bryan's starting a new college right here in Dayton."

"You don't say."

"Columbia University doesn't want to accept Tennessee students. I guess they think our kids are tainted. Anyway, Superintendent White told Bryan he ought to start his own college." He lay down the brush. "I think he's going to do it."

Nessa's voice came from below. "Trent! Vic! Tell the fellows that supper's ready!"

With no warning, the lights went out.

Chapter Twenty-Three

"Daddy!" Lori screamed in the kitchen. "It's okay, honey," Nessa called to her through the blackness. "I'll light a candle."

When the men arrived, a tiny flame had transformed the kitchen into a cave with deep caverns in the corners.

Tyson chuckled at his daughter's spooked face. "It's only me, Chickabiddy. Can a ghost give you a tickle?" He poked a finger at her ribs.

She squealed, laughing. "Don't!"

"Oh, no! The water's gone!" Nessa cried in frustration. "Micky, quick get a bucket and set it under the rain spout by the porch."

"How can I find a bucket in the dark?" the boy demanded.

Heddie snapped, "At the top of the basement steps."

Nessa struck a match. "Here. Take a candle with you."

"Things keep getting better around here," Vic said, mildly.

"It's the judgment of God," Heddie declared. She thunked a skillet of corn pone on the table and said, "The women in my prayer group are going to pray for Clarence Darrow every day. The man's an infidel bound for…" She paused. "I'd rather not say what I'm thinking." She slashed at the yellow bread.

"Mind if I quote you, Mrs. McGinty?" Paul asked, laughter in his voice.

"Go right ahead, young man. I don't have nothing to hide."

"And me without my pencil," Dick Beamish said, chuckling deep in his belly.

Paul said, "I hear Bryan's got a whopper of a speech for his closing statement."

Beamish nodded. "I heard that, too. He's been working on it for six weeks."

Heddie took a seat. "Mr. Bryan will set them all straight, you just wait."

Vic reached for the pot of beans. "St. Clair may not want to come over here in this weather."

"He'll be here," Tyson said. "Would you like to join us, fellows?"

Paul asked, "What are you playing?"

"Mah-Jongg. Usually, it's chess, but with more than two players in the house, we'll change tracks tonight."

"I'll play," Paul replied. "I belong to a Mah-Jongg club in St. Louis. Not that I'm there much."

The evening was a washout in more ways than one. The sitting room was so dark, the men had to strain to see the playing tiles. With the heat of the candles, and the windows closed against the rain, the house became close and uncomfortable. At nine o'clock Paul called "woo," and they broke it up.

The next morning, Vic came to breakfast with a stack of newspapers under his arm. The men immediately reached out for copies and ate their eggs from behind a printed page.

"Well. looky here," Beamish drawled. "Mencken's strutting his stuff."

"Read it," Bill Perry urged.

Heddie took a seat at the end of the table, her eyes on Beamish.

Beamish chuckled. "You asked for it." He grinned at Perry over the paper then read: "'There is a Unitarian clergyman here from New York trying desperately to horn in on the trial. He will fail. If Darrow ventured to put him on the stand the whole audience, led by the jury, would leap out of the courthouse windows, and take to the hills.'"

The newsmen guffawed. Tyson watched Heddie's face turn pink. He waited for the explosion.

It didn't happen. The good woman drew in a hard breath and returned to her dishpan. She let the rattle of glass and silverware speak for her.

Tyson smirked into his collar. Still another benefit of being a trial boarder.

Half an hour before court convened on Tuesday morning, a round-cheeked clerk puffed up the stairs. "Deputy Tyson, you have a phone call."

Elbowing through the stream of people climbing to the second floor, Tyson hustled down after the young fellow. He leaned on a high counter and put the receiver to his ear.

"Hey, Trent!" It was Charlie Greene's squeaky drawl. "I hear you're having an exciting time in Dayton these days."

"What's the scoop, Charlie?"

"That teenage girl you sent down…Dotty Smith? She died of an overdose of sleeping tablets. Ten partials were still in her stomach." He cleared his throat. "There was something unusual about her, though."

"Yeah?"

"She had a forced abortion three or four weeks ago. Looks like a professional job."

"What!" Tyson felt numb around the mouth.

"Trent? You there?"

Shifting the receiver to the other hand, Tyson tried to get a grip on himself. "Charlie, what about the bottle and the glass?"

"Both had the girl's prints on them, a little smudged but definitely hers. The glass was clean. Pure water."

"Thanks a million, Charlie."

"Shall we release the body?"

"Sure. I'll tell Dotty's mother she can start funeral arrangements."

Tyson joined the crowd moving upstream and took his position at the door, his mind whirling.

Officer Rice's gavel woke him out of his stupor.

Judge Raulston said, "Rev. Stribbling, will you open with prayer?"

Clarence Darrow came to his feet. "Your Honor, I want to make an objection before the jury comes in."

"What is it, Mr. Darrow?"

"I object to prayer and I object to the jury being present when the court rules on the objection."

Darrow spoke so softly that District Attorney Stewart looked up and said, "What is it?"

Judge Raulston turned shocked eyes toward the prosecution. "He objects to the court being opened with prayer, especially in the presence of the jury."

A whistling murmur passed over the startled crowd. Darrow turned and glared at them.

"I do not want to be unreasonable," Judge Raulston told him, "but it has been my custom since I have been judge to have prayers in the courtroom. I know of no reason why I should not follow up this custom, so I overrule the objection."

The lawyer wouldn't give up so easily. "Seeing the nature of this case there should be no attempt by means of prayer to influence the jury."

Again, Judge Raulston turned to the prosecution. "Do you want to say anything?"

"That matter has been passed upon by our supreme court," Ben McKenzie said. "It was commendable to the jury to ask divine guidance."

"I do not object to anyone praying in secret," Darrow continued, "but I do object to the turning of this courtroom into a meeting house. You have no right to do it."

Stewart turned steely eyes on Darrow. "The state makes no contention that this is a conflict between science and religion. It is a case of whether or not a school teacher has taught a doctrine prohibited by statute."

Malone leaped to his feet. "We believe that this daily opening with prayers increases the atmosphere of hostility to our side which already exists in this community by widespread propaganda."

With suppressed emotion, Stewart forced out his answer, "I would advise Mr. Malone that this is a God-fearing country."

Malone bristled. "It is no more God-fearing than that from which I came."

"Gentlemen," the judge intervened, "do not turn this into an argument."

Darrow said, "This statute says no doctrine shall be taught which is contrary to the divine account contained in the Bible. So there is no question about the religious character of these proceedings."

Judge Raulston drew himself up. "This court has no purpose except to find the truth and do justice. I have instructed the ministers to make no reference to the issues involved. Therefore, I am pleased to overrule the objection and invite Rev. Stribbling to open with prayer."

Because of the electricity outage the night before, the judge had not finished his written answer to the defense's motion to throw out the case. After prayer, he immediately adjourned until one o'clock so that he could complete it.

Tyson waited until the crowd drifted outside. He took a seat at the prosecution table to scribble in his notebook while Greene's call lay fresh in his mind. With electricity still unavailable, the fans stood silent and still. Drinking water was at a premium.

Twenty minutes later Tyson reached Lizzy in his own driveway. Harris had put him on patrol duty again. Today he'd swing down Front Street and ask a few questions while he was there.

He tapped on Bella Smith's kitchen door and waited. No one came, though her Pierce Arrow sat in the drive.

Finally, he crossed the lawn to Essie Caldwell's house. At his knock, the lady opened the screen door on her front porch. Around her waist hung a wide apron embroidered with cardinals.

"Good morning, Deputy," she said, delighted to see him. "Come in. Would you like some tea?"

"Thank you, Mrs. Caldwell. I've just come from the courthouse. It's as dry as the Sahara around there."

She led him into her kitchen, a gleaming place with white porcelain everywhere: counters, table, sideboard, and sink. She opened the ice box.

"I'm afraid it won't be too cold. The ice man is only giving a quarter of folks' usual orders this week. With so many people in town, by the end of the week, we may not have any ice at all." She set a tall glass on the table before him.

He took two grateful swallows before saying, "I've got a few questions about Dotty, Mrs. Caldwell."

Her eyes filled with tears. "That poor child." She sat at the table and pulled out her handkerchief.

"Don't answer right away. Think back very carefully." He took another sip of tea. "When exactly did Dotty change?"

"When did she become depressed, you mean?" Rubbing fingertips across her lips, she studied the flowery linoleum in front of the sink.

"It was shortly after the state fair. She started out with a sort of worried look. I figured maybe she had a squabble with her mother or something. I didn't like to pry."

Tyson hid a smile. Touching his mustache, he watched her seamed face and waited.

"About the time things started gearing up for the trial, she took sick for a few days, and I didn't see her at all." She drew in a long breath.

"It seems like she never got over that sickness, Deputy. I never saw her smile again. She quit coming out with me in the mornings. A week later, I asked her over to help me mark quilting squares, something she usually enjoyed. She came, but she hardly said two words."

Tyson noted down dates and wrote brief comments beside them. "Did she ever talk about any boys around Dayton?"

"When she and Bella first came here, Dotty talked about her boyfriend back in Chattanooga." Essie grimaced. "She said he was a dark-haired sheik with a long sports car."

"Did you ever see her with a local boy?"

"Never. She and Bella hardly went anywhere, except shopping trips to Chattanooga now and then."

Tyson drained his glass. “Thank you, Mrs. Caldwell. For the drink and for the information.” He stood. “I’m supposed to be patrolling the outskirts of town. I’d best get on with it.”

Tyson said goodbye then strode across the yard on a path toward his car. Halfway across, he stopped and stared. Bella’s driveway was empty.

He retraced his steps around the corner of Essie’s house. She was standing on her front step with her hand on the screen door, holding it so the spring wouldn’t bang it shut. She was staring at the lavender hollyhocks along the house.

“How’s Bella getting along since Dotty’s passing?” Tyson asked her.

She looked up, vaguely surprised. “I’ve scarcely seen her. She doesn’t have many friends around here. Some church ladies came and brought her food over the weekend, but no one’s come for two days now. I’ll go over to check on her later.”

“Don’t bother. She just left.” He touched his hat. “Thanks again.”

He crossed the grass and reached under Lizzy’s seat for the crank. On the second swing, she sprang to life with a kick that jerked his arm. He jumped back, rubbing his wrist.

Five minutes later the old Model T chugged into her parking place in front of the sheriff’s office. The door was locked. Tyson let himself in and picked up the phone.

“Get me Chattanooga police.” He sat in his chair, toe-tapping while he waited. Three minutes passed before he had his man. “Jim, I’ve got a problem.”

“Fire away,” Crabill said, his voice grating across the phone wires.

“You remember that bootleg bust at the Chinese laundry? Bella Smith spent thirty days in the hoosegow for trafficking, remember?”

Crabill grunted.

“Well, her daughter committed suicide last Thursday. I sent the body to the pathology boys and Charlie just called with the report.”

“Yeah?”

“She had an abortion.”

“You can’t charge her for it now, Tyson.”

Tyson ignored Jim’s sorry attempt at humor. “Her mother seems to be avoiding me. She wouldn’t answer her door this morning, and now she’s taken off for parts unknown. I’m wondering if she knew something about the abortion. Would you check around that same neighborhood; see if she’s gone to talk to a friend down there?”

“You want me to book her?”

“Just hold her for questioning. If you get her, I’ll try to get loose and come on down.”

"Will do. If there's some quack in Chattanooga doing abortions, I want to be the first to know. Nasty business." Crabill rang off.

Locking the office door behind him, Tyson strolled across the courthouse lawn, bought a hot dog, drank some soda, and chatted with Vic in the shade.

At one o'clock, Rice rapped the gavel and announced that court would reconvene at two-thirty. No one wanted to lose his seat, so the crowd muttered and smoked and sweated.

At two-fifteen, Judge Raulston strode in wearing a suit as black as his expression. He took his place on the bench and said, "I gave strict instructions to the stenographer that my opinion was not to be released to any person. If any member of the press sends it out before I begin to read it, I will deal with them for contempt of court."

Stiff with righteous indignation, he marched out, leaving behind a bee hive of rumors and guesses.

Time crept along on leaden feet. Pungent odors mingled and made breathing a chore.

A man wearing bib overalls brought up a case of red soda pop and sold it for a quarter a bottle. In three minutes, he'd sold out.

Kelso Rice sauntered over to Tyson and said, "You think the floor of this place can stand the strain of all these people?"

Tyson pried his mind away from Bella Smith. He focused on Rice and absorbed his statement. "I never thought about it, Kelso."

He glanced at the crowd. "Maybe we'd best have a look downstairs."

"You look," Rice said. "I'll mind the store."

Tyson shuffled down the stairs and turned toward the back of the building to the underside of the courtroom floor. The ceiling looked fine. He returned to holding up the door jamb.

At three-forty-five, Judge Raulston bustled in, a folder of papers under his arm.

His narrow tie skirted off center, Hays was before the bench as soon as the judge sat down. "Before the proceedings go further, may I present a petition to the court." He began reading something about selecting ministers to pray each morning.

Stewart lunged to his feet, interrupting. "I submit that is absolutely out of order. This is not an assembly for hearing any motion of that sort."

Hays said, "I insist on making this motion."

"I am making my exception to the court," Stewart countered.

Hays raised his voice to drown out his opponent.

Face red, Stewart said, "Will you please keep your mouth shut!"

Judge Raulston looked from one determined face to the other.

"I will hear it."

Stewart clenched his fist and cried, "I except to it with all the vehemence of my nature."

"Proceed, Mr. Hays," the judge said.

The lawyer finished reading a document insisting that clergy from various groups be called on to pray, not only fundamentalists. Charles Francis Potter's signature led the list.

Raulston said, "I shall refer that petition to the pastors' association of this town and I shall ask them . . ."

Laughter and loud applause cut him off.

Kelso Rice thumped his gavel. "Order! Order in the court!"

When the noise level dropped, the judge finished, "I'll ask them to name the man who is to conduct the prayer."

He shuffled some papers on the bench and looked over the crowd. "Now, I have a very serious matter to speak of. I dictated my opinion in this case to a reputable court stenographer in secret with the instruction that no living person know anything as to my conclusions.

"I am informed that newspapers in large cities are being sold, which state what my opinion is. Any person who sent out such information, sent it out without the authority of this court. If I find that they have corruptly secured said information, I shall deal with them as the law directs.

"When the crowd is gone, I want all the members of the press to meet me in this courtroom."

Stewart asked, "Does Your Honor want the attorneys?"

"Yes, sir, the attorneys on both sides."

The crowd shuffled. Reporters whispered to one another—some angry at being scooped, others amused.

Observing the judge's stern expression, Tyson knew that at least one person wouldn't be laughing when this session was through.

Chapter Twenty-Four

When the last spectator had cleared out, Tyson made sure no one loitered about the door to eavesdrop.

Raulston leaned forward and said, "Did you see the wire, Mr. Stewart?"

"I saw the wire." The District Attorney looked around at the assembled newsmen. "Who had that?"

A gray-haired, spectacled man waved a yellow paper at him and handed it to Rice who passed it to the judge.

Dick Beamish got to his feet. "Won't it be read out, please, so we can all hear it?"

The judge nodded and spoke clearly. "'*St. Louis Star*, carrying story, Law held constitutional by judge.'"

Judge Raulston continued, "Now, if this is a deduction, gentlemen, of course they have a right to guess. So, I think it is proper that I appoint a committee of pressmen to ascertain what these papers are carrying and ascertain if they are carrying this as a true story."

Beamish nodded. "That would be very fair."

Raulston called out five names, including Richard Beamish. "Be prepared to report to me as soon as you can." Jaw set, lower lip stretched out, Judge Raulston said, "You may be excused," and he marched out.

Tyson glanced at his watch. It was four o'clock, his usual time to knock off, but tonight he had to beat the pavement in Dayton 'til the streets cleared. As Tyson pulled into his driveway that evening, the house lights came on. The electricity was back. At least something was going right in this crazy town.

"Looky here," Paul Henderson said the next morning, holding an open copy of the Baltimore *Evening Sun* over his breakfast plate. "Old Mencken's at his tricks."

"Read it," Beamish urged. He forked scrambled eggs into his mouth, his eyes on Henderson. The other trial boarders paused their conversation to listen. Also at the table, Nessa kept her eyes on her bacon and eggs.

Henderson spoke clearly. "'The net effect of Clarence Darrow's great speech yesterday seems to be precisely the same as if he had bawled up a rainspout in the interior of Afghanistan.'" He paused to sip coffee. "'It was not designed for reading but for hearing. The very judge on the bench, toward the end of it, began to look uneasy. But the morons in the audience, when it was over, simply hissed at it.'" Henderson paused to chuckle. "'Bryan has these hillbillies locked up in his pen and he knows it. His nonsense is their ideal of sense.'"

Heddie banged the frying pan on the stove. Avoiding Nessa's flashing eyes at the other end of the table, Tyson excused himself and headed to the courthouse. He wondered how long Heddie could hold her tongue—even for a trial boarder.

When Tyson arrived at the corner of Market and Third Avenue on Wednesday morning, Bryan was posing for photographers in front of a truck with "Ask Us About Tampa, Florida" on the side.

Tyson smirked. The Great Commoner was still pushing the Florida real estate that had made him a millionaire.

Three men stopped H.L. Mencken at the bottom of the courthouse steps. All were over thirty years old and dressed in miners' clothes.

"So, we're hillbillies and morons, are we?" a short, husky man asked. "We're imbeciles?"

A wary look on his face, the reporter glanced from one stern face to another. "Gentlemen, I have no quarrel with you."

"Well, we sure 'nuff do with you," said a red-haired man, a determined look in his eye.

"Okay, let's break it up," Tyson called, striding toward them. "You fellows move on."

With a nod at the deputy, Mencken scurried up the stairs.

"He's asking for it," the red-haired one said.

"Come on, Joshua." Eyeing Tyson, the third man said, "That poison pen jockey won't always have the law around to protect him." They shuffled to the benches set up in the yard, and Tyson strode into the courthouse.

In full form, Kelso Rice called the fourth day of the trial to order. "Oyez, oyez, this honorable circuit court is now open. Sit down please."

Charles Francis Potter prayed, and Neal offered a new, lengthy objection to the opening prayer.

After the judge again overruled the objection, District Attorney Stewart stood and spoke quietly. "Yesterday afternoon, Mr. Hays was presenting a matter to the court. I desired to object, and feeling that Mr. Hays did not give me an opportunity to address the court, I expressed myself toward him in a discourteous manner. I feel very much ashamed. I apologize for it."

"I am happy to accept the apology," Hays said with a tight-lipped smile. "There are two qualities I admire in a man. One is that he is human and the other, that he is courteous. The outburst yesterday proves that the attorney general was human, and the apology proves that he has the courtesy of a southern gentleman."

Both attorneys took their seats, and the atmosphere noticeably eased.

Raulston turned his attention toward the audience. "Is the chairman of the press committee present?"

Dick Beamish stood and adjusted his glasses by holding the side near the ribbon. He read from a paper. "The sender of the bulletin did not obtain this information in any improper manner. The committee recommends that he be not disturbed in his relations with the court."

Raulston peered over his glasses. "I think the court is entitled to know how this information was had."

"The information came from the court."

"Well!" Raulston's mouth dropped open.

Beamish hurried on, "The young man met the judge upon his way to the hotel and asked, 'Will you adjourn until tomorrow?' to which the reply was, 'Yes.'"

Ignoring the chuckles behind him, Beamish said, "If the motion was affirmed, the trial would have been ended. It was pure deduction."

"Who is he?" the judge demanded.

"Mr. Hutchinson."

"Come around, Mr. Hutchinson."

A fresh-faced reporter with a round chin and anxious eyes came before the bench.

Raulston paused, looking him over carefully. "I do not think you had any right to inquire if the court would adjourn until tomorrow."

Beamish interceded. "Mr. Hutchinson is an upright, conscientious and honest newspaperman. I am sure he had no sinister motive."

"If you want information," Raulston said, "ask me directly and I will give you a direct answer." He reached for his papers. "You may be excused."

A stir went through the crowd. Hutchinson returned to his seat amid handshaking and backslapping.

Rice bellowed, "Order!"

"The court is about to read his opinion," the judge said. "I shall expect absolute order in the courtroom because people are entitled to hear this opinion." He turned to photographers. "If you gentlemen want my picture make it now."

A titter rose at Raulston's obsession with publicity. A dozen men bearing cameras marched forward. Like a team of acrobats, they arranged themselves pyramid style: a kneeling row, then a standing row, a row on chairs, and two on a table. Judge Raulston leaned back, papers in his left hand, his expression sober.

Five minutes later he carefully arranged his papers in front of him and sing-songed his way through nineteen pages, stopping often to touch a handkerchief to his face. Sheriff Harris took a fan from the defense table and brought it to the bench.

Bryan listened intently. Darrow's eyes wandered about the room.

Judge Raulston found the Butler Act to be constitutional. He denied the motion to throw out the case.

At lunchtime, spectators poured outside. When others surged in to take their places, the morning crowd forgot food and drink. They rushed back to reclaim their seats.

If possible, today's heat was the worst yet. Tyson wondered how much longer the case would drag on. He felt he had been in the courtroom forever, and the main part of the trial had yet to begin.

Shortly before one o'clock, the attorneys entered the courtroom. The prosecution couldn't find its witnesses. While Ben McKenzie, his son, and the Hicks brothers waded through the crowd in search of their youngsters, spectators snatched the prosecutors' chairs.

The boys finally came forward, and the prosecutors returned to their table. Looking around in dismay, Ben McKenzie called, "Please return our chairs. We are a necessary evil in this courtroom."

The chairs were handed over.

At that moment, in dashed John Scopes, the younger Bryan, and Wallace Haggard. They'd gone swimming at the Blue Hole and had forgotten the time.

Hays barked at Scopes, "Where have you been? You could cause a technical error by not appearing. You may even be arrested!"

John slunk to his seat like a whipped child. Until then, no one had noticed he wasn't in his place.

"Open court," Judge Raulston said.

The bailiff rapped the gavel and gave his usual spiel. The jury filled in the front row of chairs as a clerk called each man's name.

Scopes pleaded not guilty to the charge. Attorney General Stewart made a two-sentence statement that Scopes had taught man's development from a lower animal and, therefore, had violated the Butler Act.

Reading from a typed paper, Malone gave the opening statement for the defense. "To convict the defendant, Scopes, the prosecution must prove two things: First—that Scopes taught a theory that denies the story of the divine creation of man as taught in the Bible, and second—that he taught that man descended from a lower order of animals.

"The defense believes there is a direct conflict between the theory of evolution and the theories of creation as set forth in Genesis." A while later, he said, "We will show by the testimony of men learned in science and theology that millions of people believe in evolution and in the stories of creation and find no conflict between the two."

Listening closely, Tyson's brow drew down. Was there a conflict or not?

Malone spoke for several minutes about an old writing of Bryan's, trying to discredit the man's current stance. Then he listed several proofs that evolution must be true.

"The defense denies that it is part of any conspiracy to destroy Christianity. Such a conspiracy exists only in the mind of William Jennings Bryan."

Stewart objected to the barbs aimed at Bryan.

The Commoner stood and said, "I ask no protection from the court and when the proper time comes I shall be able to show the gentlemen that I stand today just where I did then."

The spectators stamped and cheered. They whistled and applauded.

Judge Raulston thumped his gavel.

When the crowd quieted, Malone droned through three more pages.

When he finished, Ben McKenzie said, "This is wholly improper. My friend is talking about a theory of evolution that took him two years to write—that speech," referring to Malone's high-blown language.

Loud laughter and hoots cut off his next words.

Malone looked down his nose at McKenzie. "The jury knows the difference between testimony and oratory."

Red around the ears, McKenzie said, "The only mistake the good Lord made is that he did not withhold the completion of the job until he could have got a conference with you," suggesting that Malone claimed to know more about the earth's origin than God himself.

Malone smiled, "You're right."

More laughter.

The judge asked for order and swore in the jury. Stewart called his first witness: Superintendent Walter White, who confirmed that Scopes had admitted to teaching evolution in biology class.

Next, round-eyed ninth-grader Howard Morgan, son of the banker who had rented his home to the Darrows, came forward. He wore a white shirt, the collar open and the tie pulled down and to one side. A dark cowlick stood up at his crown.

After the preliminary questions about his name, age, and the school he attended, the boy told Stewart that Scopes had taught him evolution.

Stewart stood near the boy and gave him an encouraging smile. "Just state in your own words, Howard, what he taught you."

"He said that the earth was once a hot molten mass. In the sea the earth cooled off; there was a little germ of one cell formed and this organism kept evolving until it got to be a pretty good-sized animal and then came to be a land animal, and from this was man."

Stewart said, "Let me repeat that. If I don't get it right, you correct me."

Hays said, "Go to the head of the class."

Stewart restated the Morgan boy's answer as it would be found in a textbook. He then held up the school's *General Science* text.

"Can you find that in this book?"

"No, sir, I couldn't find it."

The District Attorney handed the text to the defense table. "I hand it to you, gentlemen, to find it." He turned back to the witness. "Howard, how did he classify man with reference to other animals?"

"He classified man along with cats and dogs, cows, monkeys, lions, and all that."

"Did he say what they were?"

"Mammals."

Stewart turned toward the defense. "Cross-examine."

Darrow hitched his suspenders and stood. "Now, Howard, what do you mean by *classify*?"

The boy fidgeted in his chair. "Well, it means that men were just the same as them, in other words . . ." He twisted his tie towards his left shoulder.

"He didn't say a cat was the same as a man?"

"No, sir. He said man had a reasoning power that these animals did not."

Darrow smirked toward the crowd. "There is some doubt about that, but that's what he said, is it?"

Laughter filled the courtroom until Raulston banged his gavel. "Order!"

"With some men," Stewart added, grinning toward his opponent.

"A great many," Darrow agreed, glancing at Bryan.

Bryan merely smiled and fanned.

Darrow returned to the witness. "Did he tell you what distinguished mammals from other animals?"

"I don't remember."

"And you didn't know that a mammal is a species that suckled its young, did you?"

Shock jolted the courtroom. One woman covered her ears. Parents sent children out to the lawn—where they could hear the loudspeakers.

Darrow asked, "Well, did he tell you anything else that was wicked?"

"Not that I remember of." Glancing toward Scopes, the boy grinned.

Everyone, including Bryan, chuckled.

"It has not hurt you any, has it?" Darrow asked, man to man.

"No, sir."

"That's all."

His white shirt rolled up to the elbows, Hays stood, holding the text, and walked toward the boy. "Is there anything in this book that says man is descended from a monkey?"

"Yes, sir."

Hays's voice grew louder. "That man descended from a monkey?"

Howard gulped. "No, sir."

Stewart stood. "It is not in the book about man coming from the same cell that the monkey came from, either."

Howard Morgan stepped down and seventeen-year-old Harry Shelton came forward to be sworn in. Again, Stewart opened the questioning.

Holding *Civic Biology* in his wide hand, he asked the boy if Scopes had taught that text. Eyes on the floor, mouth pulled into a frown, Shelton confirmed that he had.

Stewart called for Darrow to cross-examine.

"Are you a church member?" Darrow asked.

"Yes, sir."

"Do you still belong?"

"Yes, sir."

A blood-chilling scream sounded on the courthouse lawn.

"It's a chimp," someone near a window called out.

Darrow asked the witness, "You didn't leave church when he told you all forms of life began with a single cell?"

"No, sir."

Darrow turned away. "That is all."

Shelton stepped down and F.E. Robinson, the druggist, came forward. Stewart finished his questioning in three minutes and returned to his table. Wallace Haggard leaned forward to speak with the district attorney. Sue Hicks and Bryan joined in.

Judge Raulston called, "If the counsel for the state would stop; they are talking too loud."

Stewart moved away from his team members. "Just conferring with each other."

The judge sent them a baleful look and nodded to Darrow.

Darrow took the biology text and opened it to page 195. He read the entire page, including a table. He verified that Robinson sold the offending book in his drug store, and the hustling druggist stepped down.

With that Stewart rested the prosecution's case.

The defense's first witness, Maynard M. Metcalf, was a portly, balding man who served as chief of biology for the National Research Council. An avowed evolutionist, he was also an active member of the modernistic United Church in Oberlin, Ohio, and a Sunday school teacher.

Wearing rimless glasses and a learned expression, Metcalf took the stand.

Stewart stood. A lock of dark hair fell across his forehead and he brushed it back. He informed Darrow about the Tennessee law that a defendant must testify as the defense's first witness or not at all.

Darrow said, "Your Honor, every word against Scopes is true."

"So, he does not care to go on the stand?" Raulston asked.

"No, what's the use?" He turned his attention to Metcalf and had the scientist give his credentials in great detail, then asked, "Are you an evolutionist?"

"Surely." The man's cherubic face broke into a wide smile.

Darrow paced before the witness chair, hands behind his back. "Do you know any scientific man in the world that is not an evolutionist?"

"We except," Stewart called.

"Sustained."

One elbow over the back of his chair, Stewart grinned, showing white teeth. "Of course, if you want to take a vote . . ."

Darrow's eyebrows raised. "We are talking about scientific things," he archly told him. He looked at Metcalf. "Is it or not accepted by scientific men?"

"Object."

"Sustained."

Hays got heavily to his feet. "Our whole case depends upon proving that evolution is a reasonable scientific theory."

Judge Raulston pursed his lips. "I do not know how you can prove it reasonable by proving what some other person believes."

Darrow continued, "Will you state what evolution is, in regard to the origin of man?"

"We except to that!" Stewart said, rising, "And to everything here that pertains to evolution."

Judge Raulston said, "I will excuse the jury to hear the arguments."

He looked at the jury foreman. "Do not linger in the courthouse yard. I excuse you until nine o'clock in the morning."

The jurors shuffled out at four thirty-five. Tyson watched the judge, wondering how much longer he'd hold court open. The spectators chose this break in the proceedings to stand and stretch, discuss the day's events, and relax a bit.

"Order!" Rice's gavel sounded.

Darrow led Metcalf through an extended definition of evolution.

Ben McKenzie sagged in his chair. Malone rushed over to fan him, fearful of another fainting spell. Wallace Haggard brought a glass of water, and the old warrior revived. He stayed in the courtroom.

Tyson listened carefully to Dr. Metcalf's testimony, but he could understand little of his scientific jargon.

When he mentioned that life existed six hundred million years ago, disbelieving laughter interrupted the testimony. The hour neared five o'clock, and the audience began clearing out.

Passing near Tyson, one man said of Metcalf, "He's about as authoritative as an evening breeze."

At the judge's nod, Rice banged his gavel. "Now, folks, tomorrow there is not going to be anybody let in here to stand, no standing room at all. Go out on the lawn."

Raulston wearily closed the session. Scorching temperatures and fearful responsibility were taking their toll on the judge.

Bryan ambled over to Darrow and handed him a tiny wooden monkey, carved from a peach pit. "A friend gave me this to give to you. It's so pretty, I thought you may like to keep it as a memento of the trial."

"Thank you," Darrow said. "I have one similar to this. I'll send it to you."

Returning to his table, Bryan spoke to his son while he stacked a handful of papers and pulled open his Gladstone bag. Frowning, he pressed his hand inside the case. He set the bag on the floor, stamped inside it with his right shoe to pack it down, then lifted the bag to the table and pressed the new set of papers inside. He snapped the lid shut while Will Jr. continued their conversation, following his father's moves as though nothing unusual had taken place.

Tyson left the final closing of the courtroom to Rice. His head throbbed and his back ached. He needed a cool drink in the worst way.

Heddie was cocked and primed when he reached home. She met him at the kitchen door with a giant spoon in her hand. "Did you hear what that man, that scientist, said today? I heard every word on the radio."

Tyson eased into a chair next to Micky. He was too tired to hear one of Heddie's tirades tonight. "He said a lot of things, Heddie. Which part did you mean?"

"He said science has proven evolution as a fact, they just haven't figured out how it happened." Her chin jutted forward.

"What's your point?"

"A person could say the same about creation, Trent. We know God made the world, we just don't know how."

Vic joined them. He picked up two sugar cookies from a platter on the table. "That puts us all on level ground, don't it?" he asked, smiling. He did a lot of smiling lately. "No one was there to see the first evolutionary blob or hear God's first word, either. Arguing about it isn't gonna prove anything."

"I wonder why Darrow didn't put Scopes on the stand," Tyson said, reaching for another cookie.

"I know that one." Micky spoke up for the first time. "He told us boys that he wouldn't be testifying. Darrow's afraid he doesn't know enough about evolution to talk much about it."

"You don't say." Vic's eyebrows reached for his hairline.

"Care for a game of Mah-Jongg, Pa?" Tyson asked, changing the subject on purpose. "I'd like to kick off my shoes and forget about how the world began. This business is making my head spin."

"I'll set up the game," his father said. "Help yourself to a couple of Heddie's cookies. They'll put life into you for sure."

Tyson filled a glass with water from a bucket on the counter. He drank it and filled it again.

Over the game in their sitting room, Vic continued rambling about the creation-evolution controversy, but Tyson listened with only half an ear. He was trying to figure out why Bella had left Dayton. Why hadn't she opened the door to him? Surely a mother wouldn't endanger her daughter's life by encouraging an abortion.

But then, why had she run away?

"What's eating you, son?" Vic asked as he laid down *kong*. "You haven't heard two words I've said."

"It's Dotty Smith."

"The little girl that killed herself?"

"I got the pathology report today. Dotty had an abortion less than a month ago."

Vic whistled under his breath. "There's your motive for suicide. You can shut the folder on that one."

"Not yet." Tyson told him about Bella's disappearance. "I've got Chattanooga PD keeping an eye out for her. That Pierce Arrow should lead them to her like a lighthouse."

"She may have gone to the girl's father. Or she may have wanted company. Surely she has close friends in Chattanooga."

"It just doesn't fit," Tyson insisted, tapping his fingertips on the oak table. "I get itchy when a puzzle doesn't look exactly right."

Vic laughed. "I know the feeling, son. You have my sympathy."

Suddenly, Tyson sent his father a piercing look. "What gives, Pa? You look ten years younger. Make that twenty years."

Vic tried to look sober, but a twinkle peeked out. "You've been too occupied with the trial and Dayton's climbing death rate to notice."

"It's Heddie, isn't it?" Tyson's tone had an accusing flavor.

Vic sent him a don't-get-fresh-with-me look that Tyson hadn't seen for twenty-five years.

Tyson wasn't intimidated. "She bat her baby blues at you?" he asked on impulse. His jaw dropped when his father's cheeks turned pink. "Well, I'll be . . . At your age?"

Vic grinned like a schoolboy. "A man's not dead just because he has six or seven decades under his belt."

"Heddie! Of all people." He was talking to himself, but Vic heard him.

"She's a fine woman, Trent. Caring, honest, hard-working. With a fiery wit . . ."

"And a fiery tongue," Tyson finished. "She uses it on me religiously."

Vic chuckled, then leaned forward, serious again. "Keep this between us, will you? I haven't told her yet, and I don't want Nessa stealing my thunder."

"Will do." Tyson shook his head. "And I thought *I* had troubles.

Chapter Twenty-Five

Thursday morning, the crowded courtroom rumbled with the excitement of an Olympic event.

At the defense table, chain-smoking Scopes sat between blue-coated Dudley Malone and Arthur Hays, whose knotted black curls looked much like Tyson's.

Wearing purple suspenders over his white shirt, Darrow had his elbow cocked over the back of his chair while he chatted with Quin Ryan and H.L. Mencken at the press table beside him. Ruby and Doris had chosen cooler regions and the radio today instead of sweltering with their husbands. At fifteen 'til nine, the temperature passed ninety.

On the prosecution's side, William Jennings Bryan sat erect in his collarless shirt, eyes darting across the crowd as he spoke to his son.

Will Jr. held a handkerchief over his mouth to cough. He looked pale. Before him lay several law books in a neat stack and a brief that he kept shuffling and glancing through.

In shirt sleeves and a bow tie, District Attorney General Tom Stewart sat near the end of the table where he could move out easily.

The Hicks boys and Gordon McKenzie arrived at the last minute, holding their coats and straw skimmers, their faces flushed and damp.

Ben McKenzie was standing in the center of the audience, joking with reporters when Judge Raulston strode in. The former attorney general broke it off with an upraised hand and edged between bodies to his chair at the front.

Kelso Rice banged the gavel and the games began.

After some initial haggling between attorneys about expert testimony, slim William Bryan Jr. opened the session with his prepared statement on the topic. His hoarse throat made speaking an effort. "This expert testimony determines whether we will try the case upon the indictment or whether it will be a debate about evolution," he said, stepping closer to the bench, papers in hand.

"If the court please, the only issue this jury has to pass upon is whether or not John Scopes violated the law. This cannot be the subject of expert testimony." Bryan Jr. spoke directly to the judge. "To permit an expert to testify on this issue would be to substitute trial by experts for trial by jury, and to announce to the world Your Honor's belief that this jury is too stupid to determine a simple question of fact."

Hays jumped to his feet. "First our opponents object to the jury hearing the law; now they object to the jury hearing the facts. All the scientists in the country are on one side of the question. They are not here to give opinions; they are here to state facts."

Hays stepped around the table and into the sanctum, intent on Judge Raulston. "Your Honor, this is a serious thing. The eyes of the world are upon you here. This is not a case where the sole issue is whether or not John Scopes taught evolution."

Puckering his lips and touching his bow tie, Herbert Hicks took the floor. "The gentlemen of the defense remind me of my experience as a gun pointer in the navy trying to fire upon a submarine. You will see the periscope here at one place, and it will go down and in another moment it will be here and in another moment it will be there."

Hicks's voice rose. "Evolution is unproven. An eminent scientist, Bateson accepts evolution because he cannot find any better theory."

Darrow demanded, "When did he say that?"

"In his speech at Toronto."

Raulston stared at Darrow. "Address any objection to the court, gentlemen."

Hicks continued with several legal examples of why expert testimony should be excluded, then said, "We do not want to make this a college."

Tyson glanced at Darrow, who didn't want the courtroom to be a meeting house. Now Hicks didn't want it to be a school. When were they going to get down to the real issue of whether Scopes was guilty of teaching evolution or not?

Tyson shifted his feet and wished for an icy root beer float.

Ben McKenzie pushed back his chair with a loud scraping sound. "Your Honor has held that the Butler Act was reasonable. That leaves nothing to determine except the guilt or innocence of the defendant."

Herb Hicks sat down and Ben stepped forward. "They want to put words into God's mouth and say that he issued some sort of soft dish rag and put it in the ocean and said, 'Old boy, if you wait about six thousand years I'll make something out of you.'"

Loud laughter made him grin at the audience. He gestured toward the defense table. "And they tell me there's nothing vague about that."

Hays stood to ask McKenzie a question. The old campaigner cut him off, demanding, "Do you believe in the story of divine creation?"

Hays stiffened. "That is none of your business."

"Then don't ask me any more impertinent questions."

Judge Raulston stared at Hays. "I don't think Colonel Hays's answer to General McKenzie was courteous."

Hays's bony face turned red. "That's so. Instead, I will say it doesn't concern General McKenzie."

McKenzie's manner was slightly mocking when he nodded. "I have as little concern about where you came from or where you're going as any man I've ever met."

Hays turned toward the bench. "Now may I ask for an apology, Your Honor?"

"Yes, sir."

"I beg your pardon," McKenzie said, shortly.

It was Hays's turn to bow. "It's like old sweethearts made up."

Chuckles came from the audience. Kelso Rice glanced toward Tyson. His face remained still, but his eyes laughed.

Gordon McKenzie asked for the noon adjournment so that more fans could be installed. Though it was only eleven o'clock, Judge Raulston agreed. Darrow objected to the early dismissal but the judge ignored his arguments.

Folks in the audience opened lunch bags and jars of tepid water. No one would leave his chair, certain he would lose it if he did.

Tyson left the spectators to sweat it out with two Chattanooga boys watching them. He set off for home. The smell of roast chicken met him at the door.

Vic paused his serving when he saw Tyson. "You heard the scuttlebutt?" Vic asked.

"What?" Tyson reached for a plate in his father's hand.

"Bryan's speaking after lunch."

Tyson lifted a chicken sandwich. "So that's what Raulston's up to. I was wondering when Bryan would get around to it."

"If you think the courtroom was jammed before, you ain't seen nothing yet," Vic said.

Tyson rushed back to the center of activity and saw Elmer Buntley standing on the sidewalk near a busy hot dog stand. He was sipping at a bottle of orange soda.

Elmer watched Tyson's progress toward him without moving a muscle. Without his coat, the old-timer looked like a plucked chicken. Smelled like one, too.

"Afternoon, Deputy," he said. "You want to talk to me?"

"I have a question for you, Buntley." Tyson kept his voice casual.

"Did you know Bella's daughter, Dotty?"

Elmer shook his head, sadly. "It seems like I'm jinxed, Deputy. Every time I make friends with someone, they end up dead."

Buntley ticked off a list by making a fist and stretching out a finger for each name. "First, Miss Ida, then Sammy. Then that girl of Miz Mullins. Now that cute little girl of Bella's." His rheumy eyes stared at Tyson. "I can't figure it."

Tyson moved back to the main topic. "How well did you know Dotty?"

"She used to come out mornings sometimes and help me pull weeds around the shrubbery. When she and her mother first came to Dayton she was always laughing and saying how glad she was to be away from the city. Then she got sick. She was never the same after that. Stayed in the house most of the time. I hardly ever saw her."

"Did you see her last week?"

Elmer scrunched his features and looked at the cloudless sky. His face looked like a balled-up fist. "On Wednesday I saw her sitting by the window that opens onto the porch. I stepped up on the porch and told the little girl how I was missing her help. I gave her a couple-a springs of mint and told her to make herself some tea."

"Did she ever mention a boyfriend in Chattanooga?"

"Not to me, she didn't."

"Did she mention going to see a doctor?"

"Nope."

Tyson moved closer. "This is important, Elmer, so think carefully. Did she and her mother make a trip to Chattanooga during the past four weeks?"

Buntley watched a monkey turning somersaults on the lawn.

Tyson was about to repeat the question when the gardener said, "Come to think of it, I believe they went away shortly before Dotty got sick."

Tyson made a note. "Thanks, Elmer. If you think of anything else, let me know, will you?" Tyson pushed the notebook back into his pocket and left Buntley to his warm soda.

Tyson was almost late getting back to the courtroom. He quickstepped up the stairs and took his place. Standing beside him, Dr. St. Clair leaned close to whisper, "I'll probably have to leave early, but I canceled my appointments this afternoon."

Tyson nodded and drew away as the gavel thumped.

The judge opened the session. "This floor is burdened with great weight. I do not know how well it is supported, so I suggest you be as quiet as you can." He shuffled papers and looked over his glasses at Tom Stewart. "I believe Mr. Bryan will speak next for the state."

William Jennings Bryan took center stage like an apostle facing a tribunal. "The principal attorney for the defense," he glanced at Darrow, "has often suggested that I am responsible for this case. I have been credited with the leadership of ignorance and bigotry which he thinks inspired this case."

Bryan's hand swept toward John Scopes. "Mr. Scopes violated the law. That is the evidence. This is not the place to prove that the law should never have been passed." He scanned the audience and camera lights flashed.

Ignoring photographers, Bryan continued, "They passed a law up in New York repealing prohibition. Suppose the people of Tennessee sent attorneys up there to fight that law, oppose it after it was passed, and had experts to testify how good prohibition is to New York and the nation."

He stepped toward the judge. "Your Honor, it isn't proper to bring experts in here to defeat the purpose of Tennesseans by trying to show that evolution is a beautiful thing."

His voice swelled to the rafters. "In this state, they cannot teach the Bible in school. They can only teach things that declare it to be a lie, according to the defense." His dark eyes swept across Darrow and Malone, who leaned back in their chairs and returned his stare.

Bryan went on. "There are so many kinds of evolution and so many definitions of evolution that if they made a general statement it would be useless, and if they went into detail it would create controversy."

Loud laughter and applause wafted from the audience. Hands behind his back, Bryan waited. He wasn't smiling.

"The Christian believes that man came from above, but the evolutionist believes he must have come from below." Again, laughter made him pause. "And that is from a lower order of animals."

He grinned. "Talk about putting Daniel in the lions' den!"

His features grew solemn and intense. "It wasn't until Darwin's explanations became a laughingstock that scientists began to distinguish between Darwinism and evolution. Evolutionists have discarded Darwin's idea of natural selection. But, my friends, they still teach his doctrines." He held high a thick volume.

"What is that book, Mr. Bryan?" Malone asked.

"*The Descent of Man* by Charles Darwin." Bryan read a lengthy passage concerning the progress of one life form into another. He closed the book with a thump. "The legislature paid evolution a higher honor than it deserves. Evolution is not a theory, but a hypothesis. Darwin himself said it was strange that with two or three million species they had not found one that they could trace to another."

He smiled at Herbert Hicks and took a step toward him. "About three years ago, Bateson of London come to Toronto to the American Academy for the Advancement of Science—"

He swiveled his head toward the defense table, "Brace yourselves, gentlemen. I am a member of the American Academy for the Advancement of Science." He turned back toward the center of the sanctum, his voice swelling.

"Bateson said that every effort to show the origin of species had failed—everyone. Never have they traced one single species to any other. That is why this so-called expert, Dr. Metcalf, stated that while the fact of evolution is established, the various theories of how it happened have failed. Today there is not a scientist in all the world who can trace one single species to any other, and yet they call us ignoramuses and bigots because we do not throw away our Bible."

Pacing, he continued. "I supposed Dr. Metcalf shamed them all by his number of degrees." He turned toward the audience. "He did not shame me. I have more than he has."

He whirled, pinning the defense under his gaze. "Did he tell you where life began? Not a word about it. No, they say life is a mystery that nobody can explain."

Judge Raulston leaned forward over the bench. "Mr. Bryan, if God didn't create that first cell then evolution cannot be reconciled with the Bible?"

"Of course not."

Bryan's words blasted across the courtroom, onto the courthouse lawn, and through microphones to radios across the nation and the world.

"A doctrine that refutes not only their belief in God but their belief in a Savior and heaven, takes from them every moral standard in the Bible. This doctrine gave us Nietzsche, the only great author who tried to carry evolution to its logical conclusion."

He turned toward the defense. "In the Loeb and Leopold case, Mr. Darrow pled that because Leopold adopted Nietzsche's philosophy of the superman, he was not responsible for the taking of human life. That distinguished man said that the teachings of Nietzsche made Leopold a murderer."

"Your Honor, I object." Darrow cried. "Nietzsche never taught that."

Bryan lifted a sheaf of papers from the prosecution table. "I will read you what you said in that speech."

"I want to object," Darrow said, "to injecting any other case into this proceeding."

Bryan stepped toward him, chin high. "I have never in my life misquoted a man intentionally."

Darrow stood. "I say you did."

Licking his lips, Bryan found a page. "Here it is, page eighty-four." He glanced around. "These are on sale here in town. Anybody can get it for fifty cents."

Malone called, "I'll pay a dollar fifty for yours."

Hoots and laughter broke the tension.

Bryan waited until the noise quieted then read Darrow's argument. "'Is there any blame attached because somebody took Nietzsche's philosophy seriously and fashioned his life on it? There is no question in this case but that it is true. Then who is to blame? The publishers of the world are more to blame than Leopold. Your Honor, it is hardly fair to hang a nineteen-year-old boy for the philosophy he learned at the university.'"

Darrow stretched out his hand. "Will you let me see that?"

"Oh, yes, but let me have it back."

Darrow's mouth formed a curved-down smile. "I'll give you a new one, autographed for you."

Bryan continued his speech. Darrow interrupted to again ask that the Loeb-Leopold case be put out of the record.

Instead of replying, Raulston urged Bryan to finish up.

Bryan faced the crowd. "When it comes to Bible experts, every member of the jury is as good an expert as anyone they could bring. The beauty of the Word of God is, it does not take an expert to understand it."

Wide, swelling applause. "Amen!" several shouted.

Darrow turned around and asked Hays, "Can it be possible that this trial is taking place in the twentieth century?"

Raulston called a brief recess, and Dr. St. Clair slipped out.

When court reconvened, Darrow asked permission to read the paragraph following the one Bryan had quoted from the Loeb-Leopold case.

A loud crash behind the judge's bench brought him up short.

"Just a picture machine fallen over," Kelso said.

As Darrow sat down, Malone stood. He slowly and deliberately unbuttoned his coat and took it off. He folded it neatly and laid it on the defense table. Every eye in the silent room stayed upon him.

Leaning against the defense table, he said, "I would like to ask the court if there was any evidence of moral deterioration in those school boys due to the course of biology which Professor Scopes taught them." He drew himself up to full height. "I think the prosecution should introduce at least one person whose morals have been affected by the teaching of this theory."

Clearing his throat, Tyson remembered the Leopold murder case Bryan had just mentioned.

Malone strode to the center of the inner sanctum and continued passionately, "We say, keep your Bible. Keep it as your consolation, keep it as your guide; but keep it where it belongs, in the world of your own conscience." He raised his fist, his voice booming. "Is the church the only source of morality in this country?"

Lowering his hand and his voice, he said, "We have no fears about the young people of America. They are a pretty smart generation, probably much wiser than their elders. We just had a war with the Kaiser in Germany, with twenty million dead. Civilization is not so proud of the work of the adults. For God's sake, let the children have their minds kept open."

The hatchet-faced court reporter became so caught up in Malone's oratory, he forgot to take notes.

Malone's voice swelled with every word. "There is never a duel with the truth. The truth always wins and we are not afraid of it. The truth does not need the force of the government or Mr. Bryan. The truth is imperishable, eternal, and immortal."

As he built to a crescendo, Malone's face grew red. He shouted, "We feel we stand with progress. We feel we stand with science. We feel we stand with intelligence. We feel we stand with fundamental freedom in America. Where is fear? We defy it!"

The crowd went wild. Lunging to their feet, clapping and shouting people surged forward to shake Malone's hand.

Overcome with emotion, Kelso pounded the recorder's table with his nightstick. Tyson rushed to him, thinking he needed help to quiet the demonstration.

Kelso shouted at him, "I'm not trying to restore order. I'm cheering!"

The table top split under his enthusiasm.

H.L. Mencken cried out, "Tennessee only needs fifteen minutes of free speech to become educated." He strode forward, wiping a handkerchief across his face. "Dudley," he said, pumping his friend's hand, "that was the loudest speech I ever heard."

Ten minutes later men and women returned to their seats and order slowly returned to the courtroom.

After Judge Raulston asked a few questions of Darrow and Malone, Stewart stood to finish the argument.

He left his papers on the table and paced toward the bench. "When science strikes upon that which man's eternal hope is founded, then I say the foundation of man's civilization is about to crumble. I ask Your Honor respectfully and earnestly to disallow the admission of this testimony because I believe under the law of Tennessee it is absolutely inadmissible."

The applause continued until Judge Raulston rapped the gavel and adjourned the session.

The room cleared until only three men remained: Bryan, Malone, and Scopes. All kept their seats. Will Bryan rocked in a rocking chair someone had provided for him. He fanned himself, looking at the floor before him, his expression solemn.

Finally, he spoke aloud without moving his head, "Dudley, that was the greatest speech I have ever heard!"

"Thank you, Mr. Bryan," Malone answered. "I'm sorry it was I who had to make it." He stood, shook Bryan's hand, and walked out. The others followed him.

Tyson helped Kelso carry the broken table to a storage room and find a replacement. He reached the lawn at quarter to five.

Looking south on Market Street, he spotted Nessa with Micky. Lori rode on the boy's shoulders. Smiling happily, the child waved at him. Tyson raised his hand to wave back.

He sucked in a quick breath as Micky's foot skidded on the sidewalk. Lori fell headlong into the street. Her scream pierced the air, and Tyson raced toward her.

CHAPTER Twenty-Six

Nessa knelt on the hot macadam holding sobbing Lori when Tyson reached them. White to the lips, Nessa murmured to him, "It's her good arm."

Tyson slipped gentle hands under his wailing, broken little Chicky. "Let's get you to Dr. St. Clair, honey. He'll fix you up good as new."

Vic and Heddie trotted down the sidewalk toward them. Stammering, Micky told them what happened.

With Nessa trotting by his side, Tyson fell into a long-legged stride down Market Street. Crowds split before him like the Red Sea before Moses. Conversations stopped, but plinking organ grinder music went on.

Tyson suddenly stopped in front of the doctor's house. He remembered the morning he had brought Sammy here with a broken leg. A nameless dread filled him, choking him.

"What is it?" Nessa asked. "You look like you just saw a ghost."

"Maybe I did." He gazed down at his tear-smudged daughter, then at Nessa. "I felt something evil."

She stared at him like he'd lost his senses. "C'mon, we've got to get her to the doctor."

Essie Caldwell stepped out of St. Clair's office with a fat book under her arm.

Holding Lori close to his heart, Tyson said, "I don't know what's going on in this town, but I'm going to find out if it's the last thing I do."

Essie met them at the porch steps. "What on earth happened?" she asked.

"She fell," Tyson said, shortly.

"Poor dear," Essie patted Lori's leg. "Aunt Essie will come by and bring you a lollipop tomorrow, dear." She smiled encouragingly at Nessa. "Little ones are always getting into scrapes. It's part of growing up." She trotted away.

Nessa held the door open for father and daughter.

In the waiting room, Dr. St. Clair took one look at Lori's arm and said, "Bring her into my examining room."

Tyson glanced at Nessa. "Maybe you'd best wait here," he murmured.

Biting her bottom lip, she nodded.

Steeling himself for the task ahead, Tyson carried Lori in and lay her on a narrow cot.

Sadie came toward them, a white bib apron over her dark dress.

"Lori, honey, what happened?" She smoothed the child's dress and touched her cheek while Tyson retold the story.

Lori's wails intensified when she saw the syringe.

"This will take away the pain." St. Clair said, kindly. "Then I'll put a bandage on it for you."

The next half hour aged Tyson by ten years. Letting out a deep silent sigh, he carried the dozing, sniffling child into the waiting room where Micky, Vic, and Heddie waited with Nessa.

Sadie came out, too. "Hello, Heddie, Vic," she cooed. "I need to invite you folks over for pie sometime."

Vic replied, "If it's apple or peach pie, you've got a date."

Sadie beamed at him.

Tyson handed Lori to Vic. "I'll get the car and drive you all home." He crossed the room to the door.

When Lizzy reached their block Tyson saw Sheriff Harris standing on the corner of Fourth and Market. Beside him George Rappelyea, arms crossed, leaned on his gleaming black Studebaker.

"Howdy, Trent," Harris said when Tyson braked the car beside him. "Meet Dayton's master of speed. Twenty miles an hour in a twelve-miles-per-hour zone. This is his third ticket since the trial started."

"Aw, you're giving me the business, Sheriff," Rappelyea protested. "I'm the best driver in Dayton."

Harris's pen scratched on his ticket pad.

Tyson shook his head and continued to his own driveway.

Minutes later, he laid Lori on his bed and slipped off her shoes. Nessa eased off the child's dress and pulled the quilt out from under her tiny form, so she'd be cooler on the sheet.

The child mumbled, hiccupped, and slept on, with her cast propped on a pillow. The damp halo of brown hair about her face made her look like a cherub.

Side by side, Tyson and Nessa watched her for a full minute. He turned, intending to whisper to Nessa, and she walked into his arms. Instinctively, Tyson held her close while she cried, her soft hair against his cheek. When she calmed down, he eased her to the sitting room sofa.

"I feel so guilty," she said, sniffing into her handkerchief. "I shouldn't have let Micky carry her like that."

"It was an accident, Nessa. Don't blame yourself."

"But her good arm! What if it doesn't heal properly?"

"Doc said it was a simple fracture. She'll be good as new in six weeks." He touched her damp cheek. "Please don't cry. I can't stand it."

A movement caught his eye and he glanced up. Micky stood in the doorway, shoulders hunched, staring at the floor.

Tyson came to his feet. "I don't blame you, Micky. I saw what happened, and it was an accident."

The boy took one step inside. "I should have been watching closer. Somebody dropped an ice cream cone, and I slipped on it."

Lori started crying. Tyson darted to her side. Nessa and Micky followed.

"Does it hurt, Chicky?" Tyson smoothed the hair from her forehead.

When she nodded, he glanced at Nessa, "Would you crush half a pill for her? Doc gave me this." He pulled a brown envelope from his shirt pocket and handed it to her. She hurried away, her shoes tapping on the wooden floor.

Tyson gathered Lori into his arms and moved to the rocking chair a short distance from the bed. She snuggled close to his chest, her sniffles muffled in the cotton broadcloth covering his chest.

Soon, Nessa arrived with a spoonful of strawberry jam mixed with white powder. In her other hand was a glass of water.

"Here, take this, Chicky," Tyson said.

Lori shook her head, hiding her face.

"Lori," Tyson said, firmly, "take the medicine."

With a look of disgust, she slowly turned toward Nessa and opened her mouth a crack. Nessa somehow managed to get the spoon inside. The child gulped water.

Taking the empty glass, Nessa and her brother went out.

In the quiet room with his darling in his arms, Tyson gently rocked and allowed his thoughts to wander. The courtroom… the tragedy-struck Johnson house… Elmer Buntley standing on the sidewalk sipping orange soda. What had Elmer said? "It seems like I'm jinxed, Deputy."

The medicine took effect and Lori relaxed against him. When her breathing deepened, Tyson carried her back to the bed and gently propped her tiny plastered arm on a pillow.

He pulled a sheet of note paper from the desk, picked up a book to rest it on, and returned to the rocker. Putting pencil to foolscap, he made a list.

Ida Johnson, age 72, recluse, tansy

Sammy Buntley, age 57, vagrant, tansy

Anna Joy Mullins, age 15, mentally slow, tansy

Dotty Smith, age 17, student, suicide—2nd try

In another column, he listed the ages together. Then he listed the descriptions. Beside those, he listed the causes of death. Chin on hand, he stared at the sheet until the pencil markings ran together.

When Nessa called him to supper, he folded the page and put it into his pocket with his notebook.

He eased open his drawer for a fresh shirt and draped it over the end of the bed. Struck by an inspiration, he strode to the bathroom, lathered his shaving brush, and applied it to the bristles covering his upper lip. Ten minutes later, he dried his face and returned to his room to dress for supper.

After the meal, Tyson and his father lounged in their sitting room, sipping tea. "Pa, take a look at this, will you?" He handed Vic his list.

The retired policeman read the list, then went back for a closer look.

Tyson leaned toward his father, elbows on his knees. "When Miss Ida died, I knew something was wrong before the lab report came back. Something powerful and evil . . . and hard to pin down."

He took the paper from Vic's outstretched hand. "Then Sammy and Anna Joy died." His voice tightened. "Now that teenage girl."

Vic shook his head. "That one's not related to the rest. Dotty grew up in the dregs of society. She'd seen more of life than Heddie has."

"I know." Tyson took a deep breath and let it out fast. "I wish I could bury my doubts about Dotty's death. But for some reason, I can't."

Lori cried out. Tyson stuffed the list into his pocket and hurried to her.

Deputy Tyson has to be stopped. His eternal digging and questioning is getting me riled.

The problem is, the man never needs a doctor or a nurse . . . or even a tonic. It's impossible to get to him. But Nessa now. She's a different story. When I saw Nessa McGinty holding the deputy's arm and crying over his hurt little girl, everything began falling into place.

I'll have no problem getting to her. And it will serve her right. I've warned her to stay away from him, but she won't listen. So, she has to go.

I know what I need to do.

Friday morning Tyson left Lori at the boardinghouse in Essie's care when he went to work. With the lunch Room in full swing, both Heddie and Nessa were too busy to sit with a sick child.

Tyson hated to leave her, but she didn't seem to mind. Snuggled in Essie's featherbed lap in the rocking chair, Lori slurped a lollipop and listened to a Cinderella storybook. She didn't look up when he said goodbye. Tyson hoped she'd be that content when Sadie came to sit with her at noon.

Tyson sauntered into the courtroom at two minutes 'til nine on the sixth day of the trial. He dreaded another scorching day filled with photographers and pressmen and puffed-up attorneys.

Judge Raulston opened the day by reading his ruling on scientific testimony. His face flushed and drawn, the judge cleared his throat and read from a paper: "The state has absolutely established the defendant's guilt. No amount of expert testimony can affect the final results."

Reading on, he lifted the top page and started on the second. "It is not within the province of the court to decide which is true: creation or evolution."

The gentlemen around the defense table stared at him with rapt attention, seeking a flaw in his reasoning should the decision turn against them.

Raulston continued, "The non-expert mind can comprehend the simple language, 'descended from a lower order of animals.' Therefore, the court sustains the motion of the attorney general to exclude the expert testimony."

Darrow's face turned purple. He glared at the judge.

Hays spoke out, "We say it is a denial of justice not to permit the defense to make its case."

Stewart leapt to his feet. "I except to his manner. I think it is a reflection upon the Court."

"Well, it don't hurt the Court none." Raulston drawled.

Darrow retorted, "There is no danger of hurting us."

Tom Stewart's eyebrows reached for his hairline. "You are already hurt as much as you can be hurt."

Darrow pierced him with a narrow-eyed stare. "The state of Tennessee don't rule the world yet."

District Attorney Stewart turned toward the bench. "They are entitled to enter on the record what they expect to prove, but they have no right to conduct a long, drawn-out examination and make a farce of Your Honor's opinion." He glanced at Darrow. "How many branches of science have you represented here by witnesses?"

"Six."

Raulston leaned forward, peering over his glasses at Darrow. "You are entitled to have in the record your proof for the appellate court, in case of a conviction here. I meant all the time for you to do it."

Malone spoke up, "I want to ask General Stewart to withdraw his remark about the purpose of the defense being to make a farce of the judge's opinion."

Stewart smiled tightly. "I will be glad to withdraw it. And add to it that it is a known fact that the defense considers this a campaign of education to get before the people their ideas of evolution. This case has been sensationalized by the newspapers and these gentlemen want to take advantage of the opportunity."

"The defense is not engaged in a campaign," Malone countered. "We represent no organization for the purpose of education. If the defense is representing anything, it is merely attempting to meet the campaign of propaganda by a distinguished member of the prosecution." He looked pointedly at Bryan.

Bryan stood. Instead of a collar-less shirt, today he wore a crisp madras and bow tie. "If these witnesses are allowed to testify, I presume they would be subject to cross-examination?"

"They will if they go on the stand," the judge said.

Darrow objected. "They have no more right to cross-examine…"

Judge Raulston looked at him. "Colonel, what is the purpose of cross-examination? Isn't it an effort to ascertain the truth?"

Darrow said, "No. It is an effort to show prejudice."

Boisterous laughter cut him off.

He went on, his voice heated. "Has there been any effort to ascertain the truth in this case?"

Judge Raulston continued, "Courts are a mockery…"

"They are often that, Your Honor," Darrow interjected, "…when they permit cross-examination for the purpose of creating prejudice. If the defense wants to put their proof in the record in the form of affidavits, of course, they can do that. If they put witnesses on the stand and the state desires to cross-examine them. I shall expect them to do so."

"Always expect this court to rule correctly," Raulston said.

"No, sir. We do not." Darrow's mouth set in a hard line.

More laughter.

Darrow shouted, "I do not understand why every request of the prosecution should meet with an endless waste of time, and a bare suggestion of anything that is perfectly competent on our part should be immediately overruled."

"I hope you do not mean to reflect upon the Court?"

Darrow turned away from the bench and headed for the defense table. Under his breath, he said, "Well, Your Honor has the right to hope!"

His face turning red, Judge Raulston followed Darrow's progress across the room. "I have a right to do something else, perhaps."

Darrow waved a hand. "All right, all right."

A nervous quiet settled over the courtroom, a fearful expectancy.

Raulston added, "Regardless of the opinion of counsel, I have no purpose except to be fair." Shortly afterward, court adjourned until Monday morning at nine o'clock.

Instead of rushing outside, the press carefully packed up papers, microphones, and cameras. Since the judge had blocked the experts from testifying, they thought the trial was over. Tired of heat, crowds, and legal jargon, they were eager to go home.

Tyson stepped into the sunshine like a man released from prison. The spectators must have had the same idea because the yard was clearing as fast as a baseball stadium in the bottom of the ninth with the score at zero to ten.

Tyson strolled to the sheriff's office, taking his time, enjoying the shade of the spreading trees. When Tyson stepped inside the building, Harris was dismissing the police officers from Chattanooga.

"I'll need Rice, Stevens, and Dennis back here at nine o'clock Monday morning," he said. "To the rest, I thank you for your help."

He glanced at Tyson. "I'm hanging around town this afternoon. There's another plot afoot to tar and feather Mencken."

Tyson shook his head. "I wish that wise guy would get out of Dayton." He chuckled. "Or maybe it would be best if he stayed around and took his medicine." The phone jangled, and he grabbed it.

"Tyson?" a husky voice said. "This is Crabill. We've got Bella Smith."

"At the station?"

"Right here in front of me."

At the door, Kelso Rice turned to send Tyson a thumbs-up sign. "See you in court Monday."

"Hold on a minute, Crabill," Tyson said. He turned toward Kelso. "Can you give me a lift to Chattanooga?"

"Sure. I'll tell the fellows to wait." The big Irishman ducked out the door.

Tyson spoke into the phone. "I'm coming down with your boys. Court's adjourned until Monday and they're on their way home."

"I'll see you in an hour," Jim said and hung up.

Tyson clicked the armature on the phone. "Mabel, get me my house, will you?" A moment later, he told Nessa of his plans, asked about Lori, and slid the earpiece into place.

Harris was taking down the cordon ropes across Market Street as the police car backed out of the parking lot. They shot down Third, then Market, pausing at the other end to take down the ropes at Main and pass through. Wind sailing past their ears, the men in the car joked like college boys on holiday.

Tyson drew in a belly full of fresh air and shook his muscles loose. The day had turned out better than he'd expected.

The desk sergeant did a double take when Tyson walked in. Tyson nodded to him briefly and kept walking. The station house smelled of cigar smoke and stale sweat. A hundred memories hit Tyson with every step.

"Howdy, pard!" Big and clumsy, Jim Crabill thumped his shoulder and grabbed his hand. "She's in number two." Tyson nodded.

He walked into the interrogation room alone to find Bella huddled at a bare table in a bare room. She looked at him with dull eyes that held no sign she recognized him.

"Hello, Bella," he said, as though on a social call. "I've been looking for you."

"Who hasn't." Her lips had a bitter slant. She knotted her hands and stared at them.

He scraped a chair away from the table and sat. "Why didn't you answer the door when I came by last Tuesday?"

"I didn't know you were there."

He studied her haggard face. "You left town right after that."

"Is that a crime?" A spark of defensive temper showed. "What's going on, Deputy? I didn't do anything this time."

He leaned forward, eye to eye. "Dotty had an abortion. I think you knew about it."

Bella's head jerked up—eyes wide, face sagging. Fat tears formed at the corners of her eyes. Her head lowered to the table, and deep heaving sobs wracked her body.

He dug in his pocket for a handkerchief and gave it to her. Was this an act?

Hands trembling, she finally sat up to mop her face. Her lower lip quivered when she spoke. "She had a boyfriend, a runner from the laundry, before we came to Dayton. But they broke it off. She seemed so happy at the new house, that I never dreamed . . ."

"Who did the abortion, Bella? Surely she didn't do it herself."

"I don't know." More tears. She tilted her head back. "Honest to God, Deputy. I don't know."

Tyson went to the door and spoke to an officer at the desk outside. In a moment, Tyson returned with a glass of water. He set it in front of Bella and waited for her to drink.

"Let's go over that period of time. Starting with your trip to Chattanooga a month ago."

She drew in a shaky breath, plucking at the handkerchief before her on the table. "We came to town to do some shopping. I wanted to get a new carpet for the living room."

Step by step, they went through it. Two hours and ten pages of notes later, they reached the time of Dotty's illness.

"A month before I went to jail, I left Dotty overnight at a friend's house in Chattanooga."

"That was on, what date?"

"June eighteenth."

He waited while she blew her nose.

"Dotty was still in bed at noon when I came to get her. She said she felt sick. Her stomach hurt. I gave her some bicarbonate, waited an hour, then drove her home. She lay in the back seat of the car the whole way."

Bella sniffed and dabbed at her face. "That's when it happened, isn't it?"

Tyson didn't answer.

She went on. "Dotty moped around the house for the next three weeks. I blamed it on the heat. I told myself it was teenage moodiness. I wondered if she missed her boyfriend after all."

Suddenly she reached out and grabbed Tyson's sleeve. "I didn't know what she did, Deputy. You have to believe me. I'd never allow my daughter to risk her life like that." A dry sob shook her frame.

Tyson put away his pencil. "The medical examiner has released Dotty's body. You can begin making funeral arrangements."

He paused. "Do you need help getting home? Is there someone I can call?"

She handed him his soggy handkerchief. "I'll get a hotel here tonight. I want to see about Dotty before I go."

Tyson said goodbye and hit the street, whistling for an open taxi. "Take me to the train station," he told the black cabby and settled into the back seat.

His instincts told him to believe Bella. The city offered many opportunities for an abortion. Who would do that kind of dirty work in Dayton?

CHAPTER
Twenty-Seven

The next morning, Tyson discussed that question with his father over a second cup of coffee in the kitchen. The boardinghouse had the quiet stillness of a seacoast town after a hurricane. All the trial boarders but Paul Henderson had checked out. Heddie and Nessa were cleaning vacant rooms in the upper regions.

"Dotty Smith had to have transportation to get an abortion," Vic said. "Are there any quacks living in South Dayton?"

Tyson shook his head. "I asked Harris and he said, it was the first abortion he'd ever heard of in Dayton."

"Would he know one if he fell over it?"

"You've got me there, Pa."

Tyson stretched back in his chair. It felt good to be off duty in a quiet town.

"You still have that list you made out?" Vic asked. "I'd like to take another gander at it."

Tyson pulled it out of his pocket and handed it over as the back door burst open and Micky strode in carrying a basket of string beans. He set it on the table and hurried back outside.

Vic glanced up from the paper. "You know what? None of these people had a job."

Tyson smirked. "Neither do you, Pa. Does that mean you'll be the next victim?" He sipped coffee. "I'm so tired of this court case I could spit. What does it really matter how we got here? We're here aren't we?"

Vic studied him a moment before answering. "Son, if there's a Creator, the Bible is true. If the Bible is true, there's a righteous God to answer to." He rubbed his white whiskers. "You'd never get Darrow's crowd to admit it though. That fellow Bateson is one brave man." He picked up his coffee cup. "I'm waiting to hear Bryan's closing statement. He's been mighty quiet in the courtroom up to now."

Tyson massaged his face. "I'm going up to my room to read a while. I feel like that soft dishrag Ben McKenzie was talking about."

"Enjoy your day off. You earned it." Vic handed over the list, and Tyson shambled down the hall.

Heddie met him at the top of the stairs, a folded newspaper in her hands. "Look what I found in one of the rooms."

Tyson caught a glimpse of the heading, "Monkey Trial."

"Listen to this. It's H.L. Mencken talking about William Jennings Bryan." She read, "'This old buzzard, having failed to raise the mob against its rulers, now prepares to raise it against its teachers. He can never be the peasants' President, but there is still a chance to be the peasants' Pope. One somehow pities him, despite his so palpable imbecilities. It is a tragedy, indeed, to begin life as a hero and to end it as a buffoon.'"

She turned the folded page over and read on, "'But let no one, laughing at him, underestimate the magic that lies beneath his black, malignant eye.'"

She looked up, furious. "How dare he!"

"No wonder the locals are laying for him." Tyson stretched out his hand. "Mind if I read the rest of that?"

"Go ahead. Burn it when you're through." She brushed her hands on her apron as though to clean them from touching something filthy, and marched back to her work.

With a feeling of intense relief, Tyson stretched out on the quilt and opened the Baltimore *Evening Sun*. Lori snoozed on her trundle bed with a gentle smile on her face. A few minutes later, her daddy was snoozing, too.

When blighted by disease, the plant may not show the rottenness at its core, but if left to stand it will spread its corruption to its neighbors.

Though lovely, it, too, must go.

That afternoon Micky refereed the baseball game alone. Tyson wanted to spend the afternoon with his daughter, and she wasn't up to a jaunt in the hot sun just yet. He put together two puzzles while she watched and gave instructions.

He read four story books to her and gave her sips of warm tea. Dayton's ice supply had run out, and the shipment from Chattanooga hadn't arrived yet.

That evening he carried a tray upstairs and fed Lori her supper. Nessa came in to chat with her after the meal. By the time Dr. St. Clair arrived for a chess game, Tyson was having second thoughts about their chess match. He'd rather retire early.

"Good evening, Trent," St. Clair said, slipping off his hat. He carried his black bag. "You seem tired."

"That's only because I am." Tyson led the way upstairs to his sitting room. When they arrived, Nessa was bending over a crying Lori, trying to calm her.

"Good evening, Nessa," Dr. St. Clair said. "Looks like I'm right on time."

Nessa's head jerked around. "Oh, Dr. St. Clair! You startled me!" She hugged herself. "I'm a little nervous these days."

"Is Lori having trouble tonight?"

The child's sobs subsided when she saw the doctor. She watched him, her eyes round.

Moving towards her, St. Clair said fondly, "Hello, Lori. I'm not going to do anything to your arm tonight. I just want to know if it still hurts."

Lori's hair lay matted against her damp cheeks. She said, whimpering, "I bumped it on the edge of the bed."

"I gave her the last pain tablet last night," Tyson said.

Dr. St. Clair opened his bag and drew out a small paper envelope.

"Here are a few more." He handed Tyson the packet. "Only give her one when she really needs it."

He smiled at Lori and touched her hair. "I prescribe a cool washcloth on your face and then a nice sleep. Only a few more days and the pain will be over. You'll be better than new."

Nessa hurried downstairs to crush up a pill and mix it with jam.

When she returned, Lori swallowed her medicine and reached out for Nessa to rock her. Tyson and Dr. St. Clair moved to their game.

On the sofa, the doctor asked, "Where's Vic tonight? I thought we might play another round of Mah-Jongg."

"He and Heddie are snapping beans out back under the porch light."

"Sadie wouldn't like that," he said dryly.

"Don't tell me she has a case on Pa, too." Tyson's eyebrows drew together.

"Sure as you're living." He grunted. "I've come to dislike your father heartily, Trent. I have to live with him day and night."

Tyson chuckled. "I never saw so many old-age romances in my life."

"Just because you're old doesn't mean you get cold," St. Clair said, grinning slyly.

Tyson moved a wooden knight. "I have a few questions for you."

"I'm not sure I can answer, but fire away."

"Would abortion fit the eugenics philosophy?"

"Unwanted children are unfed and unloved." An intense gleam sparked in the doctor's eye. "They wallow in the muck while they're small and join the offscouring of society while they're adults. It would be a mercy to both them and society if they were never born." He placed a knight at the center of the board.

"Alexander Hamilton was illegitimate."

"A rare exception, my friend, and hardly worth mentioning."

"Dr. St. Clair," Micky called up the stairs. "Telephone!"

Heaving a deep sigh, the doctor trudged to the door. In less than a minute he was back, a distraught look on his face. His tense words put an icy chill down Tyson's spine.

"It's Jody Riesbeck." He grabbed his bag. "I've got to get over there right away."

"I'll come along." Pausing to speak to Nessa in the bedroom, he glanced at sleeping Lori and caught up to the doctor on the front steps.

"I'm going to walk over," St. Clair told him. "It's only three doors down. By the time I start the car and back out your driveway, I could be there already."

Pale and trembling, chubby Jason Riesbeck was waiting on his porch when they arrived. The yellow bulb over his head formed dark shadows on his face.

Forgetting a greeting, he grabbed the doctor's sleeve. "I'm afraid it's too late, Doc."

St. Clair pushed past him to rush into the house. Belinda's shrill sobs led them to the bedroom.

"Jody! Open your eyes!" She was shaking the child's shoulders.

Jody's head lolled from side to side.

St. Clair grabbed Belinda from behind and pulled her away.

"Let me see her. Maybe I can do something."

Shrieking and wailing, Belinda threw herself at Jason and fell to her knees before him. Half-carrying her, he took her out of the room.

Tyson watched the doctor lift Jody's eyelids and touch her milky neck. St. Clair's shoulders drooped. "She's gone." He sank to the chair beside the bed and covered his eyes with one hand.

Tyson looked at Jody. The little girl looked like a wax doll, so beautiful with a lilting nose and cornsilk hair. Hands shaking, he swallowed hard and forced himself to think professionally. "How sick was she, Doc?"

"Her heart must have given out." Standing, he said, "I'd best give Belinda a sedative," and trudged out.

Tyson thought back to Belinda's visit last week. He didn't know much about medicine, but it didn't seem right for a child to gain strength, then just up and die.

He sat with Jody for twenty minutes, his mind working, his heart breaking. Dr. St. Clair came to the open bedroom door. "I just called Ketcher. Belinda's starting to feel the effects of the sedative, so Jason's taking her to her room. I think we can go now."

"I'll stay a while, Doc." His own words seemed far away. "Jason should have someone with him."

"He called his mother while I was seeing to Belinda."

"Thanks for everything, Doc."

"What did I do? There's nothing worse than helplessness, Trent. Especially for a man in my profession." With that, he plodded to the door and let himself out.

Tyson found Jason in the hall, standing uncertainly as though he didn't know where to go next. His hand traced a pink rose on the wallpaper. Tears coursed down his cheeks.

"Can I get you something, old man?"

"What?" He turned dazed eyes toward Tyson.

"Let's sit down." Tyson took his arm and started him gently toward the living room. On the floor beside the coffee table lay a brown leather notebook. Tyson picked it up.

"St. Clair" gleamed in gold on the cover. Tyson flipped it open. Dr. St. Clair's appointment book must have fallen out of his bag while he prepared Belinda's hypo.

Tyson tapped the book against his knee while he talked to Jason, who slumped on the sofa, eyes closed, his head leaning against the soft back.

"If you can pull yourself together, Jason," Tyson said in a moment,

"I need to ask you some questions."

Visibly trembling now, Jason nodded and sat up. "What is it?"

"I want to know exactly how Jody felt the past few days. Was she weak? Sick?"

"No." He drew in a breath. "That's why this is such a shock. She was doing better. Yesterday she cried to get out of bed and eat at the table with us. She's been sitting up to draw and look at story books."

Tyson moved forward in his chair, looking directly into the man's face. "Jason, please listen to me. I know this is hard on you, but you've got to think about what I'm going to say."

Jason watched Tyson with haunted, faraway eyes.

"I think you ought to have an autopsy done."

He jerked. "What are you talking about?"

"Something about this isn't right. A child doesn't gain strength after an illness and suddenly die."

"Why didn't Dr. St. Clair tell me this?"

"He loved Jody. Maybe he was too overcome to mention it. Or maybe he thought both of you were too shocked to stand anymore."

Jason pressed his eyes shut. "I can't stand the thought of someone cutting . . ."

"Don't you want to put the questions to rest? Don't you owe your daughter that much?"

He sighed, pressed meaty fingers into his knees, and said, "Okay, Deputy. Go ahead."

"Mind if I use your phone?"

Tyson made two calls, then people began arriving. He moved outside to the porch to give friends and family a chance to share their grief. Essie Caldwell and Jenny Mullins arrived just after Jason's mother. Next came Belinda's parents and Kate Bailey, who carried a pot of soup.

When Ketcher arrived, Tyson told him to deliver Jody's body to the train station in time for the southbound to Chattanooga in the morning.

He walked home and checked the kitchen, hoping to find Nessa.

She was washing something at the sink, her back toward him.

He dropped the notebook to the table and she turned, her eyes on his face. "What's happened?"

"It's Jody."

Stark fear stiffened Nessa's features. "Trent!"

"She's gone."

Tears rushed to her eyes. "She can't be. I was there today. She was laughing and drawing in her book." She groaned and closed her eyes.

Tyson put an arm about her and waited for her sobs to quiet.

"I'm sorry, Nessa," he murmured.

Her eyes and cheeks swollen, she looked up a few minutes later. "How's Belinda?"

"Doc gave her an injection to calm her down."

"She's got to be careful, or she'll lose her baby, too." She pressed her face into his shoulder. "It's too awful."

Stroking her hair, Tyson stared into a dark corner. His tears formed deep inside where no one could see.

After a fitful night, Tyson tossed his father Lizzy's keys on Sunday morning so he could drive the McGinty family to Pikeville to hear Bryan speak in an open-air service. Lori wasn't strong enough for a trip. Tyson would stay with her.

After they left, he read to Lori until she fell asleep. Picking up the appointment book, he went down to the kitchen to make some coffee.

While the pot perked on the stove, Tyson sat at the table and pulled out his notebook along with the list he'd made. He set them, unopened, before him and idly flipped through St. Clair's appointment book. It was a one-year calendar with twenty lines under each date, one day per page.

The doctor's hand had a crisp block style with squared edges on his "O"s. Idly turning the pages, Tyson saw Lori's name appear at regular intervals.

Miss Ida's name came under March 10. Suddenly intrigued, Tyson realized that the doctor's appointment book was a sort of health journal for Dayton. He scanned the pages, his mind ticking off the events of the past three months.

Miss Ida had seen the doctor on April 15, five days before her death. On April 24, Sammy's name had been hastily added in a different ink.

The coffee pot boiled away, forgotten.

Lori had her normal check-up on May 8. Anna Joy Mullins had a house call on May 24. That must have been the night of the girl's fracas with Elmer. Another entry for May 24, the day she died.

An acrid smell made him lunge toward the stove. Grabbing a dishtowel to pad his hand, he lifted the pot and plunged it into a basin of water in the sink. A hissing cloud of steam rose to the ceiling.

So much for coffee. He drew a bottle of milk from the warm ice box and sniffed it. Sour. The ice shipment from Chattanooga still hadn't appeared. Filling a glass with tap water, he returned to the appointment book.

On June 18, the last line read, "Dotty Smith, 5:00."

Lori's cries brought him to his feet. He closed the book and took his notes upstairs.

Half an hour later Vic walked in with Nessa. She wore a peach chiffon dress with a ribbon rose at the left hip.

Snuggled in her daddy's lap, Lori was looking at a picture book. She smiled and called, "Hi, Nessa! Want to see Old Dobbin?"

Nessa's tried to smile. "Sure, honey." She walked closer. "Mama bought some barbecued chicken from some folks cooking outside the meeting grounds."

She took off her formfitting, satin hat and held it near her waist. "Trent, I need to speak to you."

Something in her tone made Tyson look up. He saw worry and something more in her expression.

"Chicky, would you mind looking at Dobbin for a few minutes while I talk to Nessa?" he asked, sliding Lori to the sofa. "Turn the page, Daddy."

He set the book on the table, and she held the page open with her cast.

Tyson followed Nessa into the hall.

"Someone wrote on my bedroom window with soap," she whispered.

He grinned. "A teenage admirer?"

She didn't smile. "It says, 'Too Late. You're next.'"

CHAPTER Twenty-Eight

"Watch yourself, Nessa," Tyson told her, leaning his back against the white door molding outside his room. "This person is a poisoner. Be careful whose hands you eat or drink from."

Nessa shivered and moved closer to him. "I'm afraid to go to work tomorrow."

"Where are you cleaning?"

"Bailey's and St. Clair's."

He sighed and ran fingers through his curly top. The mere thought of someone hurting her made him sick to his stomach.

"Take Micky with you," he said. She was close enough for him to see flecks of gold in her blue eyes. "Keep him with you every minute."

"I'd rather have you."

He touched her nose. "Believe me, I'd much rather be with you than in that stuffy courtroom."

A curtain came down over her eyes, but not in time to hide a flicker of pain. "I'll talk to Micky." She moved toward the stairs, her steps muffled on the hall's carpet runner.

"Daddy?" Lori called from the sitting room. "I'm tired of this book. I want to rock."

"Coming, Chicky." He watched the back of Nessa's head another moment, then went inside.

Tired as he was, Tyson slept little that night. He kept dreaming of a courtroom full of vicious shadows that swooped at him and let out an evil laugh when he flinched.

After breakfast the next morning, Nessa and her brother walked with Tyson to the corner. Leaving him to cross the street, Nessa sent Tyson a parting look that made him want to get out his service revolver and stand guard over her for the rest of the day. He forced himself to turn south.

The courtroom looked the same as it had for six straight days, but the crowd had changed. Of the original two hundred, only two dozen diehard journalists remained. Most of the spectators were locals.

Looking refreshed from a weekend off, stocky Kelso Rice called the session to order.

When the preacher finished his opening prayer, Judge Raulston read the record of his heated interchange with Clarence Darrow on Friday.

"The court has withheld action," the judge said, "until passion had time to subside, and until the jury could be kept separate." He avoided looking directly at Darrow, who watched him with apparent unconcern.

Raulston continued, "Men may become prominent, but they should never feel themselves superior to the law. It has been my policy to avoid rushing to conclusions. But in the face of an unjustified expression of contempt for this court by Clarence Darrow on July 17, 1925, I feel that further forbearance would cease to be a virtue.

"I hereby order that citation be served upon Clarence Darrow, requiring him to appear in this court at nine o'clock a.m., Tuesday, July 21, 1925, and make answer to this citation.

"I also direct that he be required to make and execute a bond for five thousand dollars and not depart the court without leave."

Hands deep in his pockets, Darrow shuffled toward the bench.

"What is the bond, Your Honor?"

"Five thousand dollars."

The attorney looked at the defense team. "I'm not sure I can get anyone."

A short, slim gentleman with a press badge on his shirt stepped forward from the seats. "I'll put up the bond," he said and gave his name as Frank Spurlock from Chattanooga.

A buzz came from the audience.

Kelso Rice banged his gavel. "Order!"

At a quarter to ten, the trial got underway. With his long jaw tucked low against his deep chest, Arthur Garfield Hays continued to argue for expert testimony, though Judge Raulston had ruled against him on Friday. The whole morning passed in haggling between attorneys and the judge.

An afternoon in the Sahara would have been just as hot but not half so dry. Tyson sweated and chafed and glanced at his watch a hundred times. His mind wandered to Nessa. She'd become more important to him than he'd realized. If only he could convince her that their differences didn't matter.

A goggle-eyed young woman in a dark dress touched his arm. "You have a phone call," she whispered.

Tyson followed her down the stairs to the high counter in the lobby. "Tyson here," he said into the mouthpiece.

"Howdy, Trent," Charlie Greene's squeaky tenor filled his ear. "I put a rush on the Riesbeck child's autopsy. I have the report here."

Tyson gripped the cup receiver and waited.

"She died of an overdose of sleeping powder."

The stiffness went out of Tyson's knees. "There's no chance it was her heart?"

"Her heart was damaged enough to restrict her activities, but not enough to kill her."

"Thanks, Charlie," he murmured and slowly hung up the phone. He felt as though a thick blanket had tightened around him, smothering him. Pushing through the front doors, he stood

by the iron porch railing, breathing fresh air and trying to think.

He pulled the list of Dayton's victims from his pocket and added Jody's name in a shaky scrawl. The last shred of doubt was gone. Someone had appointed himself a cleanup committee to weed out Dayton's weak.

He stayed outdoors until the noon adjournment, then hurried home, frantic to know about a certain dark-haired young woman. He burst into Heddie's kitchen at five past noon. "Is Nessa here?"

The landlady glanced at him over a pot of split pea soup, her Irish burr in evidence. "She's serving plates in the dining room."

He took a bowl from the table, plunked a slice of cornbread on top of it, and picked up a wide spoon. Dropping into a chair, he raised the spoon to his lips, but he didn't taste what he swallowed.

He stayed tense, waiting for Nessa to come through the door.

She did so three minutes later. "Trent!" She set an empty tray on the table and smoothed her hair.

"How did it go?" he asked.

"Perfectly normal. I feel like a fool getting so upset."

"You should have been upset," he said abruptly.

"What's that?" Heddie demanded, glancing from Nessa to Tyson as she filled bowls with a big ladle. "Upset about what?"

Nessa hesitated. Her eyes begged Tyson not to tell.

He cleared his throat. "Someone soaped Nessa's window."

"I cleaned it off," her daughter added quickly, lifting the heavy tray.

Heddie shook her head. "Those O'Toole boys were behind it. Mark my words."

Nessa hustled toward the dining room with her load, and Tyson finished his lunch wishing he could skip out on this afternoon's session.

Setting down his empty bowl, he left the boardinghouse to take a turn around Market Street and arrived at the courthouse in time to hear the gavel.

Tom Stewart rose as court convened, "This morning the court read a citation to one of the defense counsel. Mr. Darrow has a statement that he wants to make at this time. I think it is proper that Your Honor hear him."

"I will hear you, Colonel Darrow."

Hitching his suspenders over his paunch, Darrow paced forward, his voice oily. "I have been practicing law for forty-seven years. I've had many a case where I have had to fight the public opinion of the people in the community. I never yet have had any criticism by the court for anything I've done in court."

He spoke to the judge in a low tone. "I have regretted my words ever since. Personally, I don't think it constitutes a contempt, but I am quite certain that the remark should not have been made. I want to apologize to the court for it."

Darrow received swelling applause as he took his seat.

Raulston's expression softened. "I accept Colonel Darrow's apology. He spoke these words, perhaps, just when he felt he had suffered one of the greatest disappointments of his life when the court had held against him."

Thunderous applause filled the courtroom.

Raulston waited for order, then said, "I think court should adjourn downstairs. I am afraid of the building. The court will convene down in the yard."

The crowd surged downward to where benches and a platform had been set up. Since they were still excluded from the proceedings, the jury filed inside the hot courthouse.

The lawn had the atmosphere of a ballpark. Boys selling hot dogs and soda pop passed through the crowd. Some fellows hung out of open courthouse windows. Others sat on the hoods of parked cars. Buzzing flies dipped and swooped among the crowd.

Fans for the home team—who claimed William Jennings Bryan as their leader—sat to the left. The visiting team's fans gathered on the right. They elbowed each other, made bets and predictions, and hunkered down for the final inning.

When everyone had found a place, Hays read affidavits from prominent theologians who tried to reconcile the Bible to evolution. When he finished, Darrow stepped forward. "Your Honor, before you send for the jury, I think it my duty to make this motion. Off to the left is a large sign reading, 'Read Your Bible.' I move that it be removed."

Ben McKenzie lunged to his feet. "If Your Honor please, why should it be removed if it is their defense that they do not deny the Bible?"

Ben's son, Gordon, stood. "I believe in the Bible as strong as anyone else here, but if the sign is objectionable to the defense, I think the court ought remove it."

Malone spoke up. "Our religious beliefs or Mr. Darrow's nonbelief are none of the business of the prosecution. We do not wish that referred to again."

Brief applause followed.

Gordon McKenzie again stood, his face brick red. "I withdraw my suggestion." He glared at the prosecution. "I have never seen the time in the history of this country when any man should be afraid to be reminded that he should read his Bible." His words became more heated as he spoke. He thrust a finger at the defense and shouted, "If they should represent a force that is aligned with the devil and his satellites..."

"Objection!" Malone shouted.

Gordon shouted over him, "I say when that time comes then it is time for us to tear up all the Bibles, throw them in the fire, and let the country go to hell!"

Shouting, cheers, and applause set the court into confusion.

Hardly able to be heard, Judge Raulston ruled that "satellites of the devil" be removed from the record.

Kelso Rice banged his night stick against a table and shouted, "People, this is no circus. There are no monkeys up here. This is a lawsuit, let us have order!"

Judge Raulston ruled that the sign be taken down. Two men in overalls came with ladders and set them against the brick wall.

Hays called out, "The defense desires to call Mr. Bryan as a witness. We want to take Mr. Bryan's testimony for our record."

Bryan's eyes widened. He turned toward Darrow who had a sly smile on his leathery face.

A startled silence settled over two thousand people. Children scuttled forward to sit on the grass close to the bench. Three reporters raced for the telegraph room in the courthouse. Tyson leaned against a tree trunk, his father beside him.

Ben McKenzie spoke out. "I don't think it is necessary to call him, a lawyer representing his client."

Bryan said, "I insist that Mr. Darrow can be put on the stand, and Mr. Malone and Mr. Hays."

Judge Raulston said, "Call anyone you desire. Ask them any questions you wish."

Carrying his brown palm-leaf fan, Bryan walked forward. "Where do you want me to sit?"

Kelso Rice placed a chair toward the front of the platform, and Bryan eased into it.

"Do you want Mr. Bryan sworn in?" Raulston asked.

"No." Still smiling, Darrow regarded his quarry. "I take it you will tell the truth, Mr. Bryan." Darrow stood beside the defense table, casually leaning forward with one foot on the seat of a chair. "You have given considerable study to the Bible, haven't you, Mr. Bryan?"

The crowd hushed, intent on the answers. "Yes, sir. I've studied the Bible for about fifty years."

"You claim that everything in the Bible should be literally interpreted?"

"Everything in the Bible should be accepted as it is given: some of the Bible is given illustratively. For instance: 'Ye are the salt of the earth.' I wouldn't insist that man was actually salt."

"But when you read that Jonah swallowed the whale—or that the whale swallowed Jonah—excuse me please, how do you literally interpret that?" He straightened and walked toward Bryan.

"One miracle is just as easy to believe as another."

"Just as hard?" Darrow said, ironically.

"It is hard to believe for you, but easy for me."

"Perfectly easy to believe that Jonah swallowed the whale?"

Bryan's chin lifted. "The Bible doesn't make as extreme statements as evolutionists do. I believe the Bible is inspired."

"Whoever inspired it?"

"The Almighty."

Tom Stewart objected to the questioning.

"Mr. Bryan is willing to be examined," Judge Raulston said, brusquely. "Go ahead."

Darrow's voice grew harder. "You believe the story of the flood to be a literal interpretation?"

"Yes, sir."

"When was that flood?"

"I've never made a calculation."

"What do you think?" Darrow prodded.

"I do not think about things I don't think about," Bryan declared.

Darrow's eyebrows lifted. "Do you think about things you do think about?"

Laughter came from the right.

Stewart said, "Your Honor, Mr. Bryan is perfectly able to take care of this, but this is not competent evidence."

Bryan said, "These gentlemen came here to try revealed religion. I am here to defend it. They can ask me any question they please."

Rousing applause came from the left.

Darrow turned toward the spectators and said, "Great applause from the bleachers."

"From those you call yokels," Bryan answered.

"I never called them yokels."

Bryan went on, "That is the ignorance of Tennessee, the bigotry."

"You mean, who are applauding you?"

Bryan said, "Those people whom you insult."

Darrow's temper flared. "You insult every man of science in the world because he does not believe in your fool religion."

Raulston finally stepped in. "I will not stand for that. Let him tell what he knows."

"All he knows?" Darrow mocked.

"I won't insist on telling all I know," Bryan said, "I will tell more than Mr. Darrow wants told."

"I object to Mr. Bryan making a speech every time I ask him a question."

"Overruled."

Bryan went on to tell of his conversation with a Buddhist teacher, then Darrow questioned him about the age of the earth.

Finally, Raulston leaned forward. "Are you about through, Mr. Darrow?"

"I want to ask a few questions about the creation."

"Be very brief, Mr. Darrow," the judge said. "The only reason I'm allowing this at all is that they may have it in the appellate court."

Bryan spoke up. "I am not answering for the benefit of the superior court. I want the Christian world to know that any unbeliever can question me any time, and I will answer him."

McKenzie spoke up. "Do you think this evidence is competent before a jury?"

Darrow said, "I think so."

Raulston shook his head. "It's not competent."

"Nor is it competent in the appellate courts," McKenzie added. "The defense would no more file the testimony of Colonel Bryan than they would file a rattlesnake and handle it themselves."

"They have not questioned legally," Bryan declared. "The only reason they have asked any questions is to give this agnostic a chance to criticize a believer in the word of God."

Darrow shouted, "I object to your statement. I am exempting you on your fool ideas that no intelligent Christian on earth believes."

Judge Raulston thumped the gavel. "Court is adjourned until nine o'clock tomorrow morning."

Both Tyson men sat on an empty bench in the back when the crowd left their seats. Dozens of people swarmed around both of the main players in today's drama. From the back-slapping and handshaking going on, both sides seemed to think they had won.

Vic looked closely at his son. "What's gotten into you? You look sick."

Tyson reached into his pocket for a handkerchief to wipe his face. "Jody Riesbeck's autopsy report came in this morning."

He had Vic's full attention.

"She was murdered." The words fell like bricks into a shallow pond.

"Who would do a fool thing like that?"

"The same person who killed Anna Joy and Sammy and Miss Ida. Someone with a deranged idea that only the fittest folks in town should live."

"Any more leads?" Vic asked quietly.

"I'm going over to Riesbeck's now to dig some out." He adjusted his hat and cut across the grass toward the sidewalk.

CHAPTER Twenty-Nine

When Tyson strolled up the front walk, Riesbeck's white frame house had a black wreath on the front door and six people wearing black on the porch. He nodded as he passed somber aunts and uncles and cousins of the grieving family.

The door stood slightly ajar, and a beefy aroma wafted from within.

"Go on in, Deputy," a stout woman in a rocking chair wheezed. "Jason's in the kitchen."

Tyson eased inside and strolled down the hall, past the closed room where the horrible act had happened, and into the spacious kitchen on the right. He found Jason at the table staring into a half-empty mug of coffee. Also wearing black crepe, Essie bustled about the kitchen wiping down wooden counters while a stewpot simmered on the porcelain range.

"Good afternoon, Jason," Tyson said, fedora in hand. He stepped closer to the table. "Mind if I sit down a minute?"

Jason waved toward a chair without looking up. "Help yourself, Deputy."

Tyson softly dropped into the chair as though even a creaking noise would disturb the mourners. "I'm sorry to bother you at a time like this, Jason. I got the autopsy report this morning, and I thought you needed to hear it."

Riesbeck looked at Tyson with a hopeless expression that squeezed Tyson's heart. He'd felt that unspeakable, gut-twisting agony just five years ago.

Tyson spoke slowly and evenly. "Jody died of an overdose of sleeping powder."

Jason let out a horrified gasp and slumped back in his chair, his lips drawn back from his teeth, his eyes closed. A deep, guttural sound started as a sob and ended as a wail. "No-o-o!" It was the cry of a tormented soul.

"Essie," Tyson said, "did Doc St. Clair leave more sedative for Belinda?"

She nodded, her second chin wobbling, and reached up into a cabinet. "Here's the packet." She handed it to him and pulled a black handkerchief from her pocket to dab her eyes.

Inside the yellow envelope lay four white tablets. Tyson shook out one and handed it to Jason. "Swallow this, old man. The dosage says two at a time, so it shouldn't knock you out."

Trembling, Riesbeck found his mouth with his hand and lifted a sloshing cup to sip. His lips hung loose. His breath came in shallow gasps. Tears washed down his round cheeks.

Tyson waited while Jason put his head on the table and cried unashamedly for his little daughter. Watching him, Tyson's sympathetic grief became simmering rage. What kind of a heartless monster would hurt a child?

When the grieving father's emotion subsided somewhat, Tyson leaned closer to him. "Jason, do you feel calm enough to answer a few questions? I want to find out who did this, and I don't mean to wait another day."

Tugging a handkerchief from his shirt pocket, Riesbeck sat up and wiped his face. "What do you need to know?" Tears continued to spring from his bloodshot eyes.

"Who was in the house that day?"

Jason fumbled with the handkerchief, his brow creased. "I…

I can't remember." His eyes sought Essie at the sink.

"Essie, who was here that day? Can you help me?"

The town gossip turned toward him and ticked off some names. "Sadie came in the morning to check on the little girl. After that, Elmer Buntley brought her a flower." She paused, thinking. "Did the doctor come that afternoon?" she asked Jason.

"I went to town," he said. "Belinda would know that, but she's sleeping."

"When she wakes up, try to ask her about it and let me know, okay?" Tyson stood and reached for his hat on the tabletop. "I lost my wife a few years back. I know what you're feeling." He gripped Riesbeck's hand. "I'll do my best. You have my promise."

Jason's eyes glowed like molten lava. "You'd best not tell me who it is, Tyson. I'd finish them off with my bare hands."

Hands shoved deep into his pockets all the way home, Tyson met Nessa in the front hallway. When she saw his ravaged face, fear brought her hands to her cheeks. "Something's happened."

Her wide blue eyes held his. "For God's sake tell me!"

He put his hands on the gray cotton covering her slim shoulders to brace her for a shock. He hadn't told her while she served tables at noon because he knew how she'd react. He said it as gently as he knew how.

"Jody was murdered."

A quick intake of breath, a startling flash of agony, and she crumpled.

He pulled her against him and edged her to the stairs. Sinking to the second step, he held her while she wailed, "Who's next?"

Shoes tapped the floor as Vic and Heddie approached. "What happened?" she demanded, touching Nessa's back.

"I got the autopsy report on Jody today," Tyson told her as Vic walked up. "She was murdered."

"Heavens above!"

It was Vic's turn to comfort a crying woman. He looked across Heddie's dark head. "Who did it, Trent?"

"I don't have any proof yet, but I have some ideas."

Nessa sniffed and looked at him. "Who?"

"I'm not ready to say just yet."

She pulled away from him. "I've got to go over there."

"Belinda's sleeping."

"I don't care." She pushed some hair off her face. "Let me get my hat. I've got to go."

Tyson shrugged. "I'll walk you over."

Red-cheeked and bleary-eyed, Heddie backed away from Vic and pulled a handkerchief from her sleeve. "Tell them I'll bring some food over later." She looked up at the older Tyson. "I'll make potato soup this evening."

Fifteen minutes later, Nessa entered the Riesbeck's home to sit with Belinda and Jason. Tyson sat under the yellow porch light with a thousand mosquitoes and moths, flipping through his notebook and staring into the lilac-scented darkness. He wanted to be alone to force some analytical thought out of his fuzzy brain.

When Dr. St. Clair and Sadie arrived, they waved a hello but didn't stop to talk. Sadie's eyes were swollen and red. The doctor carried a heavy coffee urn.

At fifteen past ten, Nessa came out the door. No closer to a solution than before, Tyson put away his notebook and stood. "Ready to go?" he asked.

She nodded, her expression pained. “I’m not feeling well. Do you mind if I take your arm?”

He lifted her hand and placed it inside his bent elbow, covering it with his own. She seemed shaky on her feet, so he slowed his pace.

In front of Jenny Mullins’s house-for-sale sign, Nessa stopped, swaying, with her hand on her forehead. “I feel faint. And sick at my stomach.” Her hand flew to her mouth. “Oh!” She leaned over the shallow ditch beside the road and retched.

Tyson held her from behind, supporting her. “Nessa, did you eat anything while you were there?”

She slumped against him. “I drank coffee, that’s all.”

“Who gave it to you?”

“Sadie. She brought a coffee urn from home.” She doubled over in a paroxysm that ended with her legs folding under her.

Lifting her in his arms, Tyson carried her home. He kicked the back door until Heddie opened it for him.

“Nessa!”

Tyson stepped inside. “I’m afraid she’s been poisoned.”

The landlady’s face blanched. “Bring her to the bedroom.” She led the way into the tiny family apartment and opened the first door to the right for him. “I’ll phone the doctor.”

“He’s at Riesbeck’s house,” Tyson called after her.

Flushed, Nessa moaned and clutched her stomach. “My mouth is burning all the way down to my stomach.” She tried to sit up. “I can’t lie still. Let me up.” An instant later she sank back to the pillow, her face white as chalk.

Sitting on the bed beside her, Tyson’s heart felt as though it would burst through his chest. He put his hands on either side of her terrified face. “I love you, Nessa McGinty,” he said angrily. “You’re not going to die. Do you hear me?”

Gasping for air, her eyes fluttered closed then opened wide. “I left my cup on the table to cool while I visited with Belinda in the bedroom.”

“Nessa!” he moaned. “I told you to be careful.”

She looked at him, confused. “No one was there. Only our friends.” Tears trickled toward her ears.

“This way, Doctor,” Heddie said in the hall.

St. Clair filled the doorway like an avenging angel, his face thunderous. Tyson backed up against the wall to give him room. The doctor felt Nessa’s pulse and looked into her eyes while Tyson listed her symptoms.

St. Clair sniffed her breath. "Camphorated mothballs." He turned toward Heddie who stood wringing her hands by the wooden footboard. "Have you any activated charcoal?" When she nodded, he said, "Get it. And bring lots of water."

"It's a good thing you vomited," he told the sick girl.

"I'm so thirsty."

"You'll have all the water you want in just a moment."

Heddie rushed in with her hands full. The doctor administered the antidote and instructed Heddie to keep an eye on Nessa. He made eye contact with Tyson. When he left, the deputy followed him out.

"Will she be all right, Doc?"

"She has a good chance, depending on how long she had the poison in her system before she vomited." He looked at Tyson with a grim expression. "How did she get it?"

Tyson stiffened. "You're the last one I'm answering questions for, Doc. I didn't want Heddie to call you, but I had no choice."

He turned away. "Sorry to be rude, but I've got to get back to Riesbeck's place." He pushed through two doors and jogged down the dark street. He could have saved the effort. By the time he arrived, efficient Essie had washed every cup and saucer. No one had noticed anyone near Nessa's coffee cup. No one was noticing much these days.

Partway through Tyson's questioning, St. Clair came in. He stood near the doorway, watching his friend with narrowed eyes. Sadie crossed the room to stand with her brother, her expression matching his.

Tyson finally ran out of questions. He pocketed his useless notes and sprinted home.

Nessa was sleeping quietly when he reached her room. Heddie sent him an encouraging smile and a nod that brought his blood pressure down a few notches. He tiptoed out of the room and moved upstairs.

Lori lay sleeping on her trundle bed without a care in the world.

Her father knelt beside her, head bowed, his hand on her blanket, for more than an hour.

The next morning Nessa was at the kitchen table when Tyson brought Lori downstairs. The sweet smell of warm syrup mingled with fresh coffee and killed Tyson's appetite.

Setting his daughter on her stack of Sears catalogs, he chose a chair across a corner from Nessa. "You gave me a fearful scare last night."

"I gave myself one." She tried a feeble smile and failed.

Lori thumped her cast on the table. "Goody, goody! Pancakes!"

Heddie slid a golden disc onto a plate for her, added hot syrup, and cut it into small pieces. "Here you go, darlin'." She held a skewered morsel to Lori's lips.

Vic stepped into the room looking fresh and cool in a white linen suit. "Morning, Trent," he said. "I'm coming to see Bryan give that old reprobate what for."

"Care to lay odds?" Tyson asked.

"Don't tempt me." He forked three hotcakes onto his plate. Tyson shook his head when Heddie offered him the serving platter.

On the way to the courthouse, Tyson bought a *Chattanooga News* from a boy on the sidewalk. Drizzling rain forced the crowd back inside. Despite open windows, the added humidity in the courtroom made smells ripen and rotten.

While waiting for the judge to arrive, Tyson read the editorial page. George Fort Milton had opposed the Butler Act from its beginning. Today, he took a different viewpoint and called Darrow's interrogation of Bryan "a thing of immense cruelty."

Judge Raulston marched in and Tyson quickly folded the newspaper. He handed it to Vic on the front row.

Court opened a few minutes early, before Darrow and Stewart arrived. Men scuttled into their seats.

Kelso Rice announced, "We opened a little earlier on account of the judge's watch, and we're waiting for counsel. The judge isn't fast. I think it's just his watch."

When the head attorneys of both sides strode in, Judge Raulston said, "After due deliberation, I feel that Mr. Bryan's testimony cannot aid the higher court in determining whether Mr. Scopes taught evolution. I am pleased to expunge this testimony from the record."

"We take an exception to that," Clarence Darrow said.

Tyson glanced at Bryan. The Great Commoner showed no sign of emotion though the judge had just stripped him of his right to question Darrow.

Vic glanced at his son, an irritated expression crossing his bearded features. A restless wave coursed across the room.

Darrow moved into the inner sanctum. He seemed pleased with himself. "To save time we will ask the court to bring in the jury and instruct them to find the defendant guilty.

"We accept the suggestion of Mr. Darrow," Stewart said.

Bryan stood to say, "I fully agree with the court that the testimony taken yesterday was not legitimate or proper."

"Yes, sir," Raulston said.

Bryan went on, "I had not reached the point where I could make a statement to answer counsel's charges as to my ignorance and my bigotry."

"I object, Your Honor," Darrow said.

"Why do you want to make this, Colonel Bryan?" the judge asked.

"I just want to finish my sentence."

Darrow smirked. "Why can't he go outside on the lawn?"

"I'm not asking to make a statement here," Bryan said.

Raulston nodded. "I will hear you."

"I shall have to trust to the justness of the press to report what I will say in answer to their charge. I shall also give to the press the questions I would have asked had I been permitted to call the attorneys on the other side to the stand."

He glanced at Darrow. "It is hardly fair for them to stand behind a dark lantern that throws light on other people but conceals themselves."

"I object," Darrow said.

"Overruled."

Ben McKenzie stood. "I suggest that the gentlemen get together with Colonel Bryan, that they have a crowd and have a joint discussion."

Malone said, "Our discussion is ended. We're ready for the jury."

The jury shuffled in looking tired and disgruntled. Men hoping for ringside seats had heard only two hours of testimony.

Judge Raulston charged the jury that the issue at stake was not whether evolution conflicted with Genesis, but whether John Scopes had indeed taught evolution in his class at Rhea County High School.

Darrow walked over to the jury. "We are sorry we've not had a chance to say anything to you. This case and this law will never be decided until it gets to a higher court, and it cannot get to a higher court unless you bring in a verdict. We cannot even explain to you that we think you should return a verdict of not guilty. I guess that is plain enough."

Stewart stood. "What Mr. Darrow wanted to say to you was that he wants you to find his client guilty. He did not want to be in a position of pleading guilty, because it would destroy his rights in the appellate court."

Kelso Rice led the jury outside into the hall. Nine minutes later, they returned.

Judge Raulston said, "Mr. Foreman, will you tell us whether you have agreed on a verdict?"

"Yes, sir, we have."

"What did you find?"

"We have found the defendant guilty."

"You leave the fine for the court?"

"Yes."

The judge looked to his right. "Mr. Scopes, will you come around here, please, sir?"

Scopes approached the bench. His clothes hung loosely about his shoulders and his hips; his cheeks were sunken.

"Mr. Scopes, the jury has found you guilty under this indictment. The statute makes this an offense punishable by a fine of not less than one hundred nor more than five hundred dollars. The court now fixes your fine at one hundred dollars." He peered at the young teacher. "Have you anything to say?"

"Your Honor, I feel that I have been convicted of violating an unjust statute. I will continue in the future, as I have in the past, to oppose this law in any way I can. I think the fine is unjust."

Tyson moved his feet, itching to go, but those word-hungry lawyers weren't ready to be quiet.

Bryan stood. "This cause goes deep. It extends wide and reaches into the future beyond the power of man to see. We ought to pray that right will prevail."

Applause filled the room.

Thumbs under his suspenders, Darrow said, "I think this case will be remembered because it is the first of this sort since we stopped trying people for witchcraft. Here we have done our best to turn back the tide of testing every fact in science by a religious dictum."

Raulston ended the session by saying, "There are two things that are indestructible. One is truth. The other is the Word of God."

A preacher stood to give a benediction, and the crowd pressed forward to shake hands with their heroes. They trickled from the courtroom.

Vic paused by Tyson on his way out. "That was a killing blow at the end there."

"What do you mean?"

"By asking for a guilty verdict, Darrow shut out Bryan's closing speech." Vic watched the Great Commoner shaking hands with Herb Hicks and Haggard. "I wish I knew what he was going to say."

"Just wait a few days and some paper will print it." Tyson glanced at his watch. "When this place clears out I'm heading home."

"I'll wait for you. I'm in no hurry."

On the sidewalk, Tyson told Vic about the doctor's appointment book. "I fell asleep before I had a chance to look through all of it." He pulled it from his shirt pocket and turned some pages. "Look here. At June 20 near the bottom."

Vic paused a moment to scan the writing. "Dotty Smith." He looked at Tyson, concern in his eyes. "St. Clair wouldn't do an abortion, would he?"

"I'd like to say no," Tyson said, taking the leather notebook back. "But I can't. Last night he made a speech about how unwanted children were better off not born."

They walked half a block in silence. The sound of rumbling automobiles and shouting children came from behind them.

At the corner, Vic stopped and touched Tyson's arm. "Hold on a minute. I've got something to tell you." He looked at his shoes and twisted his lips. "I popped the question to Heddie yesterday."

"What did she say?" Tyson asked, afraid to hear the answer.

Vic looked up and beamed. "She said, 'Yes.'" He held out his hand. "I wanted you to be the first to know."

Tyson gripped his father's wide paw. "Congratulations." He forced a smile. Maybe he'd get transferred to Nashville eventually.

Remembering Nessa, he killed that idea.

They reached the front porch. A small silver hatbox tied with a pink ribbon lay in front of the door. Tied to the bow, a tag had "Nessa McGinty" inscribed in bold black pencil.

Tyson picked it up and carried it to the kitchen.

Nessa sat at the table. Wearing a cotton robe, her dark hair hanging about her shoulders, she looked exhausted. Heddie was stirring her soup pot, and Micky was slicing roast beef for sandwiches. The Lunch Room would open for business in an hour.

At the table near Nessa, Essie prepared a tray to take to Lori upstairs. Since Sadie was tied up with Belinda, Essie had volunteered to sit with the youngest Tyson. She looked up when the men walked in, her quick eyes briefly noting the hatbox. "Your little girl has been asking for you," she said smiling.

"Tell her I'll be right up," Tyson said. "Soon as I get a glass of cold water."

"You can have water, but I doubt it'll be cold," Heddie said, lifting a glass from a stack in the drainer. "The icehouse is empty again." She paused to send Vic a wide smile. He grinned back at her.

Tyson set the hatbox in front of Nessa and sat beside her. "Maybe this will cheer you up."

She gave an irritated flick at her wild tresses. “I look a fright, but right now I don’t really care.”

He murmured, “You look wonderful to me. How are you feeling?”

“Weak and sort of shaky inside.” She shifted in the chair and touched the box. “Dr. St. Clair stopped in this morning looking for his appointment book. He’s been everywhere in town tracking it down.”

Tyson nodded. “I’ll get it to him in good time.” He looked at the hatbox. “You want me to open it for you?”

She brushed away his hand. “I’m not that sick.” Slipping off the ribbon, she pulled the lid away and held it over the box while she looked inside.

Her face twisted. Shrieking, she slammed the box to the floor.

Chapter Thirty

Drawing in a breath, Nessa screamed a second time, ending in a deep sob. Tyson grabbed her and held her as she lashed out hysterically, shouting, "No! No!"

"Nessa, stop it! Nessa!" He pulled her to him and held down her flailing arms.

Heddie rushed to her side, calling for her to calm down.

The girl didn't hear. She sobbed wildly, her head arching backward.

Tyson picked her up. "Let's get her to bed." He headed toward the family apartment. "Did the doctor leave her any medicine?"

"Yes, some sleeping tablets," Heddie said, opening the bedroom door. Hearing the commotion, Micky ran through the door and pulled up, watching his sister, a scared look on his face.

While Tyson carried her into the bedroom Nessa quieted somewhat, but she still gripped his shoulders in an iron clasp and cried shrill and long. A moment later Heddie came with two pills. She forced them through her daughter's lips and held a glass of water for her to drink.

Nessa's head sank onto the pillow—her eyes closed, her breathing rapid and shallow. Tyson rubbed his face and glanced toward his father standing in the doorway. Vic made a jerking motion with his head. Leaving Heddie to watch over her daughter, Tyson followed him outside.

"This is what got Nessa so stirred up," Vic said grimly, holding out a doll the size of his big hand.

Tyson reached for it. The thing was made of soft cotton cloth with brown yarn hair. It had no left arm. Its right arm had a white bandage from shoulder to wrist. Tyson stared at it, an icy hand running down his spine.

The tiny face and chest had been slashed to ribbons.

"Pa, don't let anyone in to see Lori. Anyone." He stuffed the doll into his pants pocket. "I've got something to do."

After cranking Lizzy, Trent turned south on Market. He didn't want to think what he was thinking. Turning left on Main, he parked in front of the Hicks's law office and crossed the street. Clarke Robinson was in St. Clair's waiting room with little Wallace when Tyson rushed inside. He whispered a few words to her. She looked shocked, grabbed her boy's hand, and marched out.

Trent turned the sign on the door so the "Closed for the day" side showed, took a seat, and waited for the current patient to leave the examining room. Five minutes later Mrs. Kate Bailey stepped out carrying a flat, brown bottle. She nodded to Trent and hurried outside.

Dr. St. Clair paused in the inner office doorway. He smiled. "Good afternoon, Trent. Did you bring my appointment book? I've felt like I'm missing my right arm all morning."

Tyson stood. "I've got it, Doc. I'd like to talk to you."

St. Clair glanced at the clock. "I've got some prescriptions to prepare, but I can spare you a few minutes."

Tyson stared into St. Clair's mild eyes and moved toward him.

Giving him a puzzled look, St. Clair backed into the examining room and leaned against his heavy desk.

Tyson's chin jutted forward. "Why Jody, Doc? Why Nessa and Lori?"

"Have you lost your mind?"

"Miss Ida and Sammy were old and feeble. But Jody had her whole life ahead of her. And Lori . . ." He couldn't go on.

St. Clair moved to his chair and sat. "Are you implying that I had something to do with those deaths?"

"You've been bumping off Dayton's lower element, haven't you? Purging the world of useless life forms to make way for their betters?" He moved closer, pushing his opponent.

St. Clair's face turned the color of beefsteak. He raised a clenched fist. "I ought to throttle you."

Tyson's chest heaved. "Why don't you try it?"

Sadie came through a side door. She looked from one to the other. "What's wrong?"

"He thinks I killed Jody and all the others."

Tyson reached into his pocket and pulled out the appointment book. He flung it to the table. "Every victim is in that book within a week of his death." He placed his hands on the desk and leaned toward St. Clair. "C'mon, Doc. You're the one who goes around talking about how society would be better off without the derelict, the deformed, and the chronically ill. Remember?"

With a flash of understanding, the doctor glanced at his sister. He held up his hands as though pushing Tyson back. "Trent, listen to me! You're not the only one I've been talking to in this town."

"Who else then? Who else has access to everyone? Who else knows about poison and how to slip it to someone?"

Sadie gasped. "Essie!" She looked at her brother. "It has to be. She's been making a nuisance of herself for months. Every time I get to a serious case she's there, acting like an angel of mercy."

St. Clair nodded slowly. "She comes here every Thursday afternoon to help me in the lab and talk science. You wouldn't know it to look at her, but she's smart as they come. Always asking me questions." His wide brow pulled down. "What set you off just now, Trent?"

Tyson drew the doll from his pocket and dropped it to the desk.

Sadie reached for it. Her face contorted. "It's Lori!"

Tyson felt a rush of panic. "Essie's feeding her lunch." He looked from brother to sister. "Both of you come with me. I'm not letting you out of my sight." He hustled them out of the office and into Lizzy idling by the curb.

They reached the boardinghouse in minutes. Keeping the doctor and Sadie in front of him, Tyson trotted into the house and bounded after them up the stairs.

On the sofa, Essie had a cup to Lori's lips when they burst into the room. Startled, she jumped and spilled water down the child's pink nightie. "Well, I never . . ." her exclamation fell away unfinished when she saw the look on the three faces staring at her.

She moved closer to Lori.

"What-sa matter, Miss Essie?" Lori asked, reaching for her hand.

"Mrs. Caldwell, would you step into the hall with me for a moment?" Tyson said, trying to keep his voice calm. He wanted her away from his daughter.

"What is it, Adam?" she demanded.

"Deputy Tyson has some questions to ask you, Essie," he said. "About Jody."

A wild look came into her eyes. She pulled Lori into her lap. "Don't come any closer."

Tyson made a move toward her.

Essie yelped and pulled a small vial from the pocket of her house dress. She pulled the cork loose with her teeth and spat it out. "Stay where you are!"

"I want my Daddy!" Lori cried, wriggling.

"Tell her to stay here," Essie said, "Or she'll get this. It's tea made with cigarette tobacco. Enough nicotine to kill a whole family. All I have to do is spill it on her skin." She held it over the girl's bare thigh.

"Stay still, Lori!" Tyson shouted.

The child froze, her face stiff with fear. She whimpered.

"Essie, please," St. Clair said, "let the child go."

"And have you cart me off to jail? No, sir."

"Why did you do it, Essie?" St. Clair demanded.

"This is all your doing," the desperate woman shouted. "You filled my head with your high-blown ideas." Her voice quivered. "And made me fall in love with you." She paused, her breast heaving. "I did it for you, Adam, so you'd be proud of me. I wanted you to care for me."

"Essie," St. Clair's voice became pitying. He took a step forward.

"What about Dotty?" Tyson cut in. "She was young and healthy. Why did she have to die?"

"I'm sorry about Dotty." Essie tilted her head close to her shoulder. "When she told me about the baby, I advised her to get an abortion. After she had it done, she wouldn't tell me who helped her." Her eyes sought the doctor's. "She woke up crying about her baby, and I thought she'd tell on you, Adam."

"On me?" he demanded, shocked. "I've never performed an abortion in my life."

"But you said…" Anger surged through her. "Why, Adam St. Clair, you are a coward. After all you said, you're afraid to follow through on it. I'm ashamed of you!"

Lips tight, the doctor moved forward.

"Stop! Don't come any closer."

Tyson's muscles screamed to take action, but a tiny glass tube no bigger than a pencil stub tied him down as tightly as a stout rope.

"It was so easy," she said. "All I had to do was act like a friendly neighbor and slip them something when no one was around." Her lips trembled. "You're the guilty one, Adam. And you want to act so innocent!" She jerked the vial to her lips.

"Essie!" St. Clair leapt for her.

At the same instant, Tyson grabbed Lori out of her arms. He glimpsed Sadie slipping out the door as he carried his darling, crying Lori to the wingback chair and sat as though his knees had collapsed.

Essie's fleshy form pitched back across the sofa, her eyes rolled up until only the whites showed. Her foot kicked Tyson's chess set off the low table. It scattered across the carpet as her body went limp.

St. Clair stood over her, a helpless, hopeless expression on his gaunt face. "She wasn't a bad person, Trent. She was trying to help."

"Tell that to Jason and Belinda Riesbeck," he said, hugging his sobbing daughter tightly to his chest. Her hair brushed his cheek and he stroked its precious softness.

The doctor sank into a chair and covered his face with his hands. "I killed those people. Just as surely as if I'd pulled a trigger."

Tyson gazed at the dead woman and thought about her last words. Several parts of another puzzle suddenly came together. "Why is Essie's crime so tragic, Doc?" he demanded. "Farmers kill deformed animals all the time and never give it a thought." He paused, groping for words to answer his own question. "I know why it's so horrible. Because people have an inborn respect for human life, that's why. We're made in God's image with a conscience. There's no other explanation."

Tyson lowered his face until it was hidden in Lori's curls. "How could I have been such a fool?" He began to tremble. *God, forgive me.*

A few minutes later Sadie and Heddie rushed in, Vic following closely behind them.

"I called the sheriff," Sadie said. She knelt beside her brother and touched his shoulder. "I'm so sorry, Adam."

He didn't answer.

Nessa appeared in the doorway, a lavender robe tied about her slim form. "Lori!" she cried, dashing toward the child. "Are you okay, honey?"

She threw herself at the child and wrapped her arms around Trent's as he held his daughter. Turning, Lori hugged Nessa and their tears mingled.

Oblivious of the others in the room, the three of them stayed close in a tight love circle, trembling with shock, basking in blessed relief that the ordeal was finally over.

When Nessa looked up, Tyson's eyes met hers. Their spirits connected in a flash of understanding that snatched the breath from each of them. Riveted, her cheeks flooded with color.

"God is real, Nessa," he breathed. "He's alive. I know it."

Fresh tears sprang into her eyes. He reached out to wipe them away then bent down to gently kiss the place where they'd been.

Lori squirmed. "Kiss me too, Daddy." She held up her cheek and Tyson obliged, his lips curving upward for the first time. "Let's get you downstairs, Chicabiddy. We've got some things to discuss."

Nessa got to her feet and Tyson stood beside her with Lori perched on his left hip. Glancing at Essie's lifeless form, Nessa's voice quavered. "Why did she do it, Trent?"

He drew in a long breath, forming his answer. "Essie believed in a philosophy called eugenics. She believed it enough to put it into practice." Slipping a protective arm about Nessa's shoulders as they headed toward the door, he said, "God help our country if it ever catches on."

About the Author

Known to her friends and on social media as Lana McAra, Rosey Dow is the author and ghostwriter of 41 titles with more than half a million in sales. She is an editor and a book coach, helping new authors bring their ideas to life.

Her first book, *Megan's Choice*, was voted a reader's favorite in 1997. Rosey was also elected a favorite new author that year. *Fireside Christmas* put her on the CBA best-seller's list. In 2001, *Reaping the Whirlwind* won the coveted Christy Award, the national Christian fiction award. Her 2004 release, *Colorado*, has 250,000 copies in print.

To date, she has ghostwritten fifteen books on business, leadership, personal development, health and wellness topics as well as prescriptive memoirs.

Lana speaks at writers groups, conferences and seminars around the world about writing as well as personal development topics such as recovering from childhood trauma, stalking and recovering from narcissistic abuse. Visit her website www.Lana-McAra.com for more information.

A free ebook edition is available with the purchase of this book.

To claim your free ebook edition:

1. Visit MorganJamesBOGO.com
2. Sign your name CLEARLY in the space
3. Complete the form and submit a photo of the entire copyright page
4. You or your friend can download the ebook to your preferred device

Morgan James BOGO™

A **FREE** ebook edition is available for you or a friend with the purchase of this print book.

CLEARLY SIGN YOUR NAME ABOVE

Instructions to claim your free ebook edition:

1. Visit MorganJamesBOGO.com
2. Sign your name CLEARLY in the space above
3. Complete the form and submit a photo of this entire page
4. You or your friend can download the ebook to your preferred device

Print & Digital Together Forever.

Snap a photo

Free ebook

Read anywhere

CPSIA information can be obtained
at www.ICGtesting.com
Printed in the USA
JSHW021430150523
41730JS00001B/5